JEN WILLIAMS lives in London with her partner and their cat. A fan of pirates and dragons from an early age, these days she writes character-driven fantasy novels with plenty of banter and magic, and in 2015 she was nominated for Best Newcomer in the British Fantasy Awards. In 2018, *The Ninth Rain*, the first book in the Winnowing Flame trilogy, won the British Fantasy Award for Best Fantasy Novel. The sequel, *The Bitter Twins*, was published in March 2018 and Jen was awarded the British Fantasy Award for the second year running. Jen's first series, the Copper Cat trilogy, consists of *The Copper Promise*, *The Iron Ghost* and *The Silver Tide* – all published by Headline in the UK – and the first two books in the trilogy are now available in the US and Canada, published by Angry Robot. Both *The Iron Ghost* and *The Silver Tide* have also been nominated for British Fantasy Awards. Jen is partly responsible for founding the Super Relaxed Fantasy Club, a social group that meets in London to celebrate a love of fantasy, and she is partial to mead, if you're buying.

The Poison Song is the third novel in the Winnowing Flame trilogy.

Find out more at www.sennydreadful.com or follow her on Twitter @sennydreadful.

Praise for the Winnowing Flame trilogy:

'Jam-packed with breathtaking inventiveness – giant flying bats! Dragons! Aliens! Vampires! In anyone else's hands, that might be an unholy mess, but somehow it just works brilliantly'
James Oswald

'Williams brings her dark and immersive narrative to life with vivid descriptive passages, a great line in sarcastic humour and human insight'
Guardian

THE
POISON
SONG

JEN WILLIAMS

HEADLINE

First published in Great Britain in 2019 by
HEADLINE PUBLISHING GROUP

First published in paperback in Great Britain in 2020 by
HEADLINE PUBLISHING GROUP

5

Cataloguing in Publication Data is available from the British Library

ISBN 978 1 4722 3524 4

Typeset in Sabon LTD Std by Palimpsest Book Production Ltd, Falkirk, Stirlingshire

Printed and bound in Great Britain by Clays Ltd, Elcograf S.p.A.

Headline's policy is to use papers that are natural, renewable and recyclable
products and made from wood grown in well-managed forests and other controlled
sources. The logging and manufacturing processes are expected to conform to
the environmental regulations of the country of origin.

HEADLINE PUBLISHING GROUP
An Hachette UK Company
Carmelite House
50 Victoria Embankment
London EC4Y 0DZ

www.headline.co.uk
www.hachette.co.uk

For Ella and Daisy,
my two favourite witchlings

Chapter One

Ink. And paper. In this tower built with the silence of women, I have been given back my voice.

The room is still a cell, in a way. The walls are still black stone and my window is still barred, but when the door – of old, blackened wood – is closed, I cannot be seen. There is a bed, a place to wash myself, and a small wooden desk, with ink and paper and pen.

They will not know what they have given me. Winnowry agents are expected to write reports on their missions, and this is what the desk and its contents are for, but in it I see an extraordinary thing.

The curse of the Winnowry is silence and forgetfulness. So many women have entered these black towers, passing out of their lives and out of Sarn, into nothingness. Their lives end here, unremarked, and they are buried deep in the cold sand. Of them and their lives, their stories, nothing is known.

I have lived in that, have felt the slow creeping terror that I am forgotten by the world. Have watched women with pasts as colourful and as unique as tapestries turn to slow and silent stone as their humanity was leeched *from them. Are you really speaking if no one can hear you?*

But, ink and paper are now mine. In a small way these women's stories will be recorded, and I will give them voices – even if they must be secret ones.

Extract from the private records of Agent Chenlo

'Put that flame away! Unless you want to go back to your cell?'

The girl looked up at her, startled, and Agent Chenlo smiled to lessen the harshness of her words. These girls, she reminded herself, were not yet used to the licence they'd been given, limited as it was, and even less used to the idea that a misstep wouldn't automatically earn them a freezing bath or a beating. The tiny lick of green flame that had been curling in the girl's palm immediately vanished.

'Put your gloves back on, Fell-Lisbet, and here, look.' Agent Chenlo gently turned the girls to look back at the Winnowry. The small jetty they stood on was chilly and damp, and the little boat docked there smelled overpoweringly of shellfish, but the Winnowry remained its black, imposing self, looming over the fell-witches like a threat. 'You see those windows there, that go all the way up the chirot tower? And those in Mother Cressin's territory? A sister or a father may look out of those windows at any time, or even the Drowned One herself,' she ignored the mutter at her use of this forbidden phrase, 'and they could see us, huddled down here on this grey day. And winnowfire, even the tiniest flicker, will draw their gaze like *that*.' She snapped her fingers for emphasis. She did not wear gloves herself today. 'It is so bright, it is like a beacon to them. And do you think that if you are caught using your abilities without permission they will allow you to become agents yourselves?'

The girls shuffled and muttered as one, picking at their scarves and casting shy glances at the towers. They liked Agent Chenlo because she gave warnings before punishments, and because she called the winnowfire an *ability* and not an *abomination* – at least when she was out of earshot of the other agents.

'Come on, let's get those barrels on board, or we'll be late. Quickly now.'

The girls returned to the task at hand. Today was the beginning of their introduction to the business of the Winnowry, the daily and weekly tasks that kept the order going. They would load the barrels of akaris up onto the little boat, and make the quick crossing to Mushenska, where they would be unloaded again. They would then accompany Agent Chenlo to the trading house, where much of the akaris would be sold in bulk to the highest bidders. A unique drug that could only be crafted within the intense heat of winnowfire, akaris gave its user a deep, dreamless sleep – unless it was cut with a variety of stimulants, in which case the effects were rather more lively. Officially, only the Winnowry could supply the drug, and thanks to this little monopoly, they could happily charge through the nose for it. Once the akaris had been changed into useful coin, Agent Chenlo and the novice agents would return across the channel of grey water, and that would be that. Small steps, but important ones: learning how to conduct themselves out in the world, showing that they could be trusted. If any one of the four girls stepped out of line, it would be up to Agent Chenlo to admonish them, which could mean anything from a severe dressing-down to having their life energy removed to the point where they passed out. She was authorised to kill them, if she had to, and she carried the silver-topped cudgel, normally worn by the sisters, at her belt, but Agent Chenlo had never had to use it.

She watched them for a moment, rolling the barrels up the gangplank, observed by the wiry captain and a spotty cabin boy. The barrels were heavy and sometimes the fell-witches found the work too difficult, weakened as they were by years spent in damp cells eating gruel, but this group were making the best of it. Satisfied that they'd be able to manage, Agent Chenlo turned away to look across the sea to Mushenska, and all of the familiar ordinariness of the day was chased away by the sight of an impossible shape in the skies over the city; a nightmare coming into focus. She made an odd noise, somewhere between a yelp and a gasp, and heard the captain shout something. One of the girls let out a little shriek.

A dragon was flying over the sea towards them. It was a magnificent thing, covered in pearly white scales, its wings bristling with white feathers. It wore a harness of brown leather and silver, and there was a young woman sitting on its back, her black hair flapping wildly in the wind and a furious expression on her face. Agent Chenlo turned back and shouted at the girls.

'Go! Get on the boat now. You,' she gestured at the captain, 'get them to the city. Cast off immediately.'

The man opened his mouth to argue, and she raised her hands in a clear threat. 'Do it, captain, or I will sink your miserable boat myself.'

The novice agents were all either staring at the dragon – it was so close now, so close – or staring at her, their eyes wide. Agent Chenlo clapped her hands together once, sharply, and the spell broke. As one, the young women ran up the gangplank, and as they disappeared below decks, she felt a surge of relief. From the towers, bells were ringing as various people sounded the alarm all at once.

Chenlo hesitated on the jetty, uncertain what to do next. Knowledge of a number of recent events jostled for her attention, but one fact was clearer than anything else: as unlikely as it seemed, the dragon had to be a legendary war-beast from distant Ebora, and the young woman riding on its back had every reason to be furious with the Winnowry.

4

She began to run towards the main buildings. The dragon got there first, crashing into and through one of the high, spindly towers. Black chunks of rock exploded into the sky as the very top of the structure was smashed to pieces, and then, with a roar, the dragon turned, coming round for another attack. This time the monster landed on the tower that housed the sisters' quarters, latching on to it with claws and tail. It brought its nearest talon up to a long window, sealed with glass and lead, and smashed it quite neatly. Agent Chenlo saw the woman on its back shouting something, and then, after a moment, she leaned forward and sent a barrage of winnowfire in through the newly gaping hole. Chenlo, still staggering towards the gates, felt her skin turn cold, as though she had been doused by a great wave of seawater. It was late in the morning, and most of the sisters would be at their duties, yet she doubted very much that the tower was empty.

Activity erupted at the chirot tower. A trio of agents mounted on bats flew out of its open roof, rounding quickly on the dragon, which was just lifting off from the sisters' tower. Down on the ground, the doors leading to Tomas's Walk sprung open to reveal several panicked-looking sisters, their faces smeared with soot. Behind them it was clear that the interior of the tower was ablaze, and one of them, a woman Chenlo knew as Sister Resn, ran up to her, the silver mask of her order still clutched in one hand.

'You! Get up there and stop them!'

Chenlo spared her a glance, then looked up to where the other agents were engaging the dragon. Bright orbs of green fire danced across the sky, and were met with jets of violet flame.

'Have you lost your mind? That's a dragon! They're going to get themselves killed.'

Sister Resn's face turned red under the soot and her wet mouth creased with outrage.

5

'You dare to speak to me this way, Agent Chenlo?'

Chenlo shook her head in annoyance, unable to look away from the scene playing out around the towers. The bats were circling, brought into line by their agent riders, but it was clear they were terrified of the giant flying lizard. The dragon stopped breathing fire for a moment and surged forward, bringing its long tail around in a whip-crack movement that connected with the nearest bat, striking it from the sky. It fell out of sight, its rider struggling with the harness. The woman was still shouting, and one of the remaining two agents turned her bat and fled, heading directly out to sea. More sisters and fathers streamed out of the furnace rooms, several of them half dressed, while the dragon circled higher. One of the fathers was Father Eranis, every inch of smugness wiped from his jowly face.

'It's her, isn't it?' he spat. He wasn't wearing any shoes, and his bare feet looked like ugly sea creatures against the sand. 'That fucking lunatic has come home.'

'Come home with a dragon,' said Chenlo faintly. The last agent had been chased from the sky. 'What did you think would happen?' Taking advantage of their distraction, she turned the full contempt of her gaze on the fathers and sisters gathered behind her. 'Sending Tyranny O'Keefe, of all people, to steal from Ebora? To steal the kin of, Tomas save us, actual fire-breathing dragons? As if Fell-Noon didn't have enough reason to hate the Winnowry already.'

Eranis looked at her blankly, just as though he hadn't been present in the many discussions where Chenlo had argued, again and again, that their plan was outrageously risky. She opened her mouth, unable to resist giving them another piece of her mind, when the dragon dropped down towards them. The fathers and sisters scattered, most running down across the sands, with a few heading back to the furnace. Chenlo stood her ground, wincing against the winds that battered her as the great white dragon landed in the courtyard, outside the enormous doors to the main Winnowry building. *All those women,* she thought, with a surge of terror, *cooked alive in their cells.*

'Wait! You must wait!'

Fell-Noon turned, and Chenlo was reminded of how young the rogue witch was – barely older than the novice agents she had been training. She was wearing strange Eboran clothes, and the bat-wing tattoo on her forehead, a twin to Chenlo's own, looked out of place, as though someone had scrawled it over a painting of a mythical figure in a book.

'What must we wait for?' asked the dragon.

Chenlo blinked. She knew, of course, that war-beasts could speak, but actually hearing that fine, cultured voice, being regarded by those burning violet eyes . . . that was something else.

'Please,' she held up her hands, too aware that such an action from a fell-witch was almost always a threat. 'Please, Fell-Noon, the women in there have done you no harm. I know you must be angry . . .'

'Angry!' The young woman grinned wolfishly. 'You don't know the half of it, Winnowry dog.'

'I urge you not to strike those who share your own miserable past!'

At this, Fell-Noon looked faintly puzzled. She shook her head.

'I'm not here for them,' she said.

With that she turned away from Agent Chenlo and she and the dragon moved closer to the enormous doors. She raised her arms, fingers spread, and an arc of green fire, so bright it was nearly white, burst from her hands. It hit the wood and iron of the doors and seemed to burn all the brighter, until Chenlo had to turn away, the heat and light crisping her hair and skin.

Such winnowfire, she thought, as the stench of burning wood

7

and melting metal reached her. *It burns hotter than anything I've ever seen.*

There was an odd, crumping noise, and where an enormous door had stood for hundreds of years there was suddenly a gaping hole, wreathed in flames turned orange and red. Hot pools of molten metal snaked across the sand and grit towards her boots, and hurriedly she stepped out of the way. The dragon and her rider stepped through into the echoing space beyond.

'Are all human structures so miserable?' asked Vostok.

Noon shrugged, distracted. They stood in a part of the Winnowry that she had only seen once before; on the day they had brought her here, when she was eleven years old. It was generally known as the processing office, where girls, often very small ones, were made ready for their lives of imprisonment. Their clothes would be taken, along with any other possessions they might have on them. Clingy parents or relatives were removed and sent out a separate door, and the girls were told the rules: you will not touch another person, flesh to flesh, unless you are given permission; you will give the remainder of your lives in service to Tomas the Drowned, the figurehead of the Winnowry's tyrannical order; you will work to heal the breach your very presence has made on the world; you are an abomination, and you will never forget it.

It was a dark and forbidding space, empty of any comforts or windows. There was the wide stretch of the foyer, and a line of doors on one side, where the Winnowry sisters kept their records and documents. In the centre of the space was a driftwood altar, where the girls were stripped and washed, and anointed with pale, powdery ash before being dressed again in the clothes of the Winnowry. Looking at it, Noon felt a fresh surge of rage close her throat.

'What is it?' asked Vostok, her voice lower than it had been. 'I have not felt such turmoil within you before, bright weapon.'

'It's this fucking place. It brings everything back.' Noon took a deep breath and held it for a few seconds. Somewhere, beyond this processing space, she could hear a great number of women – talking, shouting. They had heard the tower being smashed, had likely heard the sisters' and fathers' panicked exclamations. Some of them had probably even seen Noon and Vostok arrive through their tiny, smeared windows. 'It's like . . . it's like a trap is hovering over me, waiting to put me back into my cell.'

Vostok tipped her long head to one side. She took up much of the space, looking like a great marble statue against the black walls.

'Nonsense. This place could not hold you now. You will always be free. Remember why you came here.'

'Yes, you're right.' Noon climbed down from Vostok's harness, and stalked over to the nearest door. She threw it open to find a room oddly like a kitchen. An alcove sheltered a blackened stove, and a great steel bucket containing long, pale branches of wood sat to one side of it. There was a huge sieve on a table and a great clay bowl underneath. It was, she belatedly realised, where they burned the wood to make the powder they covered the fell-witches with. Cowering behind the table was a pair of sisters, one still wearing a blank silver mask.

'You,' Noon addressed them tersely, 'get me the keys. For the cells. Hurry up.'

The woman with the bare face cringed, but the one with the mask came around the table towards Noon, the heavy cudgel held in one hand.

'Abomination!' she spat. Her eyes, just about visible through the eye slits of her mask, were wild. 'What have you done? What poison have you leaked into the world with your self-ishness? In Tomas's name, I command you to repent! You must be purged, child.'

'Idiot. You're all so bloody stupid it hurts.' Noon lifted her hand and sent a blossom of winnowfire towards the woman, who danced backwards abruptly, letting out a little shriek. 'Did you forget we can do this?' She sent another small fireball, faster this time, and it landed on the woman's wide skirts. In seconds she was aflame, throwing herself onto the floor with a series of desperate screams. Noon watched her trying to douse the flames for a moment, a tight feeling in her throat, before she turned to the other woman.

'The keys?'

The woman nodded rapidly and led her to another room. It was well-lit and neat, with over a hundred iron keys hung on the walls, each carefully labelled.

'Give me the keys for the bottom-most cells on the south side.' When the woman hesitated, Noon shook her head. 'I don't have to burn you alive, you know, I could just feed you to the dragon.'

The woman turned white, and pressed a set of five keys into Noon's hand. As she did so, Noon touched her face with her free hand, draining the sister's life energy, and she dropped to the floor in a faint. 'This is the end of it all,' she said to the woman's unconscious form. 'I'm ending it all here.'

Back in the foyer Vostok was amusing herself by standing across the hole that had once been the front doors. There were Winnowry agents out there as well as a handful of sisters and fathers, and every time they drew closer to the building, Vostok would lower her long head and shoot great spears of violet flame towards them, scattering them all back. Eventually, Noon knew, they would gather their remaining agents together – perhaps calling back those who were in Mushenska too – and make a more determined assault. She did not have much time before everything became a lot more complicated.

Letting Vostok continue to hold the front doors, Noon went to the passage that led to the prison. This was the heart of the Winnowry. Here she found a pair of novices, young men who

10

inevitably reminded her of Lusk, the novice who had helped her escape, so long ago. They were easily persuaded to unbolt the doors before they ran off and locked themselves in one of the office rooms. Taking a deep breath, Noon pushed the heavy iron doors aside, and stepped into the gaping space beyond.

It was bigger than she remembered, and strange. To her left, the southern bank of cells began, reaching up and up into the echoing void, a spindly web of steps and platforms rising with them. To the other side were the northern bank of cells, and there she could see women, all of them standing at the bars with their faces raw and shocked. The same set of grey clothes, over and over, the same crude bat-wing tattoo on the broad plane of every forehead. She wondered what she looked like to them. High above everything, crouched in the ceiling, were the huge water vats, which the sisters would turn on the witches if they got out of line. A shocked silence hung in the vast space, so heavy that Noon almost felt it as a pressure against her face.

'Who are you?' someone called down from the uppermost cells, and the shout shattered the silence into chaotic pieces. Someone else shouted, from much closer, 'She's Fell-Noon! The rogue witch!' and then someone else cried, 'But she's dead! Agent Lin killed her, they said so.'

'Listen!' Noon raised her hands and shook the set of keys. 'We've got to be quick. I'll open the five nearest cells, and then those women can go to the lock room and get the rest. You have to let yourselves out.' There was a rising cacophony at this, and Noon found herself shouting over them. 'The way is free, for now! Help each other, and be fast.'

With that she turned to the nearest cells, and ignoring the look of shock on the woman's face, rammed the first key home and turned it. Throwing the door back, she nodded to the woman. 'Go, down the corridor. It's the room with the door left standing open. Start getting the keys! This is your only chance.'

The woman nodded and fled, and Noon moved onto the next cell, then the next. A great roar was filling the prison as the women clamoured to be freed, and Noon found that her hands were shaking. It had never been this loud in here; before, the women had always been afraid to be loud.

'Go,' she said to the woman in the fifth cell, just as the first one was coming back, her arms full of iron keys.

'There's a fucking dragon out there,' she said, her voice faint.

'Good, brilliant, very observant. Can you do this? Can you get them out?'

The witch was joined by the others, and they began taking the keys from her arms, set expressions on their faces. Satisfied that she'd done what she could, Noon left the echoing space behind, relief surging through her, and headed back to the foyer. Vostok had broken through part of the wall to give herself more space to target the agents, who were keeping out of her reach on the backs of the giant bats.

'Bright weapon?'

'Nearly done!'

Finally, Noon headed for the Sea Watch tower, arming herself with a fresh supply of Vostok's life energy as she passed by. Through another set of doors and out into the small stony courtyard that existed between all of the towers. Paved with grey slate and dotted here and there with bat guano, it was as miserable a place as Noon had ever seen. Sometimes, women were left out here overnight as a punishment, with no protection from the rain and the cold.

'Fucking place,' she muttered, feeling a shiver work its way down the back of her neck. The Sea Watch tower was the official name for the space where the Drowned One kept her rooms; you were sent to her chambers only if you had been especially bad, or if Mother Cressin had taken a particular interest in you. At the bottom, Noon blew the doors off their hinges and stepped inside. It was all too easy to imagine the old woman crouched at the top of the tower like some ancient, wrinkled spider, smelling of old salt and watching over her precious Winnowry. The spiral staircase within was lit periodically with oil lamps, and the sea-wards side of the tower was punctured with tall, narrow windows, yet the place remained gloomy and damp. At the very top she paused, eyeing the door with some unease. It stood open, just a crack, so that she could see a tiny slither of the room beyond. Had she ever seen it partly open like that? She thought not.

Cautiously, Noon moved onto the landing, her hands held in front of her. Just as she'd decided that Mother Cressin had already fled, the door crashed open, revealing the sizeable form of Fell-Mary, the old woman's personal bodyguard. A wall of green flame shot towards Noon and she half dived, half fell back down the steps immediately behind her. Several old wounds cried out in indignation, and she bellowed a few swear words.

'It's over!' she shouted. 'The women are freeing themselves, and there will be boats arriving for them soon. It's *over*.' There was silence from the landing. 'Fell-Mary, you don't have to babysit that awful creature anymore.'

Still there was silence. Noon poked her head around the corner, only to see Fell-Mary bearing down on her, her enormous hands reaching for her throat. This time, she lunged forward and grabbed the woman, skin against skin, and for the briefest moment felt the tug of a strong fell-witch trying to pull her life's energy from her.

Bad idea. I'm stronger than you.

Putting everything she had behind it, Noon tore the woman's life force out of her body, easily batting aside her own feeble attempt to do the same to Noon. At once she was filled with that vital, buzzing force, so much of it that her fingers tingled, while Fell-Mary collapsed to the floor, her eyes rolled up to the whites.

'I bloody *told* you,' she said, aggrieved. From within the room, there came a dry, rasping sound – the Drowned One's idea of laughter.

'Come in, Fell-Noon. Let me see what you've become.'

Noon summoned a pair of fiery gloves around her fists and stepped into the chamber. It was as cold and as miserable as she remembered. Narrow windows looked out across the grey sea, bare pieces of furniture made from driftwood were scattered to the corners, and a huge iron and glass tank filled with seawater dominated the room. The smell of salt was overpowering.

'The rumours that have come over the Bloodless Mountains are true, then.' Mother Cressin sat in one of her driftwood chairs, her skin the same chalky pallor as the wood. She looked wizened and tiny, a half-formed thing found under a rock, and for a moment Noon felt a sense of unreality threatening to overwhelm her. Why had she ever been frightened of this small, defenceless, cruel woman? She herself was the weapon, after all. 'You belong to the Eborans now. Do they know what they've let into the heart of their world?'

Noon came fully into the room. Distantly she could hear the roar of Vostok's fire, and the shouts of men and women. Soon, the boats she had paid for in Mushenska would be arriving at the small jetty, and she would need to be there to lead the women to their freedom. Time was getting away from her.

'I'm giving you one chance to leave now. Get out and go. Get one of your agents to fly you away on a bat, or swim for it, I don't care, but your time here is done. This whole shit show,' she gestured around the room, taking in the entirety of the Winnowry, 'is over. I'm ending it now.'

'So you are truly ready to unleash evil on this world? For hundreds of years, the Winnowry has been the thin barrier between the abomination of these fallen women, and the sanctity of the outer world. In Tomas's name, we have kept them hidden and safe, given them a chance to make up for what they are, and cleansed Sarn of their taint. You end that, and you will tear this world apart, and all for your own demented pride.'

'I don't give a shit about any of that fucking nonsense. Because that is exactly what it is – nonsense you and all the nasty little people who came before you made up to justify the torture and exploitation of women.' Noon laughed, a sour bark of amusement. 'Using us to make your drugs, offering tiny scraps of freedom to the women who would work for you. It's just so fucking *obvious*. You couldn't even come up with any good reasons! Oh, some man said it once, he was half mad from being drowned but, sure, let's found an entire order of misery on his say-so!'

The Drowned One stood up, her feet encased in papery white slippers. The faint mocking expression had vanished, and there were two points of pinkish colour on the tops of her cheeks – the first time Noon had ever seen any colour in that dour face.

'The fell-women are dangerous,' she said, her voice low and tight with a boiling fury. 'They kill, daily. They are a threat to every normal man, woman and child, and they are a threat to themselves.' She straightened up. 'You yourself are the best possible example of that, Fell-Noon. How many people did you kill at the tender age of eleven?'

'Stop it.' The dark space in Noon's memory opened up as if summoned, a yawning pit she did not wish to go anywhere near. 'Leave now, Cressin, or I *will* kill you.'

'Can you still smell it, in your dreams? The boiling meat of everyone you'd ever known or loved? Do you see their smoking corpses when you sleep?'

Without knowing she was about to do it, Noon raised her arms and released Fell-Mary's life energy in a solid ball of green fire. It shot across the room and exploded against the tank of seawater, which shattered with a deafening crash. Water surged across the chamber, rising briefly to the tops of Noon's boots. Glass glittered everywhere, and the black iron frame of the tank was a twisted thing, black and misshapen like a body when it has been burned down to its bones – *no, don't think about that*. Mother Cressin had been knocked to the ground with the violence of it, and was bleeding from a number of tiny cuts. She was a shrivelled white and red thing, her colourless hair sodden and clinging to her neck and forehead.

'I've let you talk for long enough,' said Noon. She could hear a gentle trickling noise as the escaped water made its way down the spiral staircase. 'All of this shit has been going on for long enough.'

'No!' Mother Cressin raised her hand, and it was holding a curved shard of broken glass. 'I will not die in the flames of an abomination.' And in an awkward, painful movement, she ran the lethal shard across her own neck. The wound opened up like a second mouth, and a great surge of blood poured down the front of her rough-spun shirt, turning it crimson in an eye blink. She made some pained, gargling noises, one hand patting at the new hole in her throat as though she was unsure how it got there, and then she lay back against the black stones.

Noon stood for a moment, watching the puddle of blood as it mixed with the seawater and glass – whirls of bright crimson, seeping into the cracks of the Winnowry stone. All those years of fear and anger, and the woman was finally dead. Eventually, she turned her back on the whole mess and made her way down the stairs, taking care to step over the inert form of Fell-Mary, whose own clothes were now sodden with escaped water and blood.

'Go.' Noon stood up in Vostok's harness, addressing the small crowd of fathers, sisters and Winnowry agents on the bleak stretch of sand. Behind them, a small ramshackle fleet of fishing boats were crowding the jetty while a long line of women waited to be taken away from the island. Looking at them briefly, Noon caught a mixture of expressions on their faces: joy, confusion, terror. 'The Drowned One is dead –' she ignored a handful of cries at this – 'and there's nothing left for you here. The Winnowry is finished.'

'You murdered our sacred mother.' It was a tall man with a gingery beard, his face smeared with soot. Noon recognised him as one of the fathers who had regularly escorted her to the furnace. 'This is a dark day for Sarn, a very dark day.' He shook his head mournfully.

'She took her own life, if you must know.' A thought occurred to Noon. 'What happened to Novice Lusk, the novice who was in the chirot tower when I escaped this shit hole?'

'He died. During . . . questioning.' This was from one of the older agents she had briefly spoken to earlier. To Noon she looked to be around Vintage's age, although she had a thick bolt of white threaded through her long black hair. She was tall and held herself without fear – Noon could feel Vostok's reluctant approval – and there was a tattoo of an eagle at her throat; a much finer piece of work than the crude bat wing on her forehead. Dimly, Noon recalled the people of Yuron-Kai who had arrived, with many other humans, at the Eboran palace. This woman had been taken a long way from her home. 'Fell-Noon—'

'That's not my name. Don't call me that.' Noon gestured to the women filing onto the boats. 'Don't call anyone that again.'

The woman nodded once, accepting this without argument. 'Noon, of Ebora, I'm sure the women you have freed are grateful, but you have to understand . . . they have no homes to go to, no jobs.' She paused, clearly trying to think of a way around the problem herself. 'There's no shelter for them tonight, no food in that city. They have no money to pay for it! Their families will likely not have them back, and most of Sarn

17

harbours no love for fell— for these women. For us. Where will they go? What will they do?' She brought her hands together, and clasped them in front of her in an oddly formal questioning gesture. 'You have given them their freedom, Noon of Ebora, but they do not yet have their lives.'

Noon stopped. She wanted to look again at the women climbing onto the boats, to see for herself whether they were truly joyful, or whether they were now realising that she had released them into an uncertain future – but to do that would be to let the agent know she also had her doubts. Instead, she lifted her chin, and pressed one hand to Vostok's scales. The dragon's affirmation and certainty was a balm.

'The Winnowry has money, doesn't it? All that akaris you've been selling, you can't tell me there isn't a room in that place somewhere stuffed with coin. Use it, for once, for their benefit. And tell them to come to Ebora,' she said, lifting her voice to address the entire crowd. 'Sarn might not love them, or want them, but Ebora has more wisdom than that.'

With that, she let Vostok leap up into the air and take flight, pleased with how the shivering group of sisters and fathers quailed at the movement. The agent, however, the one with the eagle at her throat, did not flinch, and Noon could not help noticing that she watched them go with a thoughtful expression on her face.

'What now?' asked Vostok. 'You have won a great victory here today, bright weapon.'

'Yeah.' Noon nodded, narrowing her eyes against the sea wind. 'It was a long time coming.' But privately she kept returning to the agent's questions, and the sound of blood trickling down cold stone steps. 'Let's go home.'

Chapter Two

Fell-Almeera

A new girl came in at the gates today. Like most new girls, she walked with her head down, her shoulders slumped. I could see from my place in the courtyard that she was shivering, although it was a warm day. The sisters and the agents with her did not seem to notice, and she was taken through to be given her new clothes, and to be instructed in her new rules. Be quiet, do not get angry, touch no one, do as you are told.

Her name is Almeera, and she is from Talrisan, a kingdom of Jarlsbad. I will add further details to this record when I know more.

Almeera is twelve years old, she had a mother and a father, and two younger brothers. When she talks of these two brothers, she cries. The ability only manifested in her recently, within the last year or so, and she is so frightened of it, sickened by it almost. You can tell she is afraid of her own self now, holding herself away from others in case the ability manifests without her say-so. I am on hand during her initial meeting with Mother Cressin, and Almeera tells the old woman that she had nightmares about accidentally hurting her little brothers; that she saw them screaming in her dreams, their smooth brown skin bubbling up like pig fat in the fire. Mother Cressin nods and tells her that she is corrupted, that she is a vessel of evil and a stain on the world, but that if she does as she is told, she can help heal the wounds she has created.

I watch Almeera for a few days. She is quiet and makes no attempt to talk to the women in the cells around her, and even as I am frustrated with her for this, I become annoyed with myself; she is a child, taken from her family. Perhaps in time she will grow stronger and find some anger inside herself, but for now I fear I can do nothing for her.

Here are some details about Almeera of Talrisan, that I was able to uncover from the agents who collected her from Jarlsbad: her mother makes beautiful, colourful pottery that they sell from a shop that is also their home, right on the town square; in the yard of this shop is a place where old clay has spilled, and, once, Almeera and her brothers pushed their hands and feet into it – their marks can still be seen in the hardened clay; the sign on the shop is a bright yellow bird. Things to remember about Almeera before she was Fell-Almeera.

Extract from the private records of Agent Chenlo

Hestillion stood on the broad back of the corpse moon, surrounded by a thick and stifling darkness. High above, an unknowable distance away, was a slither of light, and this was what she focussed on. It looked like a narrow crack, hardly wide enough to push her fingers through, but she knew that the Jure'lia ship she stood on and all the other remaining Behemoths – broken and confused as they were – had passed through it, into this underground place. She shivered, despite the warmth.

'How are you feeling now, sweet one?' Her voice in the utter silence was a pebble dropped into a silent pool. Her words rippled outwards, returned to her distorted by the uneven walls with their alcoves and hidden spaces. In the darkness, a shadow moved. The longer they stayed down here, the better Hestillion was able to see in the dark, and Celaphon's great blocky head swung into view. He had found himself a ledge on the stone walls large enough to accommodate his considerable bulk.

'I feel ill,' he said. His silvery white eyes were the brightest thing in the gloom. 'I feel ill *all the time.*'

Hestillion nodded, her hand stealing up to rest against the blue crystal protruding from her chest. Through it she could feel the constant presence of the worm people, like hot hands against her skin. 'I know. I feel it too. This conflict –' She paused, uncertain how to describe the sensation. She felt as though she kept losing her footing, as though the ground were shifting under her constantly, and in her chest her heart would beat with sudden violence at random moments. If she reached out along her connection to the Jure'lia, the feelings would only grow worse – all was discord, all was confusion. Celaphon, with his own crystal resting in the centre of his head, could feel everything she could, with the added pain of his own mutant body. 'It's tearing them apart.'

'Tearing *us* apart,' said Celaphon. The big dragon shifted on his perch, and Hestillion heard the gentle rain of debris as a small avalanche of stones and grit fell down into the space below them. 'How will you fix it?'

Hestillion rolled her eyes, confident that Celaphon would not see it. 'I? How will I fix it? Not everything is for me to fix, sweet one.'

The dragon grunted. 'You are the clever one, little green bird.'

Uncertain whether to feel flattered or patronised, Hestillion looked back to her feet, and ordered the oily skin of the

Behemoth to peel back for her. After a moment it did, revealing a grey tunnel into the interior, softly lit by the glowing fronds that grew straight out of the walls.

'I will go and talk to her again.'

'Good,' said Celaphon. The lights from within had blinded her for a moment, and the dragon became a disembodied voice somewhere to her left. 'I will stay here. The air is fresher.'

Inside the corpse moon, everything was too quiet. The ever-present hum, which Hestillion barely noticed these days, stuttered and clanged, growing louder and stopping, or becoming a vibration strong enough to turn Hestillion's feet numb inside her boots. The frond-lights flickered often too, occasionally turning off entirely, or even, on a number of unsettling occasions, sinking back into the pliable walls.

As she made her way to the centre of the Behemoth, she thought of Celaphon's words: *tearing us apart*, he had said. Although Celaphon was a war-beast born from the branches of the great tree-god Ygseril, he was now wholly a creature of the worm people; the queen of the Jure'lia had fed him, nurtured him, and when his body was sufficiently twisted, had embedded the blue crystal into his flesh and joined him to their great web of minds. And where her war-beast went, Hestillion must follow.

The wall in front of her spasmed open, revealing the enormous blue crystal that was the heart of the Behemoth. Kneeling in front of it, her mask-like face rapt, was the Jure'lia queen.

'You are still here, then,' Hestillion pointed out. When the queen didn't reply, she strode across the chamber to join her in front of the crystal. A familiar image flickered within its depths, but she ignored it, looking down at the queen instead. Her amorphous, almost humanoid body was folded and creased in on itself, her long fingers – each fully as long as Hestillion's hands – neatly intertwined in her lap. 'You must come away from it now. Can't you see? Things need to be fixed.'

The queen nodded, but she did not move. 'But it is all broken, Hestillion Eskt of the corpse moon. Can you not see it? Can you not feel it, in your heart?'

'I can, actually.' Hestillion grimaced, pressing one hand briefly to her breastbone. 'I feel like I might drop in a swoon at any moment, and it is most disagreeable. Celaphon, too, feels this illness. It is time to – to snap out of this funk.'

'Funk.' For the first time, the queen lifted her head and looked at Hestillion. The smooth white planes of her face were streaked with a watery, greyish fluid. 'What is funk?'

Hestillion shook her head. 'We must repair! We cannot hide here forever, can we?'

Slowly, the queen rose to her feet, unfolding like some elaborate paper confection such as Hestillion's mother had made when she and Tormalin had been children. 'We have always done so, before,' said the queen, towering over Hestillion. 'When we battled you in the past, and found ourselves pushed back by your creatures and your people, we would retreat, underground, and slowly we would grow ourselves anew, to be ready again.'

'Except you're not doing that, are you?' Hestillion tried to control the sharpness in her voice, and failed. 'Because of this,' she gestured to the crystal, and the new, strange memory contained within it, 'you sit in the ground and rot instead.'

The queen twitched, as if struck, then reached out one long finger towards the crystal. 'We do not understand it,' she said. 'How can this displace what we are? How can *this* be strong enough?'

Reluctantly, Hestillion turned back to the crystal. Within it, there was a shimmering image of her home in winter. The Eboran palace could just be glimpsed in the background, the shining gates standing open, the plaza crowded with people. Humans, she corrected herself. Humans dressed in thick furs and gloves and hats, while their strange lurid tents and travelling vehicles

23

were dotted around. And in the middle of this chaos stood, of all people, her cousin. Aldasair Eskt, wearing the old-fashioned blue frock coat that she had seen him in often enough, a dusty moth-eaten thing he had been ludicrously attached to. In the vision he looked lost, his auburn hair tumbling over his shoulders and an expression of faint perplexity on his face. As usual, when she saw her cousin, Hestillion was filled with the urge to grab him and give him a good shake, but this was just a memory, placed within the crystal by the human man Bern Finnkeeper. Once, the crystal had held something quite different – a memory of another world, almost too alien to look at; a memory in the great chain of memories that had held the Jure'lia together. The human man had inserted his own memory and broken that chain, throwing them all into disarray.

'It doesn't matter,' said Hestillion. 'You're the one who joined the human to the Jure'lia when we took him prisoner. Do you see now how that was dangerous?' The queen tilted her head slightly, and Hestillion moved swiftly on. She didn't wish to remind the queen that it had been her who had led Bern and Aldasair to freedom, afraid as she had been that they would turn Celaphon against her. 'What's important is that you banish this memory that is hurting us, and restore the old one. Can you not do that?'

For the first time in weeks, the queen seemed to come back to herself somewhat. Her eyes narrowed, and her fleshless lips pressed together.

'It is not so simple, Hestillion Eskt. We can banish it, but the memory that the crystal once held is gone. When the human pushed his own memory on it, it ceased to exist.'

'You can't replace it with something else?'

The queen looked perplexed. 'Like what? That unique memory of a long-ago world is lost, I cannot simply replace it. We cannot.' All the previous solidity seemed to drain out of the queen's form. 'Besides which, we must know why this memory,' she reached out to the crystal, 'is so strong. So solid. It vexes us.'

'Well, this . . . disruption is vexing me.' Hestillion crossed her arms over her chest. 'We have crawled down into this hole, and it appears we are simply rotting here, and you will not do anything to stop it. Celaphon and I did not join ourselves to the Jure'lia to be so easily defeated. Do you know what we have given up? What we have sacrificed to stand with you?' An image of the Eboran boy Celaphon had killed during the battle over the Tarah-hut Mountains briefly threatened to disarm her completely, but she pushed it away. 'We have kept our side of this pact. Now you must fight too, queen of the Jure'lia.'

With that she turned and left the chamber, heading for her own quarters while her heart thundered in her chest.

Chapter Three

Fell-Marg

Fell-witches are very rare, yet Mushenska seems to produce more than its share of them. It's as if the city creates them in defiance of the black towers that lurk across the sea from it. Today, we took a girl from a wealthy merchant family – a strange and delicate situation. Three of us were dispatched to take her in, with a sister assigned to add, I suspect, an extra layer of respectability. The parents were anxious we were not seen from the street and let us in through the back of their sizeable house (I have to wonder what are they planning to tell people? That their daughter has gone to stay with distant family? That she has gone to study at a college in Reidn? How long do they imagine they can keep up that pretence, especially when she never returns?). Their daughter, Marg, was fifteen and defiant. I knew immediately that she would give us trouble, and steeled myself while the parents greeted us with tea and fruit.

(The families we must take fell-witches from have many varying reactions. Most are sad, many are frightened. A distressing number are, as mine were, disgusted and

ashamed. A few, like Marg's parents, seem keen to treat it like an everyday, normal transaction. Their daughter could be starting a new job, or they could be selling an item of furniture. The clues to their distress are in tiny things: shaking hands, smiles that hang on the mouth a touch too long, a sweaty forehead.)

The moment came when Agent Lin indicated that we must leave. The girl Marg slapped a hand around her mother's wrist, drained her to unconsciousness in a moment, and then threw a ragged swirl of winnowfire at us, which was easily avoided. To my surprise, she jumped for the window (we were two storeys up) but it seemed there was an awning below that caught her fall.

A chase then, through a busy Mushenskan street – so much for discretion. The girl did not get far, and no one was hurt, although there was a stall of cabbages that will not see market day again. Marg was drained and trussed, and we left without further delay. Agent Lin was not happy, but I reminded her: our concerns are to be for the Winnowry and our charge, not for disgruntled parents.

Marg is an interesting prospect. Spirited, angry, but possibly too willing to take risks. The Winnowry might sap the anger from her in any case. We shall see.

Some details about Marg of Mushenska: she looks strikingly like her father, tall and dark with thunderous eyebrows. She has no siblings. Her favourite fruit is the pear – her mother asked if she could send some on, when she was settled (as if this were a boarding school). She collected seashells, and had several in her pockets when we took her down. I threw them into the sea as we passed over on our bats.

Extract from the private records of Agent Chenlo

'There's another group arriving.'

Vintage took the eyeglass away, squinting into the distance. It was possible to see them now without the contraption; seven giant bats with riders, looking like black-and-white smudges on the blue summer sky. It had been three months since Noon's little incident at the Winnowry, and still new fell-witches were arriving every few days or so. Another seven would take their witch population up to thirty-eight.

'Helcate,' said Helcate.

'Indeed.' Vintage reached up and absently patted the war-beast on the snout. Since the sun had warmed the Eboran forests into lively places once more, he had grown a great deal, and although he still clearly mourned Eri, there were signs that this fresh bonding with her was giving him new strength. 'But this is interesting. So far we've mostly seen them arriving on foot over the mountains, or there was that group that came via the Barren Sea. But on bats? Perhaps this could be our mysterious Agent Chenlo, finally come to join all the women she has apparently badgered into our company.' She grinned. 'Noon will be so pleased.'

With that in mind, she left the summer gardens, Helcate trotting at her back, and made her way to the south-eastern portion of the palace. Here, Aldasair had thoughtfully housed all their errant fell-witches close to each other, with many of their rooms facing out across a set of ornamental ponds. At its heart was one of the palace's odd sprawling rock gardens, a concept Vintage had not come across before. Rather than a place of lush grass and flowers, there was a neat lawn punctured with artful piles of white and grey stone, themselves dotted with hardy little plants which had fat, bulbous leaves and blossoms of all colours. It had become an unofficial meeting place for the women, many of whom still seemed reluctant to mix with the other peoples of Sarn. She smiled to see them, a mixture of young and old women, several sitting on the grass chatting, with a few perched on the rocks, drinking tea. She could see from the blank wonder on their faces that they were still getting used to being outside at all. One child, surely no more than fifteen, sat with her fingers buried deep in the grass, her face turned up to the sun.

'Morning, Carola.' Vintage crouched by the girl, taking a moment to enjoy how easy it was to do this now – her broken ankle, after many long weeks, had finally healed. 'How are you today?'

The girl beamed up at her. Her face, so pale and drawn when she had arrived, was gradually getting some colour. Vintage thought she could even see a few freckles.

'I am very well, Lady Vintage.' The girl's voice was hoarse still – too many years spent in near silence. 'The sun is out, I can eat what I like.' She patted the grass. 'And the *green* of it all. It's like being warm after years of being cold.' She shrugged. '*And* it's warm, of course. There's a rumour, Lady Vintage, that the Jure'lia are dead now. That your warriors killed them all with their tricks.'

Vintage felt her smile die a little. 'Now then, darling, we can't know that.'

'No one has seen them for months! They all vanished from the sky after you fought them off.' The girl tore up some blades of grass and watched them fall through her fingers. 'That's what everyone is saying, everyone who comes over the Bloodless Mountains.'

Vintage looked away, back to the smooth organic shapes of the palace. The girl was right; every piece of gossip they heard claimed that the Behemoths had sailed off out of sight – that their trickery in Ebora had somehow frightened the worm people off. No one, despite all of Vintage's questions, had been able to give her any idea of exactly where they had gone, and that was what worried her. This, she knew well from her own studies, was not unheard of. At the end of every Rain, when the war-beasts who had been born from Ygseril defeated the Jure'lia, the old enemy would disappear for a time. And ultimately, she and Bern had only been able to disrupt the memory crystal of a single Behemoth – could that have hurt the worm people so badly? Was that really enough to send them into hiding again? Somehow, she did not believe it.

'Lady Vintage, do you know where Noon is? We thought maybe she'd come and see us today.'

Vintage smiled, returning her attention to the girl. When the fell-witches had started arriving, they had insisted on calling Noon by any number of titles, much to the young woman's horror. Fell-Noon, Mistress Noon, Lady Noon, Sister Noon . . . the younger girls, at least, seemed to have come around to the idea that she needed no title, but it hadn't lessened their admiration for the woman who had liberated them.

'I haven't seen her, my dear, but I'm sure she'll pop her head around soon.'

The girl nodded seriously, her hair falling over her forehead and partially obscuring the crude Winnowry tattoo. Vintage left her on the grass, waved to a pair of older women cradling delicate teacups in their hands, and left the gardens with Helcate in tow. Together, they made their way to the central war-beast courtyard, where Tormalin, Noon, Vostok and Kirune were waiting to leave. Tor was still adjusting Kirune's harness, his long black hair loose over his shoulders. The war-beast rumbled at Vintage's approach, and Tor looked up.

'All set?'

'Please, *you're* asking *me* if I'm prepared? How times have changed.' She turned to Noon, brushing the younger woman's arm. 'They were asking after you again, my dear.'

Noon sighed, looking troubled. 'Fire and blood.'

'They seek a leader,' said Vostok. The great white dragon had been fussing at the feathers on her wings, and still had one curling from the end of her snout. Noon reached up and plucked it off. 'Which is what you are, bright weapon.'

'Give over. That's the last bloody thing I am. What am I supposed to do with them, anyway? We've given them rooms, food, clothes. What else do they want?'

'A direction, a purpose?' Vintage spread her arms wide, grinning at Noon's discomfort. 'Destiny? I saw more arriving as I left, by the way. They were flying in on bats, which is useful. I wonder—'

'Shall we make a move before we've lost all the light?' cut in Tor. He had climbed onto Kirune's back and had strapped himself in, and was now tying his hair back in a loose tail. The big cat was silent, his amber eyes narrowed in the bright sunshine. 'You can gossip on the way, if you like.'

'Oh, fine.'

Vintage climbed up onto Helcate's back and got herself comfortable in the harness, feeling, as she always did, a little shiver of wonder that she was riding a war-beast. Noon was seated on Vostok's shoulders, and she had pulled a large map from one of the packs strapped there.

'So we're heading north-west . . .'

'According to Micanal's amber tablets, that's where it should be,' said Tor.

'There's a lot of Wild out there,' said Noon, doubtfully. 'If this map is to be believed.'

'Even more by now, I expect,' said Tor lightly. 'But don't worry, you will be with me. Come on, I will lead the way.'

Vintage waited for the two larger war-beasts to get up into the sky, then leaned down to talk into Helcate's long, foxy ears. 'Come on then, my darling. Let's be having you.'

He leapt up, thick leathery wings unfurling, and in moments they were up in the sky, Vintage's stomach left somewhere in the courtyard.

'Sarn's bastard bones, I don't think I'll ever get used to that.'

They rose up over the palace, Ebora unravelling before them like an impossible tapestry. Just ahead, the elegant forms of Vostok and Kirune made strange shapes against the blue sky until Vintage and Helcate drew level with them once more.

'You will have to learn to take off at the same time as us,' said Tor, when she was back within earshot. 'It's such a scruffy formation, having you swoop up behind us.'

'Formations! You're lucky I don't fall straight off this thing.' Vintage had hold of the leather strap on the front of Helcate's harness, her grip so tight that her hands ached. 'Besides, you both take up too much room. You might accidentally knock little Helcate from the sky.'

'That would not happen,' rumbled Kirune. 'We are much too skilled.'

Vintage smiled to herself, a small blush of warmth touching her heart. Since their dangerous journey to the island of Origin together, Kirune and Vostok had grown closer, seeming to become allies of a sort. Given that both were vain, proud and easily offended, she viewed this as something of a miracle. When Kirune and the other war-beasts had been born from Ygseril, they had emerged without their vital 'root-memories', the collective memory that bound the war-beasts together into a formidable fighting force. This new bond between them, then, was especially precious. Unfortunately, this new closeness seemed to have come at a cost. Tor himself had been distant lately, morose even, his mind dwelling on the unfortunate revelations they had uncovered far across the sea. No Eboran as proud as Tormalin the Oathless wanted to discover that the history of his people was a kind of cosmic joke.

'Well, I prefer to give Helcate his space.' Vintage leaned forward and, in an act of steely self-will, unfastened her hand from the harness and gave the war-beast a scratch behind his ear. 'We're both still learning.'

They flew on. The sprawling stretch of the central Eboran city began to grow sparse, the golden threads of the broken roads trailing away into dirt tracks, the houses becoming smaller, more modest, until there were no buildings at all. Green forests lapped at these edges like an eager sea, rushing in to fill the gaps, until they flew over vast tracts of trees only broken up here and there by busy rivers and forgotten paths. Tor flew slightly ahead, leading them forward until late in the afternoon he gestured that they should land. He had chosen the banks of a wide lake, its waters a deep, lovely blue. Moving as one this time, they came to rest on its shoreline, which was made up of white sand and grey rocks. Vintage climbed down from Helcate's back with slightly shaky legs.

'Here, then? Close to here?'

'On the far side of the lake,' said Tor. 'If everything Micanal collected was true, that's where the sword should be.'

In the silence that followed, Vintage pulled one of the bags from Helcate's back, and began looking for a suitable patch of sand.

'Let's eat, then, before we start the real search.' She held up the bag. 'Wine, bread, cheese – just the essentials.'

Soon, they were seated on the warm sand, cups of wine in each hand. Noon was unwrapping the cheese, wrinkling her nose at the stink of it, while Tor absently cut the bread into pieces with his belt knife. Abruptly, and for no reason she could think of, Vintage felt overcome with a bittersweet mixture of happiness and woe. She smiled at them both; Tor's handsome face with its scars, his long fingers skilful as they wielded the blade, and Noon in her new Eboran clothes; even with her untidy hair and the bat-wing tattoo on her forehead, she was a very long way from the ragged creature they had found in the Shroom Flats. She held herself differently now, with a new confidence.

'This is just like old times, isn't it?' said Vintage, even though it wasn't. Tor looked up, one eyebrow raised.

'I'm not sure. There's not enough mud here, really, or any parasitic monsters made of light hanging around to turn us inside out.'

'And,' added Noon, taking a piece of bread from Tor, 'no giant worm ships scuttling around, waiting to feed us to a giant maggot that it has shit out of its bum.'

'What a delightful turn of phrase, my darling,' said Vintage dryly. 'I just mean that it's such a pleasure to have your company again, out in the wilds of Sarn.' She took a sip of her wine. 'And we're looking for a mysterious artefact.'

'Yeah. What's so special about this sword, anyway?' Noon addressed the question to Vintage, but she in turn raised her cup to Tor, who shrugged.

'Well, first of all, I don't have a sword anymore, do I? Not one befitting an Eboran warrior, anyway.' The Ninth Rain, the sword that had once belonged to Tormalin's aunt, and then his father, had been lost during the battle over the Bloodless Mountains – dropped from his flailing hand as the Jure'lia queen dangled him in the sky. He had looked for it more than once, but ultimately had to concede that it would likely remain forever hidden by the snows and undergrowth of the foothills.

'I don't know if you're aware of this,' said Noon, pulling a serious face, 'but there are such things as new swords. You could buy one. Or if you can't find one fancy enough for a fancy Eboran warrior, you could have one made. It's a radical idea, I know.'

Tor shook his head lightly, a genuine expression of annoyance flitting briefly over his face. 'That's not really my point. This sword, the one we're out here looking for, is legendary. Now, my old sword had a name, given to it by my idiot father, and it certainly saw some extraordinary battles, but the Ursun Blade . . . the Ursun Blade saw at least four Rains, and was carried by

34

two of our most celebrated warriors. If it still exists, it is something that should be back within the Eboran palace, near the roots of Ygseril.'

'Or, at least, hanging on your belt?' Noon stuffed a large piece of cheese into her mouth.

Tor shrugged and looked away. 'If it still exists, it's probably in pieces. Perhaps the hilt still survives . . . But I would like to try and find it, either way.' He paused, looking down into his drink. 'We went through so much to get to Origin and retrieve the amber tablets. Suffered a great deal of pain and humiliation. It would be a balm to my soul if something good came out of it. If we could retrieve something from our history that *does* still have meaning.'

Vintage glanced at Noon, and saw her looking at Tor with concern, which she quickly tried to hide with more bites of cheese.

'Besides which,' he continued, 'I am certain we're not safe from the Jure'lia yet, and legendary swords are in short supply. We need all the help we can get.'

'Well,' Vintage said brightly. She pulled a notebook from her jacket pocket. 'According to our notes, Tor, the final recorded resting place of the Ursun Blade is a short walk from here. Exactly the sort of short walk required after a lunch of cheese and wine. Isn't that marvellous?'

He smiled wanly at her and drained his cup.

Leaving the war-beasts to sun themselves by the side of the lake, Tor, Vintage and Noon ventured into the thick forest on the far side of the shore. This was Ebora in high summer, and the trees and plants were lush and humming with life. Tor made himself listen to it, breathe it in and smell it; he let himself taste it on his tongue. It was as beautiful as it had ever been when he was a child, and it was important to remember that there was more to his home than its history. Birds called to each other from all around, delicate sounds like liquid music, and other, harsher noises that brought to mind the calls of carrion birds.

It had not been easy to find this place. The information stored within the amber record, as crafted by the celebrated Eboran artist Micanal the Clearsighted, was enormous and complex, and much to Vintage's annoyance, largely poorly organised. Night after night Tor had dream-walked into the record, reporting back to Vintage what he found there, and, painstakingly, she had made notes of it all, linking everything up as best she could. Again and again Tor witnessed dream-crafted visions of war-beasts and warriors that were long dead, created anew by the artistry of Micanal, and watched a piece-meal history come together that felt empty to him. Hollow. How could it mean anything when he knew the truth? That Ygseril the tree-father was nothing but a random alien exper-iment, a diverting curiosity for a race of people that did not even know Sarn, and certainly did not care for it. The Aborans, as they had called themselves, had left similar marks on count-less worlds, and Ebora was something of a disappointment to them. But Vintage, clever Vintage, had spotted several clues and references to a legendary sword in amongst the hollow histories. Could it be possible that the Ursun Sword was not lost or destroyed at all, but simply forgotten, resting in its own distant tomb?

'Tell me about this thing, then,' said Noon into the busy forest silence. 'Who wielded it? What amazing feats, which monsters decapitated, blah blah.'

Tor glanced at Vintage, but she was looking at him, her eyes oddly watchful. He sighed, and went back to watching where he was placing his boots. There was no path here, and every step risked a broken ankle.

'The Ursun Sword. A winnow-forged blade. It was made by one of our master blacksmiths, a woman called Pelinor the

Unwavering, at around the time of the Third Rain, and given to Araiba, a great warrior of the time.'

'Winnow-forged.' Noon frowned. 'I don't suppose history records the name of the fell-witch who provided the flames?'

'It doesn't, no.' Tor glanced at Noon, then continued. 'Araiba's war-beast was a bear, and the pommel of the Ursun Sword was shaped like a bear claw clutching a huge, red ruby – like a bloody heart.' Tor grinned, suddenly taken with the ludicrousness of such a weapon. 'It's outrageous, really. By all reports, Araiba was a bit of a show-off, incredibly vain, you know the sort.'

Noon coughed into her hand. 'I suppose I can imagine it, if I try really hard.'

Tor ignored this.

'For all his nonsense, he was a great warrior, who covered himself in glory during the Third Rain. He died, eventually, in a duel, which is an especially ridiculous way to go, if you ask me, and his squire Lanamond inherited the sword. If Araiba was a respected warrior, Lanamond was beloved. She grew to be a true leader of Eborans, both a general and a queen, in a sense.'

'I thought Eborans didn't have kings and queens?' asked Noon.

Tor waved a hand dismissively. 'Our history has always been complicated. There have been emperors, war lords, even a roots-heart, who was a person elected to lead us, but we've never quite settled on one thing for very long . . . and eventually, of course, the crimson flux made all of that obsolete anyway.'

He paused, looking ahead. The forest was growing darker and damper, and he could see tell-tale patches of black bark on the trees here and there.

'The Wild,' muttered Vintage. 'I can smell it. Let's be watchful now.'

'You hardly need to remind me,' said Tor. Although Ebora did not contain as many Wild spaces as the rest of Sarn, it was not untouched, and animals that had been corrupted by the worm people's poisons could be very dangerous indeed. Despite all his posturing about the Ninth Rain, he had, of course, borrowed an old sword from the Finneral blacksmith, but it was a strange weight at his hip. He hoped he would not have to use it.

'What happened to her, then? This Lanamond?'

Tor glanced at Noon. She was wearing a set of Eboran travelling leathers, recut to her size, with a pauldron capping her shoulder; it was a beautiful thing, made of pieces of a soft bronze-coloured metal, shaped like leaves. Under the bodice she wore a pale-green Eboran silk shirt, embroidered with yellow leaping fish. It was strange, to see a human wearing items that had once been made for Eboran lords and ladies, but he could not pretend they didn't suit her. He looked away; things had grown colder between them since Origin.

'She distinguished herself in the Fourth Rain, leading the very charge that sent the Jure'lia running back to their hiding places, and after that she became a kind of queen, in all but name. There's a painting of her in the palace, hidden in one of the more obscure observatory rooms, and I've always thought she looked mildly put out – as though she didn't ask for any of the attention.'

'An obscure back room?' Vintage frowned, stepping carefully over a sucking pool of mud. The forest was growing more unpleasant all the time. 'If she was so celebrated, why is her portrait not on show?'

'Ah, well. I'm afraid she fell from grace. In her later years, she became something of a diplomat for Ebora, travelling back and forth across Sarn, agreeing trade deals and acting as a mediator in disputes – things like that. Gossip began to fester about her though, while she travelled away from home. It wasn't natural, it was agreed, that she should want to spend so much time with humans, that she should travel so far from the roots. Eventually, it was revealed that she was having an affair with one of Jarlsbad's princes, and she was cast out of her role. There was a minor revolution – we've had a number of those too, but very little ever changes.'

'Having an affair was enough to lose her her position?'

'With a human?' Tor raised his eyebrows. 'Certainly. Imagine finding out that your most admired royal leader was having a torrid affair with a servant.'

'The plains people don't have royalty,' pointed out Noon, 'or servants. So that's how Ebora felt about humans, then, is it?'

'Servants is a polite way of putting it,' said Tor, sourly. 'Which makes the truth all the more delicious, doesn't it? Half of me wishes all those old bastards were still around, so I could explain to them exactly what we found at Origin.'

Noon and Vintage fell suspiciously quiet at this, and Tor scowled to himself as they moved forward. Ever since the battle at the Tarah-hut Mountains they had been careful around him, as though he were a delicate vase that might shatter if they looked at it the wrong way. It didn't help that he often felt like exactly that: a hollow thing, a construct that was ultimately meaningless.

'Well, I for one hope she enjoyed her Jarlsbad prince,' said Vintage eventually.

'And the sword?' asked Noon.

'There was a big argument about it,' said Tor. The forest had grown quieter, and instead of birds singing he could hear the faint *rrrp-rrrp* of frogs, and the busy whirrings of insects. 'For a while it was thought that the Ursun Sword should go to whoever took over her position, but Ebora being Ebora, even her position looked likely to disappear with her. Eventually, it was forgotten, and until Vintage and I started rooting around in Micanal's amber tablets, it was thought to be lost. Something

39

like that, a piece of our history that is solid,' he waved a hand to disperse a cloud of flies, 'it could be inspiring. A reminder of what we *can* be.'

The normal forest had truly ended. All around, the trees grew taller and stranger, and even the shadows seemed deeper. A sharp, sour smell came from the pools of slippery mud under their feet, and a thick green moss covered the bottoms of the nearby trees like a virulent carpet. The sound of frogs was growing louder.

'So? What happened?'

'Micanal was intrigued enough to poke around, it seems. He discovered that Lanamond left Ebora and met up with her prince, and they lived together in secret for many years, until eventually he died. When she lost him, Lanamond returned and built a tomb for both him and her sword, somewhere out in the forests of Ebora. Once it was done, she left them both there, and became, according to Micanal, "a wandering hermit", refusing to ever return to either Jarlsbad or Ebora.'

'Here, look. What's that?'

Ahead of them the ground dropped away, and they looked down into a boggy indentation in the forest, thick with puddles of greenish mud. In the middle of it all was a stone structure, made of marble that had once been white, but which was now stained with streaks of black mould and daubs of yellow and green moss. All around it small animals were moving, hopping and swimming through the mud and reeds. The whine of insects was back, stronger than before.

'I suspect that's our tomb, darling.' Vintage moved to the front, her eyes bright, completely unconcerned by the mud. 'Shall we have a look?'

They shuffled down the bank. As they grew closer, it was possible to see that the marble tomb had been carved with a leaping buck, its horns gradually growing into a wide spread of tree branches, complete with leaves sprouting from them.

'The Jarlsbad prince,' said Tor, nodding towards it. 'His sigil was a leaping buck.'

'What are these things? Frogs?' Noon was scowling at the small green and brown creatures hopping away from them.

'I believe so, my dear, although that one there is more rightly a toad.'

One of the things hopped on top of the tomb and glared at them with gold and black eyes.

'The frogs on the plains are little green and orange things,' said Noon. 'We only ever saw them at the rivers. They were quite pretty.'

They reached the tomb and the toad shuffled away, dropping into the mud with a plop. Tor rested his hands on the edge of the cover, testing its weight and peering at the space where it met the main body of the structure.

'Is there going to be a dead body inside that thing?' asked Noon.

'Only a very ancient one, Noon dear,' said Vintage. 'It'll be all leathery and dry, I expect, or just a pile of bones. It probably won't smell at all.'

Bracing himself in the mud, Tor crouched and pushed the lid, wincing as it screeched its way off the sarcophagus. A stench, so thick it was almost visible, rose up off the dark space within. Noon swore and stepped back, holding her nose.

'*Ugh*. It definitely smells like someone died in there.'

Tor peered over the top. In the space within, there was a distinct lack of giant mythical swords. There were a few scraps of what might once have been fabric, and a rusted shape that could have been a belt buckle. And in the corner there was a large brown and green lump, about twice the size of a man's head. It was splattered with mud and was glistening faintly in the daylight.

Noon appeared at Tor's shoulder. 'Is that the Jarlsbad prince? I'm not sure what she saw in him, to be honest.'

Tor scowled, suddenly violently irritated with the whole thing; with the stench of the bog, the muck on his hands from touching the tomb, Noon's flippancy, the lack of any sign of the sword itself . . .

'I don't know what it bloody is,' he snapped, 'but it looks like Micanal's notes were full of sh—'

The brown and green lump quivered and shifted, revealing a wide, wet mouth and a pair of huge golden eyes. Tiny front legs unpeeled themselves from the front of its body, and its jaws fell open, revealing another set of puckering mouths nestling within its sizeable tongue. Tor got a brief glimpse of a pair of larger back legs, and then the thing was leaping at him.

'Fuck!'

Abruptly, he was on his back in the mud, a huge weight on his chest and all the air knocked from his lungs. Vintage was shouting, and there was the soft *wumph* as Noon summoned her winnowfire. Horrified, Tor shoved the slimy creature off him, and scrambled awkwardly to his feet.

'It's just a worm-touched toad!' he shouted, attempting to brush the filth and muck from his coat. The thing itself had scrambled off into a puddle, attempting to sink into it and vanish. 'There's no need to set anyone on fire.'

'I'm not worried about that little bastard.' Tor looked up to see Noon standing with her fists covered in green flame. Vintage stood on the far side of the tomb, her small crossbow held up and ready in both hands. 'I'm worried about this ugly brute.'

Belatedly, Tor saw where they were both looking. What he had taken to be a thick confusion of rocks and foliage between a set of close-standing trees was, in fact, a much larger version of the thing that had jumped out of the tomb. Twice his height, a worm-touched swamp toad glared down at them with three times as many eyes as it should have had. Its body was broad and misshapen, lacking even the compact shape of a normal toad, and there were moving things all over it; tiny versions of itself crawled and hopped over its glistening skin. As they watched, it shifted forward, and the long wet crack that was its mouth fell open, revealing its awful, busy tongue.

'I'm going to be sick,' said Noon.

'Perhaps if we just back away slowly, it'll leave us be. Not everything worm-touched is out to eat us, you know.' Vintage didn't lower her crossbow, but she took a few steps backwards, boots squelching in the mud. The golden eyes of the giant toad slid wetly to follow her progress. Its mouth opened a little wider.

'Vin, I don't like the way it's looking at you. Vin.' Noon raised her hands. All around, the little frogs and toads began to croak and burp, as if in protest at their leaving. Tor drew his sword, feeling a flicker of discomfort at the unfamiliar hilt. 'Vintage, maybe we should—'

The tongue shot out from between the creature's lips, flying across the bog and striking Noon with terrible accuracy. She shrieked, and instantly she was in the air, flying towards the worm-toad's enormous gaping mouth.

'Noon!'

Tor ran, sword at the ready, but with a flash of green flame Noon was already falling back into the mud. The toad bellowed in pain, reeling its singed tongue back into its mouth while its stubby front arms writhed.

Noon was on her feet by the time he reached her, which was useful, as his chest felt oddly tight. He paused at her side, distracted by a strange burning sensation beneath his breast bone. Meanwhile, Noon raised her hands, a furious expression on her face. She shot off a barrage of fireballs, which landed hissing against the worm-toad's skin. The creature shivered all over, wriggling backwards to get away from them.

'Tor, I'll have to use some of your energy.'

Tor, still distracted, opened his mouth to reply, but Noon

had already taken hold of his hand, giving it a firm squeeze. The energy drain was like a hammer blow, and before he knew it he was on his knees in the mud again, his vision dimming at the edges. He blinked slowly, looking down at his sword where he had dropped it. He could hear the toad-thing croaking, and the crashing of something huge moving through foliage, but it all seemed very distant. Instead, there was a roaring in his head and a red-hot pain in his chest.

'Tor? Tor, my darling, are you all right?'

Vintage's kind face loomed into his field of vision, and he felt her hand on his arm, giving him a gentle shake. He pressed a hand to his chest, but the pain there was fading to an ember. With Vintage's help, he clambered back to his feet.

'By Ygseril's damned roots, could you be a bit more careful, witch?'

Noon looked at him, obviously puzzled. The space where the giant toad had been was empty, and many of the smaller creatures had vanished too. Instead, there was a sickly reek of singed flesh, and a sort of oily yellow smoke.

'I didn't take that much,' protested Noon. 'No more than I've taken before, anyway.'

'You must have surprised me.' Tor looked back to the empty tomb. 'So, no sword. Knocked into the mud by a giant toad. Drained by an over-enthusiastic fell-witch, and covered in mud a second time. Also, I think there is slime.'

'What happened to the sword?' asked Noon. Vintage had returned to the tomb and was peering over its edge.

'Very likely it was never here, or someone got here first and pinched it.' Vintage grimaced. 'There's a reasonably large crack in the bottom of this thing, so I suspect our prince's body was just eaten over time by a variety of worm-touched frogs. That big toad probably crawled inside when it was a tiny baby thing, then grew to such an enormous size it couldn't get out again. Toads can live for a very long time, you know.'

'How utterly charming.' Tor coughed. His lungs felt full of swamp stench. 'You know, this feels like some sort of elaborate metaphor for Eboran history, or, indeed, my life.' He held up his hands, as though picturing it. 'A lot of misery and lies, ultimately revealed to contain nothing much save for a particularly ugly monster and a lingering smell.'

'Tor . . .'

'Come on, let's get back to the war-beasts. I don't want to spend another moment in this grim little armpit of Ebora.'

They walked back in an uncomfortable silence, although as they left the Wild-touched portion of the forest Tor felt his spirits lift a little. It was still summer in Ebora, and the forests of his birthplace were still beautiful – that had to mean something too. Perhaps enough to fill the void he'd felt inside since their experiences at Origin.

It was as they neared the clearing where the war-beasts rested that he began to feel the pain again. It flared at first in his chest, and then, oddly, in his arms, throbbing at his elbows and wrists. Annoyed, he pulled up his sleeve to massage his forearm and saw a livid red line, no more than an inch or so long, hidden in the hollow of his left elbow. He looked at it for a handful of seconds, feeling the last remnants of hope fall away into dust, and then he pulled the sleeve sharply down over it. To the others he said nothing.

Chapter Four

'Please do be careful with that.'

Bern paused with the dagger tip pressing into the scarred flesh of his hand. He wore only his loose linen trousers, and he was sweating slightly all over, perched as he was on the edge of their bed. Aldasair took advantage of his stillness to move closer.

'I can't stand it any longer, Al.' The big man spread his fingers so that the thick lump of crystal jutting from his palm caught the light. It glittered fetchingly, and Aldasair thought that in another time he might have thought it beautiful, yet instead it had become a symbol of hate and pain. 'I have to cut it out. I could stand the pain of that, at least.'

'It's not the pain I'm worried about.' Aldasair placed his hand over Bern's wounded one, edging the blade away. 'You know that we've spoken to Vintage about this more than once, and every time I come away convinced that you will only do yourself enormous harm. The delicate muscles and nerves in your hand could be damaged, you could lose all use of your hand. Please, Bern, think about this.'

'Enormous harm.' Bern shook his head. The big man looked uncommonly pale in the bright afternoon light, his blond hair dull and brassy against his broad forehead. His beard, normally so neatly trimmed, was getting wilder by the day, and his long braids were loose and uncared for. 'I've already had an enormous harm done to me, Al. I can't sleep, I can't relax, because I can hear them all the time – whispering, scratching, ticking, all the time. I can't eat, because everything tastes of ash. It's got worse. It's *getting* worse. Stones broken and cursed, what am I supposed to do?'

Aldasair pushed a lock of blond hair back from the big man's cheek. Bern's connection to the Jure'lia was killing him; he didn't need Lady Vintage to tell him that.

'We'll think of something,' he said, not for the first time.

'They're broken and confused.' Bern put the dagger down, and with a hand that was shaking slightly, he rubbed the sweat from his face. 'And it's infected me too.'

Aldasair opened his mouth to reply when there was a series of rapid knocks at the door. A face peeked around the edge; it was Norri, one of Bern's Finneral guards.

'Lords, we have some new arrivals. I think you should probably come and see them.'

Slowly, Bern got to his feet, picking up a shirt from the wooden trunk at the foot of their bed.

'Norri, I told you not to call me that. I'm no lord.'

'And I'm not really one either, truth be told,' added Aldasair.

The woman rolled her eyes a touch. 'Lord Aldasair, you are the closest thing Ebora has to a leader, and, technically, Bern is the son of a king, and, well . . .' She gestured vaguely at the pair of them standing together. 'It's just easier to call you lords. My lords.'

Bern shrugged on his shirt and they followed Norri from their chambers. Out in the grounds of the palace quite a crowd had gathered, and it didn't take long to see why; seven giant bats in full harness were sitting quite peaceably on the grass while the humans stood around admiring them. Some of the children were even being brave enough to stroke their furry flanks. One huge creature, a dusty grey in colour, bent his velvety head to be petted more efficiently.

'More fell-witches,' said Bern, uncharacteristically gruff.

'It's fine. We still have plenty of room.'

A group of women stood just near the bats, slightly apart from the crowd. Four of them wore green-and-grey travelling clothes, a uniform that Aldasair had learned to recognise as that of the Winnowry agents, while the other three wore a mixture of sturdy leather and linen, no doubt too warm for such a hot day, but necessary when flying over mountains. One of the agents spotted their approach and stepped forward. She was tall, and moved gracefully. As well as the rough bat-wing tattoo on her forehead that marked all fell-witches from the Winnowry, a beautiful tattoo of an eagle encircled her throat; picked out in vivid reds and browns and blues, it was, to Aldasair's eye, a true work of art. Her hair was long and black, with a thick cord of white beginning just above her right temple.

'Greetings,' said Aldasair, bowing slightly. 'You are very welcome here.' He looked to the other women, who looked less certain. 'You are all welcome in Ebora.'

The woman pressed a hand to her chest and bowed more formally. Now that they were closer, Aldasair could see that her clothes were slightly different to the other agents'. Her fitted leather coat, scuffed and carefully oiled, looked more like a beloved personal item than a uniform, and she wore a small bracelet of green stones at her wrist.

'Thank you, Lords of Ebora. I am Agent Chenlo. I have brought these women here on the suggestion of your own Lady Noon.'

'Ah, Agent Chenlo, it is an honour finally to make your acquaintance.' At her surprised expression, Aldasair smiled encouragingly. 'Each fell-witch who has made it to Ebora has told us how you have assisted them in their journeys. That you insisted that they come here, to us.'

'It sounds like you fair badgered them into it,' said Bern. He was flexing the hand with the stone in it, as if it pained him.

'There was little other option, since the Lady Noon destroyed the Winnowry.'

'She hates being called that,' said Bern. 'And the Winnowry deserved everything it got.'

Agent Chenlo held up her hands. 'Of course. I merely meant that there was no system in place for these newly free women, but Lady – Mistress Noon indicated that there might be places for them here. I have done what I can to make sure they made it to you safely.' Lowering her voice, she folded her hands neatly in front of her. 'There is another matter, my lords. One that more directly concerns Ebora. Perhaps we could discuss it in private?'

Aldasair nodded formally. 'Of course. Norri, please show our new guests to the section of the palace we've put aside for them. Agent Chenlo, please come with us.'

The receiving room was full of bright sunshine. Rather than the steaming pots of tea Aldasair had had prepared during the winter months, tall bottles of a chilled and watered wine stood in the centre of the table. As Agent Chenlo sat in the offered chair, he poured some into a shallow glass drinking bowl; a present from Sen-Lord Takor of the Yuron-Kai.

'Thank you.' Chenlo sipped the wine, and allowed herself a small smile. 'Cold wine after a long, hot journey. It is most welcome.'

'What is it you wanted to say?' Rather than taking a seat, Bern stood by the door, his hands behind his back. He did seem to find it difficult to sit still, currently. Aldasair fought to keep a frown from his face, and turned back to Chenlo.

'My lords, let me be clear. I am not here to speak in any

sense for the Winnowry. It is, in any way that truly matters, a thing of the past. But there are certain consequences of its actions that I believe you should be aware of.'

'What is there left of the Winnowry? Can you tell us that?'

Chenlo curled her hands under the glass bowl. 'Your Lady Noon was quite thorough in her destruction. Many of the men and women who caused the Winnowry to function in any sense were chased away, or killed.' Her face was as smooth as a summer lake as she said this. 'Mother Cressin, who was the figurehead of the order, killed herself, and much of the building has been destroyed. There are a handful of the faithful left, a few still living at the site, and, from what I've heard, arguing over who gets to be the next "Mother", although what that actually means when the cells all stand empty, I do not know. But they are a sad sight, zealots clinging on to something that no longer exists.' She hesitated, a flicker at her jawline betraying some discomfort. 'However, you should also know that a few of the fell-witches did return.'

'They did?' Aldasair sat back slightly in his seat. 'They returned to their prison?'

'As I said to the Lady Noon on that day, these women do not have homes to go to, and are not necessarily welcome anywhere else. It is not a pleasant truth, is it? I tried to send as many your way as I could, but there were those who could not face the journey, or were simply too frightened to come to Ebora.' At that her gaze flickered to Aldasair and away again, and he understood. The Carrion Wars were not so easily forgotten. To many humans, Ebora would always be home to those who had once swarmed down across the plains, massacring every human in sight. 'Those who returned currently exist in an uneasy peace with their former captors.' She drained the last of her wine, the tattooed muscles on her throat working as she swallowed. 'I do not pretend to understand it.'

'You feel no loyalty to the Winnowry? Were you not one of their most senior agents?'

At this she looked directly at Aldasair, as if daring him to call her a liar. 'It is a hard life in the Winnowry, Lord Aldasair, and I am sure your Lady Noon would tell you that you do what you can to survive. I did what I could, once I had some freedom, to keep those around me safe. But I am no fool. I can see the ending of a thing. I have no loyalty to the debris of the Winnowry.'

'Yet you continue to work to keep others safe,' said Aldasair, softly. Before she could answer, he continued. 'And I suspect you are still here on Winnowry business.'

'In a sense. There was, as you know, a plan to steal one of your unhatched war-beasts.'

'We're aware of it, yeah,' said Bern, dryly. 'A Winnowry agent calling herself Tyranny Munk came to us with a mouthful of lies, burned half our forest down, tried to kill our friends, and made off with one of our war-beast pods.'

Chenlo placed the empty bowl on the table. 'Yes. For what it's worth, I argued against this plan. Tyranny has always been unpredictable. Violent.'

Aldasair reached out for Jessen instinctively. He could feel her nearby, in the palace grounds somewhere. She was enjoying the sun and he took comfort from her contentment.

'You do realise,' he said to Chenlo, 'that what Tyranny did was no less than an abduction? A war-beast pod is not simply some valuable artefact. It contains a life that is an extension of Ygseril, our tree-father. That life is kin to our war-beasts, and, by extension, us.' He tapped his fingers lightly against the table. 'If Noon hadn't taken the matter into her own hands, it is likely that Ebora would have been forced to go to war with the Winnowry also . . . once the Ninth Rain was over.'

'You have news, don't you?' said Bern. He had crossed his

arms over his chest. 'What happened to Tyranny and her little gang when they escaped us?'

'She did not return to the Winnowry itself. They weren't so foolish as to hide something so valuable and dangerous within a place that can be found on any map. Instead, she and her charge were hidden at one of the Winnowry's lesser-known bases.' Chenlo took a breath. 'My lords, your war-beast pod hatched. The creature lives, and is healthy.'

Aldasair swallowed. He felt his own shock reverberate through the link he shared with Jessen, Bern and the others, and felt their reactions, distantly.

What is wrong? Jessen was close, and Sharrik had joined her. He could feel it.

'By the stones,' said Bern. He had finally joined them at the table, his green eyes bright with emotion. 'A new war-beast? What is it?'

'That, I am afraid, I do not know,' said Chenlo, an edge of bitterness to her voice. 'What I do know is that Tyranny rebelled. With her war-beast, she destroyed much of the remote Winnowry base, and killed a large number of agents.'

'*Her* war-beast?' spat Bern. 'What do you mean, *her* war-beast?'

'We do not know much about Ebora, truly, but everyone knows about the legendary bond between war-beast and warrior. By all reports, Tyranny has bonded with her war-beast.'

Aldasair poured another two bowlfuls of the cold wine. When he was done, Bern picked up the bottle and took a swig from it.

'That murderous liar, bonded to a war-beast.' Bern shook his head. 'Imagine what will happen when Vostok hears about this.'

'My lords, that is not all. After Tyranny destroyed the Winnowry base, she left with her war-beast and a handful of loyalists, and made her way to Jarlsbad. Once there she attacked a small kingdom known as Tygrish, decimating their standing army and taking their royal family prisoner.' Chenlo grimaced slightly. 'She has since declared herself and her war-beast queens of Tygrish.'

Bern gave a sharp bark of laughter. 'She's done *what*?'

'That is . . . extraordinary,' said Aldasair.

'Truth be told, Tyranny has never been especially stable. I imagine you know something of her background?'

'Vintage told us that she was once a gang leader in Mushenska. A feared and dangerous one at that.'

Chenlo nodded. 'And that need for power, that need to be recognised as a leader, never really left her. Sneaking around as an agent, having to pretend to be something else – these things riled her. Now she is acting out all her greatest fantasies, and with the Winnowry gone, there is no one to pull her back into line.'

There were a few moments' silence. It was possible to hear, through the tall windows, the sounds of children playing in the palace gardens.

'My lords,' Chenlo cleared her throat, 'this is a problem of the Winnowry's making . . .'

'A giant pile of shit of the Winnowry's making,' added Bern.

'But I do not think I need to tell you how this could impact on Ebora. Tyranny rules by virtue of her war-beast and has crowned it alongside her.'

Aldasair nodded slowly, a tight worm of worry growing in his chest. 'It's an enormous insult to Jarlsbad, not to mention an act of war, and with a war-beast involved, we are complicit. And this, just as we were reaching out to other nations for help.'

Bern frowned. 'But surely they will see this has nothing to do with Ebora?'

'It's not that simple, Bern. Any goodwill my people had earned was destroyed during the Carrion Wars, and we have

53

failed to protect many during this current Rain. Now, one of our own has taken land by force. It will not take much for everyone else to turn against us.'

Chenlo nodded solemnly. 'For what it's worth, I am sorry to bring you such tidings, lords.'

Aldasair smiled, and rose from his seat. 'We are very grateful, Agent Chenlo, and grateful also that you thought to bring us news before you had even had a chance to rest – my apologies. I'll have someone take you to a suite of rooms where you can wash the dust from your boots.'

When Chenlo had left, Aldasair pulled another bottle of wine out from under the table and refilled his glass bowl.

'What do you plan to do?' asked Bern.

'Speak to Vintage when she gets back,' he said immediately. 'She spent the most time with the woman, so I'm sure she'll have a few opinions.' He swirled the wine in its bowl. 'Let's hope no more problems crop up in the meantime.'

Chapter Five

Fell-Longsprite

A tiny girl, no more than five years old. She hid behind her mother's skirts when we came, but her grandmother dragged her out, screaming. These people are farmers. The child cannot control her ability and already they have lost animals and crops, have suffered burns themselves. The women are pale and watery-eyed, as if they have suffered through some sort of war, and the mother turned away when the girl screamed for her.

Agent Lin was agitated by this collection in a way I had not seen before. I have considered reporting her but she grew calm again as we reached the south coast.

As for the girl – her given name is Longsprite – my hopes are small things. The life of a five-year-old girl within the Winnowry is a particularly horrific one, with no human contact and no care. If she lives through it, I do not know how much she will remember of her previous life. In a way I hope she doesn't remember: doesn't remember her grandmother dragging her out into the light, doesn't remember her mother turning her face away.

Some details about the life of Longsprite of the plains:

she lived in a conical yurt, the felt of which had been passed down through the women of her family for generations. Her family's prize possessions were two fine bay horses, which were kept away from the child when her abilities manifested. Her mother had a tattoo on her arm of a snake, which made me think of Yuron-Kai, and my not-home, but I prefer not to dwell on that. Her people were afraid of our bats. When we took her, it began to rain.

I struggle to record much here. She was five. She had barely begun to have a life to speak of.

Extract from the private records of Agent Chenlo

The light was ghostly and weak, but it was enough to see by – although Hestillion was rapidly wishing she hadn't bothered.

The light-filled frond, which she had torn from the fleshy walls of the corpse moon, clung octopus-like to the end of her stick, casting a glow that did not so much reveal the cavern they were in, as paint it in fuzzy shades of grey and silver and green. All around her, Behemoths loomed, crammed together on the cavern floor, cushioned on spindly insectile legs that created deeply unnerving shadows. Vast oily shapes glistened and pressed in on all sides.

'It's like being inside something rotten,' she murmured. 'Like looking at the innards . . . of a frog.'

The Jure'lia collective was not as still or as silent as she had expected. Despite the queen's malaise, some of her skittering creatures were still busy enough. As she walked slowly between the giant ships, Hestillion saw spider-mothers of various sizes crawling over the surface of several Behemoths, clustering at the places where the oily skins of the ships had yet to heal completely, or slipping in and out of ragged holes. To Hestillion's eyes their movements were a little erratic, but it was clear that they thought they were supposed to be doing something.

'You're still trying to fix things, even if you're not sure why.' She held up her makeshift torch to get a better look at a churning cluster of spider-mothers. Distantly, she recognised that she was no longer so repulsed by them, and her other hand stole up to touch the blue crystal at her chest. 'What use is it all, though, if the queen never commands us to fly again?'

Since the queen had grounded them, Hestillion had largely spent her time exploring, or flying small distances with Celaphon. The humid forest that pressed on either side of their hiding place was strange, filled with odd, Wild-touched things she had decided she did not want to dwell on, and she'd been forced to go further afield for her own food and supplies. She had taught herself to hunt, in small ways; had built traps and chased down rabbits; had learned to forage. At first it had felt humiliating – that the Jure'lia's inactivity had forced her to scramble for food with her bare hands. But eventually, as she became skilled with her spear and learned where to find what she needed, her self-sufficiency became a point of pride.

But it was time to get things moving again. Time to find out what she could about the Jure'lia's inconvenient hibernation.

She walked on, her leather boots making barely a sound against the stone. Celaphon was asleep within the corpse moon, a giant dreaming mind looming behind her – it was oddly reassuring – while the queen continued her endless vigil at the broken memory crystal. It was almost possible, despite the scratching presence of the Jure'lia in her head, to feel herself alone. Just ahead, the line of hulking Behemoths ended and a great wall of darkness hung beyond them. Curious, Hestillion headed towards it, wondering how deep into the flesh of Sarn the cavern burrowed.

She walked on for some time, long enough to wonder if the place was endless, until the landscape around her began to change. Ahead of her, the rocky ground dropped away, creating a huge shallow basin in the rock, wide enough so that all of the Behemoths could have crouched in it side by side, and stretching far enough back that Hestillion was unable to see its end. Nestled in the space were countless rounded shapes, each nearly as big as Celaphon and glowing, ever so slightly, from within. They were all wrapped in tattered layers of trembling greyish foam, and the core of each was encased in smooth green moon-metal.

'By all the roots, what is this place? What are those things?'

Eggs, Hestillion realised, the knowledge dropping into her mind like a cold, wet stone. The queen had mentioned them once, might even have spoken about laying them within the flesh of Sarn, but Hestillion had not made the connection with this dark, dank place. She held up the glowing frond and tried to count them, but it was impossible; row upon row of the Jure'lia eggs marched back into the darkness, their tiny glowing cores becoming indistinguishable from the motes of flying colour behind Hestillion's eyes.

Hesitantly, because being in such direct contact with the Jure'lia was still unnerving, Hestillion reached down through the network she shared with them, seeking out their collective memories. The shattered piece that had been the memory crystal was jagged and discordant, sending shards of glass down a link that should have been smooth and strong, but she saw enough to make some sense of what she was seeing. When the Jure'lia came to this world in their travelling forms, they used the last of their energy to deposit their eggs under the skin of the land, where they would be protected, and then they underwent the seismic change that transformed them from their travelling forms to their harvesting forms. From that point onwards, their only goal was to change this world to suit the eggs, so that they would eventually hatch and leave for new spaces of sky and land, taking with them the fragile network of memories that held the Jure'lia together as one thing. In her mind's eye, Hestillion saw worlds other than Sarn harvested and smothered in varnish, until their inner temperature rose enough to hatch the eggs. Here, then, in this hidden place, the eggs had been waiting for thousands of years, their cycle interrupted by a world that dared to fight back.

Despite everything, she smiled to herself, and immediately felt a curious push from Celaphon.

What pleases you so?

Nothing. Go back to sleep.

This, then, it stood to reason, was where the worm people went at the end of each Rain. This was their long-sought-for hiding place. Hestillion left the edge of the valley of the eggs and headed back to the Behemoths, looking above to the distant crack through which they had entered. Although she had explored around the crevasse, she had gained no real information about their location. Where in Sarn was this? Where had the old enemy been hiding over all the long years? She should like to know, if only for her own amusement.

She made her way towards the corpse moon, trying to ignore the busy creatures clinging to the Behemoths all around, when a sudden burst of frantic activity to her right made her pause. The softly curving wall of the Behemoth above her flexed and twisted until an opening appeared, and something awkward began to crawl forth. It appeared to be a creature halfway between a giant burrower and a spider-mother; a long-bodied beetle with a flexible segmented body and long legs bristling with hooks and barbs. Its head was little more than a huge pair of black pincers, and it twisted this section around to look at her – she caught an unsettling glimpse of a cluster of tiny red eyes, like dots – and then it promptly fell on her.

Hestillion hit the ground heavily, all the air knocked from her in an instant. The thing was twice her size and wriggling frantically, the bristling texture of its legs catching her hair and yanking it from its braid. Belatedly, Hestillion realised the thing was poorly formed, and broken somehow. Its legs were making grasping, uncontrolled movements, and a distressed, mewling sound came from somewhere at the centre of it.

'Get off me!'

Her command had no effect. The thing whirred and twisted, digging its claws deeper into her while the gritty floor of the cavern dug into her back through the leather of her jerkin.

'Roots and stones, get off me!' A tiny shred of panic growing in her chest, Hestillion briefly considered calling out for Celaphon, but the dragon, as strong and as mighty as he was, was not known for his precision. Summoning him here, into this tight space between the Behemoths, would likely only do more damage. Or he would simply step on her by accident. Grimacing, she lifted her head and strained her neck, looking at her surroundings. Communicating with the creature writhing on her would clearly do no good – the thing was suffering from the broken connection that afflicted all the Jure'lia and couldn't obey her. She needed to try another way.

In the shadows beneath the Behemoth, something tall and pale moved. One of the queen's other experiments.

'You! Come here!'

The figure did not even turn to look at her. Muttering in disgust, Hestillion closed her eyes and reached within the busy darkness of her mind, seeking out the web of connections the crystal wedged in her chest had given her. It was like running her hands along the edge of a lethal blade – so sharp and so intimate that the pain would only be apparent later – but there it was. She grasped at the figure at the edge of her awareness, feeling the slippery clay of its mind and ignoring it, simply commanding it to *come*.

Hestillion opened her eyes. The insectoid beast was still on top of her, leaking greenish fluid from between its mandibles, but the pale figure in the distance was coming closer, its blank face oddly intent. Hestillion recognised it as one of the man-like things the queen had made not long after she had come on board the corpse moon; a thing with graceless bat-like wings and skin the colour of porridge. A thing made to be summoned.

When it arrived, she glared up at it for a moment.

'Well? Get this thing off me.'

More and more now, the things she voiced openly echoed down through the Jure'lia web, and immediately the grey man bent down and snatched up the writhing bug. There was an awful moment when the creature's bristling legs caught in Hestillion's hair, threatening to yank it out at the root, but she tore it free and suddenly she was back on her feet. A shiver of revulsion moved through her body.

'This place. These *things*.'

She stopped, realising that the grey man was still standing with the oversized bug in his arms, waiting for her next command.

'Take it away,' she told him.

He turned, his broad body glistening in the dim light, and Hestillion watched him go, her face creased in thought.

Later, when she was back within the corpse moon, she made her way to the central chamber that Hestillion now thought of as the queen's 'crafting room'. It was here, in the steaming white pools, that she and Celaphon had been permanently joined to the Jure'lia, and it was here that the queen had made her strange grey flying men. Several of them lined the walls, as silent and as still as sentries.

'You. Come here.'

There was no hesitation. One of the grey men came forward, and when she told it to get into the white crafting pool, it did so immediately, lying with its face to the ceiling. *And why should you be afraid*, thought Hestillion, as the steaming waters shrouded its body. *This is where you were born, after all.*

Hestillion pulled on a pair of leather gloves that reached to her elbows, and then sank her hands into the fluid. She waited, just in case the flesh should fall off her fingers, but the gloves seemed to be doing their job, so she reached for the creature's body. As she had hoped, it had become malleable, and when she pressed her fingers into its flesh it gave way like sticky dough. She could shape this thing. Shape it into anything she wanted.

Why? Hestillion recognised her own voice in her head, a slim remnant from the time before she had thrown herself in with the Jure'lia. It was very small. *Why do you need to change its shape at all? Who are you trying to recreate here?*

Hestillion ignored it.

Instead, she leaned forward and, mostly feeling her way, began to pull and stretch the pliable flesh into new, more pleasing shapes. Her hands caressed its blocky head, smoothing it into something narrower, more appealing. The queen did not understand the importance of faces, or the reassurance of ears, and neck muscles, the crisp shape of a jaw. She thought of the ceramic art works she had made when she was a child, and an absent smile touched her lips.

'I have missed creating things,' she said, her voice loud in the enormous chamber. 'And you will be someone very special. Someone at my back, always. Like a brother should be.'

Chapter Six

'What, if anything, can be done about Tyranny Munk?'

Agent Chenlo stood for a few seconds longer as silence grew within the war-beasts' courtyard, and then she sat on the chair they had brought out for her. Vintage pursed her lips and looked around at their extraordinary gathering. Even with this fresh pile of horse-dung dumped in their laps, it was hard not to appreciate the sight of all the war-beasts together under the bright sun, with their warriors beside them, standing still and serious. Noon and Vostok, Tor and Kirune, Bern and Sharrik, Aldasair and Jessen. Helcate, and yes, even herself. The only figure that stood apart was Agent Chenlo herself, and although Vintage resented her presence – this courtyard was private to the war-beasts and their companions, after all – she had to admit that the woman had a presence of her own. She sat now waiting for their response, her hands, bare of gloves, folded neatly in her lap. Her black hair with its bolt of white had been pulled back into a loose braid, and she held her head up. This was a woman who was used to keeping her movements in check.

Aware that the silence had gone on too long, Vintage cleared her throat.

'It's quite a story you bring us, Agent Chenlo. Please do forgive us if it takes a while to get it all straight in our heads.'

The woman lowered her head in a movement that was more of a bow than a nod.

'It's a story, all right, but I don't see what it has to do with us.' Noon stood the furthest from the woman, her arms crossed over her chest and her eyes averted, as if the bat-wing tattoo on Agent Chenlo's forehead were something obscene she couldn't bear to look at. 'This is the Winnowry's fuck-up.'

'I would agree,' murmured Bern. His posture mirrored Noon's, his burly arms crossed, his wounded hand hidden from view. 'We've enough on our plate to be getting on with, without getting involved in the leftover power struggles of the Winnowry.' He paused, tipping his head slightly to one side. 'And the Finneral people have long cast out any loyalty we might have had to your castle of fanatics.'

Again, Agent Chenlo bowed her head in acceptance. 'Your Stone Talker,' she said. 'That was an unfortunate episode.'

'Your entire history is an *unfortunate episode*,' added Vintage, and watched as a flicker of discomfort moved across the woman's features. 'The entire place should have been smashed to pieces years ago.'

'I feel I must remind you, *I* am not the Winnowry.' She had lifted her head and her gaze was direct and defiant. She had, Vintage noticed, light grey eyes, like summer clouds. 'No more than the Lady Noon is.'

Noon made an indignant noise at that, but Aldasair had stepped forward. Behind him, Jessen stood tall and still, her black ears cupped forward to better hear them all.

'It is more complicated than Winnowry business. We cannot simply let it be handled by someone else, and we cannot let things continue as they are. There is a war-beast involved . . .'

'A war-beast that is our kin!' Vostok surged forward, her violet eyes blazing. Vintage watched with interest as the

Winnowry agent stiffened in her chair. The courtyard was the largest in the palace, but it could still feel very small when it contained an angry dragon. 'It is an outrage that they were ever taken from us. What Noon and I did was the barest vengeance, a tiny taste of my anger!' Vostok huffed, and wisps of grey smoke curled from between her teeth. 'All creatures of the Winnowry should be smoking husks, in my opinion.'

'Outside of our understandable anger,' Aldasair continued, 'there is the question of how this makes Ebora look to our potential allies. A war-beast stands at the side of a despot, enforcing her will. The leaders of Jarlsbad will not stand for such treatment, I am sure.'

'That's what worries me.' Tor had been standing back under the awning, half hiding in the shadows there. When he stepped into the light, Vintage was struck by the lines of his face – did he look gaunter than he had? But then his usual half-smile appeared, and he was once again his shining, handsome self. 'Do we really have time to get into a conflict with Jarlsbad? If we go there, poking our nose in, it's only going to look like we're stirring things up.' He shrugged. 'We should let them deal with it. Keep our heads down.'

'But our sister!' Sharrik shook out his great head, the feathers on his neck and chest puffing up to make him look even more enormous. 'They must be with us. It is our way.'

'That there is a war-beast out there that we have not seen nor smelled, who has not stood with us . . . a rogue war-beast . . .' Vostok's claws flexed against the flagstones. 'Have we all forgotten the monstrous creature that flies with our enemy? That worm-touched dragon has cost us dearly. We cannot allow another rogue war-beast to grow into being out of our sight. The bright weapon and I will travel to Jarlsbad together, and we shall destroy this Tyranny as we destroyed the Winnowry, and bring our sister home.'

'My darling, it may not be as easy as that. If what Agent

Chenlo tells us is true, our rogue war-beast has already bonded with Tyranny Munk. Getting them to come back to Ebora, especially if you have just roasted her companion alive . . . well, we might lose all of you.'

Vostok snorted. 'Whatever this rogue is, it is surely a runt, while I am the most formidable of all of us.'

Sharrik made some rumbling noises at this, and Noon placed her hand on Vostok's neck. The dragon grew quiet at her touch.

'What do you think we should do, Vintage?' Noon looked as serious as Vintage had ever seen her. 'You met Tyranny Munk, you spoke to her. What do you think?'

Vintage sighed. Thinking about Tyranny's subterfuge still brought on a sharp pang of guilt, of disappointment in herself, and a little throb of pain in her newly healed ankle. Bitterly she remembered the moment Nanthema had betrayed them; the expression of mild discomfort on her face when she was found out. Ultimately, Vintage's devotion had meant very little to the Eboran woman, and Tyranny had got exactly what she'd wanted.

'I think, my darling, that I let you all down enormously, and if I had been thinking more clearly, we wouldn't have this problem in the first place.'

'Helcate,' said Helcate. Vintage reached up and scratched him behind the ears.

'But my dear friend here is right. My self-pity doesn't help us either. My impression of Tyranny was of an intelligent, if cruel, woman. Her past as a gang leader in Mushenska suggests that she is bold and ruthless, capable of anything. Being under the boot of the Winnowry can't have been easy for a woman who is used to wielding power, so now she has seen her chance, and grabbed it. Getting her to let go of it . . . will not be easy.'

'You think it's a possibility though?' said Tor.

Vintage shrugged. 'Ruthless, but not utterly heartless. She was clearly very fond of her pet assassin, Okaar, and his little sister, Jhef. They had a bond, I'm sure of it. Perhaps that suggests there are some softer places under that iron-hard shell.'

'Diplomacy,' snorted Vostok. 'This is what you speak of.'

Vintage smiled at the dragon's disgust. 'What I think, Noon, is that perhaps the very first step we need to take is to talk to her. Explain the situation. Appeal to her better nature. Suggest, very gently, that now is not the time to be a thunderous pain in everyone's rear end. And also suggest, very gently, that defying the war-beasts of Ebora would have an unfortunate outcome.' She turned to Agent Chenlo. 'You must have known the woman to some degree. What do you think?'

Chenlo looked surprised to be asked. 'I knew her a little. We did not like each other. She had no interest in the other women imprisoned by the Winnowry, only in what she could hoard for herself. If, perhaps, you could convince her that giving up the war-beast is in her own best interest . . . I suppose it may be possible.'

'So what are you thinking?' Tor pushed a loose strand of hair behind his ear. 'Are you going to send her a very sternly worded letter?'

'Darling, I don't think even my writing skills are up to that. No. I will go there, with Helcate, and with Agent Chenlo here. Familiar faces.' She grinned sourly, thinking of Tyranny Munk's face when she realised Vintage was very much still alive and very much still a pain in her arse. And would Nanthema still be with her? She thought it was entirely possible. 'Familiar faces are what's needed here.'

As the group dispersed, heading off to their various tasks, Vintage heard a polite cough from behind her and turned to face Agent Chenlo. The woman was an inch or so taller than her, and there was a wiry aspect to her frame that suggested a life of constant travel, along hard roads and across stormy skies.

'Yes?'

'Lady de Grazon, you appear to have volunteered me for something. For a task.'

'Yes, I have.'

'That was not discussed with me.'

'I suppose not.'

'And to which I have not agreed.'

'Ah.' Vintage turned and looked down the corridor to see Noon just disappearing out of sight. The young woman did not like to be in the company of other fell-witches for very long, that much was clear, and Vintage could hardly blame her. 'You don't want to help? I thought you came here to help, Agent Chenlo?'

The taller woman paused, also looking down the corridor, as if she too wished to see where Noon had gone. In the moment's silence, Vintage found herself drawn to the eagle tattoo around Agent Chenlo's neck. It was the most extraordinary work, a symphony of brown, black and blue lines. Much finer in line and detail than the tattoos of their Yuron-Kai allies. Vintage was filled with the urge to ask about it, and opened her mouth to do so, but Chenlo was speaking again.

'All I have wanted to do is see that the witches – that the women who have been freed from the Winnowry – have a chance of survival. That is my purpose here.'

'Good. Great. And you've brought them all here, haven't you? Shepherded them to the gates of Ebora, and now they have shelter, and food, and no one is locking them up in cells. We have taken these women in, Agent Chenlo. They are safe.'

'And now . . . I owe you?'

Vintage grinned. 'No one wants to see these women cast back out, my dear. And it seems to me that what is happening in Jarlsbad is a Winnowry problem.'

'Lady de Grazon, I do not believe for a moment that you

would force the fell-witches back out of Ebora. The Lady Noon is dear to you.'

Vintage surprised herself by laughing. 'You've got me there, I suppose. Come on, let's get out into the sunshine and you can tell me everything you know about our good friend Tyranny Munk.'

Outside in the palace gardens the weather had turned, bringing clouds and a freshening breeze that promised showers, but Vintage and Chenlo walked out anyway. When it did start to rain, fat drops of summer rain that thumped into the grass in an unruly manner, Agent Chenlo smiled and lifted her face to it. Catching Vintage's look, she shook her head slightly.

'When you have spent so many of your earliest years in a cell, you never quite get over the miracle that is weather. The movement, the taste of it . . .' She trailed off, and cleared her throat. 'You wanted to know about Tyranny Munk.'

'Yes. Quick, let's get under this tree. You might be all for the rain but I've forgotten my hat.'

They stood, watching as everyone caught out in the brief shower moved towards other trees, or headed back inside the palace. People were laughing, amused by this sudden change in the weather. *They think the Jure'lia are gone*, Vintage reminded herself. *It's easy for them to think that when there's no corpse moon in the sky.*

'Tyranny was turned in by a member of her own gang, the Salts,' said Chenlo. 'I assume you already know that?'

'She did tell me some of it, in a fashion.' Vintage shook some raindrops from her jacket. 'She told me all manner of stories.'

'Some of them were probably partially true. She came to the Winnowry quite late. She had managed to hide herself successfully for some time. This was unfortunate. Most women are brought to us – to the Winnowry – when they are children. They are unable to control their ability, and so they are exposed very early on. More often than not, their own families turn them in.'

'An ability, you call it. Not a curse, an abomination?'

Chenlo shrugged, as if this did not matter. 'Tyranny was too used to her freedom, and to being in charge. They had two options: keep her locked up in the strictest conditions, forever, or give her some room on the leash. Make her an agent.'

'You sound like you didn't agree?'

'I wasn't happy with either option.' Chenlo sighed. Beyond the circle of the tree cover, the rain grew heavier. 'There are several paths to becoming a good agent. Fear can keep you obedient, or the need to stay as free as you can. Some even come to see their role as a way of keeping the Winnowry in line.' Vintage looked up at that, but Chenlo was still gazing out across the gardens. 'Tyranny was not fearful. She was furious. She had had so much freedom in her life that what the Winnowry offered was a poor shadow of it. She was, in short, impossible to control. So, against my advice, she was not marked with the sigil,' at this Chenlo touched her own forehead, where the bat-wing tattoo was branded, 'and she became one of a very select number of secret operatives. Fell-witches who move in the world unseen and unknown, under Winnowry control.'

'And they trusted her to keep in line?'

Chenlo smiled thinly. 'I think she was an experiment to them. She had a number of skills, all of which were useless if she was kept in a Winnowry cell. So . . . she was assigned a watcher, someone to keep an eye on her.'

'Okaar?'

'He was trained in ways to kill, quietly, quickly. It's unusual for the Winnowry to use an outsider in this way, but Tyranny had such a hatred for fell-witches, it was impossible to get her to work with a partner. But as it turned out –'

'She and Okaar became as thick as thieves.'

Chenlo nodded.

'The stuff she told me about arranging trips across the Wild for rich men and women, about finding the war-beast armour, was any of that true?'

'No. The war-beast armour she brought here was all purchased by the Winnowry over the centuries, as a kind of investment. Tyranny was given a small portion of it to win your trust.'

'Fuck my old boots.' Chenlo raised an eyebrow, and Vintage shook her head. 'And I did trust her, like the fool I am. I was distracted at the time . . .' She thought of Nanthema, how she had been so distant, and how the need to believe that she was still the woman she had loved as a teenager had obscured things that should have been obvious. 'But that's no excuse.'

A pair of young women, marked as fell-witches by the tattoos on their foreheads, ran across the grass, laughing. The rain had eased off, but the ground underfoot was wet and their feet were bare.

'Look at that,' said Vintage, absently. 'I imagine they thought they would never touch grass again.' She turned to the taller woman. 'Agent Chenlo, I fucked up something chronic when it came to Tyranny Munk, and I need to make up for it. If that means retrieving our war-beast, then that's what I'm going to do. And our concerns about how Ebora is perceived in this aren't unique to us, you know. How do you imagine Jarlsbad will feel about all these fell-witches running around free when one of them has forcibly taken over Tygrish? If you want these women to live free in Sarn, you have to stop Tyranny just as much as I do.'

Chenlo turned to her. 'You volunteered me first, and now you are giving me my reasons?'

'You are an intelligent woman, Agent Chenlo. You would have come to these conclusions yourself, eventually.' Vintage smiled and shook some water from her boots. 'All people need, in my experience, is a little push in the right direction. Or a giant kick up the arse. I am always happy to provide either.'

Chapter Seven

Fell-Gianna

The life of a Winnowry agent is a regimented thing. We are at the Winnowry, or we are on a mission: retrieving new fell-witches, selling or moving akaris, or some other Winnowry business. Sometimes it is possible to forget the other dangers of this world, or, at least, to put them from your mind.

Not so today. There is a densely forested region of Triskenteth which is riddled with Wild, and in the midst of all that, a settlement surrounded by high, carefully maintained walls. We were warned in the missive we received that if we must approach by air, we would be advised to land outside the walls and present ourselves to be admitted. If we appeared in the skies directly over the settlement we would likely be shot down.

I can say now I forgive them their caution. We spent only a short time in the Wild-wood, but every sense I have rang with danger, and things moved in the shadows that were much too dark for the time of day. I was quite relieved when the huge wooden gates were finally opened.

This girl was quiet, calm, watchful. It had taken some

Hestillion paused to catch her breath, blinking at the sweat running into her eyes. Her hands inside her long leather gloves felt numb, and there was a solid, throbbing ache in her back from bending over the crafting pools.

She'd been working for – hours? Days? She was no longer sure. There were no windows this deep within the corpse moon, and there would be nothing to see through them anyway, save for more Behemoths. It took her a moment to realise why she had stopped, but of course it was Celaphon. The great dragon stood inside the entrance to the crafting chamber, his huge form blocking out the light from the corridor.

'What are you doing?'

Hestillion stood up straight, wincing at the knots in her back. 'I have been creating, my sweet. Making new things. As the queen does.'

Celaphon snorted, and lowered his bulky head. 'What for?'

'Let me show you them.' Hestillion walked to the far wall, where three of her creations stood waiting. 'I've made them as helpers for me. Servants who can do as I ask, directly, so I do not need to chase after any of the queen's dirty little creatures. These ones are mine.' Hestillion paused as a memory resurfaced. 'Once, before the Carrion Wars, Ebora had many servants. Humans who happily served us, even lived with us, but of course that all changed.'

'What were these Carrion Wars?'

'It . . . does not matter now, Celaphon. It's the history of a dead world.'

The dragon came closer to the far wall, his great nostrils flexing as he took in the scent of the newly created creatures.

'They look strange,' he said eventually.

Hestillion nodded absently. They did.

Her first had been a tall man-shaped thing, his face now sculpted into something sharp and angular and almost familiar. His wings she had strengthened with pieces scavenged from some of the larger burrower creatures, and the spider-mothers. Once she had hit upon this idea, it had seemed obvious. Her creature would need armour of a sort, something to protect the soft flesh of his body. She had commanded several of the larger burrowers to climb into the changing pools, and then she had slowly taken them to pieces. Useful pieces.

Curiously, they had seemed to resist this, and the strange keening noises they made as Hestillion eased their bodies apart were unnerving at first. Unsettling, almost. But the noise distracted her from the discordant music in her head – that unending broken wail that was the Jure'lia – and besides, when she saw what she could make for her servant, she quickly brushed aside any queasiness.

He stood resplendent in a shining black carapace, the sharply curving shards of spider-mother skin making fine vambraces and pauldrons. His breastplate was a flexible mesh of black scales, each picked from the body of a giant burrower hybrid. His eyes, she had to admit, were a little unnerving; a pair of slippery yellow globes plucked from another anonymous scuttling creature. But they seemed to work. They followed her wetly as she moved, and there was more life in him than in any of the queen's skittering homunculus creatures.

'This is the First,' she said, tapping the man-servant on the shoulder. 'These two, I have no names for yet.'

Her next creations had been largely female in aspect. They were smaller than the man-servant, and more encrusted in the makeshift Jure'lia armour. The top halves of their heads were covered in spiky helmets made from pieces of burrower skin, neatly doing away with the need for eyes.

'What are they for?' Celaphon asked again, and he looked slowly around the chamber. Hestillion could see him looking at the discarded remains of so many Jure'lia creatures, and she felt a sudden stab of irritation.

'They are for me,' she said firmly. 'You cannot understand, Celaphon, since you were born and raised here, but I need company. I need shapes like me, or I fear I will lose my mind. You cannot know what it is like.'

Celaphon snorted. 'I do not know what it is like to crave the company of my own kind?' He rounded on her, his silvery eyes full of an intelligence she hadn't guessed at. 'Have you forgotten that you chased my brother and sister away from here? When I wanted them to stay and be joined with us.'

'It was the wrong path, my sweet.' Hestillion walked away from the dragon back towards the crafting pools. Another figure awaited her there, similar to the others. She would have to make them distinct somehow, she realised. Amongst the connectedness and anonymity of the Jure'lia, she had a sudden craving for individuality. 'I know it hurts now, but you will come to see it as clearly as I did. We do not need the others.

They let us down.' Unbidden, a memory of the Eboran boy Celaphon had dismembered again floated through her mind; his pale hand upturned in the dirt, black blood running into gritty snow. In response to that, she plunged her arms back into the steaming pool. 'We will make our own family now.'

Tor sat alone in his chamber, nursing a glass of wine. Through the tall windows he could see that it was very late already – he seemed to be losing track of time these days – yet the full moon was hidden behind a dense bank of clouds, turning them grey and somehow ghostly. The garden beyond was a place of flat silvery light, just as it had been when he was a child. If he closed his eyes and peeked only through his eyelashes, if he sat very still and very carefully thought of nothing – not Noon, or Kirune, or the worm people – it was almost possible to imagine that he were back there, in the time before the crimson flux had left its bloody footprints through the corridors of the palace. If he sat very still.

He picked up the glass and drained it off, quickly pouring another to replace it. There was an intermittent prickling pain in his left arm, but he did not lift his sleeve to examine it.

'Who'd have thought,' he said aloud to the empty room, 'that I would end up back here after all? In this state. I thought I was running away from it all, but actually I was just getting up speed. Making sure I had enough momentum to properly land in the shit.'

The wine was rich and full-bodied, a select bottle from one of the many human travellers that arrived at their gates these days. He took a few more large swallows, wondering if it would help him sleep, when an agonised scream scattered the silence into pieces. Tor winced, swallowing hard, and waited, but the screams didn't stop – they only grew louder. Along his link to Kirune and the other war-beasts, he felt a shiver of their worry and discomfort, and so he stood up, putting the glass back on the table. He knew there was no use, that he could be of no help, but it was one thing to know that, and quite another to stand in the dark listening to a human bellowing with pain and fear.

He left his room and headed down the corridor, walking stiffly and without thought. When he arrived at his cousin's chambers he let himself in without knocking and abruptly wished he had brought the bottle of wine with him.

'Al, is he awake?'

Bern was lying rigid on the bed, his eyes open but unseeing even as he let loose one hoarse scream after another. The cords in his neck were rigid, his hands curled into fists at his side. Even in the gloomy starlight coming through the window Tor could see that he was covered in sweat, the loose strands of blond hair stuck to his cheeks and his forehead. Aldasair was kneeling next to him, his hands on the human man's shoulders. He did not look up as Tor came in.

'Bern, it's me! It's Aldasair. You are safe, you are home. This is just another nightmare.'

Bern screamed again, a terrible sound of horror and sorrow, and then some of the energy seemed to go out of him. He sank back into the bed as his muscles relaxed, but still his head thrashed back and forth, and he began moaning, murmuring disconnected words and phrases.

'Tearing it all apart . . . water rushing . . . the burns . . . new faces . . . the eyes!'

'I don't think this is truly a nightmare, cousin.' Tor had joined Aldasair at the side of the bed, and for the first time his cousin glanced up and seemed to take in that he was there. 'It's the Jure'lia link. It haunts him.'

'It's killing him,' spat Aldasair. 'As sure as a poison or a festering wound, it takes a bit of his strength each day.'

Tor looked at the man reluctantly. He had always been one of the most impressive humans he'd ever seen, easily as tall as

78

any Eboran and certainly stronger than most humans he had known, but months of living with half a foot in the worm people's hive was visibly sapping him. Inevitably, Tor thought of all the Eborans who had gradually died in these rooms, coughing up their last life's blood onto dusty sheets. He cleared his throat.

'Look, Al. He's coming round.'

Little by little, the glazed expression in Bern's eyes was receding. Eventually, he stopped moaning and began shivering instead. He turned to look at the two Eborans at his bedside, and managed a wry smile.

'Please don't tell me Tor is my nursemaid now,' he said, his voice cracked and weak.

'You wish,' said Tor. 'There are women in Mushenska who would pay good coin for attention like that.'

Bern coughed in place of a laugh and, with Aldasair's help, sat up so that he was leaning against the headboard.

'By the fucking stones, I am tired of this.'

'I will get you water. Can you stand to eat?' Aldasair brushed some hair from the bigger man's forehead. 'I can find soup.'

'Just water, please.'

Aldasair vanished into the next room, his bare torso briefly outlined in gloomy moonlight from the windows.

'What was it this time?' asked Tor, pitching his voice low. 'It sounded worse.'

'Worse. It was worse.' Bern nodded, looking down at his lap. 'Ah, stones crush me, I can't take any more of this.' He glanced up, catching Tor's eye with a look that was suddenly conspiratorial. 'You have to do it for me, Tor. I'm not accurate enough with one axe, not at this angle.'

'Bern . . .'

'A good sharp sword, take the whole thing off at the wrist. Then I'll be free of the bastards.'

'Bern,' he gripped the man's forearm, 'my cousin would

79

murder me. And Vintage would too. And Sharrik. Fuck, all of them would, probably. And besides . . .' He bit his lip, not wanting to say it. 'It might not even work.'

The big man turned his head away, droplets of sweat in his lank hair. 'You think it could be in me all over, by now. Whatever this taint is.'

'I don't know, my friend,' Tor squeezed the man's arm, and let it go. 'I honestly don't. But I think it's best we don't do anything rash.'

Aldasair reappeared with a jug of water and a fat glass, which he passed to Bern. After a few gulps, Bern shook his head.

'What did you see?' asked Aldasair. Tor winced, thinking that Bern would hardly want to relive his visions, but the human sat up a little more in the bed and faced Aldasair with an open, trusting look.

'I saw your cousin.' He glanced at Tor. 'Your sister. Just brief glances of her, like pieces of a broken mirror. I think that's because we broke the Jure'lia's link to each other when I replaced their crystal memory.' He frowned, as though talking of such things still seemed like gibberish. 'Everything is chaotic there. But what I did see – I saw them in pieces, being pulled and stretched, her long sharp hands dipping into their insides, teasing them apart.'

Tor sat back. It was suddenly much colder, as though a window had swung open.

'What do you mean? Is she killing them?'

'It's hard to describe. Because of how this link works,' Bern briefly held up the hand with its chunk of blue crystal embedded in the palm, 'I see it all from many directions. I feel her hunger and curiosity, I feel their pain and fear. She sinks her fingers into their guts, and I can feel them moving in mine. She has a great sense of satisfaction, a warm feeling of . . . fulfilment. It doesn't feel like killing. It's almost the opposite, somehow.

And they are trapped and pulled apart, unable to stop her.' He looked at Tor almost sheepishly. 'And I thought I saw your face there, just for a moment.'

'That doesn't make any sense.'

'I know.' Bern shrugged. 'I wish I could show it to you more clearly. It might help, to know what she is up to. It might help just to share the sight with someone else.' His voice grew low and quiet. 'I think I am going mad, sometimes. Maybe it is all my imagination after all.'

'It is not,' said Aldasair, firmly.

'Aldasair is right,' said Tor. 'And I know Vintage would say the same. These . . . visions. Are they like nightmares? Do they feel like dreams?'

'I thought we just agreed they were not dreams,' said Aldasair, a little testily.

'I know, it's just –' Tor swallowed. The wine he'd been drinking was now a sour taste at the back of his throat. Briefly he wondered if the people camped out in the gardens could hear Bern's screaming. He wondered what they thought of it. Perhaps they thought the Eborans were torturing someone. It was the sort of thing they were known for, at least in the more lurid stories. 'If it's like a dream, or a nightmare, there's a chance I could dream-walk into it.'

'Dream-walk?' Bern had finished his water, so Aldasair poured him a fresh glass.

'The Eboran art of dream-walking,' said Al. 'We can enter another person's dreams, and even shape them. It's how we've been exploring Micanal's amber tablets. Hestillion was especially talented at it. Tormalin too.'

'Not as talented as my sister, believe me,' said Tor. 'But I can certainly do it. If I can dream-walk into what you're seeing, I could share it with you.'

'Brother,' Bern grasped Tormalin's arm, 'I would not inflict that on you.'

It was like being punched in the gut. For a second, Tor felt the full force of his connection to the war-beasts, and to their companions – the shared grief, the shared affection. For a terrible moment he felt his eyes sting, but he blinked it away. *And to think I was so alone once.*

'But it could be helpful, Bern. Not just to your sanity, but to the wider war effort. We desperately need information, and remember, I know Hestillion better than anyone. I may be able to discern what she is up to. And through that, find out what state the Jure'lia are in. Or even where they are. I think it's worth trying. And unlike you, I can remove myself at any time.' He smiled wanly.

Aldasair looked less than convinced, but Bern nodded. 'If we can drag something useful out of this bloody nightmare, then I suppose it is worth trying.'

'Not now. Not until you've rested,' said Aldasair firmly.

'A glass of wine, then,' said Bern. At Aldasair's look, he shrugged. 'Or a few, even. I reckon it's the only way I'm getting back to sleep.'

Tor left them, walking back out into the darkened corridors with Bern's screams still echoing in his head.

'What happened? Is Bern all right?'

Startled, Tor turned to see Noon coming down the corridor towards him, her hair messy from her own bed. He felt a flush of horror that he had not heard her approach. Were his senses already becoming dull, or was he simply preoccupied?

'More nightmares,' he said. 'This link to the Jure'lia, it's killing him, I think. Or driving him insane.'

Noon frowned, looking back towards the door to his cousin's suite. 'You really think it can do that?'

'If you had horrifying nightmares every time you slept, wouldn't it drive you mad?'

Noon looked troubled. 'I've touched it, the crystal in his hand. I can feel the life of the worm people through it, like . . .

It's like touching someone sweating their way through a fever. The Jure'lia are a sickness. If I can feel that just from touching the crystal . . .'

Tor sighed. 'I've offered to dream-walk with him, to try and ease it, if I can. Once, before Ebora fell into ruin, dream-walking was often used as a way to heal people who suffered with maladies of the mind. I've never tried it, but there's also the chance we could learn something useful about what the Jure'lia are up to.'

Noon nodded, but she was watching him too closely, and he sensed she hadn't really taken in what he'd said.

'What is it?'

'You look knackered,' she said. 'Like you're not sleeping either. Do you want to . . . ?' She held up her arm, the hand bent back so the wrist was exposed, and again Tor felt dizzy. The salty warmth of her blood in his mouth, the texture of her skin under his teeth, and then the rush that followed . . . it was all that he wanted, but when he thought of taking her hand, smiling as he had in the past and leading her back to his room, the thin red line on his arm crashed over all of it, obliterating every warm feeling, every desire. He forced a smile on his face.

'Thank you, but no. As you say, I should get some sleep. We all should.'

He turned and left her in the corridor, walking as fast as he could while still being polite. He was afraid that if he looked on her face for a moment longer he would give in.

Later, when everything was green fire and agonising questions, Tor would look back on the memory – of her eyes, dark and confused in the shadowy corridor, and how he had turned away – and curse himself.

Chapter Eight

Fell-Kreed

We had a runner.

When we arrived for the scheduled pick-up, the child's family were silent and sick-looking, saying that they had kept the knowledge from the girl for as long as they could, but when she had worked it out, she had fled. Kesenstan is a wild, cold place, with the Targ mountains looming so close that it's possible to feel that they will fall on you at any moment. The girl, whose name was Kreed, had taken a horse and headed into the foothills. She will know how to hide, they warned us. There will be monsters there too, they said. When I asked why she would flee to a place haunted by parasite spirits, they shook their heads and said 'because you are worse monsters'. Agent Lin sneered at them, but I must admit I was heart-sore. Kreed would sooner risk having her body turned inside out than come with us.

We searched for a full two days, following her tracks into the Wild undergrowth. Several times at night we saw shimmering lights in the distance, and once heard a mournful wailing sound, more sad than frightening. Lin cursed the girl and cursed the Targ mountains for being unlucky. The bats, at least, seemed happy enough – Targ is their ancient home, not that any of them have ever seen it.

Eventually, we found the girl, half-starved and mostly frozen, hidden under the exposed roots of a fallen tree. She had fled her home so swiftly that she had not taken any food with her. Agent Lin, somewhat unnecessarily in my opinion, took so much life energy from Kreed that the girl did not regain consciousness until we were already some way across the plains.

Details about the life of Kreed of Kesenstan: her family were poor. How else can I say that? It sounds too raw. But they took the money we gave them gladly. She was a shepherd, with a small flock of her own to care for. The sheep (a type I have never seen, with cream-coloured wool) each had a blue-and-yellow circle dyed onto their coats, which is unique to Kreed.

Extract from the private records of Agent Chenlo

The next morning, Tor rose with the sun, washing and dressing himself swiftly and eating a quick breakfast of apples and pear jam. He left his rooms and walked quickly through the palace, deliberately not thinking too closely about where he was going, or what he intended to do. Gradually, the morning sun filled the window-lined corridors, revealing marble floors freshly washed, and he came to a quieter part of the palace, a corner that he had not visited since the fall of the Ninth Rain. *I meant to*, he told himself. *It was always in the back of my mind to do so. It's not like we haven't been busy.*

In one such corridor he met one of the healers. He was a young man from the plains, his arms bare and his black hair pulled neatly back from his face. He wore a brightly coloured horsehair tunic and simple leather trousers. At the sight of Tor his eyes widened slightly. There was a deep scar on the left side of his jaw, a twisted white line marring the smooth brown warmth of his skin.

'My lord,' he said, clearly taken unawares, 'I wasn't expecting to see anyone today.'

Of course you weren't, thought Tor sourly. *I've hardly been a regular visitor.*

'I don't want to interrupt you. I just wondered if it would be possible to see Egron. If he's well enough this morning.'

'I was just going to check in on him. Come with me.'

Tor followed the healer, trying to ignore the flush of shame he felt at the cool way the plain's man had assessed him. When Hestillion had asked the people of Sarn for assistance, they had answered, sending aid in the form of food, trade and healers. When everything had gone so disastrously wrong, many humans had, quite understandably, fled back to their own homes. But a few had stayed, opting to do what they could for the remaining Eborans still suffering from the crimson flux, and even tending to Ygseril, in the hope that the tree-god would waken from his slumber and give more of his magical sap. It was this sap that had once given the Eborans their unusually long lives, but when the tree-father seemed to die at the end of the Eighth Rain, that supply of sap had vanished. For a time, human blood had seemed to provide a solution, leading to the horrors of the Carrion Wars, but . . . Tor grasped at his aching arm, struck afresh by the particularly vicious irony that their bloodlust should ultimately lead to their doom. Vintage reported that the handful of surviving Eborans were still clinging on, made comfortable at least by the ministrations of the remaining humans. Tor had been glad, up until now, to take her word for it.

The healer opened the door to a suite and stepped inside, pulling back curtains and letting light into a spacious room filled with musical instruments. Tor stood for a moment, slightly taken aback by the sight. He remembered that Egron had been obsessed with music, that he had collected instruments all across Sarn and attempted to master them all, but for some reason Tor had assumed that, with the illness, all of this would have faded away. Beyond the room crammed with instruments was another, and it was here that Egron lay, in the centre of an enormous bed.

'Good morning, Egron,' the healer called out. 'You have a visitor.'

The prone Eboran did not reply. The human went into the chamber and bent over the figure, softly talking. He took some things from a side cabinet, small bottles and a long spoon, and for a while Tor looked away. Eventually, the healer came out, wiping his hands on a cloth.

'Go and see him,' he said quietly. 'He's awake now.' And he left the suite.

It was very quiet in this part of the palace, so far from the human habitations and the section given over to the fell-witches, but it was just about possible to hear, somewhere down the corridor, someone coughing their lungs to pieces.

'Tormalin the Oathless?' Egron's voice was surprisingly firm. 'What are you hovering about out there for?'

Feeling even more awkward, Tor entered the bedchamber and forced a smile on his face.

'How are you, Egron? It's been . . . a while.'

The Eboran in the bed turned his head to one side, laughing softly. It was clear from the thin sheets that covered him that his body was emaciated, and his skin had taken on the chalky white pallor of the flux. Much of his hair was gone, leaving a waxy-looking scalp threaded here and there with strands of yellowish hair, and there were bright red lesions on the arm that lay above the bed covers: the vital black blood of Eborans turned red and vivid with disease. Yet his eyes were bright, and he watched Tor with obvious interest as he approached the bed.

'I'm still here, which is something. I like that healer, he has a kind face. His name is Cloudwall, did you know that? The plains people have such interesting names. Musical names, I think.' Egron stopped and swallowed, and Tor clearly heard the click his throat made as he did so. 'Can you believe our fathers and mothers killed so many of them, Tormalin? Such a senseless thing.'

'It was a time of madness,' said Tor. He and Egron were of an age, both too young to have been involved in the Carrion Wars, yet both old enough to carry some dark memories. They were not related, had not been friends; had barely even known each other. Just familiar with each other's faces, really – which was inevitable when everyone around you was dying at a terrifying rate. He remembered that Egron had been handsome, and had loved music. That as a child Hestillion had harboured a crush on him briefly, which eventually had been replaced with some other fancy of hers. He remembered that Egron had caught the crimson flux just before Tor decided to leave Ebora, and consequently had been one more face he had been glad to consign to forgetfulness.

'*A time of madness*, heh. Well, so is this, I suppose,' said Egron, and to Tor's surprise he sat up in bed, reaching for a glass of water next to him. When he had taken a few sips, he plucked fussily at his nightshirt. 'To what do I owe this pleasure?'

'I wanted to talk to you. About . . .' Tor went to the chair beside the bed and sat, trying to think what to say. How to get to where he needed to be. 'About the flux.' He cleared his throat. 'You know we have so many new healers in Ebora now, humans who are eager to help us. I've offered to gather information about the flux, to help them. The more we know, the more –' He waved a hand, vaguely.

'And you've offered to do that in the midst of fighting the worm people? Of bonding to a war-beast?' Egron's crimson eyes grew bright, as if he were laughing at him. 'How generous of you.'

'Tell me about the beginning of it.' Tor folded his hands in his lap. 'Tell me about how it starts.'

Egron sank back into the pillows. His head looked like something whittled from old, diseased wood. 'My fingers,' he said. 'They started to go numb. I was not as strong as I once was. I could not lift my plains drum, one day. Odd, little things like that. I felt weak, so I sought out more blood, to make me feel better.' He grinned. 'Idiot that I was. Then, a burning pain in my chest, and then my arms. Is any of this sounding familiar yet?'

Tor sat very still.

'It took a while for the cough to come,' said Egron. His voice was mild, as though he were talking about the weather, or his beloved instruments. 'I was surprised by that. There was pain, and weakness, a slow draining away of ability and strength and life. Then the marks.' He lifted up his arm with the ragged red tears, as if Tor could have failed to notice them. 'There's no avoiding it then, of course. You can't keep on lying to yourself when your blood turns red.'

'But you look brighter,' said Tor. 'You are speaking easily with me now, and you have had the flux for how long?'

'Many years,' said Egron, nodding. 'Many, many years. Cloudwall has these mixtures and pastes that ease the pain, and a drink that coats my throat, to ease the coughing. It's quite something. Did you know, he told me that the medicines he gives me would kill a human in such dosages?' Egron seemed impressed with this fact. 'But it's all a bandage over a wound that won't heal, Tormalin the Oathless. It's the painted face of a corpse.'

'You are still alive,' said Tor.

Egron nodded, but he was looking away, as if he hadn't really heard.

'It kills quick, or it kills slow, but it always kills. This is the end of us. I didn't used to think that. I thought there was hope, and that somehow, if enough of us hung on, Ygseril would heal us somehow. Well, he's back, and he hasn't. And it comes for all of us eventually, doesn't it?'

He looked directly at Tor, and Tor felt a dim bloom of pain at his elbows and wrists. *It's your imagination*, he told himself, but the pain did not fade.

'Pass me that set of pipes,' said Egron, nodding at a low table by Tor's seat. 'It's all I can manage to hold now. I got them from Reidn, two hundred years ago. By rights they should have fallen apart, but I think much of what the humans built will be here long after Ebora has collapsed into dust.'

Tor passed the pipes over. They were light, made of hollow wooden tubes laced together, and were decorated only with a few daubs of pink and yellow paint.

Egron pressed them to his lips, and a few soft notes of music filled the room. Much to his own horror, Tor felt the hair on the back of his neck stand up; he knew this tune, had heard it over and over as a child, but hadn't heard it since. Hadn't his mother and Hestillion sung it together, some little song about the different flowering seasons?

Egron dropped the pipes, seized suddenly with a racking cough. All the remaining colour drained from his face, and the cords in his neck stood out with exertion. He rocked back and forth, wheezing desperately to get some air back into his lungs before he suffocated. The pipes dropped to the floor with a little clatter.

'Egron!' Tor stood, uncertain what to do. The lesions on the man's arms were opening up and weeping, as though they did the breathing for him now, and his eyes bulged from his head. Black blood, thin and diluted with diseased red fluid, began to leak from the edges of his yawning mouth.

90

'Shit.'

Where once there had been an ill man in his sickbed, talking quietly of the past and of music, there was a creature composed entirely of pain, of desperation and suffering. Tor backed towards the door, only realising that he had been calling for Cloudwall when the young human appeared in the chamber. He went immediately to Egron's side, easing the Eboran back onto his pillows with strong, capable arms, and Tor left them there, with the sound of Egron's music and his coughing still ringing in his head, like one terrible symphony.

'I've never been to Jarlsbad.'

At her words, Helcate lifted his snout and pushed it into Noon's hand, demanding that she scratch behind his ears. She obliged, smiling faintly. They had all struggled since the death of Eri, Helcate most of all, but the littlest war-beast grew a little brighter every day.

'Oh, it's wonderful.' Vintage was at Helcate's side, busily strapping bags onto his harness. They had to travel light, something that Vintage was used to, after all her years of exploring Sarn. 'Wonderfully varied. Strictly speaking, you see, it's a collection of minor kingdoms, with their own royal families, all under the wider rulership of the High Jarl. It makes for a unique collection of cultures. Lots of minor differences, with a larger, underpinning thread of similarity. I've travelled through the region a number of times, and I always see something new.' She frowned slightly, as though remembering something that troubled her, then yanked another strap into place. 'I may be experiencing a very different sort of welcome this time.'

'We are not likely to be welcomed at all.'

Agent Chenlo appeared, a pack already slung over her shoulders. It seemed she travelled even more lightly than Vintage. Noon crossed her arms over her chest.

'I'd be happier about this if we knew what sort of war-beast you'll be facing,' she said. 'All we really have to go on is what you've told us.'

'You mean you have to trust my word?' Chenlo's mouth twitched at the corner, as if she wanted to smile but had thought better of it. 'Your reluctance is understandable, Lady Noon. If you wish, we could wait until more gossip filters over the Bloodless Mountains.'

'Don't call me that.'

'We don't have time,' said Vintage. She had finally finished adjusting the harness, and joined Noon by Helcate's head, rubbing the war-beast's long neck. 'We need to nip this in the bud before it becomes something we have no hope of resolving quietly. The Jure'lia could be back at any time, and we'll need to be focussed on that if we've any hope of surviving them. Besides,' she sighed, 'what of the bond between our war-beasts? It grows daily, yet this new creature isn't a part of it. We have to consider that eventually it may be impossible for them to become – for them to join with us successfully. And that will be a great tragedy. I feel that strongly.'

'Like that giant brute that has joined with the Jure'lia,' said Noon. She and Vostok had fought Celaphon in the skies, and had felt nothing but flat hatred and a strange, alien desperation from him. 'Listen, I wanted to talk to you before you went, Vin. Privately.'

Chenlo nodded, and turned away across the palace gardens. After a moment, she lifted a silver whistle to her lips and a great black bat appeared in the skies, wings whirring.

'What is it, my darling?'

'Oh, lots of things. Too many bloody things.' Noon reached up and pushed her fingers through her hair. It was getting too long. 'Don't trust that one, for a start. She's one of the Winnowry's dogs.'

'There isn't a Winnowry anymore, my dear,' said Vintage mildly. 'You made sure of that.'

'You know what I mean. Watch your back, all the time. Be careful. Find out what you can but don't do anything rash.'

'Darling, I was doing rash things when you were still drooling in your mother's lap.' Seeing the look on Noon's face, Vintage smiled. 'I take your point. Believe me, after my experience with Tyranny Munk, I am not rushing to trust anyone.' The smile faded, and Noon got the impression she was thinking of Nanthema again. Tyranny Munk wasn't the only one who had betrayed a trust.

'All right. Good. We just need information, first of all. Information from someone we can trust.' She reached over and squeezed Vintage's arm briefly. 'The bond between the war-beasts, between all of us, is getting stronger, but we don't really know how it will last over such distances. And, well . . .'

'And I am new to it, and Helcate is . . . well, Helcate is himself.'

'Helcate,' agreed Helcate.

'I just can't help feeling like all this is a mistake,' said Noon. Unexpectedly, she felt on the verge of crying. 'Last time, when Tor and I left on some fool's mission, all we found was a lot of terrible stuff, and then when we came back . . .'

Vintage put her hand on Noon's shoulder. 'What you brought back, darling, was the truth. Which is rarely comfortable and never painless, but often, ultimately, worth knowing. And there is the amber record. There are still useful things to be gleaned from that, whatever Tor may think. I've asked Aldasair to do his best to keep cataloguing it while I'm away.'

'Do you think Tor is all right?' The question was out before she knew she meant to ask it. 'Does he seem himself to you?'

'Vain, difficult, self-absorbed? He seems perfectly normal to me.' Vintage smiled, a little sadly. 'He's not all right, Noon, but who is at the moment? And he's just found out that much of his own history is a lie, or, at least, is severely warped. I imagine it will take a while for him to adjust to that.'

At that moment, Noon became aware of a pair of young women approaching them across the lush grass. One of them had an arm covered in rippled, melted skin – a bad burn scar – while the other looked very frail, as though a strong breeze would blow her away. Both had the mark of the Winnowry on their foreheads.

'Oh shit,' said Noon in a low voice. 'They've caught me.'

Vintage lowered her voice to match. 'Darling, you will have to talk to them at some point.'

'Lady Noon?' The woman with the scars stepped forward, her broad face serious. 'I'm Fell-Andrea, this is my friend Fell-Stasia. I'm sorry, we haven't been here long, but we wanted to say thank you. For what you did. For getting us out of there.'

The other girl nodded silently.

'You're welcome,' said Noon stiffly.

'My darling, if you don't mind me asking, where did you get those scars?' Vintage asked.

Andrea blinked and looked down, as though surprised to see the scars herself. 'Oh! I was in the agent training programme at one point, but I, uh, didn't settle. I couldn't follow orders, you see. So one of the agents burned me, as punishment.'

Vintage looked ill, while Noon nodded towards Chenlo, who was adjusting the harness on her bat. 'An agent like her, you mean?'

'Oh no, not like her.' The pale girl was speaking, her voice soft and uncertain. 'Chenlo was the good one. You were lucky if you were in her squad. She did what she could to keep us from beatings. Burnings.' She shivered under the bright summer sun.

'What a saint,' said Noon.

'I couldn't stand with the agents, because they were the

Winnowry, and they imprisoned me when I was eight years old,' Andrea's voice was terse now, a little unsteady, and Noon felt a shiver of discomfort move down her back. She didn't want to be here. She didn't want to be having this conversation. Somewhere, distantly, she felt Vostok turn her attention towards her. 'But I would stand with *you*, Lady Noon.'

'Me too,' said Stasia, her voice barely more than a whisper. 'Just tell us when and where. We'll follow you.'

Noon swallowed and looked away. 'There's no need for that,' she said. 'I'm not leading anyone anywhere.'

The two women looked at each other, clearly embarrassed, and Noon felt a fresh stab of guilt and horror. She made herself look at them both.

'Look, you're free. That's the point. You don't have to follow anyone, you don't have to do anything you don't want to. Go and do . . . whatever it is you wanted to do with your lives in the first place.' As soon as she said it, she thought of eight-year-old Fell-Andrea, before she was imprisoned by the Winnowry. Andrea had been a child, with no idea of her place in the world yet. What was she supposed to reclaim, exactly?

Even so, the two women nodded and said their goodbyes. When they were some distance away, Vintage elbowed Noon in the ribs.

'What did you have to go and say that for?'

'Fire and blood, what was I supposed to say? It's madness. I'm not a leader. I shouldn't be in charge of anything. And I'm definitely not a replacement for the Winnowry.'

'Yet here you were just now, advising me on my mission, appraising me of our wider situation.' Vintage laughed at Noon's outraged expression. 'You might not like it, Noon, but when you're on the battlefield, when we fight, you move into that position naturally. Now, it might be Vostok's influence, but I think it's a role that's not completely beyond you.'

'Vintage, most of the time I think you're the wisest person I know. And then sometimes I think you're full of shit.'

Later, when all the packs were attached and everyone was ready, Noon watched Vintage and Agent Chenlo leave with a tight feeling in her chest. Very quickly, Helcate was a little smudge against the blue sky, and Noon found herself watching it closely, desperate to keep it in her sights until the very last moment. She had, hidden deep inside her so that the others couldn't feel it, the terrible suspicion that she wouldn't see Vintage again.

Chapter Nine

'What are you doing?'

Hestillion looked up from her work to see the Jure'lia queen standing in the doorway. Her mask-like face looked leathery and stained, but her body was in flux once more, tendrils of greenish-black fluid reaching out to support her against the walls. Keeping her own face mask-like, Hestillion murmured to her newest creation to return to her place by the wall. On the creature's bare chest the image of a green bird shimmered, unfinished.

'I am making myself some company,' said Hestillion, wiping her hands on her trousers. The figure – who Hestillion already thought of as Green Bird – had joined the First at the wall, and they watched her continually. They did not look at the queen.

'Your war-beast is not enough?'

But the queen had crept fully into the chamber, her head cocked in curiosity towards the things Hestillion had made. Oily fingers, each as long as Hestillion's hands, reached out to touch them, then apparently thought better of it. When Hestillion didn't answer, the queen oozed across the floor towards her.

'You have made things to obey you,' she said. There was no hint of judgement in her voice. It was simply a cold stating of fact. 'It is a unique pleasure. One that is not changing, or consuming. One that is . . . power. One more thing we must understand.'

'I think you already understand it,' said Hestillion, and then, 'You have left the crystal behind?'

They stood within another of the Behemoths; ultimately Hestillion had felt exposed inside the corpse moon. Too close to the teeming mind of the queen, and to Celaphon's own childish curiosity. At the mention of the crystal, the queen seemed to fold into herself.

'We have yet to understand the power of the memory. Sometimes I think I am close, and then . . .' the queen's wet eyes narrowed, 'and then it is gone. But we can feel you here, your fingers inside our flesh, working and changing.' She moved over to the wall until she stood in front of the First. Again, her long hand reached out and this time she touched the creature's cheek, smoothing a finger along the line of his jaw. 'You have made this one look a certain way. It is something that we have managed to glean from the new crystal memory – that you value the individual differences. That one face is not like another, and that is important to you.'

'To me?'

The queen waved a hand dismissively. 'All of you. The wider pestilence. You glory in the infinite differences between you all, all of which are considered valuable. That is not us. We are the whole, the many as one. We feel the human man still, the one who carries our crystal in his flesh, but curiously, the longer he is in contact with our mind, the more he is broken down, destroyed. It has become difficult to feel him in our web because of this. If we want to understand him now, to understand this human desire for difference, we would need him physically here, with us . . .' The queen trailed off, then seemed to change the subject. 'You are making use of the flesh of us. It is discomforting.'

'Yes, but I have good reason. I have an idea.' Hestillion pulled the roll of parchment from her jerkin and took it over to where the queen could see it. The map depicted much of eastern Sarn, and as far as she could tell, it had been reasonably up to date when it had been stolen from a destroyed settlement. 'You are hurt. You are healing, for want of a better word, but I am not. I can still act. Do you understand?'

The queen said nothing. At the wall, the creature called the First lifted and dropped his shoulders; almost a pretence of breathing.

'Now I am connected to the Jure'lia, let me use that. With this circle I am creating, I can control your ships. I can be your commander.'

The queen still did not speak. Hestillion hissed through her teeth in frustration.

'For thousands of years you have been trying to take Sarn, and failing. The same way each time. Any Eboran military mind would suggest that this is the very definition of madness. It does not work. Yet you are still doing it. Do you see?'

'You seek to advise us now, Hestillion Eskt, born in the year of the green bird?'

'Why not?' Hestillion threw her arms up in the air, aware that she was revealing too much of her own complicated feelings, but powerless to stop. 'I have left Ebora and pledged myself to you. We have raised a war-beast and changed him into something Sarn has never seen. I have . . . I have spilled Eboran blood, and turned away from my brother.' She thought of the days she had spent in Ebora, whispering to the voice within Ygseril's roots, convinced it was their great tree-father; and she remembered the flood of panic and guilt when she realised who that voice really belonged to. She had betrayed Ebora, and there was no walking away from it. 'I can suffer all that, I can suffer it and come through stronger, a weapon forged for your hand, but I cannot abide inefficiency.'

While the queen took this in, Hestillion brandished the map. 'Your attacks have always been random, haven't they? You emerge from your hiding place and go where the wind takes you, eating and destroying at random until the Eboran forces arrive and push you back. There is never any pattern, and never any tactical thinking.'

'There has never been any need.'

'How many times must Ebora crush you before you realise there is *every* need?' Hestillion rubbed her forehead with the back of her hand; she was sweating again. 'You need a strategy. And I can give it to you. I can even implement it, with the use of my circle.' She held up the map so that the queen could see. 'These places I have marked. These are places that have armies which will rise and fight against you. These are the places that will assist Ebora, both with soldiers and with supplies. They must be targeted, and wiped out first. Once they are removed, Ebora will be the weakest it has ever been.' Her throat contracted, and she paused, swallowing hard. She felt as though she were standing on the edge of a steep drop, an unknowable darkness yawning away below her. Then she looked up and met the yellow eyes of the First. His form was comforting, familiar. She tapped the map again. 'Do you see? Precision. Precision is what is needed.'

'And you believe that you can command our ships as we do?'

'I know I can. With my circle. While you have been studying your crystal, I have been practising. It is not easy, because the connection within us is so noisy, but I have made them listen closely to me, and I listen closely to them. We are forging our own links here, and what I speak of is possible. I promise you that.'

For a long time, the queen said nothing. She looked around the chamber instead, her gaze lingering on the discarded remains of various burrowers and spider-mothers, on the creatures

100

standing by the wall; Eboran in shape, Jure'lia in aspect. Through the blue crystal in her chest, Hestillion felt a fresh wave of discordance move through their connection.

'Prove it to us,' the queen said eventually. 'Finish crafting your *circle*. Take two ships beyond our nest, to a place that you have chosen, and make our maggots fat. Tear their worlds to pieces and cover the dust with our excretion. Make that small bit of the world ready for us, and prove the worth of this precision of yours. And leave your dragon here, with us.'

Hestillion lifted her head at this, but the queen just smiled. 'How else do we know you will return to us?'

With that, she left, oozing back through the wall. The glowing fronds dimmed slightly, and again Hestillion felt the disruption move through the network that was the Jure'lia. Making her creatures had been a welcome distraction, but it was clear that deep within, the worm people were still struggling to heal themselves.

'It doesn't matter,' she said aloud. 'I can make it work.'

She put the wider Jure'lia connection from her mind, and the figures at the wall twitched and shivered as she reached out for them instead. The one she called the First – the one that looked a little like her brother, in the right light – turned his head towards her. His yellow eyes rolled wetly; she had not managed eyelids.

'We can make it work. I will not rot in this hole waiting for the queen to make a decision.'

The First nodded, a little creakily. Somewhere, the memory of a small Eboran boy, his guts scattered in the mud and snow, kept trying to surface, but with the noise of the Jure'lia in her head and the excitement of her new plan brewing, this was easy enough to ignore. Hestillion smiled.

Vintage leaned forward to sink her hands into Helcate's curly fur, taking some comfort from his warmth. It might be high summer on the ground, but it was achingly cold this high up. Some distance to her left, the Winnowry agent was mostly hidden within the blur of her bat's wings, as she had been all morning, while in front of them it seemed like the whole of Sarn was spread like a gorgeous, shimmering length of silk.

'I doubt the plains have ever looked so beautiful,' she murmured. She had crossed them many times in her travels, often in the company of the nomadic peoples who spent their lives traversing the enormous stretches of grass and trees, and had always found them beautiful, but this was something else. Soft waves of green and gold threaded here and there with the silver of a river or a lake, and in the very far distance, soft purple hills and hints of wood smoke. It had taken them almost a week to get clear of Ebora and the Bloodless Mountains thanks to a flurry of summer storms, but now the weather had eased back into a kind of lazy serenity and the way ahead seemed impossibly clear.

One of the threads of silver was growing fatter as she watched, and with a strange thrill she recognised it: the Trick, looking, from this vantage point, very much like it did on her many maps. Clustered on this side of it was a copse of tall, spindly trees, each branch bright with small leaves. Sprawled around them, growing closer all the time, were a number of strange horse-drawn vehicles; the top half of each featured a tent shaped rather like a three-cornered hat, while the under-carriage sported a set of four large wooden wheels. There were people with the vehicles, many of which were turning to point at them as they flew closer.

'A Runningseed fishing party!' she called across to Chenlo. The woman looked up, her face blank – she clearly hadn't made sense of what she had said – so Vintage leaned down to speak into Helcate's long foxy ear. 'Take us down by the river, darling. I'm sure our friend will follow.'

They landed by the water, which was rushing quick and

bright under the sunlight, and after a handful of moments Agent Chenlo followed.

'What have we stopped for?' She peeled off her leather gloves. Her long black hair was tied back in a neat bun, but the wind had tugged much of it free. 'Are you quite well?'

'Well? I'm spectacular, darling.' Vintage untied the last of the harness straps and stepped down just in time to see the first of the plains people arriving. 'I just thought we could have a quick chat with these lovely people.'

Chenlo's brow creased. 'Is there really time for such?'

'Time to say hello? To gather information? Always. I suppose you might not have seen the need when you were running errands for the Winnowry, but believe me, this is the best way to travel.' Vintage was already in the grass, beaming at the scattering of children who had run up to greet them. Their eyes were bright and shining, but they all halted a good ten feet from Helcate, none of them quite brave enough to go any closer. A handful of adults were approaching, men and women with long colourful poles over their shoulders. 'Go on.' Vintage waved at the children. 'Go and see him. His name's Helcate, he's very friendly. He's a fiend for being scratched behind the ears.'

'You are not Eboran?' This was one of the adults. She was tall and athletic, with wiry, muscled limbs. There was a scattering of fish scales rubbed across her cheek, winking like heated metal under the sun.

'I'm afraid not, my dear, but these are strange days, aren't they? I'm Lady Vincenza de Grazon, but please, call me Vintage. This is my associate, Agent Chenlo.' She held out her hand, and the woman grasped it briefly, before adjusting the position of her fishing pole.

'We know what she is,' said one of the men. He also had fish scales stuck to his face. All of them did, Vintage realised. 'But why are the Winnowry travelling with a war-beast?'

'It's a long bloody story, darling, one I'd be glad to share with you. Perhaps we could exchange stories? A bit of lunch, a chat, some time spent with my feet on the ground. How's the fishing?'

Eventually, Vintage and Chenlo sat on the banks of the river with two of the Runningseed people while the others went back to their fishing. The woman had introduced herself as Silverbank, and her partner, a short man with startling blue eyes, as Starfault. They had cooked up some of that morning's catch with butter and salt, and despite having stuffed herself with a small pile of the little crispy fish, Vintage found herself eyeing up the rest of the haul in the hope that someone would take the hint.

'That *is* quite a story,' said Starfault. His plains speech was melodic, with different inflections and cadences; Vintage guessed he was not originally from this end of the plains. 'But it fits with all else we've heard. The worm people in the skies, the corpse moon over the mountains.'

'Gone now, though,' said Silverbank. 'No one has seen them for some moons. But you say they are not dead?'

Vintage grimaced. Chenlo had said virtually nothing during their talk, and had mostly fidgeted, eager to be gone again.

'It's not likely, I'm afraid.' She sipped a little of the milky drink they had given her. She wasn't as keen on it as the fish. 'We crawled up their asses and gave them a fright – a big one – but they always come back. The history of Sarn attests to that. And this time I don't think we'll have long to wait.'

'This is poor news.' Starfault and Silverbank exchanged a look. 'The plains need peace.'

'And what news do you have of your home?' Vintage glanced up the bank to see Helcate, surrounded by children. They had invented a game of throwing the war-beast morsels of fish, which he would snap between his jaws. Vintage doubted that Vostok would approve of such an undignified game, but Helcate was clearly having the time of his life. 'I imagine you hear quite a lot, travelling back and forth as you do.'

Silverbank nodded. She took a handful of the little silver fish and threw them into the hot pan. For a time the air was filled with the good sound of fish frying. 'Last year, a lot of the news was bad. People travelling through the plains were fleeing their homes, looking for somewhere with bigger walls. Although what help that is when the worms infest the skies . . .' She cast a hand upwards, her eyes still on the cooking fish. 'They all brought stories of people being eaten from the inside out, of giant white worms that consume the land, of abominations with too many legs.'

'All of the old nightmares,' added Starfault quietly.

'Some said that they were broken, the worm people. That their ships had holes, that they seemed confused. But who can say if that was new?' Silverbank shrugged. 'It has been so long. We only have stories of the worm people. They have always seemed like a story.'

Vintage nodded. 'It's easier to believe that, I know. Who wants to find out that the nightmare was real all along? But I have spent my whole life studying them – the Jure'lia, the parasite spirits, the Eboran resistance. It's all an important part of Sarn's history, and its future.'

Starfault smiled a little, raising his eyebrows. 'We have books and histories too, Lady de Grazon. You are not talking to ignorant people here.'

Vintage raised her hands. 'Of course, forgive me. I get carried away when it comes to this subject.'

'It was a bad time,' continued Silverbank. 'We had hoped that we had started to move out of that shadow. The plains have been a dangerous place.'

'The worm people have been here?'

Silverbank and her partner exchanged another look.

'We think our groups are too small and too mobile for them

105

to take any notice of, so we only saw them in the skies. Ugly, monstrous things. But it's war time,' said Starfault, shrugging a little. 'And people behave badly when they're afraid.'

'There have been bandits,' said Silverbank. 'Some plains people, some from the cities. At least two big groups have been roaming the grasslands, preying on hunting parties, or just smaller tribes. Taking what they want, leaving people dead, or without what they need to survive. This is why our fishing troop is so large this summer.' She gestured to the strange vehicles with their spindly wooden wheels. 'Half our group are warriors, just in case.'

'You should be careful, if you're following the Trick,' said Starfault. 'There is a gang who seem to stay close to it, looking out for anyone using the river to replenish their supplies. They are a particularly vicious lot.'

'We will be in the sky,' said Chenlo. At the unexpected sound of her voice, they all paused. Vintage half thought they had forgotten she was there at all. After a moment, Silverbank picked up the pan and shook the newly golden fish into a bowl. 'We will not be in danger from bandits there.'

'Even so,' said Vintage quickly, 'it's very useful to know. Thank you.'

Later, when they had prised the children from Helcate and said their goodbyes to the people of Runningseed, Chenlo squinted up at the sun, edging already towards the horizon.

'We have wasted quite a few hours here, Lady de Grazon.'

'Wasted? Did you taste that fish?' Vintage hauled herself up into Helcate's harness and began yanking on straps. Sensing a tension in the other woman's silence, she cleared her throat. 'You might turn your nose up at it, but we've gathered useful information here. The mood on the plains is, in my experience, a good way to gauge the mood of Sarn at large. The people here are frightened, suspicious, waiting for the other shoe to drop. And there are dangers outside of the worm people.'

106

Chenlo sniffed. She was feeding something to her bat from her hand, and it made happy snuffling noises as it chewed. 'Our mission lies in Jarlsbad, which is some way from here. Every moment we dally, Tyranny causes more damage to your cause, and the worm people edge closer.'

'Which is all the more reason to show people that the war-beasts – and Ebora – are on their side. Those children won't forget today, not for a long time, and word travels fast across these grasslands. That might do a little to alleviate Tyranny's damage, and it certainly can't hurt.'

The bat fed, Chenlo climbed into her own harness. Vintage couldn't help noticing how gracefully the woman moved. This was someone, she reminded herself, who was used to travelling alone, to doing as she pleased. *Within reason.*

'We'll have to rest tonight, and that will likely be within spitting distance of the Trick.' Vintage leaned forward and stroked Helcate's neck. For some reason, she wanted Chenlo to admit that this break had been a good idea. 'It's useful to know that we need to keep an eye out for bandits, isn't it?'

Chenlo was busily plying her hair back into its bun. 'When I travel across Sarn, I am always careful. Always cautious. That is the life of a fell-witch – endless vigilance.'

Unless you happen to be one locked up in the Winnowry, thought Vintage. *Then your life is about staring at the same four walls forever.* But she said no more, and when they left the banks of the river, it was in a stony silence.

A teeming darkness. A deafening storm.

Tor looked down at his own body, trying to reassert a sense of himself. Dream-walking into Bern's sleeping mind had seemed simple at first; the usual journey into the netherdark, finding the source of warmth that was the human man, then pushing through into that presence. However, once he was through that barrier, everything had changed. Bern was certainly experiencing a nightmare, but it was unlike anything Tor had ever known. He stood at the centre of an enormous echoing chaos. Pieces of darkness peeled away to rush at him, flickering lights crawled across his flesh, and the noise – a thousand voices that were one voice, screaming, shouting, whispering. Tor brought his hands up to his eyes, automatically trying to shield them, but it did very little.

'Bern? Are you here?'

The quality of the darkness changed, just a touch, and Tor caught sight of a slice of light cutting through the shadows. With little else to go on, he moved towards it with his head down. Something with claws grabbed at his boot, but he shook it off.

'Bern?'

Through the slice of shifting light he saw soft grey walls, pale glowing nodules; the inside of a Behemoth. Yet it was pulsing and throbbing, as though blood moved rapidly just under its skin. There was no sign of Bern yet, and Tor reminded himself that the human man was lying in his bed, Aldasair at his side. The more he concentrated on the Behemoth chamber, the more the chaotic darkness retreated; although it remained hovering, a presence at the corners of his eyes, pressing at the back of his neck.

He looked around the chamber. There was a pool of steaming white water in the ground, and moving slowly within it, one of the queen's creatures. A shining black mandible slid from the water, grasping at the air, followed by a slim white human hand. It shivered in mid-air, then returned to rest against a wide human chest. The fingers of the creature began to pluck viciously at its own flesh, peeling away ragged chunks to reveal shiny black struts beneath. Tor grimaced.

'What is this place?'

The darkness rushed in, and in the way of dreams Tor found

that he was in another space, and standing opposite him was his sister. Hestillion looked thinner than he'd ever seen her, and paler too, her blond hair oddly colourless. Her cheekbones stood out like the pommels of daggers, and her red eyes glittered as though she were in the grip of a fever. She wore a dark leather vest and trousers, her white arms bare, and she was standing next to . . .

Tor looked down at his own body again, struggling to keep a grip on himself. The teeming darkness at his back was threatening to tear him away at any second, and his own horror only seemed to increase its power.

She stood next to one of the grey men, its wings neatly folded at its back, except that that was not what it was at all, not really. The creature had been moulded, crafted into something else, a tall male figure with a slim face and a narrow waist. Its jaw was smooth and there was no hair on its white scalp, but Tor found he could recognise the face anyway, even with those eyes. In the midst of the chaos, Tor felt a cold hand walk down his back. Where had this thing come from? Bern had said before that he had seen Tor's face in his nightmares, but this was something else, some terrible hybrid. The man that looked like him was wearing a curious set of armour that appeared to be constructed from pieces of burrower and spidermother.

He tore his eyes away from the thing. Hestillion was talking, too low for Tor to make out – especially against the general cacophony of the Jure'lia – and another figure lurched into view. This one was smaller than the male, but similarly fitted with spiky black and grey armour. It looked vaguely female, from the curved bodice and the jut of its hips, but half its head was lost in a tightly fitting helmet. Curiously, there was a yellow leaf shape painted directly onto the skin of its chest. The grey wall behind them flexed unpleasantly, revealing a transparent membrane that appeared to show the view outside, such as it was; all Tor could see was darkness, and something that could almost have been rock.

'What are you doing, Hestillion? What have you done?'

His sister, of course, took no notice, and pressed her hand to the protruding lump of crystal nestled in her chest. There was an odd sensation of both movement and noise, and the skittering black shapes threatened to overwhelm Tor's awareness again. The images in front of him broke up and he saw, instead, two more of the strange Jure'lia women, apparently in separate chambers. They each stood with their backs pressed to the soft walls, and long cords of oozing black fluid flowed to them across the floor, curling up legs and swirling around arms. One had a green bird on its chest; the other, a red moth.

Another shudder, and Tor nearly fell to his knees. Once more he was in the chamber with his sister, and he could clearly see a layer of sweat glistening on her forehead. The Jure'lia warrior was still by her side, unmoving. The yellow-leaf woman had gone, but before Tor had a chance to wonder at that, the view beyond the transparent panel suddenly filled with daylight, shocking in the gloom of the chamber. Without thinking, Tor moved over to it, and got a confused glimpse of the ground falling away – thick green vegetation, a steaming swamp?

'I can make no sense of this at all.' Worse still, his head was throbbing and there was a growing heat in his chest. 'Bern, if you're here, if you can hear me, I'm getting out. I need to rest.'

He took a breath, preparing to pull his consciousness away from that of the dreamer, when the skittering black shapes swarmed him again. He gave a wordless cry, putting his arms up to shield his face, and then he was back on his knees in the chamber. Something had changed. The light outside the window was different, and Hestillion wore different clothes. She was standing by the window with a long length of parchment

110

stretched between her two hands, while the yellow-leaf woman was back. Hestillion was showing her something, pointing to a place on a map.

Feeling his stomach turn over, Tor looked back to the window. Spread out below them was a long, rambling coast line, caught in the orange light of late afternoon. It matched that depicted on Hestillion's map, although it was missing a few key things; namely the large crosses marked in red ink over each settlement.

'What is this?' Tor turned to his sister, as if demanding an answer, but she continued to murmur in a low voice to her minion. 'Is this happening now? A memory, or a dream? Are we too late?'

Back at the window, it was possible to see the Behemoth's shadow spread out below, a dark shroud moving across white sand. Tor glared at it, and then caught his breath; there was another shadow, and above it, another Behemoth, flying in formation with this one. For the first time since walking into his dream, he felt Bern near him; the humanity of him was like suddenly finding a breath of fresh air in a room filled with rotting meat.

The queen's not here, he said. *Not anywhere close.*

'Is this *real*, Bern?'

It's real. It's happening now.

Tor stepped back and with as much strength as he was able, tore himself free of the vision and its grasping, skittering presence. There was a sense of light and falling, and he found himself on the floor of Bern's and Aldasair's chamber, hair covering his face. A hand grasped his and yanked him to his feet.

'Cousin, are you all right?'

Aldasair looked gaunt, and somehow older than he had earlier that day. On the bed next to them, Bern was just waking up, his blond eyelashes flickering fitfully. They had given the

111

big man over a week to recover before Tor attempted this invasion of his mind, but he still looked exhausted.

'Hestillion has two Behemoths at her command and is using them to attack a number of settlements.' Tor took a breath. The presence of the Jure'lia lingered, like an oily sweat on his skin. 'We have to get the war-beasts and go now, while there's still some chance of saving anyone.'

Chapter Ten

Noon felt Tor's alarm through her link to Vostok, her link to all of them, and half fell, half sprang out of bed. Around her she was aware of the others via a strange combination of real, physical impressions – a lamp flaring into life down the corridor, someone shouting – and the thrum of their shared connection.

An attack, bright weapon. Vostok was both outraged and eager. *We must hurry.*

'Yeah, yeah.' Noon hopped around her room, wriggling into a pair of trousers, yanking on her jacket, a sword belt, soft leather boots. When she arrived at the courtyard everyone was there already. Tor's face was grim and thin-lipped in the moon-light, Bern looked like a newly risen corpse. The war-beasts were scrambling into their armour, assisted by a small team of Finneral guards. Aldasair was busily strapping a helmet onto Jessen himself.

'What is it?' Seeing that Vostok was being attended to, Noon went straight to Tor. 'What's happened?'

'I saw it in Bern's head,' said Tor. 'She's taking them out herself now, actually leading attacks.'

'Who is? What are you talking about?'

'Hestillion,' snapped Tor. 'My sister. Somehow, she has

control of two Behemoths and is heading for a handful of settlements along the Brindlesea coast.'

'Fire and blood.' Noon blinked, trying to come to terms with this new information. She could feel Vostok's impatience to be gone, pressing against her own fear. 'That's not far from here, is it?'

'Nope, and I doubt that's a coincidence,' said Bern wearily. 'It's a threat, all right. She brings the blade close to us, just to show that she can.'

'Shit.' Noon ran her hands through her hair, trying desperately to wake up properly. She had been in the middle of a complicated dream, something about grass and stone, a tomato . . . 'Bern, are you all right to fly? You—'

'Look like shit, I know. And aye, I'm fine.'

'Good.' She grasped his meaty forearm. 'Then let's get up there. Are we ready? Who's ready?'

She turned to the courtyard to see the war-beasts in their battle finery, the Finneral guard melting back to the walls. As one, the four of them went to their mounts, scrambling up into harnesses and strapping themselves in.

'Yes, it has been too long!' thundered Sharrik. The big griffin puffed out the feathers on his neck. 'I long to fight. My blood clamours for it!'

'There will be humans there,' said Jessen, her long pointed ears facing forward as if she could already hear their cries. 'We must save as many as possible.'

Kirune said nothing, but his head was high and his eyes glowed like lamps. The cat was ready to hunt. Noon could feel it, like a tightness under her ribs.

'What of the fell-witches?' Somehow, sitting back in Sharrik's harness, Bern looked twice as well as he had on the ground. 'Couldn't they help us? More of the witches' fire in combat could be useful.'

'No,' said Noon, immediately. 'They're frightened and

114

untrained, no use to us. I'd only have to spend my time worrying about them getting themselves killed.' She slid a final strap through its loop. 'Besides, winnowfire is mostly useless against the Jure'lia unless it's fuelled by an Eboran or a war-beast.'

A small silence met her words, which Noon ignored.

'Vintage should be here at least,' said Tor. 'And Helcate. There are so few of us. And I don't doubt that fucking dragon will be there. The last time we faced it we nearly died. We –'

Tor stopped, and Noon winced at the needle-sharp grief that pierced them all. Eri had been torn to pieces by the war-beast bonded to Tor's sister. She wondered, distantly, if Vintage could feel their pain through her new and uncertain link to Helcate, and what she made of it.

'We have to fight,' she said. 'It's what we are, isn't it? What we are made for.'

'Bright weapon,' murmured Vostok.

Tor shook his head slightly. 'Even so, we are a handful, against two Behemoths.'

'What choice do we have? Do we just sit here and let your sister throw her weight around?' Noon shrugged. 'And as Vintage would probably say, sometimes a handful is just enough.'

Tor glanced at her then, an unmistakable look of surprise on his face. She grinned at him, and then Vostok leapt up into the night sky, followed by her war-beast brethren.

It was a long and silent flight through the dark, lit by the silvery moon and stars. They followed Tor and Kirune, who had seen where the Behemoths were heading, and below them Ebora sped away into nothing, to be replaced by a land of hills and valleys Aldasair had never seen. He looked down over Jessen's shoulder as much as he was able, trying to absorb what he could about this new country, but he got only fleeting glimpses of grass and forest, all dyed silver and black by the night. When he gave up on that, his gaze wandered back to Bern most often, a hunched shape on the back of Sharrik. Once or twice the moonlight lit the human's face like a lamp, and then he was gone again. Aldasair gathered each sight to his heart to steel himself against the coming horrors.

We're nearly there. Jessen, a soft voice in his head. *I can smell the sea.*

Not long after this, Aldasair saw it for himself. A vast stretch of glittering movement, the moon hanging above it fat and round. Below, the land had evened out into a meandering coast, and the light had changed; dawn's fingers were touching the far horizon, turning the entire landscape a silvery lilac. Something about it filled Aldasair's heart with foreboding, and he sank his hands into Jessen's fur, looking for reassurance.

'What are we flying into?'

What are you afraid of?

Aldasair shook his head. The question was too large. There were thousands of things to be afraid of, and he accepted those as their lot – yet still there was something else. 'I don't know.'

Ahead, it was just possible to make out clusters of lights on the edge of the land, and then above them, two enormous bulbous shapes, each alive with a terrible, skittering movement. One of the Behemoths was significantly closer to the ground, and a stream of creatures flowed from it down towards the hapless inhabitants.

'We're here!' called Tor from the front. 'Get ready.'

Seamlessly, Vostok and Noon took the lead, picking up speed and coming in low. The newly forged link between them all thrummed, suddenly so clear: *take the lowest first. Stop that stream of burrowers. Push it away from the settlement.*

Jessen and Kirune moved up together to flank Vostok, while Sharrik brought up the rear. As they drew closer, they could hear the sound of panic drifting up from the settlement; screaming, shouting. Aldasair narrowed his eyes, following the stream of spider-mothers drifting down from the lowest Behemoth; they fell with their legs spread, twirling down like the seeds from some nightmarish tree. Once they were on the ground, Aldasair knew, the burrowers they secreted would set about turning the humans into drones, eating them from the inside out.

Unthinkingly, he sent his concerns through the link, and felt them mirrored back at him.

Get on the ground and target what's already there. We will attack the origin points.

He had time to think that the voice of the link sounded like both Noon and Vostok when the ground rushed up to them. He leaned over Jessen's neck, focussing where she was; the spider-mothers were landing in what appeared to be a market square, creating a little factory of burrowers. He pulled one of the axes, the Bitter Twins, from his belt, and squeezed the haft, bracing for impact. Above them, he could feel Tor and the others attacking the surface of the Behemoth.

Something is different. This time the voice was that of Bern and Sharrik together, deep and resonant. *The queen is not here at all.*

Surprise filtered through the link, questions from all of them at once, and then the joined voice came again: *Remember, it is the Lady Hestillion. She controls this, I can feel it.*

Aldasair barely had time to take this in before Jessen hit the ground and skidded across the smooth flagstones of the market square, her wings thrown wide to slow herself. At a glance it was possible to see what sort of place this had been – wooden stalls closed up ready for the morning, the occasional discarded fruit, and beyond the square, tall neat buildings with shop awnings curled tight for the night – but already it was a space falling to the Jure'lia. Burrowers swarmed under-foot, and a tight mass of spider-mothers seethed over the market's central well.

'Do they normally do that?' said Jessen. 'Stay together?'

'I know no more than you.'

Jessen leapt into the midst of the creatures and snapped at the nearest, shredding it between her teeth. Aldasair leaned forward and struck out at them with his axe, cleaving those that met its lethal edge into oozing pieces. Burrowers swarmed them, and once or twice Jessen rose back up into the air, flinging the scuttling beetle creatures from her with a violent shake of her fur. More spider-mothers were descending from above, but when Aldasair had a chance to glance up, he saw Sharrik attacking the hole they were emerging from: they would cease soon, surely.

'Who is that?'

Aldasair turned to see what Jessen was referring to, brushing a pair of burrowers off his leg as he did so. He stopped momentarily, a cold terror seizing his guts as the Jure'lia queen strode forth from a crowd of drones – except it wasn't, he saw a moment later. This figure was tall and humanoid in appearance, almost Eboran in its height and shape, yet it wore armour fashioned from the black carapaces of Jure'lia creatures. A helmet that made him think of summer beetles cupped the angles of her face, and there was, of all things, a green bird painted on her chest.

'Oh no,' he said. 'Roots save us.'

The figure raised one arm, a long pale finger extended towards them, and the horde of drones closed in, following her command.

Noon leaned back in the harness and raised one arm, releasing a barrage of green fireballs over the underside of the Behemoth. A number of small creatures that had been moving there grew stiff and fell to the ground; a short rain of many-jointed legs and shell turned to ash. She could see Sharrik attacking the aperture where the spider-mothers were emerging, and she was

118

pleased to see that it was slowly closing. Tor and Kirune were some distance to her right, fighting some large burrower-like creatures with wings – more of the queen's new toys, no doubt. Smiling grimly, she siphoned off a touch more energy from Vostok and summoned it into a pair of bright fireballs between her hands. And then her smile faltered. There was a sensation inside her she had never felt before; a painful spasm within her chest, deep in that place where the winnowfire energy curled, waiting to be released.

'Did you feel that?' she said aloud, knowing perfectly well that Vostok had not felt anything.

'What? What are you talking about?' The dragon sent a stream of violet fire arching over to the giant burrowers. 'What is it?'

'I just . . .' Noon absently dropped the fireballs over the side, and placed one hand against her chest. A hiccup. It was like a hiccup. 'Something's not right.'

Tor was close enough when it happened to see everything – everything there was to see, anyway. Close enough, he realised later, for Kirune's harness to suffer scorch marks and his own cloak to be singed at the edges. Not close enough though, crucially, to do anything about it.

'What are these bastard things? The queen has been busy.' He neatly dissected one of the giant burrowers with his sword – a borrowed one, nowhere near as graceful or as swift as the Ninth Rain – and the pieces of it fell away below. Next to them and above, Noon and Vostok were bathing the under-section of the Behemoth in green and violet fire, and sections of its oily green surface were turning black.

'You have not seen,' growled Kirune, in between bites. He shook his big blocky head, flinging pieces of burrower every-where. 'None of you have.'

'What are you talking about?'

'How many snakes do we have in the sky with us?'

Tor blinked, and for the first time since seeing the ominous red line on his arm, he broke into a genuine grin. 'There's no fucking dragon!' They had been attacking for some time, certainly long enough to summon a war-beast from its nap, or whatever it was up to, yet the newly dawn-touched sky remained free of that particular monstrosity. He leaned back in his harness and waved his sword at Noon, forgetting, briefly, the link between them all. 'Hoy! There's no fucking dragon! Celaphon isn't here!'

He saw her look down at him, her face caught in the lilac light from the east. She looked, he thought, perplexed, as though she could hear something he could not, and then Noon exploded in an enormous blossom of green fire.

Chapter Eleven

Fell-Tyranny

What a disaster this has been.

I knew as soon as we received the tip that it would be difficult. There was the fact that it came in from a street urchin, a thief, no less, along with the startling information that the fell-witch we needed to take in was a grown adult. This does not happen often. The ability is so obvious, so difficult to control, that it has almost always shown itself in public by the time the girl is sixteen. The fact that this Tyranny O'Keefe had successfully hidden her winnowfire for so long told me that she would not be taken in easily. That she would make us suffer. It is hard, when you have managed to evade capture, to admit that your time of freedom has come to an end. You start to believe you are untouchable. Or so I imagine.

We took her at one of her own warehouses, on the docks of Mushenska's old town. Under my advisement, we brought twice the numbers we normally would, and it seems I was quite correct (they are beginning to listen to me, at least). It was dawn when we started, yet the sun was at its highest point in the sky by the end of it, and the warehouse itself was a flaming wreck. The crowds that inevitably gather at such things kept well back. Several of the woman's 'employees' were killed in the fight, and that in itself is interesting – who fights on behalf of a fell-witch? Clearly she inspired loyalty in many.

Not all, though. Afterwards, we met with the child who had given us her location, a tiny scrap of ill-fed muscle and eyes too large for his face, and he showed us some of the other children under the 'care' of the Salts. It is a hard start in life for them, and they all look older than their years. They have become skittering and rat-like, living in the alleys and nooks of Mushenska, hiding themselves in the city's dirt and surviving on its leftovers. This is how Tyranny O'Keefe lived, how she came to adulthood. I think of my own childhood in Yuron-Kai – the horses, the endless blue sky, the scent of our yurt, the taste of salted meat – and I am dizzy with the difference between the two. Yet both Tyranny and I have ended up in the same place: the black towers of the Winnowry.

She fought wildly, with great ferocity. One of our agents died, every part of her exposed skin burned away, her clothes welded to her body. I saw a wildness and a rage in Fell-Tyranny's eyes I have rarely seen, and I believe she would have killed us all if she could – would have burned down the entire city of Mushenska, if it had allowed her to escape. This one, I have no doubt, will be kept in the darkest, lowest cell of the Winnowry, carefully monitored and controlled for the rest of her natural life. She will not see the sky again.

Details to remember about the life of Fell-Tyranny: she was the leader of a gang called the Salts, who appear to have specialised in the sale of stolen goods and the sale of illegal akaris (Mother Cressin will be glad to hear that this particular line of supply to the city has been *stopped); I could glean no information about her family from the other gang members we spoke to, so I must assume she has no living relatives; she had a great love of spicy food, and spent a lot of money at a nearby Reidn restaurant – the owners specifically expressed regret at her incarceration.*

Extract from the private records of Agent Chenlo

Aldasair slumped forward in the harness, pushed there by the heat of the explosion above his head. A moment later, he was hit by a wave of confusion and shock, travelling down through his connection to Jessen like the deep, solid note of a struck bell. He looked up in time to see the last glow of the winnow-fire before it sank into nothing. He could see Vostok, falling away as though she had been struck a mighty blow, and some distance away Tor on Kirune, half standing in his own harness. As he watched, the sword dropped from his cousin's hand and twirled away towards the ground.

'What's happened? What is it?'

'A terrible thing,' said Jessen. They were surrounded by drones, and had been cutting their way through as best they could. The Jure'lia figure with the green bird on her chest had retreated, apparently happy to let the drones detain them. Of the humans they had wished to save they had seen little sign. 'We have to go to him.'

Aldasair kicked away the nearest drones and they leapt up into the air. Sharrik had also broken off from his attack on the surface of the Behemoth, and they reached Tor and Kirune at more or less the same moment. Tor's face had entirely drained of colour, and his hair had come loose, swirling around his head in chaos. He was shouting one word over and over.

'Noon! Noon!'

'Where is she?' Aldasair looked around. Below them, Vostok appeared to have recovered and was flying in frantic circles.

123

It was clear that Noon was not on her back; the harness itself had been reduced to a few tattered and blackened straps.

'She –' Tor shook his head. 'She was there, and then –'

'The witch exploded,' said Kirune. Even the great cat sounded distressed, and through the link they all shared Aldasair could feel the growing panic of Tor, and approaching slowly but with deadly force, Vostok's outrage. All around them the onslaught of the Jure'lia continued, gaining a new speed now that their attacks had ceased. A renewed stream of spider-mothers was floating down towards the settlement, and just above them, a new aperture was opening in the side of the Behemoth. It would be a maggot, he was sure of it, or even Celaphon, finally.

'I don't understand,' said Bern. 'How can she have just . . . gone?'

'I saw it!' cried Tor, and there was an edge of hysteria in his voice that Aldasair did not like. 'She looked at me, was looking at me, and then—'

'WHERE IS SHE?' Abruptly, Vostok was in their air space. 'WHAT HAVE YOU DONE WITH HER?'

The dragon was furious, pale tongues of lilac flame curling over her teeth as she spoke. Hesitantly, Aldasair reached out to her with everything he had, leaning over in the harness and holding out his hand even as he grasped after the link between them all.

'Vostok, did you see it? What happened?'

Tor spoke. 'She died. She died right in front of us. Roots be fucking damned forever.'

Vostok shook her head violently. 'No. No. She did not.'

'But Vostok –' Aldasair looked again at the tattered remains of the harness, where Noon had been sitting.

'She is not dead, she is gone. Which I will not stand for.' The dragon turned an agitated circle in the sky, dawn light glinting off white scales. 'I will not stand for it.'

With that she turned her back on them and beat her great feathered wings, speeding away.

'Vostok!'

The dragon did not reply. Next to them, Tor slumped forward in his harness, his face in his hands. A wave of despair moved through Aldasair like a physical blow, and he turned to Bern to see his own pain reflected in the big man's face.

'It's too much,' he said in a low voice. 'Vostok's rage, Tor's grief, all the confusion . . . I can barely think.'

There was a wet tearing sound, and off to the right of them a huge glistening maggot, looking oddly metallic in the first blush of sunrise, slithered out of its aperture. Within moments it would be falling onto the settlement – what was left of it. More creatures were gathering all the time, giant burrowers and enormous spider-mothers with elongated bodies, and there were just three of them; three against two Behemoths, and one of them seriously compromised. Aldasair shivered, and felt Jessen shudder beneath him.

'Roots forgive us, we have to retreat,' he said. His lips felt numb. 'We have to get out of here.'

Vintage paused with the bread halfway to her mouth and looked out across the shadowy plains. Curled next to her, Helcate raised his head, his long snout twitching. There was still some residual warmth from the day before – it was always warm on the plains, but in the summer it was an oven, slow to lose its heat – yet Vintage felt abruptly cold. She put the bread down.

'What is it?' asked Chenlo. She had been staring into their small fire. 'Do you see something?'

'No, I thought . . .' Vintage turned to the war-beast and stroked his neck. He whined. 'Helcate, what is it? What's happened?'

The link between them was still so new, and half the time

Vintage wasn't sure it was there at all. Their situation was unknown in Eboran history; not only was she a human, riding an Eboran war-beast like a hero out of an old book, but Helcate himself had already been bonded once before, a connection that had been brutally severed with the death of Eri. She did not know truly if their bond would ever work as it should, and with Helcate's peculiarities, she wasn't sure that it even could. Yet she had felt something as she looked out across the plains, a sudden throb of despair that had not originated with her.

'Helcate,' said Helcate. She sensed fear from the war-beast, but also confusion. Whatever was happening, he did not understand it.

'Well?' demanded Chenlo.

'I don't know. This isn't a precise science.' Vintage scratched Helcate behind his ears, then dropped her hand. 'Whatever it is, it is happening far from here.' Some way to their left, the Trick river was a reassuring murmur. They had stopped to eat and to get some sleep, but all of them had woken early, dawn just beginning to kiss the horizon. 'Perhaps we should turn back.'

Chenlo raised her eyebrows, creasing the bat-wing tattoo on her forehead. 'On a hunch?'

Vintage plucked at her hair; it was especially wild after days of flight. 'Darling, this isn't a mere hunch. This is part of the intricate web that binds the war-beasts with their companions, a near mythical connection that is unknown in human society.'

'But you don't know what it is.'

'No.' Vintage sighed. *If one of them had died, I would have felt it. I am sure of it. That, at least, should be unmistakable.* She remembered their faces when Eri had been murdered; despite all the differences between them, they had looked oddly similar in grief. It had cut them all deeply, a severing that was as much a physical pain as anything else. *I would know. I would.* 'No, I don't. We'll go on as we are for now, then. If we can get this war-beast back, it could be the thing that turns the conflict for us. I can't abandon the attempt before we've even reached Jarlsbad.'

Chenlo looked for a moment as though she might reply, but instead she sipped from a small tin cup. The fragrance of it reached Vintage across the fire.

'Yuron-Kai tea?'

'You have a nose for scents.'

Vintage snorted. 'Darling, I used to run a vinery. The grapes, the fermentation, the bouquet, the taste . . .' Her voice trailed off. The despair she had briefly felt had left a residue, and it wasn't helped by the thought of the vine forest and Catalen. She had written to her nephew Marin many times, and never received a reply. Even Ezion hadn't replied, and he should be safe at the House. Surely the House was safe? But when she thought of that, she thought of the scattered pieces of Behemoth remains that had always haunted the vine forest, turning the woods around them strange and Wild. Nowhere in Sarn was truly safe. She should know that by now. She dragged her thoughts back to the conversation at hand. 'I know much less about tea, of course. Have you been home? Since you were taken, I mean.'

Chenlo put the cup down and laced her fingers in her lap. In the firelight her face was a beautiful mask, all the lines by the corners of her eyes smoothed into nothing.

'It is an unofficial rule of the Winnowry that agents are to avoid missions that take them back to anything that might be considered *home*. The last thing they would want is for a fell-witch with some small freedoms to start feeling homesick, to start thinking that perhaps they might just return to their old lives. I have not been back.'

'Not since the Winnowry fell?'

'There has hardly been time, Lady de Grazon. But I did stop and buy some tea in Mushenska. A little taste of home.'

'But you were a very high-ranking agent, were you not? And still they did not trust you?'

'The Winnowry did not survive by being trusting. It was a needless concern of theirs, anyway. There is nothing for me in Yuron-Kai. Besides more tea.'

'But you must have family there, people who knew you before . . .'

'As I say, nothing.'

Vintage picked up her piece of bread and chewed on it. What she knew of the Yuron-Kai suggested that there was more to the story; they generally lived in close family units, each member marked with the family sigil. Orphans and outcasts were given a special mark that replaced or covered up a family tattoo – something that marked them as the extended family of the tribal horselord – yet Agent Chenlo did not have that. There had been a family once, at least, and their sigil had been an eagle.

Vintage was just trying to think of a way of asking her about this when the other woman stood up on the far side of the fire. Behind her, her bat snuffled and raised his head, black eyes as wet as ink.

'What is it?'

'I think I see movement.' Chenlo narrowed her eyes. 'Something is out there.'

Vintage slipped her seeing-glass from her pack and stood up to join her. When she pressed the cold brass to her eye, though, she could see very little. The grasses of the plains looked ghostly in the half-light and they shivered constantly with the winds, but it was still too dark to make out much else.

'Where are you seeing it? All I'm seeing is a lot of bloody grass.'

'May I?'

With only a moment's hesitation, Vintage handed the glass over. Chenlo looked through it, twisted it a little to adjust the lens, then peered through again. Her mouth turned down at the edges.

'There are lots of people on these plains, yes?'

'Oh many,' said Vintage brightly. 'A remarkable variety, really.'

'How many keep worm-touched giants with them?'

When Vintage looked at her, she passed her the glass back. 'There. Where I point. Just up from that stunted tree.'

This time when Vintage lifted the glass to her eye, she saw something immediately. She couldn't make out details, but there was certainly a group of dark shapes moving, something in the long grass. She might almost think them a herd of fleeten or some other plains animal, but the way they moved was so familiar as to be unmistakable. In their midst, something even bigger moved; a huge, confusing mass. There appeared to be a lamp on top of it.

'Sarn's bones, what is that?' She bit her lip, willing the shape to resolve itself into something knowable. 'It could be a very large caravan? A mobile tent?'

Chenlo sniffed. 'One giant tent? Keep watching it.'

'You never know. Perhaps they think it's safer to travel that way.' Vintage turned the eye-glass slightly, following the group's progress. They were heading west, as far as she could tell, yet also appeared to be bending south towards the river. She squinted, wishing for just a touch more light, and the huge mound at the centre of the movement shook itself all over, just like a dog would. A tent could not move that way. 'Ah. Yes. I think I see what you mean.' She lowered the glass.

'Something that large must be worm-touched,' said Chenlo. 'Do plains people generally travel with worm-touched animals?'

'Well, darling, there's a question.' Vintage seated herself back at the fire, ignoring the faintly startled look on Agent Chenlo's face. 'Almost all wild animals have been ever so slightly worm-touched, I believe. The poisons this world has had to bear have seeped out all over. The Priat people of the Singing Eye Desert farm a kind of over-sized rodent for its meat and its coat. The kings and queens of Finneral ride giant bears. Not everything worm-touched is lethal, or at least, it can be tamed.' She thought of the giant grapes in the vine forest, sweltering under the Catalen sun. 'It's the human way, to try and make use of all things.'

'That thing looks too big to be tamed,' said Chenlo. She was still standing and looking out across the grasslands. 'I don't trust it.'

'You may be right,' said Vintage. 'Let's hope we don't have to find out.'

Hestillion stepped down onto the smooth green surface, her boots slipping slightly. It was hard already, this stuff, yet she had seen it pumped from the rear end of a maggot only moments before.

'It must harden on contact with the air,' she said, and next to her the First nodded slightly. Around them, the settlement that had once sat on the coast of Brindlesea had almost completely vanished; in its place were great sloping acres of the Jure'lia's green resin, and the occasional broken piece of masonry or wood. There were darker lumps under the varnish in places where some humans, or their livestock, had failed to get away quickly enough, and a handful of drones still stumbled around, their eyes empty black holes. On the very edges, the Jure'lia creatures continued their work, breaking down the remains of people and homes, and feeding them to the maggots. Where there had been such noise and panic only hours before, there was now an eerie silence.

'Did we kill them all?'

The First turned to her, a touch awkwardly, and she smiled

slightly at his face. She thought they had very likely killed all the humans here, or so many that it made no real difference. There was a water-road leading away to the sea, and perhaps some of them had escaped that way, on fast little boats, or perhaps some had been close enough to the settlement gates at the time to get away before the killing started. Here, today, she had killed more humans than any single Eboran had since the Carrion Wars. She took a few more steps on the green varnish, letting that sink in.

'We were delayed a little, by my brother and his cohorts,' she said. Some distance to their right, there was a shack half standing, and in its shadows, there was movement. She began to walk towards it. 'They can cause plenty of trouble when they wish. Yet they didn't stay. I wonder what happened?'

The First had no answer for that. They walked on. It was curious that Tormalin and the others had vanished, but then was she really surprised? He had always been weak. It was inevitable that he would not be able to handle the responsibility of bonding with a war-beast; it was a wonder he had lasted as long as he had. Hestillion lifted a hand to her head and rubbed at her temples. Controlling the circle, and therefore both the Behemoths at the same time, had been exhausting – a balancing act of putting herself in several places at once whilst carefully ignoring the general chatter of the Jure'lia at large. It was a matter of focus, of pinpointing one mind amongst many. Green Bird, who had been on board the Behemoth taking part in the initial attack, had controlled it, yet Hestillion had controlled her. The Jure'lia creature's mind had been familiar and easy to find, because in some way, Hestillion had formed it. Despite the headache, she smiled again. Her talent for dream-walking had made it easier, she was sure of it. And, gradually, she would get better at it.

'With the circle I have created so far, I could control five Behemoths at once. Eventually.'

They had reached the shack. A cluster of giant spider-mothers skittered outside it, weeping burrowers onto the floor, while a human man crouched inside the remains of something that looked like it had once been a shed for smoking fish. His face was dark with soot, and he was shaking all over. When he looked up at Hestillion, the shaking grew worse.

'What – what are you?'

Hestillion ignored him. Instead, she frowned at the spider-mothers. While her attention had lapsed, they had fallen back into the confusion that was afflicting the Jure'lia. They had got as far as chasing the human down, and then promptly had forgotten what they were supposed to be doing. The burrowers crawled in confused circles, leaving marks in the dirt with their sharp legs. She would have to try harder to blot out the presence of the larger Jure'lia hive mind.

'What *are* you?' The man stood up. The expression on his face was changing from fearful to a strange kind of outrage. 'You aren't worm people.' His eyes moved to the First standing next to her, then back again. 'I don't know what he is, but you're one of those bloodsuckers. An Eboran.' He pulled his shoulders back. 'You're supposed to fight these things!'

Hestillion touched the crystal at her chest, wondering what the man saw. She no longer wore her Eboran silks or any fine Eboran jewellery, and her feet were clad in functional leather boots instead of delicate slippers. She remembered the room at the palace where she had kept her gowns, which she had spent so long cleaning of dust and mould. With those images came a memory of Aldasair, sitting at a table in a forgotten room, the corpse of a spider long-dead sitting atop his stack of tarla cards. It all seemed like ancient history. And when was the last time she had seen Aldasair? He had been here moments ago, riding his magnificent flying wolf, no longer the lost soul he had been in the Eboran palace.

It was all so long ago, and she had changed so much, yet

her eyes were still crimson and she was still taller, stronger. Still *more* than this human.

'You,' she snapped a finger at the nearest spider-mother, reaching out for the piece of the web where its mind dwelt. 'End this.'

She turned away and walked out across the varnish again, listening absently to the man's screams as the burrowers pulled him apart. It was easy, really. Just a matter of focus.

'All of this,' she said to the Jure'lia at large, letting her mind and her voice echo down through the connections that linked them. 'I want all of this covered in the resin. When the queen comes, let her only see a giant mirror, free of blemishes.'

Chapter Twelve

I received a letter today.

It is the first I have been sent in the fifteen years I have been at the Winnowry, and it was sealed with a smear of gold wax. I looked at it for some time before opening it. I peeled the wax off and pressed it between my fingers. You learn, in this place, to take advantage of any unusual tactile experience, and that urge does not vanish when you become an agent. I rolled the wax into a little ball and put it on the ledge under my window, in the hope that the sun would eventually make it liquid again.

It was from my once-sister Shen. In the top right-hand corner was her family sigil, the eagle, drawn in black and red ink, and her handwriting was so familiar that for a moment I could do nothing but attempt to swallow a painful sensation in my throat. It was like hearing a voice from my earliest childhood.

In the letter, she explained that she had married and had children, two little boys, and I felt a surge of happiness for her: two boys, and no chance of the winnowfire touching them. Yet in the letter she also told me that watching her sons together has given her a different perspective on what happened to me. It has taught her that some bonds go beyond horror and disgrace, and that such bonds are only ever severed at a price. She has asked to renew our family ties, and has applied to the Sen-Lord to do so. She wants to come and visit me at the Winnowry. 'Sisters,' she writes, 'should not live as though the other doesn't exist.'

Later, when I was given my dinner, I took a little of the remaining life energy from the vegetables and saved it hot in my chest until I got back to my room, and there I burned the letter. I'm not certain if I should reply to my once-sister, demanding she not approach the Sen-Lord with such a thing, or if I should pretend I never received it. Likely it is too late anyway.

She cannot know, but it is much easier to be here when I know – I know – there is no yurt for me in Yuron-Kai. No warm welcome or sentimental memories, just flat hatred and banishment. What she has sent me is a kind of torture, and I hope that over time the image of the letter that now hangs in my mind will fade, and I will no longer recall what her handwriting looks like, or even that she had two baby boys. Shen will go back to being my once-sister, a memory from a life that didn't happen.

Still I find myself touching the ball of wax on the windowsill. It smells a little of once-home.

Extract from the private records of Agent Chenlo

'What happened?'

Tor looked down at the tin cup Aldasair had pressed into his hand. He could tell from the smell that it wasn't wine. It was something harsher, stronger.

'Drink it,' his cousin urged, but Tor looked away across the flats to the sea. It was full daylight now, and off to the south-east it was possible to see the faint brown haze of the Reidn

135

delta, impossibly busy with ships and the faint glint of its myriad waterways. The two Behemoths were gone, silently easing their way back across the sky when the sun had fully risen. Directly to the east there was smoke, and the tiny orange embers of fire. He found himself watching it, willing the fire to turn green.

'I told you,' he said, carefully controlling his voice. 'She was there. She was looking down at me, and then . . . she wasn't.' With his free hand he brushed the edge of his cloak where it was singed.

Bern cleared his throat. 'It was a mighty explosion. Do fell-witches – Has that ever happened before? I've never heard of it.'

'Has what happened before?' There was a dangerous tone to Vostok's voice. It had taken them some time to coax her away from the settlement; the dragon had been convinced that Noon must be there somewhere, that she must have fallen from her harness and was lost on the ground, even as the ground itself was slowly turned into a shining mass of hardened green resin.

'An explosion.' Bern flexed his hand, grimacing. 'An accident, I don't know. Did she lose control of it?'

'The witch was always controlled. Always thoughtful.' Kirune had been pacing around them, his big grey paws nearly silent in the thick grass. 'She would not allow it.'

'I agree,' said Jessen. Aldasair reached up and stroked her snout fondly. 'Noon was a skilled warrior.'

'You didn't know her as long as I did,' said Tor. He took a sip of the drink and frowned as it burned its way down his throat. Rum of some sort. The worst sort. 'There was a time when she was a mess, didn't have a clue what she was doing with the winnowfire. It was Vostok who gave her that disci-pline. She was a menace before that.'

'Why are you all speaking of her as if she is dead?' Vostok

glared down at them all imperiously, her violet eyes burning.

'I saw it, Vostok. I wish I hadn't, but I saw it. Nothing could survive an explosion like that, not sitting as she did at its heart.'

'I did,' snapped Vostok.

Tor laughed weakly. He felt untethered somehow, as though he were floating up above them all. The rum was helping with the sensation, so he downed the rest of it.

'Then where is she, dragon? Tell me that. Because you know, in your heart, she'd never leave you. Would never leave the battle before we'd won.' Curls of grey smoke leaked out from between Vostok's bared teeth, and Tor wondered if she would roast him alive. It seemed as reasonable an end as any at this point. 'So where the fuck is she, Vostok?'

The dragon bridled, flames glowing in the back of her throat, but Aldasair began speaking, his soft voice like water on embers.

'I've never heard of a fell-witch blowing herself up. By all accounts, they are actually protected from the flame, at least a little – how else could they form it and sculpt it between their hands as they do?'

'You sound like Vintage,' said Tor.

'There was no – forgive me – smell of burning flesh. No debris that I could see. And Tor, we would have felt it if she had died. Remember the pain we felt with Eri.'

'It was like being stabbed,' said Bern, with feeling. 'Or having something ripped out of you.' He flexed his hand again.

'Before it happened, she was confused,' said Vostok. She lowered her head to the grass, as though the answers were there somewhere. 'She said that something was wrong.'

A small chilly silence settled over the group. Tor's arms were aching again, a deep, sharp ache that throbbed outwards from his wrists.

'Let's face it, none of us know much about fell-witches, or the Winnowry. Anything could have happened, and we'd be

137

none the wiser.' Tor ran a hand over his face, feeling abruptly exhausted. 'Is there any more of that rum?'

'We should ask the fell-witches at the palace,' said Aldasair, his face brightening. 'There are Winnowry agents among them. If anyone will know if this has happened before, it will be them.'

'Are you seriously suggesting we leave?' snapped Vostok. 'She's out there somewhere, possibly confused and disorientated. We have to find her.'

'Can you feel her, Vostok?' Bern looked pained by the question, but he faced the dragon nonetheless. 'Do you sense her nearby? Could she have been taken by the worm people?'

The dragon did not answer. Instead she hissed at them all and turned her back on them, before battering them with the wind from her wings. She headed back east, towards the coast, and was soon a glinting white shape against the searing blue sky. Through the connection he shared with Kirune and the others, Tor felt a deep sense of unease rising up, as though they stood in brackish flood waters. *The group is falling apart.*

'She was not on board those Behemoths, I'm sure of it. We would have felt her, so nearby. If this was not just a terrible accident . . . Listen, if anyone can find her, it's Vostok,' said Aldasair, a forced note of cheer in his voice. 'But we should not leave Ygseril undefended if we can help it.'

Tor stood up, stumbling slightly as the world weaved and ducked around him.

'Agreed,' he said, ignoring how they all looked at him. 'Let's get back to the palace.'

When they arrived back, Tor left them all in the courtyard and headed directly for Vintage's apartments. There was a guard on the door, one of Bern's people, who he waved away, before lighting a couple of lamps in the living room – it was dark, and the place seemed especially gloomy without her there. It was filled with the usual Vintage chaos, books and papers everywhere, pots of ink and sticks of charcoal scattered on most flat surfaces, and on one large desk there was Micanal the Clearsighted's journal. Next to it there was a pile of papers, which Tor glanced at. They listed, in exhausting detail, everything they had managed to glean from the amber record so far. Tor stood with a sheet of paper pinched between his thumb and forefinger for some time without reading it, and then dropped it on the floor.

He went through to the adjoining room, where a huge wooden trunk sat at the foot of Vintage's unmade bed. It was a heavy thing, lined and sealed with iron, but Tor lifted the lid with no discernible effort. Inside were wood shavings and a large number of carefully packed bottles of wine. Some were from Vintage's own vine forest, a few from elsewhere. Tor stood staring at them until he realised that he did not care which ones he drank. He picked three at random, plucked a dusty glass from the sideboard and got to work.

At the third glass he paused, wondering if he should retire to his own rooms before he no longer felt much like walking, but the thought of leaving Vintage's suite was a cold one. She wasn't here, but the sense of her was, like a warm and slightly annoying ghost. The ink and the papers, even the smell of wood shavings; all of it took him back to their earliest days together, when she was just an aggravating eccentric traveller, and he was just her bodyguard. He remembered the first time he had seen her; a warm face dazzled into darkness by the sun as she stood over him. He had been drunk and half asleep outside a tavern, and of course she had demanded to know what he was doing. He was, ultimately, one more Eboran artefact for her to pore over.

'Another dusty relic,' he said to the room at large. 'Should have bloody left me there, Vintage. Look at all the fucking trouble we've caused.'

Noon might still have escaped the Winnowry, but she wouldn't have been found by them, wandering in the Shroom Flats like a dispossessed urchin. She wouldn't have followed them to Esiah Godwort's compound, wouldn't have absorbed the life-energy of a parasite spirit, which would turn out to be the soul of a dragon called Vostok. Without Noon, he would not have gone back inside the Behemoth wreck and retrieved the golden growth fluid, would not have taken it back to Ebora, would not have accidently released the Jure'lia queen from the roots of Ygseril . . .

'I've no doubt, Vintage, you would have got into plenty of trouble without me, but this –' he gestured around, as if taking in all of the palace and all of Ebora, perhaps all of Sarn – 'this level of fuck-up is an Eboran speciality.'

He thought, then, of how Vintage's face would change when they told her that Noon was lost, so he filled his glass up to the top and drank it off in one go. When that was done, he opened the next bottle. This wine was so dark it looked black, and it smelled of blackberries and winter. He shivered in the warm room.

'It's all falling apart,' he said. Absently, he rolled up his sleeve and peered at his arm in the gloom. The red mark there was a little deeper, and it had a new line branching off from it. Still very small, still barely noticeable, but there. 'Vintage, if, by some miracle, you can hear me, you're better off not coming back. Stay in Jarlsbad, or run. And keep running.'

Chapter Thirteen

There has been a great deal of discussion about the woman Fell-Tyranny since she was brought into the Winnowry. She has, as I predicted, been secreted away into the smallest chambers in the underground section of the towers, and, as I also predicted, she has made life as hard as possible for everyone. She refuses to eat, smears her food over the walls, bellows obscenities at anyone passing, lunges for any sister or agent who comes close. Yet, as the activities of the Salts are gradually revealed to us, I can't help noticing that when the subject of her future arises, a speculative look appears on certain faces.

They were producing illegal akaris, we know this. They were transporting it out of the city and across Sarn, undercutting the Winnowry on the price as they did so. Tyranny herself had multiple contacts, was owed untold favours. She was a power in the city, and now, some are saying, it is foolish to throw that power away. The woman has skills, ones that the Winnowry rarely comes across in its prisoners. The implication is clear: they intend to make her an agent, somehow. There is talk that Agent

The taste of ash, black and sour. Beneath her fingers, something soft and pliable. Patches of heat, coming and going, flickering and then dying.

Noon sat up, coughing. There was black sand on her face and hands, all over her clothes, and directly in front of her were softly undulating dunes, broken up here and there with spiky white plants with tiny red buds on them. The sky overhead was grey and flat – and empty. It was empty.

'Vostok? Tor?'

She tried to stand up but her legs wouldn't hold her properly, so she stumbled, turning as she fell. There was a ruin behind her, some sort of old castle built of . . . built of . . .

Noon dropped her head and looked at the black sand some more. Her head was spinning, and the sense of being utterly alone was stark, as though she had fallen naked from her bed in the middle of the freezing night. Where was Vostok? Where was Tor? Where was the Behemoth they had been fighting? *Where was the sea?*

She shivered violently all over despite the warmth of the day, and a tiny flicker of winnowfire moved over the palm of

142

her hand without her summoning it. As she blinked at that, another tongue of green flame marched up her forearm and disappeared.

'What the *fuck* is going on?'

The only answer was a soft, breathy sigh, the sound of the wind moving over the dunes. Still shivering as though she were in the depths of a fever, Noon forced herself to stand and look at the ruin. Her first thought was that it was made of shadows, a thing of dying light and hidden depths, but as she took a few steps towards it, she saw that it was actually made of a kind of dark grey glass. Translucent and impossibly delicate, it sprawled away in front of her in a series of towers and battlements and peaks that seemed to make very little obvious sense, while the light of the day pooled and shone in odd places, turning structures smoky and insubstantial. As she walked towards it she noticed that there were patches on the sand that were also hard and glassy, as though someone had once tried to make a path of the same material but had given up.

'Hello! Anyone in there?'

Noon raised her hand to shield her eyes – despite the greyness of the day, the place felt filled with light and heat – but winnowfire licked around her fingers and she hurriedly dropped her arm.

'I remember the fight,' she said aloud, still moving towards the ruin. 'I remember looking down at Tor. He had noticed that Celaphon was missing, and he was happy about it, but I didn't feel happy. I was worried. Because something felt wrong. And –' She paused. Ahead of her was a sort of arched gateway, which led to the main building beyond. Now she was close to it, she could see the sand the glass erupted from; it was covered in thick black bubbles. She leaned down to touch it, and felt hard, slick glass under her fingers. She stepped away, frowning. 'Vostok was angry with me because I wasn't paying attention.

And then – green light, a roaring sound, and this place. Fire and blood, did I just leave them there?'

Something twinkled above her line of sight and she looked up just in time to see a flicker of greenish light at one of the windows. Her heart stuttered in her chest. Was the Winnowry responsible for this? Balling her hands into fists, she strode towards the opening in the ruins – there was no door – and quickly found herself in a wide, echoing hall of sorts. More grey glass, darker the closer to the floor it was, and lots of doorways, leading off down shadowy hallways. There were stairs too, leading up to a series of precarious ledges, but the steps were slick and shiny and oddly ill-formed – almost as if they were the idea of steps rather than the real thing.

'Is anyone here? If you're from the Winnowry, I swear, you will undo what you did to me or I will find every last one of you and – and –'

Another flicker of green light, this time down at the end of one of the corridors. Noon set off at a run, frowning at how her boots squeaked across the glass, but the light had already gone by the time she got there. Instead, she found herself standing in an unsettling corridor of dark glass, the surface of it slick and cold under her fingers.

'I've lost my fucking mind.'

Laughter echoed down the hall towards her, and she snapped her head around to see the source, but there was nothing save for a sheen of greenish light in the distance. The laughter faded; it didn't sound cruel, or mocking, just genuinely amused. And female. Noon turned and followed the light, which disappeared around two corners before leading her to a set of wide, curving steps. Noon eyed them warily before following, going slowly and leaning against the wall for stability. The steps under her boots were slippery and uneven, threatening to send her sliding back down on her face. Her head down and her brow creased in concentration, the landing took her by surprise, and she looked up to find herself in a wide chamber with a low ceiling. There were windows along one side, or at least, holes in the glass, and the grey daylight from outside filtered its way inside to become a soft, uncertain glow. And she wasn't alone.

There was a woman sitting on a chair in the centre of the chamber. She was tall and rangy, leaning forward with her elbows on her knees. She wore a dress made of layers of knitted material, a mixture of black and red and blue, and although Noon could see her hair – it was long and brown and untidy – it was half hidden under an aura of green flame that flickered from the top of her head. Her eyes were bright green lights, and seeing Noon's expression, she smiled.

'There you are.' Her voice was warm and friendly, as though greeting an old friend.

'Who – what are you?'

The woman stood up, revealing the chair she sat on. There was nothing really remarkable about it – just a wooden chair, painted yellow, with a woven straw cushion – but it was so incongruous in the castle of glass that Noon could only stare at it. The woman stood to one side, as if presenting the chair for her consideration.

'Do you like it? I like bringing things back here sometimes. Odds and ends. They don't last, but I suppose that's the point.'

'I . . . it's a very lovely chair.' Noon pressed her fingers to her eyes, wondering if perhaps she had fallen from Vostok after all, and hit her head very hard. 'Who are you? And what am I doing here?'

The woman turned away from the chair and walked towards Noon slowly. She was barefoot, and as she got closer, Noon realised the woman was ill. Her skin was sallow and thin, bruised black and purple under her eyes.

'I think you know who I am, Fell-Noon. Don't you? Deep in that head, don't you know?' The woman tipped her head

145

to one side, and the flickering aura of flames around it rose a little higher. 'You people usually know, when I come to you.'

Noon looked into the woman's fiery green eyes and for a moment could say nothing at all. Because, on some level, she did know this woman. Not the face, but the *energy* of her. After all, didn't she carry it with her every day?

'I don't know,' she said eventually. 'I feel like I've known you forever, but I've never seen your face before. How can that be?' She shook her head. 'You're not surprised to see me here, and you know my name. Did you bring me to this place?'

'Noon.' The woman laid a hand on her shoulder. Noon could feel the heat of it, like a cooling iron, through her jacket. 'I brought you here, yes. Shall we go outside? I should like to walk on the sand.'

'I'm not going anywhere with you.' Noon shook her hand off. 'Tell me why you've done this, and send me back. I was in the middle of a fight! Tor and Vostok, they will think I've left them, they will think –'

The woman raised her hands, palms facing out. 'I brought you here, Noon, because you woke up the Aborans' Seed Carrier with your clever fire, and I wanted to see who would do that.' She paused, and grinned. 'Wasn't quite enough to power it up, but I bet it gave those old fools a shock.'

'That thing on Origin? You mean you know about that place, what it was?'

'Come on, let's go outside. Things make more sense under the sky, I think.'

Noon followed the woman through the castle, her mind racing. Back out on the sand, some of the clouds had cleared from the horizon to reveal the sun on its way down, filling the small bare patch of sky with orange light. Stretching away in front of them was an apparently endless desert, although Noon thought she could see the shadows of mountains to the

146

west. The aura that surrounded the woman's head seemed to grow in the daylight, stretching out and collecting other colours, a corona of rainbow lights. Noon found she had to look away from it.

'Did you see the things that lived inside the Seed Carrier, Fell-Noon?'

'No. I mean, there were monsters, and I killed those, but the people? I saw one of them, and Tor told me it was long dead, like it was a ghost of itself. And it didn't like me very much.'

The woman laughed hugely at that. 'I bet it didn't. I knew those people once. Travelled with them. Dusty, self-important. *Boring*. They thought what they were doing was so incredible.' She raised her arms and spread them wide, as if indicating the landscape around them. 'But they knew nothing about the worlds they played with.'

'You're – you're not human, are you?'

'No. Well, this bit is.' She reached up and lightly patted her own cheeks, not seeming to care that the skin on them was loose and yellow. 'This *flesh*. But otherwise, no.'

Noon thought of the strange surface of the Seed Carrier, etched with symbols and lines that she hadn't understood, yet had found oddly compelling. She thought of how her winnow-fire had sunk into the skin of it, running around patterns in the surface as though it had always been meant to do so. The faces in the alcoves, laughing . . .

'I brought them here, and then I left them,' continued the woman. 'I'd had enough of that. Of being tethered to their ship, a thing for them to use. I was tired of the coldness of the outer-black, the long spaces. All that nothingness tastes the same, you know? A world tastes different. All over.' She grinned again.

'I've no bloody idea what you're on about.' Except that Noon had a horrible feeling she did. Tor had told her about the Aborans, the beings that had spoken to him even though they were long dead; how they had travelled to Sarn over unimaginable distances in some vast sort of ship, and then how their means of powering their ship had left them somehow; had left them stranded on the island that would eventually be Origin. A memory came to her in sharp relief: the way the Aboran called Eeskar had reacted to her – or had reacted to her winnowfire. He had been angry, and afraid. As though she had personally betrayed him somehow.

'You can do better than that, Noon,' the woman said, mildly enough. 'I know for a fact you're good at figuring things out.'

'You're not human,' Noon said. 'You came here with the . . . people who planted Ygseril and created the Eborans, but you're not one of them. Somehow, you are . . . you're winnowfire.'

The woman laughed again, delighted. 'I love that word for what I am. You see? This is why I had to get out of there. Words and skies and chairs and feet and – here, look at that.'

She pointed out across the dark sands to where several shapes were moving in the distance. It was a small herd of four-legged animals that Noon had never seen before. They looked a little like shaggy goats with long necks, and they had black-and-white piebald coats.

'I've seen them in pictures, in books,' said Noon. 'My mum used to – Is this the Singing Eye Desert? Is that where we are?'

The woman nodded. 'That's right. Isn't it something?'

The thought of maps and her mother's books made Noon think of Vintage. What would she say about all this? The memory of sitting in Esiah Godwort's kitchen rose up – their cobbled-together meal of potatoes and preserves, the strange quiet of the mansion, and the knowledge that Tor was upstairs, unconscious. She had been half out of her mind at the time, with both guilt and the strange new voice in her head, and talking to Vintage had been like reaching for a lifeline while drowning.

'There were people,' she said quietly, 'people a long time ago who thought that the winnowfire was a gift. That it was sacred. They worshipped a woman, or a goddess, I suppose. They called her She Who Laughs. That's you, isn't it? I mean, assuming that I'm not leaking my brains out on a beach somewhere, having one last weird dream before I die.'

The woman turned to her. Her smile now looked satisfied, almost smug. 'See? I knew you were good at figuring things out.'

'Wait, wait. This still doesn't make any sense. If you're She Who Laughs, the, I don't know, goddess of winnowfire, then why do I also have it? Why do all those women in the Winnowry have it? And what are you doing out here in the middle of nowhere? Why are you an old woman?' Noon pinched the bridge of her nose; she felt perilously close to passing out. 'And why do you keep saying I'm good at figuring things out?'

'Ah, well, you see . . .' the woman held up one hand, and then sighed. Green fire was crawling over it, spreading rapidly as they watched, up her arm and across her shoulders, while a similar sleeve of flame covered her other arm.

'Wait, what are you doing?' Noon took a hurried step back.

The fire raced up over the woman's face, meeting the crown of emerald flame on her head, and abruptly she was burning all over; not the dirty orange flame normally born by the touch of witch's fire, but a green that grew brighter and brighter by the moment. The woman tipped her head back and lifted her arms, as though she were standing in a particularly pleasant patch of sunlight, and her body began to break apart into pieces of swirling white light.

'Stop it!'

But it was too late. In a flash of shimmering green, the

149

woman was gone. Where she had been standing was a small, sad pile of grey ash, and a blackened skull that looked like it had been sitting on the desert sands forever. Once again, the place was filled with an eerie silence, and a breeze began to scatter the ashes. Noon glared down at the remains, her arms rigid at her sides.

'You have got to be fucking kidding me.'

Chapter Fourteen

Yurt fires were terrible things. Rare, but not unknown. An old family yurt, the walls built from layers of deer fat and horse hair – a new layer applied for each new betrothal – and an untended fire. They were feared because they could go up so fast, and because you might not know about it for some time. If the people inside were asleep, taken by the smoke, they could be caught in their own private inferno for some minutes, and all that those on the outside would see would be the thick stream of black smoke escaping from the small hole in the top. Then, eventually, the yurt would collapse in on itself, releasing a huge gout of flame. A fire that burns in secret, a lethal conflagration that you only discover when it's too late to save anyone.

I thought about yurt fires a lot today. One of the young girls, a Fell-Jereen, has been quiet for some time, listless almost. I tried to talk to her once or twice, tried to engage her attention with talk of purgings and Tomas (not great subjects, I know, but we are limited here) and she only looked at me with dull eyes, as though I were not really there. She did not resist being taken to and from the

151

furnace, patted her face with the ashes without complaint. She was, to the sisters, a model fell-witch, but it worried me all the same. Something was burning underneath.

Today, she lunged for Father Isles as he was leading her from her purging, and by chance made contact with his naked face. She drained him in a moment and directed a great blast of fire at the nearest sister.

When Fell-Jereen was captured she was raving, her face wet with tears and marked where she had tried to claw herself. She swore she would kill us all, that she would burn us all to soot and piss on what was left, that she would do it to Tomas too if she could . . . She was taken to see Mother Cressin. Later, I saw her body laid out on the sand, her lips blue and her hair and clothes soaked through. She will be buried in an unmarked grave, some-where on this little sandy island – where all of them will end up eventually. And I will join them, no doubt.

Look for the darker smoke, is what my once-father used to tell me. The hidden fire.

Extract from the private records of Agent Chenlo

'Not that I've ever seen or heard of, no.'

Aldasair nodded politely. All day he had slowly made his way around the part of the palace given over to the fell-witches, asking questions and receiving mostly blank looks. The first woman he had spoken to had been older, in her sixties at least – reasonably aged for a human – and he had been half certain she would have heard of such a thing, but as soon as he attempted to describe what had happened, her face had gone very pale.

'Has someone exploded? When? Who?'

Realising his mistake he had begun to backtrack, insisting that all was fine, that he was simply collecting information. The woman had been shaken by his words, and now he was being careful to hide that particular question amongst other, less upsetting ones. 'We know so very little about it in Ebora,' he told them. 'Eborans have never been blessed with the witch flame, after all.'

And although he had had several very interesting conversations, he hadn't found anyone who had ever heard of a fell-witch causing her own explosion, and no reports of anyone actually vanishing in a storm of their own green flame. What had happened to Noon remained a mystery.

He thanked the last woman and made his way back to the courtyard, where Bern and Sharrik waited for him.

'No luck?'

Aldasair shook his head. 'And I don't believe it was such a great idea to ask them, after all. I've clearly upset some of them, and many are suspicious. Eventually, they will notice that Vostok has returned to Ebora without Noon.'

'And are we keeping that a secret?' Bern looked better than he had done in days, but then he always looked better when he was near Sharrik; the great griffin seemed to lend him some of his own strength.

Aldasair shrugged. 'It would be such a blow to them. She has become something of a hero, as much as she tried to ignore it.'

'It is a blow to us,' rumbled Sharrik. 'The witch was a mighty warrior. Almost as mighty as I.'

'We may as well chuck it all in.'

They all turned at the sound of Tor's voice. He leaned against the entrance to the courtyard, his long black hair hanging in his face. His clothes were creased and crumpled, as though he'd slept in them.

'Tormalin, we mustn't give up hope.'

'Really? Mustn't we?' He smiled and came down the low steps towards them. 'I can't think of any particularly compelling reasons to feel especially hopeful right now. Noon is dead.

153

Vintage has gone to Jarlsbad, probably to get herself killed by a maniac. Vostok is too angry to be of any use to anyone. And although the Jure'lia are meant to be *broken*, apparently they are still entirely capable of causing plenty of trouble.'

Aldasair sighed. 'You have been drinking.'

'Tell me I'm wrong, then. Bern, tell me how I'm wrong – except I'm not, am I? Word has already reached us that the Jure'lia went back and destroyed the other settlements on that coast.'

'It's true, the worm people are lively again.' Bern reached up with his good hand and pulled his fingers through the thick feathers on Sharrik's neck. 'But that's not the whole truth. I can feel them – broken stones, I can feel them all the time – and I can feel their pleasure at the destruction they're causing, but the queen wasn't there. It was just Hestillion.' He glanced uneasily at Tor, who shrugged.

'That matches up with what I saw in your head, doesn't it? My sister taking command of a pair of Behemoths. We thought we'd finally had some luck and managed to deal the Jure'lia some lasting damage, but instead my sister has lost her mind and decided to resurrect them herself.' He pushed his hair back from his face. 'I've half a mind to find a decent tavern and start drinking. Perhaps I can be unconscious by the time the spider-mothers come to pull us to pieces.'

'My cousin,' Aldasair took his arm and squeezed it, 'you tried running away before, remember? It wasn't the solution then either.'

Tor gave a short bitter bark of laughter. 'And I thought things were bad *then*. What an idiot I was.'

'You are sad about the witch,' boomed Sharrik. 'We are all sad about the witch. But she was a being crafted for war, and she would want us to fight, Tormalin the Oathless.'

Aldasair winced. They all felt, on some level, the special bond Tor and Noon had, and they had all very carefully not mentioned it – yet Sharrik was not especially blessed with tact. Something about Tor's posture changed, and he turned his face away from them, but not before Aldasair saw the expression of pain that passed over it.

'If you want me, I'll be drinking heavily somewhere. Enjoy your fight, cousin.'

The Trick river dwindled and then grew again underneath them, becoming fat and wide and slow; becoming the Ember, with its famous orange and red stones glinting just below the surface. From there the river headed directly into the patchwork lands of Jarlsbad, so Vintage and Chenlo simply followed it. Their days were filled with the sound of wings and the whistling of the wind, their nights with the quiet crackle of a campfire, the soft wheezes of Helcate's snoring.

Their first hint of Tygrish, the kingdom supposedly captured by Tyranny Munk, was a small settlement amidst the yellow grassland. It was circular, its walls made of white stone and reaching up to the sky, while to the north of it sprouted a great land bridge, also made of white stone, reaching out across the tall grasses. Within the walls was a collection of tightly packed buildings, including a few with the green conical roofs so associated with Jarlsbad. This place was a small satellite of Tygrish, and following the graceful land bridge, they soon flew over another; this one was a little larger, and in the golden morning light Vintage could see men and women below looking up at them in wonder. Tiny figures on the land bridges paused in their hauling of carts and sacks, faces turned upward.

'The grasslands are so dangerous?'

The question was shouted across from Chenlo, who was leaning over her bat's shoulder to get a better look at the land bridge. As they journeyed into Jarlsbad it was possible to see many of them in the distance, tall elegant structures looking as delicate as lace against the hot blue sky.

'Wild-cats!' Vintage shouted back. 'Worm-touched and lethal. The lands around Jarlsbad are infamous for them, and this far to the south it is preferable to avoid travelling directly through the grasslands if you possibly can. Hence, the bridges.'

'They are very beautiful.'

Vintage looked up in surprise, but Agent Chenlo had already turned away. It was possible to see where all the land bridges were heading to – a great sprawling city to the north, a place of shining towers topped with green and blue domes and spires. It was nowhere near as large as Mushenska, or even many of the other Jarlsbad kingdoms, but there was no denying that Tygrish was impressive in its own way. As she watched, a number of small shapes peeled away from the tallest tower – they looked like moths from this distance, but Vintage had a good idea what they were.

'The welcoming committee are on their way!'

'Helcate,' said Helcate.

The light across the plains was clear and bright, bringing everything into sharp focus, and it wasn't long before Vintage could make out the furry hides of the giant bats approaching them, and the serious faces of the women in their harnesses. She forced herself to sit back and adopt a relaxed posture – or as relaxed as she could manage, this far up in the air. Nevertheless, she found her hands had balled into fists around Helcate's reins, and her head was full of a forest night not so long ago; when she had followed Tyranny's little gang into the woods and nearly been murdered for it; when Nanthema had betrayed her.

'What will they do?' she shouted across to Chenlo. 'What if they try to turn us away?'

'If they take their orders from Tyranny, then there's no telling what they will do.'

'Well, if they try to blow us out of the sky, they've got a

surprise coming.' Vintage leaned down and scratched Helcate behind the ears. 'Haven't they, my darling?'

There were four Winnowry agents, three hanging back while one came forward to address them directly. She had short, red curly hair and the fair skin on her cheeks and nose had turned a shining pink under the hot sun. At first glance she looked, to Vintage's eye, unspeakably young, but as she drifted closer it was possible to see a fine network of scars across her hands and arms, as well as a ragged slash of white scar tissue across one cheek. Her eyes were narrow and suspicious, but she smiled as she spoke.

'Agent Chenlo! You've come to join us? Seen some sense at last, have you?'

'This is not what I would call sense, Agent Kreed. We're here to see Tyranny. Where is she?'

'You think you can just waltz up and demand an audience?' Agent Kreed showed her teeth in something that fell quite short of a smile. 'You're not in charge anymore, and Tyranny is a *queen*. She has a war-beast at her command.' At that the young woman glanced at Vintage, who smiled and waved. 'This is a restricted air space. What do you want?'

'We're here on Eboran business,' called Vintage. 'This is Helcate, and you have one of his siblings hidden somewhere in Tygrish. He'd like to meet them. I think that's fair enough, don't you?'

Agent Kreed's smile had vanished. 'We wish you no harm, and certainly no harm to . . . Helcate, but due to the current Jure'lia situation, Queen Tyranny has ordered the borders of Tygrish closed.' She pushed her carroty hair away from her forehead, revealing the crude bat-wing tattoo. 'That includes sky borders. You must leave.'

'Oh, but we've come such a long way, darling.' Vintage rested her hand on her crossbow, wondering what would happen if they had to fight their way in. 'And, well, let's be frank with each other, your Queen Tyranny stole something incredibly valuable from Ebora, an act that is both an unpardonable insult and an act of war. I could go back to Ebora and tell the rest of Helcate's brothers and sisters that Tyranny hasn't got time to see us today, and see how they take it –' she shrugged extravagantly – 'or we could have a nice little chat about it before things get out of hand.' She leaned forward in the harness, composing her face into an expression that suggested rueful sympathy. 'I know you are very skilled with the winnowfire, ladies, but we have a dragon at home. And just between you and me, she has a temper at the best of times.'

To her surprise, the woman smiled and raised a hand. A glove of green fire flared into existence around it.

'We've asked nicely. Now you need to go.'

'I don't want to fight you,' said Chenlo, her voice tight. 'We were sisters once, Kreed.'

'Sisters?' A strange expression passed over the woman's face. Vintage looked at the other women, who were still hovering some distance away on their own bats. They were watching their leader closely. 'Sisterhood? You could have left me in the Targ mountains, but you hunted me down and put me in that prison yourself. All that is over, Chenlo, and I don't have to do anything you say anymore.'

'Don't you trust me?' Chenlo's voice was tight, and Vintage felt a fresh surge of alarm as the agent produced her own ball of flame. Beneath her, she felt Helcate murmur with unease. This was all going south quickly. 'After *all* I did for you, you don't trust me?'

'This isn't the time or the place for this!' Vintage raised her voice and urged Helcate into the space between the two women. 'We're just here to talk, Agent Kreed. Honestly. Tyranny will want to see me, I promise. She won't be able to resist. Just tell her who's here, and we'll—'

One moment the sky was full of warm light and the sound

of wings beating; the next, it was an inferno of green fire. Vintage swore and ducked down against Helcate's neck even as the war-beast dropped away from the barrage. She didn't see who had fired first, but when she looked up she saw the three agents coming forward to join their leader, missiles of green fire streaking across the blue sky towards Chenlo, who had surrounded herself with a shield of flame. Each fireball that met it hissed and crackled, and was absorbed, but it was clear to Vintage that the woman couldn't keep the structure up for long.

'Shit.' Vintage raised her crossbow and fired up at Kreed's bat, taking the creature in the wing. It squealed its outrage, and Vintage winced, but the wound did not seem to slow it. 'Helcate, darling, we might have need of your talents here.' Even as she said it, she felt a sinking feeling in her chest. Where would this end? With more dead women, dead bats? Beneath her, Helcate began the odd hiccuping motion that summoned his acid spit. Above them, Chenlo had dissipated her shield of flame and was busily flinging out discs of fire so fierce that they were ringed with white heat. One of the agents at the back cried out and her bat dropped away, wings beating fiercely. A moment later, one of Kreed's fireballs connected with the flank of Chenlo's bat and terrifyingly quickly there was a burst of orange fire as the creature's fur caught. Chenlo leaned down and beat it out with her own gloved hands, the expression on her face stern and determined.

'Do it, Helcate. Take down Kreed if you can.'

The war-beast stretched out his neck and shuddered, and a glistening stream of translucent liquid flew from his open mouth, striking the underside of Kreed's bat. There was a fresh barrage of squealing and the thing flew upwards, wings beating frantically. Vintage felt a pang of guilt as a thin, oily smoke bled from the creature's fur.

'Stand down!' called Vintage. 'Everyone, stop! Please, we have to—'

A shadow fell over them. Vintage blinked, and then gasped. The sky around them had turned abruptly frigid, so cold that the breath in her throat felt like shards of glass. Helcate's curly blondish fur was turning white, rimmed with frost.

'Enough!'

The voice thundered down over all of them, and Vintage squinted upwards at the huge shape hovering above. Amazingly, swarms of what appeared to be ice crystals were stinging at her eyes.

In Jarlsbad? Sarn's old bones, what is happening?

The shape above became clear. It was a bat, but a bat at least four times the size of those the Winnowry agents were riding, and although her mind automatically scrambled for an explanation – *Wild-touched, some new strain of Targus bat* – she knew the truth in an instant. It was the war-beast they had come looking for.

Its fur was a silvery white, and the skin stretched between the fine bones in its wings was pale blue, the colour of a songbird's egg. Its head was bulky and muscled, with a ridged, pointed nose ringed with grey velvet, and its huge ears were lined with rings of flexible muscle. Eyes, huge and blue and shining with intelligence, glared down at them all above a mouth rammed with alarming teeth – and at the back of its throat, it was still possible to see the glittering remains of the icy magic it had summoned. The creature had no harness and no rider, but curiously there was a band of silver across its broad forehead, and this was studded with diamonds, each the size of Vintage's thumb.

'Helcate!' said Helcate.

'You see?' Kreed's voice drifted down from above, exultant. 'We have no fear of you. Fell-witches don't need to be afraid of anyone, anymore. Meet our queen – Queen Windfall of Tygrish.'

Chapter Fifteen

Noon sat on the black sand, her arms circled around her knees. After the being calling herself She Who Laughs had vanished, she had spent a couple of agitated hours exploring the strange glass castle. She had ventured up into its battlements, moving as quickly as she dared over the smooth, shadowy surfaces, and had looked out across the desert in all directions. There had been nothing but the softly undulating dunes, little clumps of the fleshy white plants, and the occasional desert animal – no people, no human structures in sight. As the sun sank out of the sky and the stars came out, the sands grew chill and desolate, yet the castle itself seemed to retain heat. It was possible to feel it where she sat, on the very threshold of the thing – if she stretched out her leg to reach the sand not covered by the glass arch, her foot would grow cold. When she brought it back, warmth flowed through her again.

The contents of the castle had not been reassuring. There were lots of strange glass objects, huge glass discs that were distorted in myriad ways so that the dying light of the day was shattered into unsettling shapes and colours, and in one echoing hall, there stood a series of tall greenish grass pillars of varying sizes; when Noon touched them, she thought she

161

could hear music. She had found the yellow chair again, although now it looked old and broken; Noon had dismissed this, assuming it must be a trick of the light. There were a handful of other objects, left in apparently random chambers – a single red slipper, embroidered with black silk; a simple wooden cup, oddly charred around the edges; a hand mirror with a brass handle. On one windowsill, Noon had found a brightly painted string puppet, its limbs lying all about it like it had fallen from a great height. Each wooden piece had been painted with great skill, and inevitably Noon was reminded of Mother Fast's puppets from when she was a girl. The thought gave her a chill, and she had left that particular room a little faster than the others.

Every now and then she had spotted more of the green lights, but had quickly learned that she could not catch them, or spy their source. They seemed to be a sort of floating sprite, a little like the parasite spirits she had once fled from with Vintage and Tor.

Vintage and Tor. Thinking of them, Noon drew her knees closer to her chin. What would they believe had happened to her? Were they even alive? Her link to them, and to Vostok, felt intact, yet somehow muffled. She was sure that if, for example, Tor had died in the battle at the settlement, she would have felt it, yet not knowing for sure was an agony. Where was Vostok? Could the dragon sense her? Could she find her? If she didn't, it seemed likely her fate was to die of thirst out here in the middle of nowhere.

'Fire and fucking blood.' Her throat already felt too dry.

The last discovery had been the most unnerving. Just as it was getting too dark to see anything properly, she had stumbled across a small courtyard in the middle of the castle. In this narrow space, open to the sky above, the glass floor relinquished its hold and turned back to black sand, and here were a large collection of charred bones. Curving fragments of skull hinted at empty eye sockets, broken jaws grinned at her, half hidden in the sand. Were these the remains of other people She Who Laughs had summoned? The ones she had become bored with? Or perhaps her intention all along had been to kill Noon, and leave her blackened bones in this lonely place. There was no way to guess at the intentions of a creature like that. After all, she had the power to bring the Aborans across unimaginable distances, and then had happily abandoned them to die slowly, trapped on a distant island.

With this on her mind, Noon stood up, brushing black sand from her trousers, and headed cautiously back inside the glass castle. It was a place of dizzying darkness and uncertain walls, but as her eyes adjusted, she started to see soft glimmerings of light in hidden places; bleeding around corners, seeping half-seen across ceilings. It was green, this light, emerald and witchy, and the floating orbs of winnowfire were there too, still moving through the glass corridors. Using this to navigate by, Noon made her way back to the small bone-filled courtyard. Here, starlight left a hard glitter underfoot.

'You're not really gone, are you?' she said aloud, looking around at the slippery walls. 'A thing like you – a thing as old as you – doesn't just burn to pieces. Part of you is still here. Well, it's rude. Why bring me here and then hide from me? What do you want?'

For a long time, there was a great aching silence, broken only by the sound of the winds moving across the desert. Then an ember of green light sparked into life in the centre of the courtyard, glowing hot and quick and then expanding, growing both lighter and darker. As Noon watched, the light took on a shape, and then weight, and soon there was a figure in front of her, bathed in swirling green light.

'You see,' said She Who Laughs, 'you're good at figuring things out. I knew it.'

The swirling light faded, leaving only the corona of emerald flame at her head, and her burning green eyes. She was younger now, and rounder, with skin the same deep tan as Noon's. She wore a tunic of grey leather that had been embroidered all over with colourful beads, and there were matching cuffs at her wrists, yet her broad face was creased with pain, and there were dark circles under her eyes.

'Why are you different now? Where did you go?'

She Who Laughs stepped over the broken bones a little gingerly; her legs did not look stable. When she reached Noon she patted her arm gently.

'If you are not too afraid of the bones, shall we sit here? I am rather tired.'

Grimacing, Noon nodded, and together they sat down, their backs against the wall.

'Remember you spoke of the women who used to worship me?' She Who Laughs folded her hands in her lap, and Noon had the strangest sense of familiarity; it was like sitting at Mother Fast's knee, waiting to hear a story. 'Well, they still exist. Not so many as there used to be, but they are still clinging on, in small pockets all over Sarn.'

'The Winnowry hasn't found them?'

'The Winnowry.' She Who Laughs paused, looking up at the night sky. 'No. I suspect they think my women are all gone now. Tiny communities hidden away, where my fire is loved and celebrated.'

She turned to Noon and smiled, and Noon found she had to look at the ground under her boots. She wanted, abruptly, to cry, and she couldn't have said why.

'It's hard for them. Keeping themselves hidden, yet still living full lives. I exist here as light and heat, mostly,' she lifted one arm and gestured around at the walls, 'but sometimes I will go to them when they are dying, and ask if they will come back with me. It is interesting to walk around in your flesh for a while.'

164

'When they are dying?' asked Noon, startled.

'Yes. When death is close and certain, I ask if I may borrow them, use up their final energies.' She brightened, and nodded towards the dusty bones. 'They see it as a great honour.'

'Fire and blood. So that woman who was here before . . . ?'

'She was taking her last breaths. And this brave woman . . .' She patted her own chest. 'A bad growth inside is eating her away. I can feel it, nasty thing. But now she feels no pain at all, and her bones will rest here with those of her sisters.'

'That . . . I can hardly believe it. All my life I've been told that the winnowfire was an abomination and a curse, that everyone lives in fear of it and that we should be ashamed. But there are places where it's just accepted.'

'It is true. Secret places.'

Noon looked at the bones littering the floor, trying to take this in. Everything she had thought was real and solid suddenly seemed insubstantial and temporary; stories told by puppets around a fire at night. The feeling made her think of Tor, and the misery he had suffered since he'd discovered the truth about Ebora.

'Before. What were you before? You could not have been human when you brought the Aborans here. I saw the Seed Carrier, and the shapes carved into it. I saw how my fire crawled into those shapes . . .'

'Child, I *am* the fire.' She lifted her hand, and as if to prove it, a blossom of emerald flame curled into being above her fingertips. 'I am the Hunger that Takes, and I am Creation, both at once. I am the act of change itself.'

'That makes no bloody sense to me.'

'Well.' She Who Laughs flexed her fingers, and the green fire began to bend and stretch in strange ways. 'I once looked like this, when I was home, so long ago. Does this help?'

The flames crawled and stretched until a shape began to emerge, a leaping, lithe thing on the tips of her fingers. To

Noon it looked a little like Vostok – there were snapping jaws, a long, tapered body – but there were many whip-like tails, and four pairs of short, scurrying legs. Looking at it made her feel deeply uncomfortable for reasons she didn't understand.

'Please,' she said, looking back at her feet. 'Stop that. I don't want to see it.'

She Who Laughs shrugged, and the cavorting creature winked out of existence. Noon cleared her throat.

'Then what about the Winnowry? Why do they exist?'

'There's a question.' She Who Laughs shrugged. 'Humans are very strange. They choose to be frightened of something rather than understand it.'

'No, I mean, why didn't you stop it?' Noon turned and looked directly at the woman, trying to ignore her flickering crown of fire. '*Your women*, as you call them, have been suffering for centuries! Locked up, treated like animals, told that they are scum, and worse, and where were you?'

She Who Laughs frowned. 'I cannot be responsible for every child who bears my flame.'

'What?' Noon scrambled to her feet. 'So you care for the ones who love you, who know about you, but everyone else can get stuffed?'

She Who Laughs shook her head gently, her eyes downcast. 'I gave this gift, Fell-Noon, only to the strongest of Sarn. *Only the strongest*. My fire seeks you out when you are in the womb and finds that strength. *Only* the strong can carry it. I'm not giving them anything they can't handle.'

Noon felt her breath lodge in her throat. She thought of the sound of a hundred women breathing at night, punctuated by the sobbing of the newly arrived. Of being beaten with a silver-headed cudgel, and eating tasteless gruel, day after day. She thought of reaching her hand down through the grill separating her cell from Fell-Marian's, forever just out of reach. For a moment she considered draining something of its life force and

166

summoning the winnowfire – even if it was pointless, blasting this woman into ash would be satisfying.

Apparently oblivious to Noon's anger, the woman had continued talking.

'The Aborans thought that they were so clever, touching each world and making it different.' The smile that creased her face now was a bitter one. 'Over and over, they sowed their seeds and stood back, just watching. Observing. Everything was beneath them – even the one who gave them the very ability to travel between worlds. Ungrateful, short-sighted. *My* gift was to be something else. Something truly unique.'

'Do you have any idea what you have done?'

The woman looked up, unconcerned. 'I have done many, many great things and many small kindnesses, Noon. All the terrible things have been done by your weaker brethren. I have imprisoned no one. Persecuted no one.'

Noon shook her head slowly. Her anger seemed to drain away into the dark desert sand.

'Why? Why have you brought me here?'

The old woman laced her fingers together and smiled. The boiling green light of her eyes smoothed away the creases at their edges.

'I can help you, I think. There's something you – and you alone – came very close to understanding, and then you wandered away from it. I felt it,' she tapped her chest, 'in *here*. And I want to help you find it again.'

'And it was a glorious battle?'

Hestillion smiled, pulling her wet hair back into its now customary braid. She and Celaphon were on top of the Behemoth, carefully sitting in the shard of daylight that made its way down from the crack in the distant ceiling. The great dragon was as attentive as a puppy, his huge blind-looking eyes trained on her constantly.

'It was, my sweet. We took both settlements, as easily as picking flowers, and my new circle obeyed my every command. They are extensions of me now, like extra bodies I can wear.' This wasn't entirely true; although the settlements had been destroyed, their remains sealed over with the greenish resin, commanding the circle and the two Behemoths at once had not been easy at all, and Hestillion's entire body seemed to thrum with fatigue. As easy as picking flowers, it was not. But the satisfaction she carried in her heart was a balm to those aches and pains. Celaphon snorted.

'I should have been there! Where you summon glory, so should I. We are warriors together, little green bird.'

'I know, my sweet, and you will be there next time.' She smiled, thinking of how Celaphon had once admired the human man Bern, as his soul was 'that of a weapon'. Perhaps now he would give her the deference she was due. *Now I am master of the battlefield.* 'I just had to prove myself to our queen. But now she can see what I can do . . .'

'We see what you do, Hestillion Eskt.' A shadow split the dusty light in two, and the Jure'lia queen appeared from behind them. 'We saw with many eyes how you threw down the humans, how you consumed them. Even your brother and his cohorts were frightened away. Impressive.'

Hestillion stood and faced the queen, lifting her chin slightly. The creature that was the heart of the Jure'lia looked a little more solid than she had done, her long rangy limbs grown greenish and spongy, and her long hands laid curled at her sides like dead spiders.

'I can proceed, then? With my plan?' Hestillion cleared her throat; she felt oddly like a child reporting to her tutor. 'Settlement by settlement, city by city. Until Ebora remains, alone and friendless. It is the only way.' She took a breath. 'I am confident that eventually I will be able to command even more Behemoths at once.' Behind her, Celaphon snorted again, louder this time. 'And of course Celaphon will be our central force, driving all before him.'

For a long time the queen didn't say anything at all. Her yellowish pond-scum eyes moved from Celaphon to Hestillion and back again. When finally she spoke, Hestillion found herself blinking in consternation at the question.

'And what of your brother?'

'What?'

'He will try to stop you, again and again. You will have to kill him. What do you think about this?'

'I . . .' Hestillion felt her throat grow tight. All at once she was too angry to speak. 'I *told* you, I have broken all bonds with Ebora, that I—'

'And you.' The queen twitched her head towards Celaphon. 'Your brothers and sisters, the griffin and wolf and dragon, who grew in the tree with you. What of your bond with them?'

Celaphon looked to Hestillion for guidance, then down at his own feet. He said nothing.

'Bonds. You things are made of them, strengthened by them. It is almost –' The queen lifted her long hands and looked at them. 'It is almost like our connections, almost, but so difficult to see, and much less reliable.'

'It's the crystal still, isn't it?' Hestillion felt her own hands curling into fists. There was a sick roiling in her stomach. 'Still you focus on that, to the detriment of everything else.'

'Yet we almost understand it,' said the queen softly, picking up on none of the anger in Hestillion's voice – *or perhaps*, thought Hestillion, *she chooses to ignore it*. 'The force that enabled the man Bern to supplant our own memory. So invisible, yet so powerful. Lord Celaphon,' she turned her attention back to the dragon, who was still sitting with his head lowered, 'you once called the connection we all share "a poison song". Will that be enough for you? Can it be?'

Hestillion felt Celaphon's dismay, as sharp as a dagger under her own ribs – she knew he still felt something for the other war-beasts. Underneath the cacophony of the Jure'lia it was there still, a faint itch, a distant sorrow, like phantom pain from a severed limb.

'I am mighty,' said Celaphon, in a very small voice. 'I will fight in battles again and show you that I don't need any of them.'

'We feel your uncertainty, Lord Celaphon.' The queen's tone was sympathetic, which only made Hestillion angrier. 'That which is not Jure'lia seems riddled with uncertainty, and I fear the crystal memory has infected me with such.' She turned to look at Hestillion, her face unreadable. 'I am certain nothing else could have touched me in such a way. *Us*, in such a way.'

'Enough of this nonsense.' Hestillion threw her hands up, dismissing them both. 'I don't have time for it. My brother and his friends might have fled at our last battle, but they will be working relentlessly to get stronger, faster, more lethal. And I must make us stronger to match.' She turned away and summoned an opening in the hide of the Behemoth. 'I will be in the room of creation. There at least I can be sure of having company that will listen to me.'

Chapter Sixteen

As of this morning I have requested to be removed as one of Fell-Tyranny's mentors.

It's not a decision I take lightly, as it's very clear she needs a great deal of guidance and instruction (and even kindness) but I fear we are just completely incompatible. She is sly for the sake of it, often creating tension and conflict between her sister witches just to watch the fallout; she bristles constantly at being told what to do, even when the commands are simple, common-sense things; she is looking continually for ways to break the system, pushing at the places where it is weak – she is, in short, much too used to being the leader of her own gang, and entirely resistant to being part of a team. This morning was the last straw. The girls had a small number of rabbits, bred specially for the purpose, and were teaching themselves to take a series of tiny sips of life energy from them – it's an exercise in self-control and restraint, and I should have known Fell-Tyranny was unsuited to it. Again and again she drained the animals until they were cold and stiff, and then shrugged when I asked her why she couldn't control her impulse. To her, control is something for other people to worry about, and this is all wrong: control is the very foundation of a Winnowry agent's life. Having hidden herself on the streets of Mushenska for so long, she is considerably older than the other girls in training, and I wonder if this is a factor too; she is offended by what she sees as 'child's work'.

I have also noticed that she has yet to be given the bat-wing tattoo, and each time I ask about this, the sisters and fathers deflect my queries. My fear is that they have plans for Fell-Tyranny, yet they don't truly understand her nature. It will end badly.

Extract from the private records of Agent Chenlo

The amber tablets had been laid out on the desk in a long line. To one side there was a pile of parchment, already covered in scratchy writing, while to the other was a pile of parchment waiting to be used, as well as several colourful pots of ink. Tor stood admiring the precision of it all for a while. So scholarly, so organised. Just like everything hadn't gone to shit. Some of the used parchment bore Vintage's handwriting, with its cheerful slant and elaborate loops, while some of it had been used by Aldasair; his cousin's handwriting was more functional, with more words crammed onto each sheet, but still beautiful in its own way.

It was another bright day outside, and a slice of sunshine had fallen across the desk, turning the tablets to glowing slabs of honey. Smiling faintly, Tor picked one up and turned it over and over in his hands, ignoring the persistent burning ache in his arms and chest. He had been drinking since sun-up, but he had a terrible suspicion that the drink wasn't working anymore. The pain couldn't be ignored.

'Time to try something else.'

He sat in the padded chair by the desk and closed his eyes, seeking out the netherdark with the relief of sinking into a hot bath. The amber tablet he had selected burned like a beacon, impossible to miss, and he stepped gladly into its warmth. There was a moment of pressure, resistance, and then he emerged, blinking, into the midst of a pitched battle. He stood on the steep incline of a grassy hill, some unknown landscape sweeping away in front, while all around him the teeming hordes of the Jure'lia scuttled and teemed. He saw at least three enormous maggots, glistening under the sun, and hanging in the sky above, a Behemoth; fat and whole, it looked like an overfed grub. Drones were everywhere, and Tor saw that Micanal had used some artistic licence there; they barely looked human at all, their skins grey and discoloured, their heads all free of hair. Perhaps Micanal had sought to reduce some of the horror in this, his paean to the glory of war-beasts and Ebora.

'Or maybe he just didn't get out much,' Tor murmured. He felt good. Despite the crawling horrors on the grasses below him, it was clear that this was not reality, and that was deeply reassuring; there was no smell of mud and blood, no imminent danger. And his veins were warm with wine. The pain and the sorrow, which had been hanging over him like a mouldering shroud, had been boiled away in this new chaos of sound and sight. He looked around. He was standing, he realised, in a long line of war-beasts and their warriors.

'Look at you,' he said. 'Look at you all.'

They were all bigger, and more glorious than they had been in life, he was sure of that, but somehow that only added to his feeling of awe; in the end, Micanal had seen them more clearly than anyone. Micanal had known them in his heart. This was why, after all, they called him 'the Clearsighted'.

To his right stood a magnificent dragon, her scales a dizzying rainbow shading from red to blue, and her eyes were pools of liquid gold. On her long, noble head she wore a helmet specially shaped for her, and everything in her bearing spoke of strength, power and intelligence. There was an Eboran on her back, and of him Tor could not see much; he wore a full set of enamelled armour, and he carried a long spear under one arm. They shared an expression, though, one of expectation and patience.

Tor looked at them and smiled. To see them like this really was a gift. He wondered, if he could spend long enough here, whether his actual memories of Ebora – of the empty palace and broken roads, of the people dying slowly in their own beds, of the gradual falling away of everything he'd ever known – could be replaced with this instead. It was an attractive thought.

Movement. The army of war-beasts behind him surged forward, galloping down the hill to meet the ancient enemy, and Tor watched them pass, a ghost in their midst. They met the Jure'lia on the fields below, and here again Tor recognised Micanal's hand, because this battle was like a dance, or a performance. The drones fell back like a tide, and each beast and warrior moved in beautiful unison, almost as if they weren't killing at all.

'Maybe this was what it was really like.' Tor rubbed at his arm, then forced himself to stop. 'When our war-beasts had their own memories, when there were more than five of them. When we knew who and what we were. Before we'd fucking poisoned ourselves.'

Abruptly, he wanted a drink.

Below, the battle was drawing to a close – this was evidence of more artistic licence from Micanal, as such battles had often lasted for days. Those Jure'lia that weren't crushed into the ground were scuttling back to their Behemoths. Slowly, the giant ships began to move across the bruised sky, heading south and passing over Tor's head. This then, was their famous retreat, at the end of every Rain, vanishing again for a generation only to come back repaired and renewed. Tor watched them go, admiring the slow trickle of daylight moving across the ships' oily skins. When he looked back, the battlefields had vanished and he stood instead inside a cavernous hall of shining marble. Huge windows lined either side, letting in a bright, cold light, and elaborately embroidered carpets lay on the flagstones all around, leading in softly curving lines to the figures of various war-beasts. They stood as still as statues, yet their eyes glittered and their flanks moved softly with their breathing. Tor wandered over to the nearest one, and read the plaque that sat at its feet: *Crowblossom, war-beast of the Fourth Rain, bonded with the warrior Lady Gweneer. Died of great age four decades after the end of the Rain . . .*

There was more, meticulous details of all of Crowblossom's achievements, including a note at the end that mentioned his celebrated poetry. Tor smiled faintly, wondering if any of Crowblossom's poetry had survived. This war-beast had come from a period of Eboran history where poetry had been considered its highest art form. The beast was a griffin as large as Sharrik, with silky black feathers and bright yellow eyes. His heavy paws were tipped with lethal copper-coloured talons.

'Such a beast,' murmured Tor. 'For all Micanal's faults and mistakes, I am glad he did this. I am glad he gave me the chance to look on you, Crowblossom, in all your glory. What a brighter and better world it was, so long ago.'

Despite the glory, Tor felt despair seep into his heart. There would be no hall of champions for him and Kirune, he was certain of that. Even if he managed to die somewhere other than a fetid sick bed, his final battle would see the victory of the Jure'lia, and his legacy would be one of disgrace and horror. He turned away and wandered down the carpet, letting it lead him from one lost hero to another as the light through the windows remained unchanging.

In the end they were flown into Tygrish with an escort of fell-witches, the magnificent war-beast leading at the front. Below

175

them, the land bridges were thronged with people, and as they passed over the city walls, Vintage saw almost all the faces looking up at them, their mouths wide open in neat little 'o's of wonder. Some of them were waving, she noticed. Cheering. *Two war-beasts in their skies*, she thought, smiling grimly. *A day of note for Tygrish.*

The enormous white bat flew above them, and Vintage found that her eyes were drawn to it again and again. Her fur was blindingly white in the sunshine, making Vintage think of Noon's old friend Fulcor, yet there the resemblance mostly ended. Windfall's eyes glittered dark blue, like the night sky caught in glass, and the translucent folds of skin between her wings held a bluish tinge too. Everything of her spoke of ice and snow, of long, lethal winters, yet here she was under the relentless Jarlsbad sun. Every war-beast was a wonder, of course, but something about this one made Vintage uneasy. Her fragile link with Helcate suggested that he was also uncertain about this newest sibling, and the fact that she was bat-shaped felt especially ominous. What sort of forces were at play when a war-beast happened to take the same shape as the symbol of the Winnowry – an organisation her bonded partner was a member of? *It's just a coincidence*, she told herself. *You have seen paintings of war-beasts shaped like giant bats before.* Even so, she couldn't help feeling like everything had suddenly become more complicated.

The city itself was beautiful and busy, a thing of white walls and green-topped towers. There were several gates leading in from the land bridges that Vintage could see, and an elaborate system of viaducts sent water all across the city. Much of it was familiar to her from her travels through Jarlsbad, but this far east there were enough differences that she found herself itching to make notes; the roofs of the towers were different shapes; there were fewer church buildings that she could see, and a great many more flags, long pennants in all colours. As they approached the palace itself, a tall central building with towers like flutes, Vintage noticed that here the flags were all shades of green, and each carried an image of a bat, drawn in white. She frowned at that, and glanced over at Chenlo, but the other woman was sitting low over her own bat, her face drawn and tense. One of the tallest towers, she noticed, had wooden scaffolding clinging to the top like a precarious web; it looked as though a set of windows was in the middle of being expanded to a proper, war-beast-sized entranceway.

Presently, the bats escorting them began to lose height, and they all landed together in a paved courtyard behind the palace walls, dotted with small fruit trees. A handful of guards came out to meet them, dressed in the flowing robes typical of Jarlsbad, although Vintage noted each also wore a green sash with the white bat emblazoned on it. Agent Kreed climbed down from her bat and began ordering them about, while Windfall only alighted on the ground briefly before taking back off into the air. Vintage lifted her head and watched her go, noting that she flew to the towers and disappeared into the hole she had spotted earlier.

'You. Hand over any weapons.'

Vintage looked down into the face of one of the other agents, an older woman with brown hair going grey at the temples.

'We're not here to fight you, darling.'

The woman raised an eyebrow. 'And we're not here to set you on fire. So how about you don't give us any reason to?'

Vintage sighed heavily and unstrapped her crossbow from her belt. She felt a real tremor of dismay when she handed it over – her companion over so many years, so many travels – but, she reminded herself, both Chenlo and Helcate were living weapons. After giving up Chenlo's bat to the guards, Kreed led them within the palace itself, and they were soon marched down wide, echoing passages lined with gently curving archways. The floors were covered in delicate mosaics constructed of tiny pieces of orange, brown and black clay, and tall, elegant vases stood in every corner, yet Vintage also spotted signs that the palace had recently seen trouble. Black marks that looked very much like burns could be seen on the walls, and there were dents in the floor that indicated something heavy had landed there. This time she did catch Chenlo's eye, and she caught the tiniest nod in response. The Tygrish royal family had fought desperately to retain their property, and lost.

Eventually, they were led, to Vintage's surprise, into a wide interior garden. There were neat green lawns, and more fruit trees, and ornate benches scattered about. At the end of the central path, lined with a mosaic that glittered under the sun, was a raised dais and a throne. Sprawled on it, with one leg hooked over an arm, was a very familiar figure.

'Hello, ladies.' Tyranny gestured lazily to Chenlo. 'Seize that woman immediately.'

'Wait!' Vintage came forward, her hands held up, but Kreed shoved her back. 'There's no need for any of that!'

Three guards approached them, and Vintage belatedly noticed that they all wore gloves up to their elbows. They grabbed Chenlo and forced her arms behind her back none too gently.

'You will both kneel to Queen Tyranny,' snapped Kreed.

'I will do no such thing,' said Chenlo in a low, even voice, but the guards forced her down onto the path while birds chirped from the fruit trees. Kreed made as if to do the same to Vintage, but she shook her head and got to her knees, cursing Tyranny and all of Sarn for this nonsense. Helcate remained where he was, watching silently, and Vintage took a moment to be glad that they weren't forcing him to kneel too; that could end badly.

'It's good to see you again, Helcate,' said Tyranny, cheerily enough. 'Last time I saw you, you were some sort of terrible monster in the night, spitting acid all over us. But in the daylight, you actually look like a big scruffy dog.' She grinned. 'I've kicked better-looking strays than you on the streets of Mushenska.'

'Hel*cate*,' said Helcate.

Tyranny, Vintage noted, had changed a little herself. Her white-blond hair had grown long and messy on top, although it seemed she was still shaving the sides, and her neck and a small portion of her right cheek were discoloured – a darkish purple colour, very striking against her pale skin. Vintage pursed her lips, remembering how Helcate's acid had spattered across her clothes and throat, sending up an oily smoke and leaving the woman bellowing with pain. *Curse our luck*, she thought, a sinking feeling in her gut. *Resentment for that injury could change everything.*

She was also much better dressed than when Vintage had seen her last. She wore blue silk robes, and there were several chains studded with glittery jewels strung around her throat. Across her forehead there was a thin gold band, similar to the one Windfall wore, and her fingers too were thick with rings. Despite all this, there were still some nods to the practical in Queen Tyranny's outfit; she wore a thick leather belt at her waist, which cinched in the robes and carried several knives that did not look at all ornamental, and her feet were clad in soft leather shoes, laced up to the knee.

'Lord Helcate has some unusual talents,' said Vintage evenly, reaching up to pat the curly fur on the war-beast's neck. 'And his siblings value him greatly.'

Tyranny ignored this thinly veiled threat and tipped her head to one side, smiling at Chenlo.

'Wasn't it a war-beast that destroyed your cosy little club, Chenlo? How are you coping without your precious Winnowry? Without your precious girls?'

'It was Lady Noon who destroyed the Winnowry,' said

Chenlo, her voice still even, devoid of emotion. 'And it was not to last. It chose to make you an agent, Fell-Tyranny, and such decisions only revealed the poison at the heart of it.'

Tyranny's mouth twitched, the smile dropping away. Vintage stood up hurriedly, raising her voice.

'Queen Tyranny, we are here to talk to you about the war-beast known as Windfall, and about the Jure'lia threat. You must realise –' she forced herself to take a breath – 'you must have known, darling, that this conversation would come up eventually? You stole from Ebora. There will be consequences.'

Tyranny laughed at that, apparently delighted. She pulled her leg down from the arm of the chair and leaned forward, her elbows resting on her knees.

'Do you understand what I've done, Lady de Grazon? I have done the bloody impossible. I hatched the war-beast pod myself, with my own hands. I pulled that war-beast free and I held her in my arms and told her her name, and then I fed her and kept her close to me. I raised her from a tiny thing, and made her strong. Windfall is mine, and I am hers.' The mocking smile shivered on her lips, then reasserted itself. 'Together, we came to Tygrish and we saw the stupid people who were in charge, saw the riches that were here, and we bloody took it. Because we could. And now we are queens of Jarlsbad.' She grinned, leaning back on her throne. Sunlight glinted in shards off the jewels around her neck. 'I'm a fucking queen, *Lady* de Grazon.'

'You murdered the royal family here?' Vintage let the question hang lonely in the air. Out of the corner of her eye, she watched to see if the guards reacted, but they stood still, their faces impassive. Tyranny shrugged.

'They're in prison. They haven't even left the palace. The people of Tygrish like their history, so I've kept it for them, but they also like to be safe.' She nodded up at the sky, which was currently clear and blue and blameless. 'They have their

180

own war-beast, one who sees Tygrish as her own personal property. Who is safer during this Rain, I ask you?'

Vintage shook her head in disbelief. 'You mean to hold off the Jure'lia by yourself? I know you're not stupid, Tyranny . . .'

'You will address the queen as your majesty,' put in Kreed. Vintage made a strangled noise.

'*Your Majesty* is not, I know full well, a dim-witted fool – she must be one of the most cunning and tricksy thieves I have ever had the misfortune to meet –' Kreed muttered at this, but Vintage ignored it. 'Yet you think you will be safe here? The war-beasts work as a team. As an army. You know this. All of Sarn knows it. You must allow Queen Windfall to return to her rightful home so that she may help to protect it. To protect us all!'

'And leave Tygrish open to attack?'

'All of Sarn is in danger,' said Vintage quickly. 'Or do you mean open to attack by neighbouring kingdoms of Jarlsbad who might like to see their relatives back on the throne?' She sensed Chenlo looking at her, but she didn't dare make eye contact with the woman. She was being too forthright, and she knew it.

'Send Windfall home, to a place she has never known? To be without me, the only human who has ever cared for her?' Tyranny looked away across the rows of fruit trees, as if truly considering it as an option. The garden was baked with heat, protected as it was from the winds by four tall walls, yet Tyranny looked entirely at her ease, her brow smooth and free of sweat. 'Why don't we ask her?'

She whistled, a quick, trilling note a little like that used by the Winnowry to summon their own bats. Vintage looked up. A huge white shape emerged from the tower and began to slowly spiral down towards them, leathery wings spread. The blue of the skin and the blue of the sky were too similar, and she blinked rapidly, trying to make sense of it. It was like a ghost was floating down towards them.

However, when Windfall landed just behind Tyranny's throne, there was no doubt of her solidity. On the ground she looked muscled and powerful, and even a touch larger than Helcate, Vintage noticed.

'Windfall,' Tyranny gestured to where Vintage stood, and Chenlo still knelt. 'These people have come to talk to you about returning to Ebora.'

Vintage cleared her throat, and sketched a quick bow. 'Your Majesty, Queen Windfall, I am Lady Vincenza 'Vintage' de Grazon and I come as an envoy for Ebora, your birthplace.'

'I was born on the plains.' The giant bat's voice was sharp, strident almost. Vintage nodded rapidly.

'Of course, Your Majesty, but your pod was birthed from Ygseril the tree-father.'

'I don't care for trees.'

'You will not know, because you and your siblings were born without your root-memories, but it is the birthright of all war-beasts to share a bond and fight together against a common enemy.'

The bat sat up on her haunches, and dropped her wide mouth open. Vintage had a moment to contemplate the alarming array of jagged teeth on display, when the creature's throat began to glow from within.

'Wait!'

It was too late. A column of blinding blue and white light shot from Windfall's gaping maw and struck the ground between Chenlo and Vintage. Instantly, Vintage felt her entire left side grow stiff, rigid with cold, and the breath seemed to freeze in her lungs. She fell awkwardly onto the ground, where she saw rimes of frost growing across the tiny mosaic tiles. She gasped, and saw her own breath in a white cloud.

'You don't tell me what to do,' said Windfall. 'I am a queen.'

'Damn right,' said Tyranny, clearly very pleased with herself.

'You can't just waltz into our kingdom and start ordering us about, Lady de Grazon.'

Vintage opened her mouth, suicidally intent on telling Queen Tyranny to cram her kingdom up her arse, but the words were strangled in her throat. Something warm nudged at her neck, and she reached up and stroked Helcate's snout. *Don't do anything*, she warned him, hoping he would understand. *Darling, don't fight her, not yet. We're outnumbered.*

With some difficulty, Vintage turned her head to look at Agent Chenlo. The woman was still kneeling, although now her head hung down, and her black hair was white with ice.

'The nice thing about being a queen,' said Tyranny, adjusting the gold circlet on her head, 'is that I get to employ lots of fancy advisors now. It's like your second hands when you're running a gang, only they talk fancier and are less worried about offending you. I think, Queen Windfall, we should ask one of our advisors what to do with our visitors.'

There was a small flurry of movement as someone was summoned from within the building. Vintage lifted her head and straightened her shoulders; some of the stiffness was easing out of her body, but, she reminded herself, she hadn't even been hit by the beam of cold directly. Windfall's talent would be formidable on the battlefield. *If she was on the right bloody side.*

A figure approached the throne, initially difficult to make out in the bright sunshine. She wore a loose silk shirt with a hood that covered her long black hair, and she was tall and long-limbed. There was a small pair of spectacles on a long gold chain around her throat, and she was Eboran. Abruptly Vintage found that her legs were full of strength again, and in an instant she was on her feet.

'They are dangerous,' said Nanthema, her voice calm and devoid of any emotion. 'I wouldn't trust them. You can hide them in the deepest cells, but it might be simpler to have them killed.'

'You absolute cow!' Vintage took a step forward, and Kreed's hand was on her shoulder immediately. 'You scheming, lying, untrustworthy, rotten, feckless creature! I should have left you in that fucking Behemoth to rot.'

Tyranny was laughing, tipping her head back so her blond hair flashed in the sun. 'Take them each to a cell. We'll have to find something special for the war-beast.'

Vintage spun and sent a single thought to Helcate – *fly!* She felt him hesitate, wanting to take her with him, but there were guards swarming them already, men and women in tough leather armour, and several of them carried a huge muzzle.

'Go!'

Helcate leapt. There was a terrible moment when one especially burly guard leapt for his back leg and dragged him back down, but the war-beast shook him off and, after bouncing somewhat less than gracefully off the courtyard wall, turned and flew up into the clear blue sky. Vintage watched him go with a strange combination of despair and triumph like a hard knot in her chest. The great bat unfurled her wings again, her blue eyes intent on the retreating figure.

'Never mind,' shouted Tyranny, looking at Windfall then back to the guards. She had stood up and was brushing a fine layer of dust from her robes. 'Let the runt go. His acid will have little effect on my palace walls, after all. Put the other two below.'

Swallowing down her own anger, Vintage forced herself to speak in a level tone. 'This is unnecessary, Your Majesty. We're not here to fight you, or to steal away Queen Windfall. We're just here to talk to you.'

'Fell-Tyranny does not talk,' said Chenlo. The ice had melted on her hair and she stood with two guards at her side, each wearing long gloves and masks. 'She just takes what she wants, because that's all she's ever known.'

'Well, thank you very much for that diplomacy,' hissed Vintage, but it was too late. The guards were dragging them towards an archway leading off from the courtyard, and Tyranny herself was walking casually away, stretching her arms above her head as if she'd just done a good morning's work. Before they were moved to the dark interior of the palace, Vintage managed to get one last look at Nanthema. The Eboran woman's red eyes returned her gaze without a flicker of shame, and then she was lost to sight.

Chapter Seventeen

'So. Tell me about your childhood.'

'What?'

Noon looked up from the plate of pastries. She had slept overnight in the entrance to the castle, under the stars but still within the strange cocoon of warmth that surrounded the glass castle. When she had complained of being thirsty and hungry this morning, She Who Laughs had produced breakfast out of apparently thin air – cheese and delicate pastry twists, berry preserves and a large jug of clear water. She didn't ask where it came from. For a being who could inhabit different bodies at will, she supposed that sourcing breakfast from miles away was easy enough.

'It's important. For the figuring out.' They sat again in the courtyard of bones, and the square slice of sky above them was a hot flat blue. She Who Laughs was still in the body of the dark-haired round woman, and the crown of green fire cast lively shadows against the glass. 'You're from the plains,' she prompted.

'I'm from the plains,' repeated Noon. 'When I was eleven the Winnowry took me from there, and then I spent the rest of my childhood in one small cell in a big tower full of miserable people.'

'That is a summary,' said She Who Laughs. 'I want details. Did you have brothers or sisters? What were your parents like? What are your clearest memories?'

'I don't have time for this.' Noon gulped down a mouthful of water, and shook her head. 'I'm supposed to be fighting a war, not having a cosy little chat about people who are – people I haven't seen for a very long time.'

She Who Laughs didn't respond. Instead, she shifted so that her short brown legs were folded under her, and she interlaced her fingers in her lap. Noon chewed down another bite of pastry, then sighed noisily.

'I didn't have any brothers or sisters. My father died not long after I was born, and I don't remember him.'

'How did he die?'

'It's not an easy life out on the plains. He fell from his horse on a hunting expedition and broke his neck. My mother told me he was a good man, but reckless with his riding. He trusted his horse, and his horse trusted him, but the ground wasn't in on the deal. He was chasing something down and didn't see a hole in the ground. The horse broke its leg, too.'

'And your mother? How did she die?'

Noon blinked. 'How do you know my mother is dead?'

She Who Laughs tipped her head to one side. 'What do you remember of your earliest childhood?'

Somewhere outside the castle, the wind was picking up, and it sang through the empty battlements like a lost spirit. Noon looked down at her hands, at the buttery pastry crumbs clinging to her fingers.

'I remember the smell of grass and horses, more than anything,' she said eventually. 'That hangs over every memory. It's on the inside and outside of it, all over.' She had not slept well, and her dreams had been plagued with images of Vostok, frantic and searching, flying over a cold and stormy sea while waves leapt up to lash at her belly. Despite the sand on her skin and the heat beating down on the top of her head, Noon felt as though she hadn't quite escaped those dreams. 'I remember my mother's tent too, full of books, and herbs drying in the roof. It was the one place that didn't smell of horse.'

'There were lots of tents?'

'Lots. We weren't a big group, but each family had a tent, and each family had horses, and a few fleeten that we kept all together in the herd. In the winter we built huge fires to keep the wolves away, and in the summer Mother Fast put on puppet shows at dusk. We had a tent-cat once, but she ran away.'

'The group. Your people. What happened to them?'

Noon looked up sharply. She felt like she'd just been pinched awake. 'What do you mean, what happened to them?'

'Did they travel, your people?'

'With the seasons, we did. There were better places for grazing at different times of the year, and we would seek out the Trick and the Ember too. The other groups would gather there, and when we met up sometimes there would be big festivals.' She smiled, despite herself. 'I remember thinking the other plains people were *so weird*. Their clothes were different, some of them had tattoos. Their voices, too, were strange, and some of them travelled in these huge wheeled carts. There would be fights sometimes, and disagreements, but mostly we would trade with them and drink. Fermented mare's milk, mostly.' She frowned. 'I never liked the smell of it but the children who were older than me, they liked it a lot.'

'What's the last thing you remember of them? Your people?'

Noon paused with a pastry halfway to her mouth. Slowly, she put it back down.

'Why do you want to know all this, anyway? It was a very normal childhood on the plains. Nothing interesting or unusual about it.'

'Is that so?'

She Who Laughs leaned her head back against the courtyard wall, her eyes narrowed like a pleased cat.

'Yes, it is fucking so.' Noon sat up. 'What are you getting at?'

'The last memory you have of them . . .'

'I don't have one. That's the truth of it. There was –' She leaned forward, the skin on the back of her neck prickling with discomfort. 'You clearly know what happened, or you wouldn't be asking. There was an incident. An accident. They died. I killed them. That's it.'

'And the memory.'

'There is none!' Noon stood up, letting the remains of her breakfast fall to the sand. 'I don't remember it, and thank blood and fire I don't. They all died, and then next thing I knew, I was in the hands of fell-witches, being bound for the journey to Mushenska. I don't have any memory of what happened at all.'

'Ah, but we need that memory, Noon.' She Who Laughs unfolded her legs and stood in one fluid movement.

'Why? What possible reason—'

'You have to trust me.'

'Trust you?' Noon threw her hands up into the air. 'The woman who has abducted me to the middle of bloody nowhere? Listen,' she took a breath, trying to calm herself, 'you should just take me back. I'm sorry, really I am, but I genuinely don't remember what happened. There's just a black space where that memory should be. Even if I wanted to tell you, I couldn't. And that's the truth.'

'You're not going anywhere until you tell me.'

The words fell like knives. Noon took a step backwards. Abruptly, her situation seemed precarious, dangerous even. What was she doing here, with this strange woman who called herself a god? This was not where she was supposed to be.

'That's where you're wrong. I can go where I like, actually.'

She bent down and snatched up the last of the pastries, stuffing them inside her jacket heedless of the grease. When that was done she picked up the jug of water, holding it awkwardly by the neck.

'If you go into the desert, you will die,' She Who Laughs said simply.

'Well? What choice do I have, if you won't send me back?'

'Tell me about what happened to your people – your mother – and I will take you back, wherever you want to go.'

Noon turned her back on the woman and walked out of the courtyard. She expected, for a moment, to be turned into a screaming pillar of fire, but She Who Laughs said nothing, and she walked the rest of the way through the glass castle until she came to the arches. The Singing Eye Desert lay beyond, a vast stretch of black sand fading to a brownish white in the distance. The sky was blue and unmarked by clouds, and a shimmering haze lay between the two as the desert slowly baked under the sun. Noon pursed her lips and stepped beyond the threshold. Heat hit her like a physical blow, and she staggered slightly.

'You'll die out there,' said a low voice from behind her. Noon didn't turn, and instead lifted her head and walked straight out into the desert.

Vintage sat and glared around the finely appointed room. As prisons went, it was difficult to imagine a more pleasant one. It had smooth, cream-coloured walls and a worn embroidered carpet on the floor, and it had a few pieces of annoyingly fine furniture; a low bed in the Jarlsbad style, covered with a thin, plain sheet; a small dresser of dark wood, and a heavy pottery sink, glazed blue and white. There was a jug of sweet-tasting water on the dresser and even two small windows in the adjoining walls. They were criss-crossed with thick pieces of black lead and filled with diamond shards of multi-coloured glass, so thick it warped the view beyond. There was a similar one in the locked door, but squinting out of it had revealed very little, save for a well-lit corridor.

She shuffled over to the window in the easternmost wall and rapped on the glass with her knuckles.

'Chenlo? You there?'

There was a beat of silence, and then a blurred shape appeared beyond the glass. Vintage could see the woman's dark hair, and a portion of the eagle tattoo at her throat, twisted and pinched by the window.

'I am here. What do you want?' Her voice was muffled but audible.

'This is going well, don't you think?'

There was a longer period of silence this time. 'Is that supposed to be a joke, Lady de Grazon?'

Vintage sighed and drummed her fingers on the glass. 'You know Tyranny, a little at least. What do you think she will do?'

'She will not keep us down here forever. This is her showing her strength. Demonstrating that she can have us taken out of the game at will. We'll be down here just long enough to make us worried, and then there will be something else.'

'Like what?'

'I don't know. She will likely kill me – she won't want any reminders of the time when she was subordinate to others.' Agent Chenlo's voice was flat and unemotional. 'What she will do with you, I cannot say. You've annoyed her, but she also beat you.' Vintage scowled. 'She would probably enjoy humiliating you some more.'

'Well, that's great news.' Vintage looked away from the little window and cast her eyes around the room, considering. 'The situation here isn't quite what I thought it would be. There are still people going in and out of Tygrish. We saw them on the land bridges. There wasn't a particularly large military presence in the city, no obvious unrest.'

'What's your point?'

'It doesn't look like a city that is shivering under the boot of a dictator, is my point. Of course, appearances can be deceptive.' She tugged at her hair, so wild after days of flying. 'But there are those flags everywhere too, the green ones emblazoned with the white bat. They're not just outside the palace, they're dotted throughout Tygrish.'

'And?'

'It's a time of huge uncertainty for Sarn. We've seen the Jure'lia return. We know that Ebora is dead, or as close to it as makes no difference. What if your royal family have never seen a real war? Certainly never a real Rain. What if in your heart of hearts you believe them to be feckless, a bit useless? Perhaps even a liability? Perhaps then a newcomer might seem like a blessing.'

'Fell-Tyranny is a mad woman. A dangerous and cruel witch.' Through the small warped window, Chenlo shifted on her own bed. 'She is a criminal, not a queen.'

'I'm not arguing that she isn't dangerous. But she's also clever, and adept at spinning yarns.' With bitterness Vintage remembered how she had listened, rapt, to Tyranny's tales of taking rich clients through the Wilds. 'She might have used force to displace Tygrish's rulers, but I strongly suspect it isn't force alone keeping her on that throne.'

'The war-beast.'

'Yes. Such an extraordinary creature, and the first they will have seen here. There can hardly be another status symbol like it.'

'And . . . so? What does all this actually mean?'

Vintage rubbed her hands over her face. Nanthema was here too, apparently in an advisory capacity. That would have leant Tyranny's cause a fair amount of legitimacy too – an actual, living, breathing Eboran standing at her side. She wondered if Nanthema had simply been bought, or if she had decided she couldn't abandon the war-beast pod after all; the woman had been desperate to get out of Ebora, but she had always had a taste for the finer things in life. A position in the court of a newly crowned queen would be tempting.

'It means, darling, that the situation here is vastly more complicated than we initially thought. Tyranny could well have the backing of the people. We came here with the threat of war with Ebora as punishment for stealing their property, but what if Jarlsbad stands behind her? The truth is, Ebora is in no state to fight a war on two fronts. We need Windfall on *our* side, helping to destroy the worm people.'

Chenlo had no response to this. For some time, they sat in silence, separated by the wall. Vintage reached out for Helcate, and felt a thin thread of confusion and alarm from him. Their connection was still so delicate, so newly forged, that this violent separation had scattered it, like dry leaves blown by autumn winds. With everything she had, she sent him comforting feelings, a reminder that he was not alone.

Stay close, but stay safe, she told him, not knowing if he would hear it or not. *Be wary of the long grass beyond the city walls, it hides Wild-touched creatures. And darling, remember your family are still with you. Vostok, Sharrik, Jessen, Kirune. They are all out there somewhere, waiting for us to rejoin them.*

'That other woman who was there. The Eboran.' Chenlo's voice was careful now. 'You had quite the reaction to her. There is a history between the two of you, yes?'

Vintage half laughed, surprised by the sting of pain in her chest at the reminder. 'Nanthema and I were lovers, once. That all ended rather spectacularly, though, when she helped Tyranny and Okaar rob us blind.'

'Oh.' There was another long silence. 'I see.'

Vintage raised an eyebrow, but before she could say more, a narrow slot in the door rattled open, and a bowl of stew appeared. Vintage jumped off the bed and scrambled to the door to take it, peering out through the slot as she did so. She caught sight of a slim brown hand, a flash of black hair.

'I wanted to see if it was really you,' came a cool voice from outside. 'If you'd really be stupid enough to come here.'

'Who is that? Jhef?'

The girl dipped into sight, smiling. She wore a silver clip at her ear, studded with blue gems.

'Why did you come here? She's quite happy, you know, playing the queen. You've just given her another way to demonstrate her power.'

'Jhef, darling, we had no choice. You know what you stole from us. Did you really think it would be without consequences?'

'What, consequences like you ending up in a cell?'

Teenagers, thought Vintage, rolling her eyes. 'You still serve her then? You and your brother?'

It was difficult to see the young girl through the narrow slot, and now she seemed to move away. The corridor was quiet, no sounds of guards talking or marching, and with a lurch Vintage remembered how she had last seen Okaar; badly wounded, barely conscious.

'Jhef? Is Okaar . . . ?'

'Tyranny is going to kill you both. Maybe not publicly, because these Tygrish people don't seem to have the taste for it. Quietly, she'll do it, but not too quietly. You know what she's like.'

Vintage leaned down closer to the slot, trying to get a proper look at the girl. The Jhef she remembered hadn't seemed especially bloodthirsty, but then, things changed.

'Why hasn't she done it already? Why not just kill us in your courtyard, in that case?'

'Oh, she needs time to think of a really *good* way.'

And with that Jhef was gone from sight, her footfalls as quiet as a cat's.

Chapter Eighteen

In the dream, Tor was standing underneath a night sky so huge it was frightening; a terrible black void lit with a multitude of uncaring stars. He was in a vast desert, grey sands stretching away to all sides, and Noon lay at his feet, curled up on one side like a sleeping child. There was a small fire burning low next to her, and she shivered violently in her sleep, as though she were dreaming of something unspeakable.

'Noon,' he said. 'I miss you.'

She had covered herself with her jacket. There was an empty glass jug sitting incongruously by the fire, and several severed pieces of some sort of plant. Odd dream details. The mind was strange, sometimes.

'I'd burn the bloody tree down myself if I thought it would bring you back,' he said quietly. 'Everything is so hopeless anyway, why shouldn't we be happy for a bit? We could have done that, couldn't we? I think so. It would have been messy, but . . . Instead my mind gives me this.' He gestured around at the dream desert, the dream sky. 'A fucking *dream* of you. As if that would be enough.'

Far on the horizon, a sinister green glow was bleeding up into the night, like some sort of eldritch sunset, and there was a sense of being watched; as though just out of sight something was observing him, or observing Noon. There were strange fleshy white plants dotted here and there, looking far too much like grasping corpse hands for comfort. Tor could not recall ever travelling across a place like it. His unconscious mind appeared to have crafted its eerie landscape to reflect his mood.

'What a shit hole.'

Noon shifted again in her sleep, hands grasping at nothing, and suddenly it was just too painful to look at her face, the black hair messy across her forehead and her skin greyish in the starlight . . .

He woke up sprawled in a chair, a half-empty bottle of wine propped in his lap. The surge of anguish in his throat had woken him, almost choking him, and then he realised that it was a real, physical pain, splitting his chest in two.

Crying out, Tor lurched from the chair and fell to the floor, wine bottle spinning away under a table. On his hands and knees the pain spread through him like a fire, searing down his arms and into his stomach. The place on his arm where the red threads had first started to show throbbed with particular agony.

He curled up on his side, much as Noon had been doing in his dream, and waited for it to pass. When finally the agony began to fade, he was covered in a fine sweat, and his muscles were twitching and cramping. There was, he belatedly realised, early morning daylight coming in through the tall windows, and he was not in his own room at all, but the office lately shared by Vintage and Aldasair. The desk was still littered with papers and the faintly glowing amber slabs.

'Ah. Good. Great.' He crawled to his feet and pushed his lank hair out of his face with trembling fingers. 'Exactly where I need to be. Well done me.'

There was a full bottle of wine on the desk, so he opened it and filled a tall goblet, which he stood and drank down in one go. *A tonic*, he told himself, *for my pains*. When that was gone he poured a fresh glass, and began to run his free hand over the amber tablets, considering. At first, he had been vaguely methodical about it, trying to figure out if the tablets had been created in any sort of order, taking note of which Rain they depicted, and which war-beasts and Eboran heroes Micanal had taken time to recreate. Vintage and Aldasair had already made notes, and he had read through those too, at first. It was diverting.

But just lately he had found himself picking up the tablets at random, dipping in and out of the crafted memories they contained. He stopped making notes, or even taking much notice of what was happening around him while he dream-walked within the tablets. It was enough to be somewhere else; some*when* else. In this glorified past of Ebora there was no Jure'lia – not one that was a real threat, anyway – and no humans, no dead witches and no crimson flux. The glory of Ebora was real, within Micanal's vision, and not a sad experiment conducted by beings who didn't even really care about the results. Within the amber record, the world was as it should be.

'Why would I ever want to leave it?'

He picked up one of the amber tablets, and took it back to the chair where he'd been sitting before, pausing to set down the glass goblet on a side table. There was a clatter at the door, and Aldasair strode in. He looked preoccupied and his arms were full of the tubes that carried messages from across Sarn, but when he spotted Tor, he stopped, his eyebrows raised.

'There you are! Kirune has been looking for you, cousin.' Tor saw Aldasair looking at the open wine bottle, the full glass on the side table, the splashes of wine on the floor. It was also possible, he considered, that his cousin was noticing his crumpled clothes and unwashed hair. He straightened up, half hiding the amber tablet behind his back.

'I've been searching through the amber record for useful information,' he said.

'Is that what you've been doing?' Aldasair looked doubtfully at the mess on the table, then carefully put the pile of letters in the one unoccupied space. 'If that were the case, that would be very useful. Because things are bad, Tormalin, very bad, and I need your help.'

'Everything is bad all the time,' Tor said, turning away to look out the window instead. It looked to be another bright morning. 'What can I do about it?'

Aldasair hissed between his teeth, such an unusual gesture for him that Tor turned back, surprised.

'What can you do? Be ready to fight, to lead. Stop drinking yourself into oblivion and get your head out of those stones. We both know you're not doing any actual research in there.'

Tor bristled. 'I'll have you know I have been very thorough . . .'

'Nonsense. You are mooning about in there looking at pretty things.'

'Al . . .' Tor frowned. His normally placid cousin had two spots of bright colour on his cheeks, and his eyes were too bright. 'It cost us a lot to find that record, I refuse to just ignore it.'

'You left us before,' said Aldasair shortly. 'Went off into the world because everything was hopeless here, and spent your time drinking and pleasing yourself. Do you think I've forgotten that?' He gestured to the wine bottle. 'You have lost hope, so you are doing it again.'

'Hope, cousin, was always something we were in very short supply of.'

'I am sorry, I should have been more specific. Noon, you have lost Noon, so you are back to your old habits.'

Tor found he had nothing to say to that. Aldasair shook his head, dismissing him, and turned back to the letters. 'We are getting reports in from all over Sarn of new Jure'lia attacks.

The small grace period Bern and Vintage bought us with their tricks is over, it seems.' He scattered pieces of parchment on the table, and then rolled a long map over the top, which he began scratching at with a leaky pen. Despite himself, Tor moved to stand at his shoulder, watching. 'They are focussing on small settlements and towns, all over – the Reilans and Catalen, the Elru valleys – and each attack features a set of three Behemoths, led by an Eboran woman riding a dark dragon.' He coughed lightly into his hand. 'I think we can guess who that is. These aren't huge losses, but she's working her way up. Do you see?' He scratched several crosses on the map, obliterating settlements with unfamiliar names: Boritnor, Dawnhaven, Kotrafen, Hope's Lease. 'Small places, but prosperous. Surrounded by successful farms and productive land, even mines and lakes. And all of it, Hestillion covers with varnish. She is very meticulous about it. Here, look.' He picked up another brush from the table and dipped it in a small pot of dark orange ink. With this he began to daub sprawling shapes across the map. 'These are the places she has covered with varnish. Do you see what she's doing?'

Tor pressed his fingers to his temples. The wine had sent a pleasant warmth through his aching limbs but it had also dispatched a couple of daggers to dig behind his eyeballs.

'I don't know. Being the worst sister imaginable?'

Aldasair pushed a loose lock of auburn hair back behind his ear. 'In previous Rains, the Jure'lia attacks were more or less random. They went where they wanted, attacked whatever happened to be there. Sometimes they would concentrate on quite innocuous targets, allowing our armies to gain serious ground.'

'Have you been at Vintage's books?'

'This, however, indicates a pattern. Hestillion is deliberately targeting places she knows she can take, and which provide a great deal of food and supplies for Sarn in general. Tor, these places are far away, yes, but eventually the enormous loss of farmland is going to have an impact on us. At the moment we import almost everything, remember. And when we start to go hungry, we get weak. All of Sarn will become weak, less able to fight. All the people who have come here to help will go hungry too. Which is exactly what she wants.'

Tor leaned over the desk, peering at the map. 'What about wine supplies? How are they doing?'

Aldasair abruptly turned on him, his eyes wild, and for a strange moment Tor was sure he was going to strike him.

'Cousin!' He held up his hands. 'I'm sorry. You know I make terrible jokes, and at the worst of times.' With a surge of dismay he saw that Aldasair was trembling, and the hectic colour had vanished from his cheeks. *If he has come down with the crimson flux too, we truly are doomed.* 'What is it, Al? What's wrong?'

The younger man's shoulders dropped. 'Bern. He is in so much pain, all the time, and it's only getting worse. Now that the Jure'lia seem to be split, his connection to them is even more chaotic. He barely sleeps, so I barely sleep . . .' He turned back to the letters on the desk, and touched one with his long fingers. 'All these reports, Tor, are terrifying. Every one of them is begging for help, and what can we do? We are a tiny resist-ance barely clinging to life, half afraid to leave Ygseril in case Hestillion attempts to destroy him.'

'I don't think she will do that, at least,' said Tor quietly. 'That abomination she calls a war-beast is as connected to the tree-father as the rest of them, and will die just as quickly if Ygseril falls.'

Aldasair continued as if he hadn't heard him. 'And we're missing half our forces. We've had no word from Vintage or Chenlo, Vostok is out searching for Noon again, and Noon . . .' He stopped, and briefly squeezed Tor's arm. 'And Noon is lost to us. We cannot face the Behemoths with just the six of us, but Tormalin, if I must read another letter detailing these

201

horrors, I think I might actually lose my mind. Again.' He half smiled at his own weak joke. 'What can we do? I am at my wit's end.'

Tor looked at the map, at the letters scattered across the desk. He dearly wished that Aldasair had not come in here, had not shown him these things. It was significantly harder to ignore the heavy weight of despair in his chest when the evidence of their doom was laid out in front of them.

'We shall think of something, Al.' He grasped his cousin's shoulder and squeezed. 'We're not giving up just yet, I promise you. I am going to go outside and get some air – I've been in this room too long – and I'll go and speak to Kirune. Perhaps the war-beasts have some ideas.'

Aldasair nodded, smiling hesitantly, and Tor left him there, rifling through letters. Once out in the corridor he headed not towards the gardens or the main courtyard, but to an old suite he knew to be empty. Inside, it was dusty, the thick embroidered curtains still pulled across the tall windows, and there was no wine, but here at least he could be fairly certain Aldasair wouldn't think to look for him. He slipped the amber tablet from his pocket and lay down on the musty bed. The glories of ancient Ebora were waiting.

This land was a land of smouldering fires and steaming forests, of black soil and hot, flat skies.

Vostok did not like it.

The fire was not clean and bright like her fire, or even strange and unsettling like Noon's fire; it was smoky and constant, filling the air with a dark taste and staining the sunsets strange, violent colours. The black mountain responsible for the fire burst up through the middle of the green forests, and the closer she got the more she felt the heat of it pushing against her wings, carrying her easily up and up. Rivulets of molten rock, bright red and orange, moved slowly down the mountain, oozing from its broken peaks and chasms almost lazily.

It was hot here. That was the point. She knew, was almost certain, that wherever Noon was, she was too warm, so it made sense to go to the hottest places. This place, south and east of Ebora, was so hot it was like moving through soup, yet her sense of Noon had grown no sharper, and her repeated calls to her still went unanswered.

Bright weapon, where are you? Can you hear me?
Nothing.

Sometimes, however, she became convinced that Noon was actually really cold, that she was lying somewhere shivering. At those times Vostok would feel her heart beating faster, almost panicked, because none of this made any sense. And if it made no sense, there was a chance – no, it was not a worthy thing to think about.

She banked low over a thick cloud of treetops and came upon a human settlement. There was a tower of dark orange clay, and branching off from it a tall wall of the same substance. Within that, she could make out a busy village, various cooking fires adding to the general smokiness of the area, and there were people patrolling the walls. All of them, now, were looking at her, their eyes and mouths round like moons. Pleased, she spread her wings wide and did a slow loop in the air, letting them see the full glory of her brilliant scales and her glorious feathers. Voices were raised in welcome and she saw more people waving at her from the top of the tower. None of those she could see were Noon.

Regardless, she flew closer, watching with faint amusement as the humans gathered on the smooth top of the tower scattered backwards, not quite daring to get so close. Delicately, she landed on the very edge, grasping with her claws – she wasn't sure she would fit on the platform without knocking a few of the humans off.

'I'm looking for someone,' she called to them. 'A fell-witch, you would call her.'

There was a great deal of talking amongst themselves, and then a tall man with bright yellow hair was pushed out of the crowd as a general spokesperson. He wore only loose cotton trousers and a thick leather belt, and he had a beard, like the human Bern, although he wasn't nearly as large or as impressive. Vostok sniffed.

'Greetings, glorious one!' The man's voice wavered, and she saw him clear his throat and try again. 'Greetings, and welcome to our home, glorious one! Can we – can we help you?'

Vostok twitched her tail, feeling it slap against the surprisingly cool clay. Did humans need everything repeated to them? It was very tiresome.

'Do you have any fell-witches here? Has a woman recently arrived? She is young, with black hair. She is kin to me.'

The man looked blank, and on the back of that, worried. 'No, great one. All fell-witches . . . Fell-witches are taken by the Winnowry as soon as they are discovered.'

'Yes, I know that,' snapped Vostok. Perhaps this was, after all, the wrong kind of heat. Too wet, too cloying. There was no moisture where Noon was. 'This one has already been to the Winnowry, and left it. And the Winnowry is no more,' she added, with some satisfaction.

This didn't seem to have the response she had expected from the crowd. Voices were raised, and people were looking at each other in surprise and consternation. While the tall yellow-haired man was considering what to say next, a woman came forward, short and round with so many freckles she almost looked brown all over.

'You have come to fight the worm people though?' she called. 'We saw them, just four nights ago, passing over. They'll come back. You'll stay and fight them with us?'

Vostok shifted on the edge of the tower, her claws digging

great furrows in the soft material. She sensed it would not hold her much longer, and that only added to her irritation.

'Do you have Noon here or not? Noon! Bright weapon! I am here!'

The crowd edged back again, and Vostok thought she recognised new expressions on their faces: fear, confusion, frustration, even annoyance. A flicker of violet fire danced around her teeth.

'But that's your job!' The freckled woman had not moved back with the rest. 'It's what you're supposed to do! How can you let this happen?'

'You know nothing of us, tiny creature. Do not presume to tell me what my "job" is.' Vostok began beating her wings to dismount, and was pleased to see a few of the humans holding up their arms to cover their faces. *I could burn you all now*, she thought, *and it wouldn't matter.* 'Noon is not here. I would feel her if she was.'

She pushed away from the tower, causing several cracks to splinter across the smooth surface of the clay, and then she was in the air again and the faint cries of the humans were nothing to her, already forgotten. What did they know of the duty of a war-beast? Or the bond between her and her companion? She was simply in the wrong place. She would find the hot place that was also sometimes freezing cold, and there she would find Noon.

The bright weapon was not dead. Could not be, because Vostok still felt her within her own heart.

Spreading her wings wide, Vostok turned her back on the burning mountain and headed further south.

Chapter Nineteen

It was a particularly tough plant. That was the only explanation for it.

Noon frowned at her knife, willing it to break the skin, but all it seemed able to do was press a narrow line into the flesh. She took a deep breath, trying to breathe past the throbbing in her head, and redoubled her efforts. Finally, the knife edge sank into the plant, and a thin line of watery liquid oozed up. Noon bent her head to it and licked up what she could – don't waste it, don't waste it – and then got back to sawing the appendage free.

The plant water was thin and tasted awful, but it was better than nothing. The water in her jug had gone alarmingly fast, and each journey to the next plant copse seemed longer and more fraught. It did not help that she was light-headed, and uncertain on her feet. She didn't like to think what would happen if she fell over in this desert.

The plant section free, she sat back on her haunches and sucked at it, gazing blankly out across the sands as she did so. The Singing Eye Desert was, she had decided, pretty dull. Just sand, these plants, lots of sun, and then at night, lots of cold. Even the sky didn't change much; brilliantly blue, no clouds in sight, or pink as the sun sauntered off, or black, when the cold came.

'Fuck this place,' she croaked. 'Fuck it in the ear.'

The taste of the plant water sour in her throat, she closed her eyes and tried to think clearly. 'Targ is to the north,' she said aloud, picturing one of Vintage's maps in her head as she did so. She remembered the mountainous region because it was said to be home to the species of giant bat flown by the Winnowry – home to her old friend Fulcor, or her distant ancestors, at least. To the west was Kesenstan, which had cities and farms and people and *water*. And to the south, she was reasonably sure, was the Thousand Tooth Valley, but she didn't know how far south, or even what was actually there. Vintage had mentioned it once, she was sure of it, but why? '. . . And go far enough south and you get to the plains eventually.'

The thought of the plains was a weight in her chest. She Who Laughs' keen interest in her childhood was unnerving to say the least, and a whole set of memories that she had hidden from all her adult life were trying to resurface; the tent-cat with its soft black fur and the tender pink pads on the bottom of its paws; roasting birds over the communal fire, ten of them at once sometimes, skewered and dribbling hot fat; the sound of her mother's laugh.

She rubbed the sweat from her forehead with the back of her hand, and not for the first time, reached out to Vostok.

Where are you? I've been taken. You need to come and find me.

There was no response, although whether that was simply because she was too far away, or because She Who Laughs was disrupting their bond somehow, she couldn't have said.

'I have to get back. They *need* me.' She didn't even know if they were still alive. When she had been taken, they had been fighting desperately against the Jure'lia. For all she knew, the war could already be over. Aldasair and Bern dead or prisoners. Tor lying broken in the surf, the war-beasts torn to pieces . . .

The plant nub was dry. She threw it on the ground in disgust and then spent some moments picking the knife back up; her fingers weren't working properly. As she started trying to hack off another piece of plant, she was suddenly reminded of the hours after she had escaped the Winnowry; when she and Fulcor had landed on the roof of a tavern and found a little garden there. There had been a tomato plant, covered in ripe fruits, and Noon had picked one and eaten it, her hands still grimy with ash. That tomato . . . a taste like being alive, finally. Like being able to see after years of blindness.

Sitting in the dust of an unfriendly desert, Noon shuddered violently. Abruptly she wanted to cry, and that made her angry enough to be able to cut off several lumps of plant in a row, letting them drop to the black sand in sticky lumps. Viciously she sucked the fluid from them, ignoring the other memories this summoned – *Tor's head bent to her wrist, the slight pressure of his teeth against her skin, and the powerful wave of desire she had felt for him* – before standing up unsteadily and turning to look west. There was another copse in the distance, and gathered around it, a group of the strange long-necked creatures she had first spied from the castle. She had seen signs that they ate these plants – tooth marks in hard, white flesh – and she had entertained many fantasies about blasting one to bits and eating its flesh, but they were twitchy bastards who vanished long before she got in range.

'But I just want to be friends,' she said aloud, staring at the distant beasts. 'Get to know you. Have little chats. Share some manky plant water. Eat you a bit.'

As if in reaction to her imagined feast, her stomach cramped violently, and for a few seconds she was bent at the middle, her head spinning. A few days in the desert, that was all, and she was close to dead.

'So useful,' she muttered as she set the copse behind her and set out west again, 'so useful to be able to summon fire. In this place. Great. Hooray for me.'

Except that wasn't entirely true. When the sun vanished, the temperature dropped, and then being able to summon her winnowfire wasn't just useful, it was life-saving. And even curled around the tiny fire she would wake several times in the night, shivering so hard she had cramps in her legs and back.

As expected, the strange long-necked creatures fled when she was still far enough away that a fireball would do little good, and she plodded the rest of the way with her head down, her eyes on the black sand. When she reached the little copse, she swayed for a moment on her feet, trying to remember what she was doing there, who she was – and then she sat down next to the plants, trying to make the most of the small amount of shade they provided. When she had her breath back and the throbbing headache had quietened a little, she reached down for her knife, ready to harvest more bits of plant – only to find that her knife wasn't there.

She had left it behind, discarded on the hard desert floor back the way she'd come.

A shudder moved through her body, like a sob that had no moisture left to express itself. She would have to go back there, waste what little energy she had left to retrieve the bastard thing. In a sudden movement, she stood up, furious with herself and everything else, and began to half walk, half run back to the small copse of white plants. She had got just beyond the outermost plants when the faint wobbles in her legs became tremors, and the world span around her: the ground beneath her feet was blue, her sky was grey, and then everything was black.

When she came round, it was to a painful burst of green light. Groaning, she pushed her face into the sand, hoping that she could escape her thumping head in more sleep, but a strong hand gripped her shoulder and shook it. With enormous reluctance, Noon opened her eyes and squinted up at the figure that stood over her.

'Look at you,' said She Who Laughs. 'You have fair cooked yourself.'

Noon groaned and sat up. The sun had gone down and the only light was the eerie eldritch crown of flames that flickered around the woman's head. She was crouching next to Noon, no longer in the body of the short, stocky woman; instead she inhabited someone tall and lithe, her hair a listless pale colour. Her cheekbones were stark under her skin.

'My knife.' Noon's voice was a shrivelled thing. 'Was going back. For it.'

'I think you're done out here, don't you? Made your point, whatever it was.'

'My point is. Fuck you.' She coughed. 'I can't do what you want me to do.'

'You didn't even try,' said She Who Laughs. There was a smile in her voice, as though she were talking to a cheeky child who had refused a plate of vegetables. 'If you die out here, Noon – and you will die out here if you stay, I can feel your body breaking itself down as we speak – then you will never be reunited with your precious war-beast, and Sarn will have to cope without you. Normally, that wouldn't mean very much in your little human life, but you've managed to make yourself quite important, haven't you?'

Noon opened her mouth to reply, but her throat was much too dry.

'Come back with me, try to do as I ask, and you may yet return to win your war. If you're not going to do it for me, or yourself, do it for the conflict that is eating your world alive.'

In the silence that followed, a harsh barking sound echoed

across the desert. Whatever it was, it was clearly some distance away, but Noon did not like the wild, hungry sound of it. After a moment, she raised her arm, and She Who Laughs looked down at her. She smiled.

'I will take you back now.'

Vintage shifted on the dresser, pulling her knees up under her elbows and ignoring how the furniture wobbled under her weight.

'Tell me more, darling. I've never been south of the Elru mountain. Didn't think there was much to see there, if I'm truthful.'

The voice on the other side of the tiny window chuckled warmly. 'Perhaps not for a woman as widely travelled as you, Lady de Grazon, but for me it was a wonder.' The prisoner, who had introduced himself as Harlo, tapped on the window. 'I can tell that you have seen the world, handled its trinkets and found them wanting. The beaches of Zanth are covered in scuttling, jewelled crabs, all with the sweetest meat and none of them Wild-touched, can you believe it?'

'Zanth is pretty remote,' said Vintage, nodding. 'A little untouched corner of Sarn. How few those are now. What were you doing there, Harlo? And how did you end up in here?'

'He is a thief.' Chenlo's voice floated across from the other side of the cell. 'I will give you three guesses.'

'There is a little temple to Tomas there, in a clearing in the forest overlooking the beach. There, the monks make these exquisite statues of the prophet, made, they say, with wood that has been blessed by his spirit specifically.' Harlo cleared his throat. 'How that works, I couldn't tell you, but the monks certainly believed it. Believed it enough to sell me a great crate of the things, all earnest and eager for the coins I gave them back. I shipped those blessed statues all the way to Jarlsbad

211

and told people that Tomas's blessing would protect them from the Jure'lia. Sold out in a week.'

Vintage shook her head. 'Desperate people in desperate times.'

'Exactly.' Harlo sounded pleased with himself. 'If you know just the right place to pinch a desperate person, you can get a decent profit from it. I was clearly onto a good thing, so I had a new batch of statues made.'

'From the monks of Zanth?'

'Not as *such*, no. More like some sympathetic tradesmen of Jarlsbad. Ones who, I'm sure, felt the spirit of Tomas moving within them when I offered them a decent chunk of coin for their labours.'

'A thief *and* a con man,' added Chenlo. Vintage flapped a hand dismissively at her unseen associate.

'So why has Tyranny locked you up in here? I'd not imagine her to be one to persecute blasphemy, or even thieves, for that matter.'

'Ah, well, it seems she took exception to me telling everyone that these statues would protect them against the Jure'lia. Apparently, that's her job. Hers and that giant freakish bat of hers.'

Vintage winced. 'Be careful what you say, Harlo. Bats have freakishly good hearing. Still, that is interesting.' She looked away from the small warped window. 'It sounds as though Tyranny is taking her role here seriously.'

'Or,' said Chenlo, 'she is simply taking the opportunity to "throw her weight around", as you might say. She has spent years having to do whatever the Winnowry said. Now she is having fun casting her shackles off.'

'You could be right.' Vintage turned back to the window. 'Queen Tyranny was once one of the most feared gangsters in Mushenska. Did you know that, Harlo?'

'No, I bloody didn't.' Harlo no longer sounded so pleased

with himself. Now he sounded sick. 'Royalty and organised crime. All a shower of bastards, if you ask me.'

Vintage snorted, amused, and then was startled to see her cell door swing slowly open. She had not heard anyone approach, and had not heard the sound of a key in the lock.

'Who is it?' She jumped down from the dresser and approached the door cautiously. A figure stood in the shadows there, coming no further into the room. It wore a dark grey hooded cloak, with most of its face hidden in shadow, and fine, pig-skin black gloves. The rest of the outfit that Vintage could see was made up of soft dark leather, carefully mended and patched. Something about it rang a bell at the back of her mind.

'What is it?' called Agent Chenlo.

'Be quiet.' Vintage took another cautious step forward, but the figure did not move or lift its head. This was not a guard. 'Who are you?'

The hood shifted as the figure tilted his head to one side. 'I cannot be here long, and I cannot move as fast as I once could. I . . . helped you find a masterpiece once, Lady Vintage.'

'Okaar?' She came towards him but he stepped back. All of his old fluid grace was gone. Now he moved with caution and pain. 'You are alive, then.'

'More or less.' He nodded and she caught a glimpse of his face; no longer bearded and smooth, but deeply scarred. Helcate's acid, Vintage remembered. It had left his face a purple, rigid ruin.

'Are you here to kill me for her, Okaar?'

He laughed, a quick, choked noise. 'She does not even know I am in the palace, Lady Vintage. Over the course of her little adventure here, we fell out. I thought it best to make myself scarce before she . . . made me scarce herself.' He leaned back cautiously and looked down the corridor. 'The guards here are slack, and they have many breaks.'

213

'You objected to her plans?' Vintage put her hands down by her sides. She found she was filled with the urge to push back his hood and take his face in her hands, as if she could heal it herself.

'I felt that stealing control of an entire kingdom was overly ambitious, even for Tyranny. And it is an insult.'

'But you aren't from Jarlsbad.'

'A neighbour,' he said, smiling faintly again. 'But I have family in these kingdoms, family who are close to the royal family. If they fell, their lives would get harder. I wanted to rest, and to hide for a while. We had all been injured, in various ways, and needed to recover properly. With the Winnowry gone, I thought we finally had our chance to be free.' He grimaced. 'But once Tyranny has an idea in her head . . . And being a queen was such an appealing idea, you see.'

'I'm sure it was,' said Vintage dryly. 'So what are you doing, without Tyranny to order you around? What does a masterless assassin do with his time?'

He tipped his head to one side. 'I sharpen my knives, I craft my poisons. In the city of Jarlsbad, I entertain those with the coin and the appetite for unusual pastimes. Those who like to gamble with their lives.' He shrugged a little awkwardly, and Vintage frowned, sure she was missing some hidden meaning. 'It is a very different life.'

'And Jhef? We saw her, she delivered food –'

'I do not have much time, Lady Vintage, and neither do you.' He glanced once more back down the corridor, then came into the room properly for the first time. He took hold of Vintage's hand, and squeezed it. 'She has picked the way that you will die, so prepare yourself. The fell-witch who was taken with you – she is a friend?'

Vintage resisted the urge to shrug. 'She is an ally, at least.'

'Take this.' From within his cloak he produced something wrapped in cloth, no longer than the palm of his hand. He passed it to her. 'Get your fell-witch friend to drink what is within, just before. It might help.'

She blinked at this strange instruction, before shaking her head. 'I can't trust you,' she said, half regretfully. 'You must know that, my darling?'

He grinned, and there was a flash of the handsome man she remembered. 'Why should you? Who, by Sarn's bloodied bones, trusts an assassin?'

He turned to go, and suddenly Vintage found that the little cell was not so cosy. She followed him to the door.

'If you want to help, why don't you get us out of here? You can unlock the doors and we'll make a break for it.'

He shook his head and pulled at his hood, twitching it to cover more of his face. 'Lady Vintage, it has taken everything I have just to get these to you, and give you these small words. I no longer have the skill or the strength to fight my way past the guards coming back this way. You must fight for yourself. Be ready.'

He shut the door in her face, quite abruptly. Vintage scrabbled at it but the locks had already slid back in place, and when she peered through the food slot, she could see nothing at all – only a slightly darker patch of shadow at the far end of the corridor. And then that was gone too.

'Who was that?' demanded Chenlo through her small window. 'An associate of Tyranny's?'

'It was Okaar, the assassin your Winnowry assigned to keep an eye on her. Another brilliant decision from them, it has to be said.' Vintage took the package over to the bed, ready to shove it under a sheet should a real guard suddenly appear. 'If they've really fallen out, it could explain Tyranny's unchecked megalomania. I always got the impression that he was her voice of reason.'

'And what was it he gave you?'

Vintage peeled back the cloth and unwound the package.

215

The material itself appeared to be a bar towel from The Shining Coin, which surprised a smile out of her; she knew it well – everyone who travelled through Jarlsbad knew it. The Shining Coin was an enormous pleasure palace within the central kingdom, dedicated to alcohol, dancing, and above all else, gambling. The name of the establishment was printed across the material, with its sigil beneath; the Jarlsbad symbol for luck, which looked a little like a bee. Wrapped inside the bar towel were three long vials, each containing a smoky orange liquid with dark inky globules moving through it. They were stoppered at the top with wax and cork. There was also a long, slender key, much too delicate for the locks on their cell doors.

'My darling, I've no fucking clue.'

Later, just as Vintage was beginning to slip into an uneasy sleep on the low, flat bed, the door to her cell opened again, revealing Jhef. This time, however, she was accompanied by a pair of burly guards, and she held her head up straight with no hint of amusement on her finely wrought features.

'Come on,' she said. 'She wants to see you.'

Vintage got off the bed slowly, considering her options. The vials and key Okaar had given her had been concealed inside her shirt, and there was the chance she would be searched by the guards – yet if she left them in the bed, there was also the possibility she wouldn't be returning, and then what use would they be? In the end she went to the door and left with Jhef and the guards, the little package from Okaar feeling heavy against her stomach.

They led her through a series of sharply angled corridors until they came to a set of spiral steps that led up and up, lit with blazing oil lamps that cast buttery light against more of the brightly coloured windows. It was late, and Vintage could see nothing but darkness beyond them.

'So, any clues as to what sort of mood she's in? I don't suppose she's had a change of heart, decided that being a despot is actually too much like hard work and retired to the country?' Vintage watched Jhef's face for a response and was rewarded only with a brief quirk of the eyebrows that she couldn't interpret. When they reached the wide doors at the top of the tower, Vintage felt a slight tremor of panic. No crossbow, no Agent Chenlo, no Helcate. She was completely out of weapons.

'Listen, Jhef darling, whatever conflict there is between your brother and Tyranny, you must know that he still cares about you greatly. Taking her side, well . . .' The guard stepped forward and opened the doors. 'I have siblings too, I know how difficult they can be, but ultimately you will regret –'

Jhef rolled her eyes at this. 'I'd hurry up and get in there, if I were you.'

The girl stayed at the door with the guards, and Vintage walked into a dark circular chamber. After the dazzle of the oil lamps, it was difficult to make out where she was, but as her eyes adjusted she realised she had been quite wrong about the nature of the meeting. There was a huge bowl filled with over-ripe fruit in one corner, and a massive brass basin of water next to it. The topmost edges of the walls were covered in odd implements, hooks and shelves and thick leather straps, and on the far side of the room, the chamber was partially open to the still night air. A huge pale shape shuffled towards her out of the shadows.

'Not too dark for you?' said Windfall. 'I prefer dark. I can see my city better.'

'Your Majesty,' Vintage inclined her head. 'You must have quite a view from up here.'

The war-beast lifted her large, blocky head. 'I can see anything coming. Any enemy. I see it. Tygrish is protected.'

'From most enemies, yes,' said Vintage carefully. 'Your

217

Majesty, there may be some aspects of this war you're unaware of.'

'You suggest I am lacking somehow?'

'No, not at all . . .'

'That Queen Tyranny has kept secrets from me?'

Vintage held her hands up. In the gloom of the tower room, it was possible to see a chilly luminescence at the back of Windfall's throat whenever she spoke.

'You misunderstand me. When you and your siblings were born from the tree-god, it was without your root-memories, a kind of shared family memory that passes down with you throughout your forms. That instinct, if you like, would have given you knowledge of the old enemy, of the Jure'lia. It would have told you how to fight them, how to defeat them. You don't have it, and apart from Vostok, none of your siblings do.'

Windfall did not move. Despite the warm summer night, Vintage felt gooseflesh break out across her arms.

'But they have learned to work together anyway, and have had some success. Ultimately, the bond they share carries them through. It is something . . . it is something you could be a part of.'

'I do not want it,' said Windfall sharply.

'We would not separate you from Tyranny,' Vintage said quickly. 'You have clearly bonded, and that is important. But you are part of a team, Queen Windfall. A family. There is a home for you in Ebora, and a vital connection to those who share your blood.'

'Ebora.' The war-beast raised herself up on her wings. She wasn't wearing her jewelled headband, Vintage noticed. 'Tell me of it.'

'Ah, well.' Vintage cleared her throat, playing for time. 'It's an extraordinary place, a land of lush forests and fearsome mountains, and, of course, the city that sits at the heart of it.

There is no other place like it in Sarn, and believe me, I have seen most of it. Only a place as extraordinary as Ebora could birth someone like yourself, and Ygseril, the tree-father, is a sight perhaps everyone should see once in their lives –'

'Ebora is nothing. Nothing to me. It is laughable, to go back there. An insult, that you insist. Tygrish is ours, our home.'

'Tygrish has belonged to generations of humans before you came along, throwing your weight around.' The bat's mouth fell open a little wider, revealing rows of jagged teeth. Vintage hurriedly continued. 'If you want nothing to do with Ebora, Your Majesty, then why did you wish to speak to me?'

For a long time there was silence. Eventually, Windfall scuffled over to the bowl of fruit, and spent some time with her head bent, noisily chomping her way through the food. Vintage stood and waited, wondering what it all meant, when abruptly Windfall called out to the door.

'Take her back now.'

Jhef had gone, but the two burly guards came back from the doors. As they took Vintage's arm, Windfall's cold voice washed over her.

'I want nothing of Ebora. It is dead.' The munching sounds resumed. 'I do not eat from carrion.'

Tor stood in the midst of the battle, watching with polite interest as clouds of dust and a mist of blood rose around him. The Eboran men and women surrounding him were dressed as warriors at their peak, their enamelled armour glinting in the sunshine, their swords and axes and spears all wickedly sharp and running with ichor, but Tor wore a long sleeping gown, belted at his waist, and he carried only a wine goblet. He sipped at it passively as the chaos boiled around him. There was no real wine here, not in this dreamscape, but he found it pleasing to have it with him nonetheless; it turned out he was quite good at imagining the taste.

War-beasts reared and thundered on all sides, crashing their way through the Jure'lia. A dragon with sapphire scales swept overhead, sending down a beam of yellow fire that seared through the worm people with deadly precision. A great bear stood on its hind legs, jaws open impossibly wide in a bellow of rage that was lost in the general hubbub. Tor waved at him.

A chorus of horns blared into life from behind him, a sound that made all the hairs on the back of his neck stand up, and the great force of Eboran warriors surged forward as one. There were men and women on horseback here too, their faces and clothes not quite as well defined – Micanal, an aristocrat to the last, hadn't quite been able to bring himself to lavish the same attention to detail on the general rank and file of the Eboran army. Ahead of them, the various dreadful creatures of the worm people fell back, and in a little while it was all over. Spider-mothers and burrowers retreated back to the fat grubs that were the Behemoths, and they began to move slowly across the sky – seven of the things, huge and bulbous, all inching in the same direction. As they got further away, they seemed to move faster, until they were little more than dots in the sky.

Tor stood and watched them, as he had watched so many similar scenes before. Always at the end of the battles, the Jure'lia would retreat. All at once they would gather themselves and scarper, like a human woman gathering her skirts and running from a room after a particularly stinging insult. The Eboran army was rejoicing in its victory, with much cheering and singing of songs, but for once Tor found his attention caught by the distant marks in the sky. How often had he watched them do that? Always, always they left that way, retreating to the sky that birthed them . . .

Without really thinking about what he was doing, Tor pulled his consciousness out of the netherdark and awoke, finding himself sitting back in Vintage's study. He blinked rapidly and stood up, brushing himself down absently. He appeared to be covered in a fine layer of dust, and his head thumped in a dry angry way that was either a hangover or another symptom of the crimson flux.

The maps and papers were still flung haphazardly over the desk. Tor pulled a map of Sarn towards him, and with a stick of charcoal taken from a ceramic pot of them, he began to mark little crosses, all across the map. After some minutes of this, he picked up a book from off a nearby table, and consulted that for a while, before adding more crosses.

Eventually, he stopped and looked at what he had made, picking absently at the long length of bandage that covered his left arm from elbow to wrist.

'Always. Always they were heading in the same direction.'

Frowning slightly, he rescued a long thin wooden rule from underneath a pile of papers and spent some time drawing lines across the map.

Again he stopped and looked at it, feeling more and more sober.

Kirune? Kirune, where are you?

There was a moment's stony silence, but Tor could feel the big cat in his bones. Eventually, the rumble of his voice came bouncing back down the strange connection they shared.

You remember I live, then.

Tor rolled his eyes. *Where are you? I need to talk to you.*

In the winter gardens.

The map rolled up under one arm, Tor pulled down his sleeve to cover his bandages and ventured out into the corridors. To his faint embarrassment, it took him a moment to remember where the winter gardens were, but soon he was out under the cloudy sky, wincing at the daylight. The winter gardens were an odd mixture of lawn, stones and evergreens, artfully arranged by the great garden masters of the past, and he found Kirune stretched out on a bed of white stones. Sharrik and Jessen were with him, and Tor felt a flush of shame he didn't understand. How long since he'd seen them all together? Days, at least. He smoothed a hand through his hair and went to them. Kirune lifted his great head, yellow eyes flashing as the pupils narrowed.

'You have come to drink outside?'

Tor bit down his initial reply and brandished the map at them. 'I think I've figured something out, and I wanted to talk it through with someone. Vintage isn't here, so . . .'

'I have little time for maps,' boomed Sharrik. The big griffin was sitting on top of a huge boulder, just like a statue of an ancient war-beast; one paw stretched out in front of him, claws extended. 'You should show Bern, or Aldasair. They both know those sorts of drawings well.'

'He doesn't want to talk to them,' said Jessen, quietly. Her wolf's eyes were too perceptive for Tor's liking. 'He's been avoiding them.'

'Yes, all right, how about you all stop giving me the evil eye for a few moments and let me tell you what I think I've found? I think it could be important.'

He knelt down in the gravel next to Kirune, and spread the map across his knees.

'I've been studying the amber record—'

'Studying,' coughed Kirune.

'Be quiet. I've watched so many battles now I think I can see them in my sleep. Micanal managed to recreate many of the major battles of the first eight Rains, and each time, at the end of each battle, the Jure'lia leave in the same direction. Here, look.' He touched his finger to one of the crosses. 'This was the Battle of the Blind Bird, in Kesenstan. And you see this line? That's the rough direction that the worm people headed in when they were defeated. And here,' he touched another cross, on the far side of the map. 'A battle from the Third Rain, which took place in what is now the Reilans. You see the line? It's on the other side of Sarn but it's heading the same way – south.'

'So?' Sharrik had shifted to the very end of the boulder and lowered his head, so he could see what they were all looking at. 'You have tracked the progress of the cowards as they flee from our might!'

'Look, though.' Tor took a piece of the charcoal from his pocket and used it to continue the lines, making them longer and longer until, eventually, they began to intercept each other. 'The Behemoths are extensions of the Jure'lia, aren't they? All part of their hive mind. They don't make decisions for themselves, they just follow instincts. And we know that after every Rain, the Jure'lia vanish for generations to heal themselves. We've just never known where they go.'

'Vostok says they would go too high, too fast,' said Kirune. Much of the bitterness had dropped from his voice. 'They would go where the air stopped being air, and we could not follow. Into darkness they went.'

'You think you've figured out where they go,' added Jessen.

Tor leaned forward and circled the place where the lines intercepted. 'There's got to be something here. Some sort of, I don't know, clue. That's what Vintage would say. And what else do we know about the Jure'lia at the moment?' He sat back on his haunches, looking around at them. 'That not all of their force is in the skies. My sister leads a handful of Behemoths, but where are the rest? Where is the queen?' He tapped the circle on the map. 'I think it's worth going to look, don't you?'

Jessen stood up and unfurled her wings. 'I will summon Aldasair.'

'Good.' Tor stood up. 'And I'm going to find myself a decent sword.'

Chapter Twenty

They were roused from their cells so early that the under-palace was thick with silence, and as they were marched along the corridors, glimpses out of windows revealed a cold morning of lilac light and grey cloud.

'Can you tell us where we're being taken?' Vintage asked one guard gamely enough, but she was met with sullen indifference. Next to her, Agent Chenlo was composed and calm, looking annoyingly fresh for someone recently imprisoned. Her thick black hair with its bolt of white was tied neatly back into its thick braid, and she looked only ahead of her. Harlo, who apparently also shared their fate, turned out to be a short, pale man with a wispy blond beard and a shaved head. All the smooth confidence of his patter seemed to have left him, and he said nothing at all as they took him from his cell.

Eventually, they left the main palace building through a tall anonymous door, and were marched briskly through a series of more utilitarian-looking gardens; here, Vintage noted, they grew medicinal herbs, things for healing and poisoning. Seeing them made her think of the three mysterious vials, each tucked safely within her vest. Luckily the guards had not deemed it necessary to search them a second time.

There were gates ahead, tall and spindly and bronze, and beyond them several land bridges broke away, elegantly leading the way to the satellite towns of Tygrish. One such bridge had a second gate, with many locks, and it was only once they were through it that Vintage realised it wasn't a bridge at all but a gently sloping stairway, leading directly into an enclosure of long Wild-grass. Vintage frowned.

'So you're just letting us out for a little walk, is that it?' She tried to catch her guard's eye. 'Bit of fresh air. How civilised of you.'

At the bottom of the walkway was a raised platform with another ornate bronze fence, and there Tyranny was waiting for them, with more guards at her side. For the time of the morning she looked slightly careworn, as if she'd been up all night, yet her eyes were bright with amusement. She had lost much of her regal finery, wearing only a loose silk shirt and a pair of billowing trousers, but the thin golden circlet was still on her head.

'There you are! Hurry up, bring the Winnowry agent here, I've got something special for her.'

Vintage tensed, desperately missing the weight of her crossbow at her hip, but the guards led Chenlo over to Tyranny, who brushed the older woman's face with the knuckles of one hand. Instantly, Chenlo buckled at the knees, almost fainting.

'Just a touch, that's all. I should think you can take that, given your training and everything. Here.' Tyranny took something from one of the guards, and had them turn Chenlo so her back was facing her. The contraption looked like a smooth silver cylinder with two narrow holes at either end; into these Tyranny forced Chenlo's hands, and then pushed a small metal lever home. There was a thick, metal clunk.

'Do you remember these, Agent Chenlo?' Tyranny turned her around, still smiling. Chenlo looked as though she had recovered from the blow, but the large metal cuff was obviously

225

uncomfortable. The older woman stood up straight, her face still carefully blank. 'You lot had me strapped in these all the time, do you remember? When I was thrown into the dungeons of that shit hole. It wasn't enough to keep me in a cell like all the other women.'

'You sound quite proud of that,' Vintage said quietly.

Tyranny briefly turned her sharp blue eyes on her – it was like a cold slap. 'They were afraid of me, Lady Vintage. You wouldn't agree with it, I'm sure. Keeping women like animals. Like worse than animals. I reckon that offends your *fine sensibilities*.'

'Of course it does,' said Vintage sharply.

'Well, Agent Chenlo here didn't want me out and about working for the Winnowry. She told them I should be locked up forever, in the deepest darkest shit hole they had.'

'And I was right.'

Tyranny turned back to Chenlo and slapped her backhanded across the mouth. The blow was hard enough to split her lip, but Tyranny seemed barely to notice what she had done, carrying on the conversation without a break.

'The others saw the usefulness of me, thankfully. They weren't as blind as this idiot.'

'And where did that get them?' asked Chenlo, but Tyranny only shrugged at this.

'I had to wear those cuffs day in and day out for months. They're not comfortable, let me tell you. I still have the scars on my wrists. Lots of scars, me.' She seemed to lose her train of thought, and she moved over to the bronze railing, leaving Chenlo to stand with blood running down her chin. 'Lady Vintage, you'll like this. Look. Come and look into the grass here.'

Reluctantly, Vintage joined her at the railing. The grass below them was around six or seven foot tall, and a yellowish-green. In some places the grass grew thicker, in solid clumps, and here the wide blades were spotted with red and orange – Wild-touched grass. There was a smell too, both the simmering vegetation smell of all the grasslands and something else. A smell that put Vintage on edge.

'Can you see them?' asked Tyranny pleasantly.

Vintage peered through the gate. She could see nothing but grass. On the far side, there were the softly curving walls of the enclosure, white stone just like all the land bridges, but that was all she could see.

'What am I supposed to be looking for?'

'Seven Wild-touched giant cats,' said Tyranny, with real pleasure. 'They're in there, somewhere, but they are extremely good at hiding themselves. Isn't it great?'

'Bloody marvellous,' muttered Vintage.

'They're all over the place out here – it's why we have the land bridges, after all – but you never see them. Not until it's too late, anyway. So I had a few captured and brought here. I wanted to see them properly, you know.' She turned to Vintage with her eyebrows raised. 'And I don't mind telling you that they are properly fucking terrifying, Lady Vintage.'

'Quite.'

''Ere.' It was the first time Harlo had spoken since he'd been brought out of his cell. He was sweating profusely, his bald head glistening in the sun. 'What's all this about? Because I don't think I've done anything to deserve, to deserve, whatever it is you're doing to these women.' He glanced at Vintage apologetically. 'I just made some dolls!'

Tyranny looked at him briefly, as if trying to remember who he was, then carried on talking. 'I keep them hungry, which doesn't put them in the best of moods, and of course they're already pretty annoyed at being kept—'

'This is all fascinating, darling, but if you're going to throw us in there, then I'd really rather you just got on with it.'

'Hey,' cried Harlo. 'I'd rather not, actually, if it's all the same to you.'

Tyranny smiled at Vintage; a genuine smile this time. 'Oh go on, then. Since I like you so much.' She gestured to the guards, who unlocked a small gate in the bronze railing.

'Can I ask you one question though?' At Tyranny's nod, Vintage continued. 'Why? Wouldn't it be much easier to chuck us back out of your city with a boot up our arses? Killing me will only anger Ebora more, and you could need them soon. You could need them very soon.'

Tyranny shrugged again, as if it was no matter at all. 'I said I would kill you before, and I didn't quite manage it. That's not something any leader should let pass, or you start to look weak. Whether you're the leader of the Salts or a queen of Jarlsbad. And her –' she nodded at Chenlo, who was being pushed towards the open gate – 'I've wanted to kill that bitch for fucking *years*. This is too beautiful an opportunity to pass up.'

Chenlo stood at the gate, her arms behind her back and her hands encased in steel. She hesitated there, trying to hang back, but one of the guards gave her a hard shove and the woman dropped down out of sight. Vintage pressed her lips into a thin line. Harlo followed her down, kicking and shouting and screaming. He landed in the grass with a thud.

'If you were hoping for assistance from above, Lady Vintage,' Tyranny nodded to more guards arriving behind them, all carrying great bows, 'we'll be on the lookout for your little friend. I would like his head mounted on my wall, and maybe a nice fur rug, although he looks a bit mangy –'

Vintage kicked her hard on her unprotected shin, and the queen of Tygrish bellowed with rage. In the confusion, Vintage made to land another blow, but it was too late; one of the guards grabbed her by her hair and in short fashion she was dragged towards the gate in the fence.

'You absolute bloody idiot!' she yelled, grabbing on to the bronze railing with both hands. 'How you ever ran a gang in

Mushenska I have no idea, I've seen rats with more sense than you!'

One of the guards punched her in the stomach, driving all the air from her lungs, and the last she saw of Tyranny as she fell backwards was her bright shock of blond hair. She hit the ground with no grace at all, and for a few moments was too dazed to do anything but look up at the sky.

'Did you strike her?' Agent Chenlo's face appeared in her field of vision, a frown creasing her forehead. Vintage took a deep, painful breath and got to her feet.

'I did, but sadly I did not strike her stupid head from her shoulders.' She looked around. Behind them was the solid white wall of the platform, and beyond that, tall shadowy grass in all directions. Harlo was crouched by the wall, his arms over his head. 'Have you seen anything? Down here?'

Chenlo shook her head. 'Nothing definite. But there is movement. The grass moves too much for a place protected from the wind.'

Vintage grimaced. She was right. The faint susurrus of the grass was constant, and once you looked into its green and yellow depths, it was all too possible to imagine huge, lithely muscled shapes moving back and forth, ready to pounce.

'Hoy! Move away from the wall.' They both looked up to see Queen Tyranny leaning over the bronze railing to grin at them. 'Don't you want to explore the grass? If you don't, we'll drop some buckets of cow's blood over here, get the cats moving ourselves.'

'Come on,' Vintage took some cautious steps forward. 'It'll be best if we get out of their sight, anyway.'

'Why? So we do not suffer the indignity of their witnessing our disembowelling?'

Vintage turned to Harlo, who was still shivering by the wall. 'Come on, my good man. On your feet. You're dead for certain if you stay there.'

Harlo looked up at her. His eyes were wet and round. 'I just sold some statues . . .'

'I know, darling, I know.' She grabbed his arm and pulled him away from the wall. 'The queen of Tygrish doesn't care for souvenirs, it seems.'

Soon they were hidden within the grass, and the platform was lost to view. Vintage unbuttoned the bottom of her shirt and reached within her vest, where she had stowed the package from Okaar. She unwrapped it, her fingers numb. The back of her neck prickled continually. Eyes in the grass, watching.

'I can't believe this.' Harlo's voice was shrill and wavering with fear. 'I can't fucking believe it. That bitch is mad, out of her mind. I've done nothing, barely anything at all and I get thrown to the Wild-cats?'

'Dear, please keep your voice down, you'll excite the wildlife.' Within the roll of material lay the three vials, and the slender silver key. Looking at it now it was obvious what it was for. 'Chenlo, turn around, let me get at that cuff.'

Chenlo turned, and as she did so, a low rippling growl oozed from the grass to their right. Harlo yelped, jumping backwards into the two women, and the delicate key dropped from Vintage's hands onto the ground. Instantly, she scrambled after it, all the hair on the back of her neck standing on end.

'Lady Vintage,' said Chenlo. 'It is coming.'

'Yes, yes, of course it bloody is.' A glitter of light amongst the grass and Vintage had it, but as she stood up with the key in her fist a dark shape moved through the grass next to them, impossibly large and silent. The thing was furless, with leathery greenish skin and a collection of long whiskers across its snout and forehead. Its eyes were a painful, watery pink, and when it peeled its lips back to emit another liquid growl Vintage caught sight of a collection of teeth that looked wrong somehow; too narrow and far too many, all packed in in rows that marched back down its throat. Trying to ignore her instinctive reaction, which was to run blindly in the other direction – run where, exactly? – she grabbed hold of Chenlo's steel cuff and slid the key home – a second or two too late.

It wasn't the one they could see that jumped. The attack came from the left, the creature moving faster than Vintage would have thought possible. One moment Harlo was with them, crouched and sweating, and the next he was on the ground, being dragged rapidly into the grass. Blood spattered, hot and quick, across the dry ground. The cuff slipped off Chenlo's hands and instantly she grabbed and drained a handful of grass, sending a ball of green fire after the Wild-cat. It hissed through the grass, sending much of it up like a torch, yet it seemed to pass harmlessly over the skin of the cat, which looked oily and strange under the winnowlight.

'Oh, you've got to be bloody kidding me . . .'

Harlo screamed, a high and terrified sound, and back up above them somewhere they heard Tyranny laughing; delighted, like a child watching a dog do a trick. The tall grasses, lush and strange in this Wild-touched region, were smouldering and throwing out a bitter-smelling smoke. The second Wild-cat was circling, and there were other shadows coming towards them, drawn, no doubt, by the screaming and the blood. Once again Vintage's hands itched for her crossbow. Chenlo held up her arms, wreathed in emerald fire.

'Here, wait, drink this. It could help.' Vintage wrestled one of the vials from the cloth and held it out to Chenlo, who barely glanced at it.

'What? No. I can burn them all.'

'Yes, but can you burn them all before they get you?' At that moment one of the cats in the grass at their backs made a quick foray towards them. Chenlo spun and threw up a wall of fire at it, and it retreated. 'Or before they get me? Drink it, Okaar will have given it to us for a reason.'

'You said this man was an assassin.'

'I did. Drink it.'

'You want me to drink poison from an assassin?'

'Yes! No, listen. If he wanted to kill us, he'd have done it then. He has no taste for this drama.' Vintage gestured around at the burning grasses, the lethal cats. 'I trust him. Do you trust me?'

Chenlo looked at her then, a direct and appraising look. Something in her eyes changed, a softening Vintage did not understand, and then she nodded once, briskly.

'I trust you, Vintage.'

She took the vial, popped the cork out with her thumb and downed it. She grimaced, and water ran from her eyes. Vintage watched her closely.

'Oh Sarn's bones, please tell me it isn't poison.'

Chenlo glared at her. 'It tastes,' she said tightly, 'like a horse's ass.'

Two of the cats leapt at once. Vintage scrambled back, and felt the claw of one rip neatly through her boot and pare her skin open at the shin. The bright shout of pain was not quite enough to distract her from the sight of the creature's drooling jaws and the bunching of muscles as it prepared to jump again, but then the entire thing was knocked sideways in a blinding blast of fire. Pieces of hot cat rained all around her, spattering and hissing like things left too long on the stove. Chenlo staggered over to her, her mouth turned down at the corners. She held up her hands, which were still ringed with fire, but the green flame was dirty, flickering with black. It hurt Vintage's eyes to look at it.

'What did you give me?'

'Quick! Get the rest of them!'

They were standing now in a blasted section of burning grass, and a few of the cats had retreated; their tough skins were no match for this newly lethal winnowfire. Distantly, Vintage could hear Tyranny shouting something – evidently she was not pleased by this turn of events. Chenlo raised her arms and sent a great arc of fire into the remaining grasses. Watching it, Vintage felt her stomach turn over; it was not the clean eldritch fire she so readily associated with Noon. This fire was wild and chaotic, tinged at the edges with a smoky blackness, and it blasted into the grass and the animals hidden within it with an uncompromising roar. Soon, all the grass was burning, and the enclosure was filled with smoke and burning lumps of flesh. Harlo's body was revealed, his ribcage open and his guts a pink and yellow collection on his knees. Vintage had a moment's gratitude that they had been spared that fate, but of course their situation was hardly much better – death by smoke, shortly, or death by arrow when Tyranny lost her patience and had the guards slaughter them.

Helcate! Helcate, my darling, are you there?

The thought of putting the war-beast in any danger stabbed at her heart, but it was clear they would be dead in moments if they didn't get assistance swiftly. There was more shouting over by the bronze fence, and Vintage looked back to see Tyranny opening the gate, a look of boiling fury on her face. The guards were behind her, their arrows trained on the enclosure now.

'Where did you get that?' she shouted as she came out of the gate and stood on the very edge of the wall. 'I'd know that fire anywhere, and you shouldn't have it.'

Vintage, still frantically calling Helcate in her head, turned and smiled at the fell-witch.

'I'm sorry, did we spoil that for you?' For emphasis she kicked the metal cuff where it was still lying on the ground. The grass and the Wild-cats were a smoking ruin; even the white walls had been blackened with the force of the fire.

'How did you get it? Who are you working with?' Tyranny raised her hands, and two balls of green fire whooshed into life around her fists. 'Tell me now or I will burn you.'

'Oh make up your bloody mind.' Vintage rubbed the underside of her wrist across her forehead. Sweat was pouring down her face, stinging her eyes along with the smoke. 'Burn us to death, feed us to your pets, stick us with arrows. There is such a thing as overdoing it, you know.'

'It's Okaar, isn't it? That sneaky fucking bastard, he can't just let me have this, he can't just *leave me alone* . . .'

Two things happened at once. A shadow fell over them, and there was a flurry of arrows from the guards. Some of them went wild, thumping into the ash and smoke of the burned grass, and some went up, sailing too close to Helcate for Vintage's comfort. Even so, she felt a lightness in her chest at the sight of him.

'Darling, be careful!'

Helcate landed, none too gracefully, as the air filled with more fire and arrows. Vintage ran for his back and jumped, scrambling to get a hold of the harness while Chenlo threw up a curtain of the terrible black and green fire to shield them.

'Get on, quick!'

Chenlo turned, her face streaked with soot, and as soon as she had a hold, Helcate began to beat his leathery wings. A few arrows still came, one piercing the skin between the war-beast's wing bones, but it passed straight through, and although he grunted with pain, he made it up into the air.

'Up, up, and away, as fast as you can, darling, we—'

Coldness hit them, silent and lethal. Helcate's coat turned white with frost and he whined like a kicked dog. Vintage looked up to see Queen Windfall, her fanged mouth still open and glowing blue with the force of her icy breath. She was blindingly white against the blue sky, powerful and enraged. Sunlight glittered off of her jewelled crown.

'You do not leave,' she called, imperious. 'You are our prisoner. A prisoner of Tygrish.'

Vintage opened her mouth, willing breath into her frozen

lungs so that she could tell the giant bat to fuck off, when Chenlo leaned forward and pressed her hand to Helcate's rigidly curled fur. Through her link to him, Vintage felt the sapping of his life force, and then Chenlo unleashed an enormous blast of fire up at Windfall, almost propelling Helcate back down to the ground. There was a scream so high-pitched that Vintage was sure she felt it rather than heard it, and then Windfall was falling past them. Tyranny was screaming again, enraged.

'Go,' she urged Helcate, 'go, while we still can, my darling.'

Helcate flew up into the sky and out across the grasslands, leaving Tygrish and its queens behind.

Chapter Twenty-one

'Pass me the wine please, brother.'

Hestillion sat at the table and watched as her creation considered this. Was it a request? A command? After a long moment, he picked up the bottle of wine and set it down on the table nearer her. She nodded. He was getting better at this.

'Thank you,' she said.

'Thank you,' he replied.

She had collected the items for this dinner herself, from the last handful of battle sites. Fresh fruits, taken from trees before they were consumed by the maggots, and freshly slaughtered lambs from a field before the varnish eased its way across the raw earth. With the help of her circle – seeing through their eyes as they searched a variety of homes – she had also found an acceptable set of plates and cutlery. Nothing as fine as what she'd eaten from in Ebora, or even the pieces she'd made herself as a child, but they looked well enough under the frond-lights.

The wine they'd found in an actual cellar, and it was very fine indeed. She watched her worm-brother's face carefully as he sipped at it, trying to spot if he enjoyed the taste or not, but his face, as finely crafted as it was, was still difficult to read. Twice now she had taken him back to the pools and pushed her fingers back into his flesh, seeking to make him closer to the vision she had in her head. Although the Jure'lia armour was welded directly to his body, for this dinner she had dressed him in loose green robes, and had even attached a long silver earring to one ear. When she had pushed the pin through the solid flesh of his earlobe, he hadn't moved at all; when she had done the same for Tormalin as a child, he had shrieked like a banshee. For herself she had found a beautiful silk dress, hemmed at the edges with a repeating geometric pattern – from Reidn, no doubt. It was the only place close to Ebora when it came to producing silks, and it felt exquisite against her skin, yet she found herself plucking at it, pulling at her own sleeves. She felt oddly naked, and missed her leathers and her furs.

'The wine is exceptional, is it not? Roots only know where humans got something like this, it's as good as anything we had in Ebora. A shame we could only save a few bottles of it.' A tiny voice at the back of her mind, almost hidden under the cacophony of the worm people, asked who would continue to make such wine when she had neatly erased all of the human settlements on her map? But it was a small voice, annoyingly concerned with human lives and Eboran history, and she easily ignored it.

'Wine . . . is good,' agreed her worm-brother. She smiled, pleased, and cut up a piece of the tender meat. After a moment he copied her movements, muscles bunching in his slender forearms.

'I'm not sure quite how your digestion works. I suppose you don't really need food or drink? But I imagine it does you no harm, and—'

A shiver passed through her and the distant hum that was the background noise of the Behemoth changed slightly. Her awareness left the chamber and she was in three Behemoths at once, her circle whispering their information to her through

237

the link they shared. She touched her fingers to the blue crystal in her chest, and came back to the table with a blink.

'We are here,' she said simply, and her worm-brother stood up immediately. She followed suit, taking a moment to wipe her hands on a cloth before pulling loose the cords on her silk dress. It dropped noiselessly to the floor and she stepped over it, naked, to reach the clothes she had laid out on a chair, ready for this moment.

'Go to Celaphon,' she told her worm-brother, who had also removed his robes. 'Be ready.'

When he was gone, she dressed quickly, pulling on the worn leather trousers and the fur vest with relish. She strapped on a pair of vambraces and pauldrons made of Jure'lia carapaces, and pulled her hair back into its braid. The thought of letting the wine go to waste tugged at her, so she finished off her own glass, then carefully wedged the cork back into the top of the bottle. She crossed the chamber and pressed her hand lightly to the wall. It flexed away from her touch, and in a few moments she was in the giant space that housed Celaphon.

'Time to fight!' he said excitedly, pawing at the ground with his clawed feet. Hestillion's worm-brother and one of the circle had been readying Hestillion's weapons for her; a short sword, a long spear. She did not often use them, but it felt wrong to go into battle with no weight at her side. Hestillion took the sword and slipped it into the scabbard at her belt, and climbed up onto Celaphon's harness. She felt his joy at being with her through both the Jure'lia link and the war-beast bond, and allowed herself to feel some of this joy with him. *Poison song indeed*, she thought. *The queen knows nothing of what we are now. What I am doing is making the Jure'lia stronger, better. She will see that eventually.* When she was settled, she held out her hand and her worm-brother passed her the spear.

'Lady,' said Yellow Leaf, 'we await your command.'

Hestillion closed her eyes and reached out to them. Each of her creations stood within their Behemoths, looking through clear walls down at the town below them. There was a delicious sense of doubling, and Hestillion saw the world laid out beneath them through several pairs of eyes. She sent them their instructions and then, still holding the thread of their awareness in her head, flexed the side of the ship open. Wind roared in, a flash of blue sky. Hestillion smiled.

'This is going to be interesting.'

Celaphon, eager to be outside, thundered forward and out, his wings opening and catching the wind with a crack, like sails on a ship. They were dazzled briefly by sunlight, and then the dragon turned, and the town below them revealed itself.

'Look at them all,' said Celaphon, in genuine surprise. 'What are they doing?'

Hestillion smiled. It was good to be back in her battle-leathers, good to be out under the sun.

'They are resisting, my sweet.'

This town, according to the maps Hestillion had been poring over, was just south of the Reidn delta – close enough to benefit from the vicinity of that rich city state, but far enough away to not be protected by Reidn's armies. It was called Stourhands, and it was nestled to the east of a set of rocky hills, within which the people of Stourhands had been mining for generations. They produced metals and ores, and sold them all across Sarn, and now the people were lining up in rows below them, wearing many of their metals as armour, and brandishing a range of pointy weapons. Like most human settlements, it was a walled town, and as they flew lower and closer, Hestillion could see men and women lined up on the tops of the walls, bows lifted and aimed at the incoming threat. There were siege weapons too, mighty wooden trebuchets weighted down and ready to fire, as well as a reasonable number of people on horseback. It was easily the biggest force she had faced so far with her circle. Hestillion grinned with genuine pleasure.

'The others didn't do this,' pointed out Celaphon.

'Well, they tried, but they weren't as organised.' She leaned forward in her harness to speak more directly into the dragon's ear. 'We have seen humans rushing with panic, and desperation. These humans, I suspect, have been watching for us, and planning what they will do when we arrive.'

'And will that help them?'

Hestillion laughed. 'No, my sweet.'

At her word, the three Behemoths began to convene on the walled town of Stourhands. On the far side of the town it was possible to see a thin line of people moving hurriedly down a distant road; the young and the old, probably, those too sick to fight. They were fleeing the town. Hestillion hoped they knew where they were going – if they were still in open ground in an hour or so, they would face death along with the rest of their people. Hestillion called her commands, and Celaphon swept down towards the first rows of men and women gathered outside the town. There was a shout from somewhere, and a shadow moved up from the walls; hundreds of arrows arching up towards them. They clattered harmlessly against Celaphon's hide – although he snorted with indignation – and Hestillion herself ducked, feeling a thrill of danger as the lethal arrows shot up through the air and past them. Next, the trebuchets fired, and abruptly they shared the sky with a volley of smoking debris. With a couple of beats of his wings, Celaphon brought himself up above their range.

'They are shooting at us!'

Hestillion laughed again. 'Of course, but it will do them no good. It will take them some time to load up again, so why don't you show them your tricks?'

Celaphon needed no more telling than that. The dragon

dropped down through the sky, his jaws wide open. The neatly formed ranks of soldiers below them wavered, and then scattered. Hestillion heard screaming, shouts for order, but it was too late. The enormous muscles beneath her bunched and flexed, and Celaphon spat down a crackling beam of blue lightning onto the army. Those directly under the beam were blown into blackened pieces in an instant, while the fallout spread outwards in a flickering circle; white forks of lightning jumping from one piece of armour to another. As Hestillion watched, men and women jerked and screamed as the electricity filled their bodies and threw them down into the dirt.

'Excellently done, my sweet,' she called to Celaphon, who was already coming around for another blast. A fresh hail of arrows flew over them, and Hestillion threw her awareness back to the circle, checking that they were following orders. One Behemoth had positioned itself over the centre of the town, leaking a steady stream of burrowers and spider-mothers down into the market square. The two others had taken up position on the east and west sides of the town wall, and the creatures they released were eating their way through any humans caught fleeing. A crack of thunder, and Celaphon's lightning blasted a hole through the town gate. More screaming. The shouts for order were both fewer and more desperate. Hestillion smiled.

Later, she stood in one of Stourhands' towers and leaned over the balcony, watching as a tide of varnish oozed its way down the street below. Celaphon was away, flying after the people who had fled from the far side of the settlement, and in her head the circle were quietly reporting their successes. Everything was as it should be.

At the front of the tide of varnish there was a shifting foam of debris, items caught and pushed along by the fluid before being overtaken and consumed by it. She saw carts and wooden buckets, heaps of straw, a broom, a sword. All of it eventually fell underneath the varnish, and there it would stay, caught forever. It was neat, really. Tidy.

A figure down the street caught her eye. It was a little human girl – impossible, with their ridiculously short lives, to guess its age, but it was small – and she appeared to have fallen and hit her head on the cobbles. Left behind in the scramble to leave, was Hestillion's guess; left for dead, probably, but she was coming around, her movements slow and confused, while the tide of varnish inched towards her, smothering everything in its path.

Hestillion felt a tremor of something. A memory was trying to resurface, an image of a young Eboran boy lying on ground turned hard with snow, but she retreated from that and reached for the circle instead. They were there, as they always were, and she sank herself into their certainty and their love for her. In a few moments, the shining green tide overtook the little girl, and she was lost beneath it. Hestillion watched until the small body stopped moving, then nodded. It was neat. Tidy.

Yet again, there had been no sign of Tormalin and his pet witch, no sign of the other war-beasts that caused Celaphon such distress. Even the human man Bern, with his connection to the Jure'lia, felt very distant from her, a tiny seed in the vast jungle that was the worm people. It was harder to find him in their chaos than it had been. Perhaps he was hiding. Perhaps, she mused, her brother and his friends had recognised that with her as their leader, the Jure'lia were more lethal than they had ever been. The thought was a pleasing one.

'Now. I believe I have a dinner to finish.'

Chapter Twenty-two

For a time, Noon experienced only darkness, with small snatches of light, and the light itself was strange, greenish, not reassuring. Eventually, she began to smell things too, and these were older, well-known smells, the scents of memory and long ago. The warm peppery smell of dried harla root; paper, lots of it, bound in leather; the little wildflower hearts-kiss, which her mother had gathered in thick bales whenever they came across it – tiny and pink, the petals made a sweet paste when mashed together. Familiar scents from a distant time. When Noon awoke, it was to see the peaked, busy ceiling of the tent, and a figure bending over her. There was a yawning sensation in her gut, like being pulled backwards very suddenly. Had her whole life been a fever dream? She was certainly unwell; she could feel it under her skin, a thick hot illness weighing her down, keeping her to the bed.

'Mother?'

The figure grew still, her head tipped to one side. It was such an alien gesture that Noon felt cast into dreams once again. She struggled to sit up, fighting against the urge to sleep.

'I suppose you could call me that,' said the figure, her voice, as ever, amused. 'But I don't think you'd really want to.'

'No.' Noon squirmed away from the woman's touch. 'What have you done? What is all this?'

'I collected together a few reminders, that's all,' said She Who Laughs. 'I suppose I got a little carried away. And it wasn't easy, if I'm truthful. Not easy to be authentic, anyway, because of course the tents and belongings of your people – well, they're not around anymore, are they?'

And it was all slightly wrong, now that Noon looked at it properly. The books were not her mother's books; Noon had memorised the spines and titles of every one, long before she could even read. And although the herbs were right, they were hanging in the wrong places. The thick embroidered rugs lining the tent walls were alien to her, the blankets did not smell of horse, and, of course, She Who Laughs was not her mother. She still wore the body of the thin blonde woman, although she looked pinched around the eyes and cheeks, and there were shadows under her skin.

'I need a drink.' Noon attempted to sit up again, but She Who Laughs placed one hand on her chest and pushed her back firmly.

'Don't move. You nearly killed yourself out there, in that heat. So stubborn. But then I never did give my gift to any pushovers.'

She fetched a bowl from the side and lifted a spoon to Noon's lips. Rather than water, the bowl was full of a creamy sort of soup. Noon swallowed a mouthful, then grimaced. It was hot.

'I don't want that. I need water.' She coughed. The soup had left a strange aftertaste. 'Listen, I don't feel well . . .'

'I'm not surprised.' She Who Laughs picked up a cloth from another bowl, and pressed it to Noon's forehead. It was warm and damp, and all at once Noon felt like the small amount of strength she had left was seeping away into the blankets underneath her. 'You need to lie quietly and relax now, wait for your body to heal itself, Noon. Noon, my little frog.'

'Wait, what have you . . . what have you done . . .' Noon reached up and took hold of She Who Laughs' arm, but her skin was feverish too, and somehow that was too much. She slumped back into the blankets and the darkness swarmed in, hot and hungry.

Her awareness, when it came back, was as bright and as cool as the plains on a spring day. It was the old nightmare, or at least, the setting of it; she stood, a young girl with a wooden sword shoved through her belt, on the edge of her people's territory. The wind was moving in the long grasses like an unseen animal, and it tugged at her hair – still long and currently free of the braids her mother habitually tried to tame it with. The smell of the grasslands under the sun was in her nostrils, as well as other familiar scents, like wood smoke, tanning leather, horses, meat cooking somewhere. Her people were as busy as they ever were, tending their animals, fixing tents, fetching water. Some of the young people were teaching their horses tricks, laughing and teasing each other, while many older people gathered in groups to talk. Noon took a few steps forward, looking at their faces. She was remembering things she hadn't thought of in decades. Names drifted up like burning embers in rising smoke.

Grasschance, an old hunter with a lean and wiry frame. His back was a mess of scars where he had fallen into a thicket of brambles as a young man. If you asked him about it, he would spin a wild tale of being captured by his enemies and tortured, but everyone knew the truth.

Father Bird, almost as old as Mother Fast. He had trouble walking, and was cared for by his two sons. He liked rude jokes, Noon remembered, and would tell you one if you brought him sips of stonefeet, no matter how old you were or whether you would understand it or not.

Onlyleaf was tall and fierce, their best and most feared warrior. She could sing too, in a high, wavering voice that she kept for them tribe alone. She was their public weapon and their secret song. Onlyleaf, young and angry and joyous.

Brittlesky had four children, and Noon only ever remembered her with a bundle at her breast and a toddler clinging to her skirts. She was also the tribe's expert on plants and their mysteries; no one planted anything without asking Brittlesky first. She had a curl in her hair, unusual for plains folk, and all her babies had it too; a little gathering of curly tops.

Hareslife, an irritable old woman who knitted hats for them in the autumn. She lived alone and hated company, but every year, those hats would start to appear . . .

Noon took a sharp breath. All of them had been waiting here all the time. She hadn't forgotten any of them, not really. Faces and voices she had known every day of her early life, hands that had always been there to help her up when she fell, to brush her down. It was good to see them, it *was* good, but . . .

'What am I doing here?'

With great reluctance, she looked down at her bare arm. There was an angry red mark there, as if someone had smacked her recently. Reaching up to touch her face, she felt tears on her cheeks, already drying in the sun.

'We were playing around, with the horses. Just pretending, like the bigger kids. But I –' She shuddered violently, and her stomach cramped. She was edging closer and closer to the abyss in her head, so close now she could hear the whistling noise it made as it sucked all the light into itself. 'I did it wrong, I messed up.'

Another memory: of a hard, flat anger inside herself, and her own hand reaching down towards the short grass.

'NO!'

Noon lurched up out of the blankets, kicking and fighting as though she were drowning in a pond. Hard, hot hands pushed her back down, pinning her to the ground.

'You were nearly there!' She Who Laughs' face was close to her own, close enough for Noon to smell the illness in the body she wore. 'Just a little bit further you have to go, that's all.'

'No! You don't understand, I can't see that again, I can't, it'll kill me.' She struggled violently, but the strength of She Who Laughs was implacable. She held her down without effort, and eventually Noon lay still, although her heart was thundering in her chest. Panic bit at her with rats' teeth. 'Why are you doing this to me? Why?'

'You have to remember, child, that's all.' She Who Laughs smiled serenely. She pulled over a couple more rugs and covered Noon's chest, tucking her in up to her chin. 'Will you take more soup? It will help.'

'No, I don't want any soup, I'm boiling my blood over here.' Noon gasped. It was getting difficult to breath, and the ceiling of the tent looked hazy, unreal. A flush of nausea moved through her, and she began to shiver. 'You're trying to kill – to kill me.'

'Little frog, if I wanted you dead, do you not think you'd already be a cinder?'

Noon tried to focus on the woman's face, but it was shifting, and strange. The halo of green fire around her head was bright, too bright, and all the shadows in the room were mocking her.

'Don't call me that,' she croaked. 'My mum used to call me that.'

She Who Laughs tipped her head to one side again, considering. 'Perhaps a touch of death is what you need, though. Perhaps then you will look it in the face, finally.'

She Who Laughs pressed her hand to Noon's cheek – hard, calloused hands – and Noon felt all the remaining strength drain out of her. Her vision turned grey and her lips numb, and then . . .

. . . back in the sunlight, in the young horses' paddock. She

247

was there with a handful of children roughly her own age, and they were admiring the colts, letting them sniff their hands and feeding them handfuls of chopped vegetables. They were happy; the day's lessons were over, and it was hours until dinner. The adults were content to let their children spend time with the horses and the fleeten, because they too would grow up to be riders and hunters. A child who was afraid of horses was of no use to anyone.

Noon looked at the faces of the children who were with her. Her first friends, long forgotten.

'Hey, Noon, can you do this?'

A boy with a long nose and a pair of healthy purple bruises across his shins slipped from the paddock fence onto the back of a waiting horse. He tucked his feet in and the animal trotted in a neat little circle. Noon grinned, reluctantly. Purefoot was a couple of years older than her, and she wasn't anywhere near as clever as he was with the horses. He slipped off the animal's back and brought it back round to the fence.

'You know I can't,' she said mildly enough.

'Noon is too little,' said another girl. 'She can't do any of this yet. She's not old enough to do tricks.'

The other girl, Sunsflower, was only a few months older than Noon herself, and so Noon felt that this was a bit of a cheek. She shifted in her space on the fence, feeling too hot. Her cheeks were flushed.

'I can do loads of tricks,' she said easily. 'Just not stupid ones with horses.' The colt pushed his nose into her hand, and she rubbed the velvet strip between his eyes.

'*Sure* you can,' said Sunsflower, witheringly. 'Nothing as good as Purefoot can do, that's what I think.'

Noon smiled, because of course she had the *best* trick. One none of them could do. It was a secret, her mother was forever telling her how secret it must be, but these children had grown up with her, they were family. They were all family. It suddenly seemed very strange and even unnatural that she should keep any secrets from them.

'Oh yeah? Well, watch this.'

She pressed her hand flat to the horse's head, and *took* a little from him, just a touch. She held out her other hand and *pushed* the flame out there. It was a perfect diamond of flame, green and blue and clear, but her friends weren't looking at it. Instead, they were looking at the horse, who had sunk to his knees in the paddock, head bowed.

'What have you done?'

Noon blinked. 'Look at my fire,' she said. 'Can't you see it?'

'Who cares about your stupid fire!' exclaimed Sunsflower, who was already scrambling down into the paddock. Purefoot was at the horse's side, trying to lift his big, heavy head. The animal's eyes had rolled up to the whites.

'You mean you know about it?' Uneasily, Noon climbed down into the paddock herself. She hadn't meant to take so much – she hadn't thought she had, but the small horse was clearly in a bad way. *Why didn't I take it from the grass?*

'You've hurt him,' said Purefoot, his voice full of anguish. 'Why would you do that?'

'I didn't mean to. I just wanted to show you – Did you know about the fire?'

'Everyone knows about your stupid fire, Noon,' snapped Sunsflower. 'And we know you're not supposed to use it.'

Uncertain what to do, Noon reached out to touch the horse. Instantly, Purefoot struck her on the arm – one hard slap, like a mother chasing a baby away from the hot surface of a pan.

'No!' he said. 'You'll make it worse.'

Her vision doubling with tears, Noon sprang up over the fence and ran blindly through the settlement, not stopping until she had left the tents and the people behind. The grass rose in front of her, and the plains swept away forever north, unbroken until the soft purple mounds of distant hills. Noon stared that way until the tears stopped rolling down her face, and looked at the sharp red mark on her arm. Purefoot had never struck her before. He had never looked at her in fear before.

Slowly, her humiliation and sadness filtered away, to be replaced with something else. A hot, flat anger. The unfairness of it, the injustice. She had thought her fire was special, a special thing that she would use one day to protect her people, but they already knew about it, and didn't care. They thought it was nothing, a trick or an amusement, of no more use than Mother Fast's puppets.

'It is bigger than that, though,' she murmured. 'I *feel* it. Bigger than everything. They just don't know it.'

Slowly, she turned back to face the settlement. The anger left her as quickly as it had come, and the sadness too, until she felt only curiosity. As she stood with her feet in the grass, this thing that she carried inside her had opened itself up to her, like a tiny bud bursting open to reveal petals, pollen, and new alien colours. Everything now looked slightly different.

She could take the life energy of any living thing that she touched. She made a connection with it, skin to skin, and she took.

But wasn't everything connected? Weren't they all connected, one to the other?

Blades of grass growing next to each other, sharing the same soil. Men and women, children, living together on this land. They shared blood, and air. And that air they shared with the plain itself, with its sunshine and its soil. Her people could not exist elsewhere, could not be the same without this plain.

'It's all connected,' murmured Noon. 'Everything is.'

She just needed to move through those connections.

As if in a trance, Noon knelt down and placed her hand in the grass . . .

She had not done it in anger. Wrapped in blankets and moaning with delirium and fever, Noon nonetheless felt a small blossom of relief at that. She had just had the thought, and had acted on it. She hadn't killed them out of rage after all.

The energy from the grass flowed into her, as easy and as quiet as water from a creek. From blade to blade her thirst travelled, turning each brown and dead as she went. A circle of browning grass bled out from her hand and seeped away, towards the tents, and she urged it on, her thirst growing, rather than being sated. A small group of fleeten stood in one of the grass paddocks, and she *felt* them, warm and vital on the grass. It was no effort at all to take her hunger to them, and one by one the little goat creatures dropped to the ground, their eyes rolling up just as the horse's had. One or two of them shuddered and spasmed as they fell, dying where Noon took too much, but she barely noticed – still the life energy flowed into her cool and quick, even as she knelt on the grass outside the settlement. Curious, Noon pushed her awareness of the connection in another direction; Lightspun, a young man who tended the fleeten, was leaning down to touch one of his charges, an expression of shock creasing his smooth features, and Noon slipped up his questing fingers to drain him, too. He stumbled on his feet, crying out in fear and alarm, but Noon barely noticed; an entire world of connections had opened up to her through Lightspun. There was his mother and father, traders both, his little brother Glow, the girl Sewnseed whose hand Lightspun held sometimes when no one else was around – all of them were open to Noon, their life energies ready to be taken. What she had taken so far had filled her like sand in a sack, running to every corner, making her solid, making her real. Finally.

On some level, she knew this could not be contained. The life energy always had to be released in fire, there was no denying it; if she didn't let it out, it would burst out of her of its own accord. But this new sensation was dizzying, obliterating all other thought. She was drunk on it.

251

Thrilled with her own power and cleverness, Noon reached out at once to Lightspun's parents, his brother, and the girl Sewnseed. As she suddenly spun in all directions, four figures dropped to the ground in the middle of their tasks. Sewnseed dropped the clay cups she was carrying and crashed into the mud; Glow, who had been teaching himself to play the pipes, slid limply off the wooden gate where he'd been sitting and broke his neck. Aside from the fleeten, he was the first to die.

From there, Noon lost control – if she had ever really had it in the first place. Life energy streamed into her faster and faster, while new connections opened up as quick as snapping bones: Lightspun's father had three brothers, his mother was riding a horse, the horse was moving through the same grass as Brittlesky was moving through, two of her children were at her heels, two were back in the tent, being tended by Noon's mother, who was helping out for the afternoon.

Connections crashed into her, one after another. She felt her mother's life energy stream into her, so fast it almost seemed like it was returning home, and she felt her stumble to her knees, crying out in fear. Noon cried out back, badly frightened now and unable to stop. The deep reservoir she had found within herself was filling up, yet her winnow-thirst moved faster than she could follow. Deep in her feverish slump, tended by She Who Laughs, grown Noon convulsed in her blankets, too filled with horror to even make a sound – she had torn her mother's life away from her, unthinking and greedy. *A thief and a murderer.*

All across the settlement, men, women and children were staggering to their knees in the dirt, fainting dead away, their faces turning slack and numb. Those still conscious began to scream, rushing from neighbour to loved one, crying out against this sudden plague, this curse from out of a clear blue sky. Somewhere in the grass beyond the tents, Noon heard them, even as thin streams of blood ran from her ears and nose.

Meanwhile, her hunger was snaking out across the plains, tendrils of dead grass reaching out as fast as lightning strikes.

I can't, she thought. *I can't stop . . .*

The answer, ultimately, was obvious. Even as the adult Noon shuddered and cried within She Who Laughs' castle, willing her past self not to do it, there never was any other way.

When life energy was taken, winnowfire must be released.

The young girl on her knees in the grass raised her arms compulsively and became the centre of a mountain of fire. A mile across in all directions, the dome of green and white rose up and up, too bright to look at, too loud to hear. The settlement was instantly engulfed as the very air turned to flame; people, animals, tents, plants, all structures, became fiery beacons, burning impossibly hot. Hair and fur crisped off in an instant, flesh melted, bones turned black and brittle. Connected to them all as she was, Noon felt the terrible flash of agony that moved through her people, felt it as though her own body were cooked, and in her last moment of awareness before she blacked out completely, she felt her mother clearly – dying, her last thought was that it had been Noon, that it had been her little frog, and that she was sad, and sorry.

Sorry.

Back in She Who Laughs' fake tent, Noon howled with anguish and curled up on her side, shivering violently. The smell of burning flesh was everywhere, in her nostrils, her hair, her skin. For the first time in her life she longed for the cold damp walls of her Winnowry cell, to be hidden and alone and forgotten again. *It's where I belong, it's where I belong, blood and fire, they should have killed me. Why didn't they?*

'Noon. You did it. You remembered. My clever girl.' She Who Laughs reached over to push her hair back from her sweaty forehead.

'Don't touch me!' Noon scrambled away, and abruptly bile

was surging up her throat. She vomited noisily into the corner, her whole body clenching with the effort of it. When it was done she wiped her lips with the back of her hand. 'Why did you make me remember that? Why –' she stopped, crying too hard to speak – 'why, when you already know?'

'What good does it do me to know? I could never have explained it to you. Do you know, Noon, that you're the only fell-witch to have glimpsed what this power really is? The only one, in so many centuries.' She Who Laughs shook her head ruefully. 'Do you have any idea how frustrating that has been for me?'

Noon opened her mouth to reply, but there were no words. She still felt incredibly weak, barely able to lift her head.

'I felt it, when you figured it out,' the woman continued. She had sat back on the far side of the blankets, her thin face serene. 'All the way out here, I felt it. Like years of watching a barren patch of earth, waiting for something to grow, and suddenly there you were. A little green shoot, there and gone again. And when I felt the old ship awaken, I knew that had to be you, too. Isn't it amazing?'

'Leave me – leave me alone.' Noon lifted her head with some difficulty and met the dancing green eyes of She Who Laughs. 'Get out now, or I swear I will kill you, or myself. Myself is probably easier, so if I am of any value to you –'

The woman stood up easily, her hands held out in front of her. 'Don't fret, Noon, I'll go. You need to rest. It's a lot to take in, my child, I understand that.'

The woman stepped out of the tent and was gone. Noon watched the space where she had been for some moments, her face blank, and then she lay back down in the blankets and prayed for the darkness to take her.

Chapter Twenty-three

When finally they landed, the towers of Tygrish were not as far behind them as Vintage would have liked, but Helcate's suffering could not be ignored much longer. With a tear in his wing and twice as much weight as he was used to, the flight had been fraught and uncomfortable for everyone. The war-beast put them down below a small rocky outcrop, hiding them from the skies at least for a little while. Vintage climbed down, a little shakily, and went to stroke his long snout.

'Darling, what a fine job you did. You saved us both, do you know that?'

Behind her, Agent Chenlo stumbled to the ground and bent over for a moment with her hands on her knees. Her skin was glistening with sweat, and belatedly Vintage noticed that her left sleeve was soaked with blood.

'Goodness! What happened to you?'

'Nicked by an arrow.' Chenlo straightened up. 'Just as we got up in the air. I barely noticed myself at the time due to the – the –' She gestured vaguely, and shook her head. 'I cannot describe it. The potion you made me drink made everything unpleasant.'

'How bad is it?' Vintage went to the woman and made to

take hold of her arm, but Chenlo stepped back. 'Oh give over. Are you a child? Let me look at it.'

Chenlo opened her mouth as if to say something, then thought better of it. With obvious reluctance she held out her arm to Vintage, who peeled the sodden material back with her fingers. The cloth had stuck to the wound, which was shallow but long. It had started to scab up already in the heat, but it looked less than clean.

'Get some air to it, that's it. We need to give it a wash, but given how abruptly we left, we find ourselves in the middle of nowhere with no supplies, no water, and no bloody crossbow.'

'The beast? Will he fly again soon?'

Vintage looked at Helcate, who had sat himself down in a patch of dusty earth. Tentatively, she reached out to him.

Darling, how are you? Tell me honestly now.

His reply came not in words, but a series of impressions: *His time spent flying the perimeter of Tygrish, frightened and uncertain. He had found no food, little water, and had been too worried about Vintage to venture far. Her summons, when it came, had been like a bell, clear and welcome. Now he was sore, exhausted, needed rest. But there was a river, very close – he had seen it as they had come down.*

'Helcate,' said Helcate.

'He needs rest for now, as you do too. There is, however, a river not far from here. We'll have to get there on foot, that's all.'

In the end, the river was an hour's walk away – Vintage made a mental note to have a word with Helcate about the tricks of perspective possible when one was sighting something from the air – and they got there as the day was reaching its hottest point. It appeared to be a tributary of the Ember, a slow and shallow section of water, glittering with orange and yellow stones beneath. All three of them drank from it gladly, and while Helcate bathed downriver, Vintage made Chenlo sit on the bank with her arm held up for examination.

'This isn't as clean as I would like, of course, but it will have to do.' She had torn a section from her shirt and folded the material over to form a rough sort of pad. She soaked it in the clear river water and held it up. 'Give me your arm then.'

Again Chenlo hesitated. She had gained some of her colour back during their walk to the river, and now her cheeks grew pinker.

'When you met the Lady Noon, did she ever describe to you the restrictions of life at the Winnowry?'

Vintage put the pad in the water again to stop it from drying out. 'Some of it, yes. And I'd heard plenty myself, over the years. Bloody awful place.'

'It's very solitary,' Chenlo said, looking away over the river. 'There can be solace in that. Grace. If you accept it. We were kept apart, and we kept ourselves apart.' She sighed suddenly. 'My point, Lady Vintage, is that I spent many years not being touched. I am not used to it. It worries me a little. People do not generally trust skin-to-skin contact with a fell-witch.'

Vintage frowned slightly. She held out the pad to Chenlo. 'My apologies. Please, I did not intend to make you uncomfortable. You can of course attend to your wound yourself.'

For a long moment, Chenlo didn't say anything. Downstream from them, Helcate splashed his wings in the water, washing the dust from them.

'No,' she said eventually. 'I appreciate your help, and I would be glad for you to do it. Thank you.'

Vintage dipped the pad again, and then carefully wiped away the sticky blood on Chenlo's arm, taking special care around the wound itself. To her relief, once the blood and dirt was washed away, the injury did not look too serious, and she used another section of her shirt to bandage it. Chenlo nodded her thanks. They sat for a while looking out across the river and the grasslands; Vintage found her eyes drawn to the sky again and again. Tyranny hadn't sent her fell-witches to pursue them, but that didn't mean she couldn't change her mind.

'So,' she said eventually, 'how would you say that went?'

Chenlo raised her eyebrows. 'Forgive me, Lady Vintage, but in Yuron-Kai we would have called that "a corpse too fly-blown for leather".'

'How colourful,' said Vintage dryly. 'And please do call me Vintage, dear. All this ladying reminds me too much of home.' She threw a stone into the water. 'We failed to get any sense out of Tyranny, but I don't think either of us were surprised by that. I was a little surprised that it escalated so quickly, and almost getting eaten by Wild-touched cats is not a success by anyone's measure.'

'Your friend Harlo *did* get eaten by the cats,' pointed out Chenlo, and Vintage winced.

'Yes, poor Harlo. However, despite all that, we learned quite a lot, I believe. We've seen our newest war-beast and she has a power none of us could have expected. She also appears to be somewhat unfriendly, and not especially interested in her home or her siblings. Tyranny seems to be taking this queen business reasonably seriously, and she is not without public support.' She paused to throw another stone. As quiet as the river was, it was running too fast to provide the satisfying little *plop* noise she was looking for. 'More interestingly, perhaps, she is no longer in league with her old partner, Okaar, and if anything they now seem to have opposing aims. Jhef I'm not sure of – I would have thought she would stay loyal to her brother, but she is young, and has probably had a somewhat lively childhood. Perhaps the stability and opulence of a royal palace appeals to her.'

'That potion he gave you.' Chenlo leaned forward, her elbows on her knees and her hands clasped loosely together. Her bare arm was smooth, the skin marked by a tiny fingernail-shaped scar at her elbow. 'It was like throwing oil on the winnowfire. How is that possible?'

'I really don't know, but it's certainly interesting, isn't it?' Vintage slipped the rolled-up piece of material out of her jacket, and held the vials up to the light. The orange fluid within rolled thickly up and down the tubes. 'We do know that Tyranny once dealt a lot of akaris in and out of Mushenska when she was still the leader of the Salts. Perhaps she was involved in other drugs.'

'A drug that makes winnowfire more powerful?' Chenlo shook her head. 'She must have kept it very quiet. The Winnowry would have killed for it.'

Helcate came splashing back up the river towards them. He had a golden fish in his mouth, held delicately at the tail – it wasn't very big, no longer than a human hand, but Vintage smiled at the sight of it.

'That's it, darling, good work! Can you get us a few more? Chenlo, let's get a fire going, and we'll have fish for tea.'

They decided to wait where they were and rest for the night, and later, as the last light of dusk seeped out of the sky, Vintage found herself sitting by the riverbed, the only one left awake. Helcate slept curled up by the fire, his leathery wings folded close along his back and his nose tucked neatly away. The Winnowry agent had made herself as comfortable as she could, and lay with her injured arm held stiffly at her side. Judging from her faint sighs, she had managed to sleep anyway.

The plains were a peaceful place at night, if somewhat eerie. Winds moved softly through the grasses, and a variety of insects set up a chorus of chirps and hums. It was, Vintage thought, tempting to sit and attempt to forget all the horrors of Sarn – the Wild and the Jure'lia, the wars and the blood-soaked land – but it was never quite possible. Sarn still wore its scars openly, and many of them were fresh wounds. As the sun had gone down, distant parts of the plain had shimmered an ominous deep green as the dying light reflected off great stretches of varnish.

'A little more poisoned, a little more ruined, with every Rain.' Vintage ran a hand across her face. Despite her well-practised optimism, it was hard to avoid the fact that the Jure'lia would inevitably win, if they couldn't find some way to rip them out at the roots. She sighed heavily and stood up, intending to move closer to the fire, when she spotted something moving in the distance. It was too far to see clearly, but the last light of dusk glinted against large pieces of an oily-looking metal.

'Sarn's bloody bones.'

It was much too small to be an actual Behemoth, and Vintage could not recall any instances of the worm people's ships moving across the ground in such a manner, but there was no doubt that it was moon-metal she was looking at. There was no mistaking that unsettling, bruise-coloured sheen.

She watched it for a long time, but whatever it was moved out of sight, and when she returned to the fire, Helcate raised his head, big blue eyes blinking curiously. She felt him offer to keep watch so she could rest, and despite herself she smiled, scratching him behind the ears.

Thank you, darling. Stay alert – there are monsters out there in the dark.

'Are you ready to talk about it? What this power means?'

Noon did not turn her head to look at She Who Laughs. She had left the fake tent and wandered out into the castle some hours ago, letting her feet take her where they would. Eventually, she had come to an upper chamber with several long narrow windows in the glass walls, and she had sat down next to one and looked out across the desert, watching as the sky changed colour and the winds moved the sand in little flurries. It was possible to see a clump of the white fleshy plants from where she sat, and she wondered if it was one of those she had run to when she'd tried to escape.

'Are *you* ready to talk about it?' Noon said eventually.

'Of course.' She Who Laughs came to stand next to her. 'I want to know what it is like, to feel that, as a human. As a person from this world. How it feels to understand it as I do. You alone of my children have started to understand what it means, this gift.'

Noon nodded absently. 'Don't you want to know what it was like afterwards, though? The things that I saw. Because I remember that too, now.'

'What?'

'And the things I smelled. When I woke up. I don't know how long I was asleep, but things were still burning when I woke up. There was smoke everywhere, and, you know, I almost didn't know where I was, because nothing looked the same. There was no grass, no tents, no people. There was smoke, great clouds of it, more smoke than I'd ever seen, and ash everywhere underfoot. White ash, that was still hot to touch.'

She Who Laughs grimaced. 'I have seen burned things before.'

Noon turned her head sharply. '*Have* you, though? I wonder. There were twisted things all about, still glowing in places. Those were the metal things we had, although I couldn't have told you what any of them were. The sky was gone too, did I say that? Hidden in the smoke. I got up eventually, because I was frightened and I wanted my mum. I wandered for a bit, feeling the heat of the ash through my boots, retching at the smell. I found twisted shapes on the ground, things that had been people I knew once. That much heat all at once melts the flesh straight off your bones, and turns your bones to charcoal, but you can still make out, you know, skulls and things. Teeth and eye sockets. What about those things? Did you want to know about those?'

'Noon –'

'Because you *forced* me to remember, and I think you should know about this, too. Because you ripped away all the careful little scabs I had built up over this memory.' She held up her hands; they were shaking. 'I was there for a few days. I didn't know what I was doing, but eventually someone alerted the Winnowry and they came and got me. I haven't thought of it since then, but . . .'

'I understand that this is difficult for you, but the power—'

'Mother Fast used to tell these stories, about dark spirits that would come and steal the souls of naughty children. She had puppets of them, little things with white faces and bodies made of black rags. When I saw the bats in the sky, I thought that's what they were. The *sky wights*, come to take my soul up to the storm clouds. I was relieved when I saw them. Which is funny, in a horrible way.' Noon paused, thinking. 'Mother Fast survived. Did you know that? I think she must have been on the very edge of it, caught by the outer ring of the blast, because otherwise I don't see how. Everyone else died. Everyone else died screaming.'

She Who Laughs said nothing. The blonde woman she was inhabiting looked much older than she had; used up, thinner.

'Did you make me do it?' Noon asked eventually. 'Did you show me how it worked somehow? Whisper it in a dream?'

'No.' She Who Laughs smiled warmly. 'You figured it out. Like I said before, you're good at figuring things out.'

'Oh.' Noon looked back out the window. She wanted a strong drink, or akaris. Akaris would be good. 'Hooray for me. Can you get me something?'

'What do you need?'

'There's a drug, called akaris. The Winnowry makes it. It makes you sleep, without dreams. Bring me as much of it as you can find. And wine, lots of that. I know you can get it.'

She Who Laughs narrowed her eyes, banking their emerald fury into a pair of glowing green slits.

'I do not want you to harm yourself, child.'

Noon flew at her, knocking her bodily into the far wall.

'You don't want me harmed?! What do you think you've done to me?' She raised her fist to strike the woman, but She Who Laughs took hold of her wrist in a vice-like grip and the life energy was torn out of her in one ragged pulse. Noon made a strangled noise and dropped to her knees, yet she lifted her head even as her vision turned grey at the edges. 'I had the beginnings of something like a life in Ebora, you monster, and you fucking took it from me. You've destroyed me all over again.' With the last bit of energy she had left, she pressed her free hand to the woman's bare arm. 'Go on, take the rest of it. Do me a favour and finish the job.'

She Who Laughs shook her off and stepped away. She stood for a moment, her face taut with a very human expression of anger and disgust, and then she left the chamber. Noon watched her go, and then crawled back to sit against the wall, her knees drawn up to her chest. *She calls it power, but it is a curse, just like they always said.* The memory of her mother's life energy, the exact moment she slipped away, seemed to hang over her like a physical weight. She hadn't burned them *all* to death accidentally, as she had always assumed – such things were not unheard of with fell-witches – she had ripped their lives from them just to feed a terrible emptiness inside her. And there was no forgetting that now. Not ever.

Chapter Twenty-four

Vintage woke to the feeling of Helcate's cold nose pressing into her neck. She groaned and batted him away, before catching the stream of feeling emanating from the small war-beast –

Danger, danger!

She rolled over and sat up. It was still early morning, the sky overhead a bright and brittle blue while the east was gradually waking into a symphony of white and yellow clouds. Agent Chenlo was fast asleep, curled up on herself like a child, her brow faintly creased as though she were having an argument in her dreams. At first Vintage could not make out what had so alarmed Helcate, and then she felt the vibrations coming up through the ground. Something was coming towards them, something big.

'Shit.'

She scrambled to her feet and looked back, away from the river. Three huge shapes were thundering towards them; Wild-touched bears, by the looks of them, each a good ten feet tall, and each wearing cobbled-together armour of moon-metal which winked greasily under the early sunlight. There were riders too, faces peering over the blunt heads of their steeds, and they brandished a variety of weapons. Vintage saw swords, spears, and even a few crossbows.

'Well, *shit*.' Vintage shuffled backwards and kicked Chenlo in the shin. 'Wake up!'

The woman groaned, and seemed to curl up tighter on herself. 'Leave me alone. I feel unwell. It's that gods-cursed potion you made me drink.'

'Bloody get up now or your stomach's biggest problem is going to be that it's smeared all over the grass.'

Chenlo got to her feet. Helcate was whining in the back of his throat, and Vintage hauled his harness over from its place by the fire. 'I know you don't like it, darling, but you might want to ready some of that acid of yours. Chenlo, help me with this.'

They hefted the harness up over Helcate's back and began pulling straps into place, but the bears were almost on them. Vintage stopped what she was doing and stood in front of Helcate, holding up her arms.

'There's no need for the show of force!' she shouted. 'What do you want?'

The bears slowed down, and the largest came to the front. Up close the thing was gruesome: white fur stained yellow by running eyes and the drool that seeped from its jaws, and it was swollen and ill-proportioned with muscle. Black claws dug furrows into the red earth of the plains. There were, from what Vintage could see, three people on each bear. The man at the front of the largest was tall and wiry, with a scrawny chest and several missing teeth. He grinned at them and held up his spear, which he pointed directly at Vintage.

'Whatever you've got,' he said in thickly accented plains speech. To Vintage's ear he sounded as though he were originally from somewhere to the south, not far from her own home of Catalen. 'Is that a gods-damned war-beast?'

'It doesn't matter what he is, you can't have him,' said

Vintage, keeping her tone conversational. 'In fact, it just so happens we've recently escaped prison, and don't have anything much to trade with you. So perhaps you should just carry on your way, find someone else.'

'Trade!' This was from the woman sitting at the head of another bear. She was small, with one arm covered in tattoos. 'We're not about trade, *dearie*.'

Vintage sighed. 'No, I thought not. Hard times on the plains?'

'Bad times,' agreed the man, nodding. 'You got to take what you can, when it's war in the skies. No more moving from you, now. Move any more, and our pets will taste your guts. Give us what you got. Or maybe we just take the beast.'

'He will fight you,' said Vintage. 'I will fight you.'

Chenlo leaned into her shoulder. 'I can blast them back,' she said, her voice very soft.

'The moon-metal . . .'

'Give me the vials.'

Vintage smiled. 'Helcate, give them your welcome, please.'

'Helcate,' said Helcate.

'What are you doing?' shouted the woman. She urged her bear forward a little, and Vintage saw faces behind her, eyes wide. 'We want no tricks.'

'No tricks,' agreed Vintage, as Helcate began hiccupping to one side of her. 'Certainly not tricks. I feel it would be disrespectful to describe the abilities of a war-beast as a trick, wouldn't you? They are blessed abilities, surely, blessed by the tree-father himself.'

'What the fuck are you talking about?' shouted the man, just as Helcate spat forward his stream of acid. Immediately the men and women on the first bear ducked, bringing up shields of moon-metal to cover themselves, and the acid splattered over the bear's armour, mostly missing the creature's patchy fur and raw skin. As Helcate leapt awkwardly up into

266

the air for a better angle on the next shot, she reached into her jacket and passed the vials to Chenlo.

'What are you doing?' came the muffled shout from behind the shields.

'This is your last chance,' shouted Vintage. 'If you leave now, we won't hurt you.' Next to her, Chenlo was choking down the contents of one of the vials.

'Piss off! What sort of broken war-beast *spits* stuff? We'll skin him for his bloody fur!'

An arrow thumped into the ground at Vintage's feet.

'Well, I tried. Chenlo?'

The fell-witch held out her hand, and, oddly touched, Vintage took it. At once she felt a weakness travel through her body, like swooning on a hot day, and then Chenlo was in front of her, arms held up. The vast wave of fire that flew from her was a nightmarish thing, tinged with shadows, and it crashed into the Wild-touched bears with a roar. There were screams, and two of the bears fell back, pieces of molten moon-metal flying from them. The last was still standing, although it hung its head low between its legs. Blood oozed from its eyes, while two of the people who had been on its back picked themselves up off the ground and began to run back the way they had come. Parts of the grass were on fire, while Helcate hovered above.

'Sarn's bloody bones,' muttered Vintage. 'I told them. I told them to go.'

'And they refused,' said Chenlo quietly. The last bear raised its head and its jaws flopped open, revealing mismatched yellow teeth, but Chenlo threw a barrage of super-hot fireballs, blasting it back at least twenty feet until it fell, smoking, into the grass. The bears, and the people – save for the two who were even now limping rapidly into the distance – were dead. 'Those were the bandits we were warned of.'

'At least they won't be robbing anyone else.' Vintage glanced at Chenlo, who was sweating slightly. 'It makes you ill, this stuff?'

She looked down at her hands. 'Yes. Like I am slightly poisoned. A headache, sickness. But it passes gradually.'

'Like a hangover,' said Vintage. Chenlo looked at her.

'You would have fought for him, your war-beast. Even with no weapons.' She smiled, just a little. 'You are brave, Lady Vintage.'

To her own surprise, Vintage felt her cheeks grow hot. 'Well, thank you, Agent Chenlo. Although I do miss my crossbow somewhat. Do you think any of their weapons survived?'

They picked their way forward carefully, stepping over chunks of bear meat and the corpses of the bandits. Some bits and pieces had survived; a spear had been flung far from the wreckage, and even one of the crossbows looked like it might fire again. Vintage paused by a pool of molten moon-metal. It looked black under the sun, and flickered with rainbows like a raven's wing.

'This strange fire Okaar gave you. It destroys the moon-metal.'

Chenlo looked over at her. 'It destroys everything.'

'No, I know, but –' Vintage grinned. She reached inside her jacket and pulled out the bar towel Okaar had given her. The words on it were stained with both beer and wine, but it was still possible to read them: Welcome to The Shining Coin. 'Let's grab what we can from these idiots, and get some fresh water from the river. We're going back to Jarlsbad.'

'I have a bad feeling about this.'

'Relax, cousin.' Tormalin looked up from where he was securing Kirune's harness to give Aldasair a quick smile. 'This is simply a little exploratory mission. To see if I'm right about the Jure'lia and their hiding place. All looking, no touching, and then we'll report back. I give you my word.'

Aldasair had to admit that his cousin looked better than he

had done in days. He had bathed recently, put on fresh clothes, and there was a brightness about his eyes that had been completely missing since they had lost the fell-witch, Noon. Once, Aldasair knew he would have found it difficult to imagine forming such an attachment to a human, with their frail bodies and short lives, but a lot had changed since Ebora had come back to life. Which was the other issue.

'If it is just looking and not touching, then why must Bern travel with you?'

'Bern will help me find them. His link to them could be invaluable. Could even work as an early warning system.'

Bern, hearing his name, came over from where he had been filling their packs with supplies. He still looked too tired for Aldasair's liking, and there were shadows on his cheeks where his face was growing gaunt.

'Aldasair, try not to worry,' he said. 'We will be careful. And Sharrik has been driving everyone spare lately – it'll be good for him to stretch his wings. That's an animal that was born to fight, and it chafes at him, this waiting and planning.'

Aldasair nodded, trying to take comfort from his lover's words. Without Noon, Vostok, Helcate and Vintage, they had been limited in what they could do. Bern was able to give them a vague idea of what Hestillion was up to, but they were in no shape to take her on. They had to think, defend and plan; none of which were satisfying to their beloved griffin. The news about Noon had, somewhat inevitably, filtered through to the human camps, and wherever he went in the palace he saw worried faces. People had taken to watching the skies again. Valous the Stone Talker had arrived from Finneral, and she had been spending her time with the fell-witches, trying to bring them through the loss of their liberator, coaching them towards forming some sort of fighting unit, but even with the wisdom of one of Finneral's greatest leaders, he feared they had lost Noon at exactly the wrong moment. With everything against them, any action they took that could get them more information was valuable, he understood that. He also understood that two of the dearest people in the world to him were flying out into untold dangers. Along the link he shared with her he felt Jessen's discomfort. She had refused to come and see them off, and was hiding in the courtyard somewhere.

'Fine. I will keep watch over Ebora and Ygseril. But you must promise me you will be careful, and safe.' He heard the plaintiveness in his own voice and inwardly grimaced at it. 'Not just for my sake. Ebora needs all four of you if we've to have any chance of surviving this Rain.'

Tor nodded distractedly, adjusting the sword belt that held his new weapon, but Bern came and took hold of Aldasair's arms, before kissing him firmly.

'I promise, my love.'

When finally they left, Aldasair stood in the gardens with his arms crossed over his chest, watching Kirune and Sharrik spirit them away. He felt Jessen's presence behind him before he saw her, and held out his hand. She pressed her nose to it.

'They will be fine,' he told her, but he knew that she could feel his own uncertainty as well as he could feel hers.

There were tiny colourful lizards in the desert. Noon did not know how she hadn't seen them before, but they moved in quick little bursts across the black sands, and sometimes skittered silently across the walls of the glass castle. She sat by the battlements and watched them, the heat beating down on the top of her head; a yellow lizard with black feet, a lizard as blue as the sky. Tiny and perfect.

She had recently come to the end of a period of crying, simple exhaustion leaving her empty and marooned on the shore of her grief. Her head ached and her mouth was dry, even though she sipped periodically from the great glass jug of water She Who Laughs had left her. *I've wrung myself out*, she thought. *Cried until there's nothing left*. Except that the image of her mother's face would not leave her, nor the memory of her sorrow when she realised what her daughter had done. All she'd ever asked of Noon was that she not reveal her fire to anyone, and she had let her down. All those people, all of them good, innocent people, had died because of her own selfishness and stupidity. There was no coming back from that, no redemption and no forgiveness.

The little blue lizard vanished over the wall, and Noon heard footsteps at her back.

'Have you finished with this performance yet?'

She Who Laughs came across the glass towards her. She still wore the body of the blonde woman; she was tough, whoever she was.

'Leave me alone.'

'I thought you were cleverer than the rest of them, Noon. Your affinity for the power I have given you should be proof of that alone, yet here you sit, crying over people who have been dead for more than a decade.'

'People I have killed, you mean. It hardly matters how long ago it was when you add that bit.'

There was a period of silence. Wind whipped up across the castle, blowing flute-like through its strange structures. When She Who Laughs spoke again, there was a clear note of disgust in her voice.

'Humans are all so weak. I have given you all so much, yet you are a world of keening, mewling infants who hide from power rather than grasp it. If you only—'

Noon picked up the glass jug and flung it, over arm, at the figure behind her. She Who Laughs twitched away and it sailed past her to shatter into pieces on the floor. The yellow lizard, which had been peeking back over the battlements, skittered away. Without saying anything more, She Who Laughs left.

Later, when the skies gave up their sunset colours and settled into darkness for the night, Noon stood up, intending to make her way back inside. She had fallen into a kind of trance for a while, reliving, again and again, the moment she had torn her mother's life energy from her body, and had quite forgotten the pieces of broken glass all over the floor.

'Oh *bastard*!'

She hopped away again, holding one foot out in front of her. A long shard of glass had slipped through the leather of her boot and stabbed her in the soft pad of flesh just below her big toe. The pain, bright and sharp, drove everything else from her mind for a moment.

Moving away from the broken pieces, she sat back down and removed the glass and her boot. The wound was bleeding merrily, although it did not look too deep. Noon grimaced, and looked at her hand, now covered in her own blood.

The smell of it, sharp and mineral, made her think of the night in the cave with Tor, when she had offered up her blood and he had taken it. She had given him something then, something vital; not just her blood and her body, but the knowledge that he was someone she desired, even needed. She had saved him, in an odd way she was only just beginning to understand, and he had given of himself in return. The memory of that night, and the night they had shared together on Origin, eased something in her chest. The sharp-edged grief that was lodged in her heart seemed, just for a moment, to soften. Yes, she had made a terrible, unforgivable mistake, but once she had also been vital to someone else's life, had been what they needed when everything else was lost.

'It's worth something,' she said to the night. 'It has to be.'

She thought of their faces – Tor's handsome, scarred face, his luminous skin; Vintage and her wise eyes, her easy smile. If nothing else, they needed her.

'And I love them,' she said, still looking at the blood on her hands. 'If anyone should judge me, it should be them.'

The wound was no longer bleeding so freely. Somewhat gingerly, she put her boot back on, and, taking care to walk around the broken glass, headed back inside the castle, limping slightly. She Who Laughs was back in her bone-strewn courtyard, the fires of her halo painting green light up the translucent walls.

'Have you come here to throw more things at me?'

Noon shrugged. 'I'm ready to talk about it.'

She Who Laughs raised her eyebrows. 'You are?'

'The power, how it felt.' Noon rubbed her hands up and down her arms. It felt like the night chill of the desert was in her bones. 'It was . . . extraordinary.'

'My child, that's all I wanted.'

'I'm sorry,' Noon walked towards the older woman, her face downcast, 'it's been hard for me, to go through all that again, but I'm willing to tell you what I can.'

'You are stronger than I thought.' She Who Laughs nodded. 'I should not have underestimated you, Noon. Tell me, when you moved through the living connections, what did that feel like?'

'It felt like . . .' Noon shook her head, wonderingly, and laid her hand on She Who Laughs' arm as if to steady herself. 'It felt like *go fuck yourself.*'

In one movement she ripped all the remaining life energy from the blond-haired woman, holding back nothing. She Who Laughs dropped to the sandy floor, her skin abruptly grey and cold – the green fire that had been dancing in her eyes and around her head flickered out.

'That's how it fucking felt.' Noon raised her hands and released a great cone of green flame into the night, burning off everything that had been held briefly inside her. A few moments later, light began to gather in the courtyard again. A new body was forming, snatched somewhere from her remaining cultists. Noon waited, watching as the green halo of flame swarmed back into life, and as soon as she could see a solid arm, she grabbed it. Again she ripped away everything the woman had, siphoning it into herself as fast as she could, and again the body fell onto the black sand, lifeless.

The third time a new body formed, she took hold of the wrist again, and She Who Laughs spoke in a quick, urgent voice.

'You know you cannot kill me this way. You cannot kill me at all, little girl.'

'No, but it's annoying, isn't it? And I can do it all night.' She tightened her grip on the woman's wrist, intending it to hurt. 'Send me home, or kill me. Those are the only two options. I'm not something for you to poke and prod. I'm not even a victory in your weird grudge match with the Aborans. Give me back to my people.'

'Your people?' She Who Laughs smiled coldly. 'You killed them all, remember?'

'The people I love. Send me back, or just end it. I promise I will be nothing but a problem for you as long as you keep me here.'

The woman scowled. Her newest body was young, no more than a teenager, and Noon felt a twisting in her gut. This vessel may be dying, but she had no wish to kill her, even so.

'Fine,' she snapped. 'If that's what you truly want . . .'

'It is. It might make me weak or a coward or whatever you'd like to call me, but if I must grieve all over again, I'd prefer to be where I'm supposed to be.'

'Very well.' She Who Laughs shook her off. 'I will send you back to your heart's dearest desire, then.' She frowned at Noon, looking as if she might say something more, but instead the woman raised her arms, and the halo of fire grew larger, filling up the small courtyard with its glow.

Tor, thought Noon, and then blinked as a rush of green light enveloped her, blotting out She Who Laughs, the glass castle, the desert night above. There was a sense of weightlessness, a rushing sensation through her whole body, and then she was somewhere else . . .

Daylight, more sky. There was nothing holding her up and she was falling, falling through an empty sky towards the very distant ground, which looked alarmingly solid and full of rocks. Noon opened her mouth and screamed.

Chapter Twenty-five

'Did you feel that?'

Tor leaned back in the harness, trying to make sense of what he was feeling. A surge of strong emotion, out of nowhere, then gone again. They were flying south over the arid plains of the Yuron-Kai, the only features of the landscape the clusters of yurts and herds of horses that indicated a settlement. Far to the east was the distant strip of blue that was the sea, and just before that, a haze on the horizon where the mighty city-state of Reidn squatted. Bern brought Sharrik up as close as he could get to Kirune, and shouted over the wind.

'Was it Vostok?'

'It felt like her,' Tor muttered, distracted.

'What?'

'The snake is very far away,' said Kirune. 'And she thinks of us barely at all. Our connection . . .' He growled low in the back of his throat. 'Vostok alone truly understands it. But she is very faint. I cannot tell what she thinks.'

'Bern?'

'I don't know. The bastard worm people make our connection harder to hear.' He held up his hand with the blue crystal embedded in it as an explanation. 'I can barely be sure of anything while they are caught in their own chaos. Apart from Sharrik.' He ruffled the feathers on the back of the griffin's neck. 'I can always hear Sharrik clear enough.'

There seemed to be no more to say. They flew on across the ever-changing landscape, heading always south. Tor had spent so long over his crosses and lines that he could picture the map in his head. Every account he'd been able to draw together suggested that the Jure'lia habitually withdrew to a place in the southern hemisphere of Sarn, a place so distant that Ebora's maps didn't have a name for it; there was just a vast expanse of forest, marked in anonymous green.

It was getting late in the day when Tor saw the first patch of varnish. The sun was going down, turning the sky to the west of them into a glowing anvil of heat and cloud, and at first he thought he was looking at a particularly large lake. Then the angle at which they saw it changed, and he recognised the shining, warped surface for what it was. It was an enormous stretch of varnish, right out in the middle of nowhere, but Tor could see many dirt roads leading into it. Evidently the place under the varnish had once been a town, and quite a big one, by the look of it.

'By the stones,' Bern's voice was thick with horror, 'there's more beyond it, look.'

He was right. As the sun sank and filled the landscape with dying light, the patches of varnish lit up, reflecting a sickly yellow. This region had once been filled with small settlements and bustling towns, but the Jure'lia had come for them and quite neatly erased them from the map.

Hestillion came for them, Tor reminded himself. *My sister has done this.*

'I want to take a look,' he called across to Bern. Kirune growled, but he ignored it. 'Let's land.'

Bern didn't object. They came down lightly, skittering across the slippery surface and coming to rest near a mound of rubble given smooth sides by the varnish. Tor unstrapped himself from Kirune and stepped down, touching a hand to the sword on his back as he did so. The place was eerily silent, without even birdsong to break it up, but a sense of danger remained, as though the Jure'lia were hiding just out of sight.

'I do not like it,' said Kirune. Even the big griffin looked uneasy, his paws taking big elaborate steps across the varnish.

'I suspect the people who died here liked it even less,' said Tor. All around them were signs of regular human life – straw, buckets, cloth, bricks – all caught and frozen by the solid resin. There were bodies too, men, women and children ensnared in a stillness they would never escape. He saw terror on some faces, those who had been trying to get away and had failed to evade the grasp of the worm people, and he saw those who had already had their insides eaten away by the burrowers; their eyes were black holes, their mouths were expressionless. Once this had been home to lots of humans. It had had its own name, its own identity. Now it was impossible to tell what it had been like. The buildings were all crushed to dust and rubble, the people all dead.

'Aldasair is right,' he said eventually. 'She is being methodical. Working her way through the continent, wiping each human place off the map. They ran, probably,' he gestured vaguely to the south, 'when they realised that their neighbours were being eaten alive. When they spotted the Behemoths in the sky, they probably ran to the next settlement, the next town. But she kept coming back. How far can you run?' He thought about that moment, so many years ago, when he had left Ebora. He had intended to run then, but it had all caught up with him. 'Maybe some of them got away. I can't believe she would have gone to the trouble of chasing the stragglers down the road. But then –' he lifted his arms and dropped them, laughed a little – 'what do I know about my sister? Fuck all, it turns out.'

278

'Have you seen enough?' rumbled Kirune.

'This probably means we are on the right track, you know,' said Bern. He was massaging one hand with the other, frowning slightly. 'If she is starting with places close to where they're holed up. But brother Kirune is right. We should get moving. It'll be dark soon, and the last thing I want to do is camp on top of this stuff.'

Tor nodded. The idea of sleeping on top of varnish was obscene somehow. He touched his sword once more, for luck, and they prepared to leave.

It was like Noon shouted in her ear.

Vostok turned sharply in mid-air, every sense alight. Out of nowhere, bright weapon was in the sky with her. She could feel her as clearly as she ever had, as clearly as when the girl had carried her soul within her.

'Where are you?'

There was no answer but a singing note of terror. Vostok cast about desperately, trying to sense where she was. The land she currently flew over was a strange, barren place, riddled with springs of water that ran boiling hot. Steam and mist clung to the rocky ground, making everything look much the same, and barely anything lived there. The acrid smell of it, she had privately decided, was enough to send even the lowest creature away.

Yet it was movement that caught her eye; a tiny figure in the distance, dropping through the air like a stone. Vostok, her heart thundering in her chest, parted the air like an arrow.

Bright weapon! I am coming!

Vostok!

It was close. Vostok ploughed into Noon, catching her only ten feet from the ground. For a time she just flew, barely in control, and narrowly avoided crashing into the rocky earth herself, then she let her wings take her up, and up. Noon was crushed against her scaly chest, held there with her front legs.

'I knew it!' she called, exultant. 'I knew you were not dead!'

They were on solid ground again. Noon opened her eyes and pressed her feverish brow to Vostok's scales, taking comfort in her touch.

'Where are we?'

The dragon had flown her up and away from the place of rocks and streams, and now they rested on the slope of a small hill, covered in patchy, sick-looking grass. When she lifted her head, she could see across the stretch of rocky ground to the sea. There was a lot of sea.

'An island somewhere,' said Vostok dismissively. 'There is no one here, but it is hot. I thought you might have been here, and then you were.' She sounded pleased with herself. Since they had landed, she had curled herself about Noon protectively, like a mother-dog with puppies. Her long white tail twitched in the scrubby grass. 'I have been looking in all the hot places. Where have you been, bright weapon?'

'I was in the Singing Eye Desert,' said Noon.

'There?' Vostok snorted. 'There is nothing there. And it is very far from *here*. In future, I would prefer that you do not suddenly go to strange places without consulting me first.'

Noon smiled weakly. Vostok's presence was solid and reassuring, a suit of armour holding her together, but she felt like she had had her life energy ripped from her. It was difficult to concentrate, or think clearly.

'It wasn't my choice, Vostok. Someone took me there, and then they sent me back. It was strange there, in the castle. I think that time was wrong, somehow . . . They sent me back to you, I think, although I doubt she would have cared if I had smashed my brains out all over these rocks instead.'

'Who was this person? Did you destroy them? This is an enormous insult to me, and to Ebora!'

Noon sighed. Already her time with She Who Laughs in the desert felt like an especially strange dream, while the memories that she had forced back onto her felt all too real.

'I'm not sure I can explain it,' she said eventually. 'At least, not yet.'

Vostok was quiet for a moment. The silence was filled with the sound of raucous seabirds, and for a while Noon lost herself in it.

'I do not understand what has happened to you,' said Vostok, her voice unusually soft, 'but I can feel it. You are broken in new places, bright weapon. I will have vengeance on the person who has harmed you so. I will bury them in fire.'

Noon almost smiled, thinking of Vostok trying to burn to death a being who essentially was fire.

'I am broken,' she agreed. 'But it's a break that's been waiting to happen for a long time.'

Vostok blew soft grey smoke through her nostrils. The birds, Noon noticed, were still all squawking madly, possibly because there was a dragon sitting in their nesting area. 'I don't pretend to know what that means, bright weapon, but we shall certainly heal you. And to do that we must go home, back to the tree-father and our brethren. There is a lot still to do.'

Noon nodded, although even the idea of standing up seemed an unanswerable challenge. She shifted, curling up closer to Vostok's side.

'I know, I just need to rest some more first. Sleep, and then home.' She thought of Tor and Vintage and smiled, even as sleep shut her eyes for her. 'Home very soon.'

Chapter Twenty-six

The lobby of the Efrinka Counting House was cool and shady, an oasis of apricot marble and artful little pools of trickling water. Vintage patted at her hair, too aware that they had been travelling through the grasslands of Jarlsbad for days, and the orange dust of the region had apparently bonded itself to every part of her body. Chenlo seemed less concerned, looking around the lobby with keen interest, while Helcate they had left to the skies.

'Madam,' the man behind the desk pressed his lips together, preparing to say something mildly impolite, 'you will forgive me, but this is an old family account, one of our most treasured, and we cannot simply take your word.'

'I have told you once already. I am Lady Vincenza de Grazon and I am the key holder of this account. As it happens, I don't have my identifying papers with me and this particular key has been mislaid, but I assure you, I have been here many times before to withdraw funds.' When the man only looked more pained, Vintage sighed noisily. 'Haven't you got anyone who has worked here longer than a week?'

The man retreated into the labyrinth back rooms and returned with a stately-looking woman with sooty black eyelashes and a gold key around her neck. She looked as though she had been interrupted during something important and her mouth was pursed into a forbearing expression, but when she spotted Vintage her eyebrows shot up and she scampered forward.

'Lady de Grazon?'

'Ah, darling, at least someone remembers me.'

'We could hardly forget one of our most celebrated customers. But Ernes here tells me that you do not have your key or your papers?'

'I have had a rough week or so, my dear. Which is partly why, of course, I must access my account immediately.'

The woman nodded vigorously. 'Absolutely, and we will be pleased to help you in any way we can, Lady de Grazon. However, you would not trust us with your funds if we weren't very careful about our security, so perhaps on this occasion we could see . . . the mark?'

Vintage grimaced. She glanced once at Agent Chenlo, who was now watching with interest, before lifting the ragged tails of her shirt and pushing down the top of her trousers. Low on her hip was a tattoo of the de Grazon family crest, combined, through a series of flowing lines, with the sigil of the Efrinka Counting House. It was drawn with very special inks, crafted from the bones of Wild-touched sea creatures, and at the sight of it, all hesitancy vanished from the woman's face. From within her shirt she pulled a long brass chain, on the end of which was a small round lens. Very briefly she pressed it to Vintage's tattoo, and for a moment another pattern was revealed within the inked lines. It looked a little like a bunch of grapes – Vintage had chosen the shape herself, years ago. The woman straightened up.

'Very good,' she said shortly. 'What can we do for you, Lady de Grazon?'

Vintage gave her the request, and then turned back to Chenlo, who looked faintly amused.

'I did not realise you had a tattoo also.'

'Yes, well. I'm full of surprises.'

'And I'm not certain why we need to go through all of this. Surely if your friend Okaar is in this city, you can go and ask for him.'

'First, I would like to eat something that hasn't been crawling about in the grass recently, and second, we will have to throw a lot of money around even to get into The Shining Coin. If Okaar is there, he is hiding, and we'll need to get through the layers of lies he will have built up around himself.'

'But why? Why would he be hiding?'

'Because, my dear, the queen of Tygrish wants him dead, and anyone here could sell his location to her for a healthy profit.'

'How do you even . . .'

'The bar towel. It was his way of telling me where to find him if we survived. Do you think an assassin habitually keeps souvenirs on his person in case he needs to hide a key? Okaar is a very clever man and we could do with him on our side.'

Chenlo looked unconvinced, but said no more as the woman with the sooty lashes returned carrying a soft leather pouch and a simple bag with a strap.

'I hope you don't mind, Lady de Grazon, but I took the liberty of acquiring a bag for you to put your funds in. Walking the streets with one of our withdrawal pouches on display may not be entirely safe.'

Vintage beamed. 'My darling, you are a wonder. If we aren't all eaten alive by the worm people's monsters by next week, I shall absolutely write a letter of praise to your superiors.'

Nodding merrily at the woman's slightly strangled expression, Vintage left the great airy building, Chenlo at her heels.

'Was that necessary? You upset that woman, I think.'

'Oh, I'm just having a bit of fun.' Vintage pulled the bag strap over her shoulder and settled it into place. 'Speaking of which, we shall need new clothes.'

'Clothes?' Chenlo looked stricken. 'I am quite happy with these. They are quite adequate.'

Vintage glanced at her again; they were good clothes, well made and solid, but they were also very obviously the travelling clothes of a Winnowry agent.

'Nonsense. We have to dress the part, you see. Come on, it won't take a moment.'

The streets of the central city of Jarlsbad were heaving, as they had been every time Vintage had visited it. Delicate green and white towers rose all around them, while the smaller, squatter buildings, with their mint-green roof tiles and elaborate shop signs, spilled even more people; men and women shopping for goods, children chasing after their parents or their brothers and sisters, merchants with heavy satchels full of change. There was the scent of cooking food on the air, mixed with a fresh floral scent. Jarlsbad was known for its perfumes, crafted from flowers growing on roof gardens all over the city. They moved up the street, heading towards the fabric quarters, where the best clothes were to be found.

Despite herself, despite everything, Vintage felt her heart soar. There were few things so fine, she thought, than to be in a city that is busy living its own life. It was possible here to feel that no matter what happened, Jarlsbad would continue on its way, that the sheer frenetic activity of such a place could never really cease. As a young person she had dreamed of exploring these streets with Nanthema at her side. That particular dream had ultimately not survived the rigours of reality, but it was fine to be here with a new friend. Perhaps, it was even better. She looked over at Chenlo, who was looking around at the busy shops with an uncertain expression.

'Tell me, Chenlo – did you never come here when you were an agent? Did you never collect a fell-witch from Jarlsbad?'

'We did,' said Chenlo, somewhat hesitantly. 'More than once. But we never stayed longer than we had to. Mother Cressin's rules on what the agents were allowed to do were very strict. I have never seen it quite like this. And certainly not without the knowledge that I was about to take a girl away from her familiar life, forever.'

Without quite knowing why, Vintage took the woman's arm and squeezed it briefly.

'Here, look. This is the place we need.'

Vintage breezed through the shop, falling easily into old habits. After years of travelling, she knew by sight clothes that would fall apart after a few steps on the road, and clothes that would last and suit the wearer. She bought for herself a fancier version of her usual clothes: some fine leather trousers and boots, a silk shirt, a fitted jacket with many pockets sewn on the inside. For Chenlo she allowed herself a little more indulgence. With the agent's vaguely bemused permission, she purchased a fine black silk frock coat with a scarlet stripe and a red silk shirt. With her striking black hair with its bolt of white and a new pair of delicate pig-skin gloves, Chenlo looked, well . . . beautiful.

'This is quite inappropriate for the weather.' Chenlo plucked at her sleeves. The eagle tattoo at her throat peeked out from the red shirt, as though the bird were rising from a wall of flames.

'You look exquisite.' Vintage cleared her throat. 'Besides which, it's what the rich here do – wear clothes inappropriate to the weather. Only people with pesky jobs have to worry about being out in the sun too long.'

Chenlo raised her eyebrows. 'And that's how the rich live, is it?'

'Some of them. Come on, we've got an assassin to find.'

It was possible to hear The Shining Coin long before it was visible. Set in the centre of a busy plaza, the enormous gambling house was much more like the buildings of Mushenska. Rambling and built of wood, it featured balconies that sprouted all over, from which men and women would shout down the odds of various games to the people still in the plaza. These 'small games' could be bet on by the general public outside, and fees and winnings would be collected and distributed by men and women with tall conical hats. Many of these 'small games' involved the spinning of wheels, where punters could bet on which painted section the clattering peg would land on. The result was quite festive, in Vintage's opinion. Spinning wheels painted all colours whirled all night and all day.

'That is . . . that is quite the thing,' said Chenlo. It was early evening, and lamps were being lit all over the building and the plaza.

'Isn't it, though? The real games are inside, of course.' Vintage prodded at her hair. The clothes seller had allowed them to use her small bathroom, and she felt ready for a night on the town. Chenlo turned to her.

'Lady Vintage . . .'

'*Please* call me Vintage.'

'Is this necessary? Or even wise? We should be returning to Ebora as quickly as possible.'

'With what?' Seeing Chenlo's aggrieved expression, Vintage shook her head a little. 'Listen, I lost Windfall for them, and it looks like she's staying permanently lost. How can I go back with that failure on my hands? I need to bring back something useful.' She took a breath. 'And that potion Okaar gave us could tip the war in our favour. Do you not see? Historically, the winnowfire had little to no effect on Behemoths, or anything protected by moon-metal, but this stuff changes that. It boiled the armour right off that bastard bear, and, Chenlo,

287

my dear –' she grasped the woman's arm again – 'we have a small army of fell-witches waiting in Ebora for us.'

'I see.' Chenlo took her arm away. It was done gently enough, but to Vintage's surprise she felt dismayed all the same. 'That is your plan. To use these women who have come to you in good faith.'

Vintage looked away. 'Come on. I don't want to leave Helcate on his own all night, and this shouldn't take too long.'

The doors to The Shining Coin were tall and elegant, almost an afterthought in the face of all the gaudy balconies. A pair of guards stood outside them, and Vintage clocked immediately that they weren't just for show. Their armour was clean but obviously well-used, and they both stood with the easy confidence of those at home with swords and the severing of limbs.

'How much is the door price to The Shining Coin these days?' she asked the first guard. He was a tall white man with short gingery hair and a pleasant, open face. He smiled and nodded at them both.

'You've been here before, my lady?'

'More times than I'd care to admit, and more than my coin purse cares to remember. I am Lady Vintage de Grazon, and this is my friend.'

The guard named a price, and once Vintage had finished wincing and had paid up, he waved them through into the welcoming lounge. Inside, the place glittered with lights and polished brass, and a long bar circled the entire central room, which was filled with low tables and cushions. Many of these tables were covered in drinks and cards, while in the very centre there was a great dais, on which a very complex-looking game was taking place, involving multiple raised boards and large game pieces made of glass of all colours. The room was hectic and busy, filled with the voices of the rich looking to get richer, if only briefly.

'There are other rooms,' said Vintage, raising her voice a little over the general hubbub. 'More exclusive games going on elsewhere. There should be a list at the bar.'

They stepped through the crowds – Vintage spotted several people glancing curiously at the bat-wing tattoo on Chenlo's forehead – until they stood at the bar. There was a long board lining the far wall, covered in chalk scrawls. As they watched, one of the staff came over and neatly rubbed out one room's activity and replaced it with something else.

'There are new games all the time, you see,' said Vintage, peering at the board. When a bar person came in range, she waved at the woman. 'Anything particularly special on at the moment, my dear?'

'Depends on what you're after,' the woman said in a cheerful Mushenskan accent. 'High stakes or just a bit of novelty?'

'Well I suppose—'

A man lurched up to the bar next to them. He had a carefully waxed moustache and wore a jacket with a multitude of shiny silver buttons. Catching sight of Chenlo, his eyebrows shot up towards his hairline.

'Are you with them, then?'

'I'm sorry?'

'The *bat women*,' he said, an oddly urgent tone to his voice. 'You know. The ones who worship the new queen in Tygrish, the one with the giant snow bat. You *must* have heard of it.'

'I most certainly am not *with them*.' Chenlo's hand reached up to touch the bat-wing tattoo on her forehead, as if she'd forgotten it was there. 'I am an agent of the Winnowry. Or I was.'

Vintage leaned towards the man. 'Queen Tyranny's guard used to belong to the Winnowry too, but now they follow her. What do you think about it, if you don't mind me asking?'

The man looked pleased, and took a sip from the drink he was holding. 'Well. It was a shock, I can tell you that. Some woman on a war-beast chasing the royal family out of their palace, hoisting up her own flags. There was a lot of angry talk here, and in the other outlying cities. How dare she, how dare Ebora, and so on. But . . .' He took a bigger gulp of his drink. 'But it's been quiet since. And, you know, the bloody worm people are back in the skies.' Some of the pleasure faded from his florid face. 'Queen Tyranny is not kind, or benevolent, but maybe that's not what the world needs, in a time of war. Between you and me, I've thought about making my way to Tygrish. We all know a regular army is fuck-all use against the worm people.' His cheeks turned faintly pink. 'I do beg your pardon, ladies.'

Vintage grinned wickedly. 'I am absolutely scandalised, my dear, and demand that you buy me a drink in recompense.'

The man gestured to the bar person, looking pleased again, while Chenlo leaned towards Vintage.

'Do we have time for this?'

'I can drink very fast. Here, look.' There was a section on the games board marked as 'invitation only', and one of the games was called CHOOSE YOUR POISON. 'That's got to be it. Excuse me, dear,' Vintage grabbed a passing waiter, his tray laden with extravagant drinks, 'how do we get into Choose Your Poison?'

'I'm sorry, madam, but that particular game is invitation only.'

'I can see that, but I've been here before, and I know very well what "invitation only" means. How much?'

The waiter continued to demur, but when Vintage opened her withdrawal bag and began counting coins out onto the counter, he seemed to change his mind, and in moments he was handing Vintage and Chenlo a pair of wooden tokens, painted black and red.

'Take them to the topmost room,' he said. 'It's where our most exclusive games are played.'

In the meantime, the man at the bar had purchased a drink for Vintage, and was smoothing down his waxed moustaches.

'Now, ladies, may I ask where you have come from on such a fine –?'

'Oh thank you, most kind.' Vintage picked up the drink. 'See you later, my good man.'

Leaving the man spluttering into his facial hair, Vintage and Chenlo headed across the gaming room to the far stairs, which led up to the balcony that encircled the upper portion of the chamber. From there they found another set of steps, then another, until Vintage was sure they must be in the roof of the building. All along the way they spotted other rooms, many with their doors shut, the sounds of merriment seeping out into the corridor. Others revealed men and women crowded around tables and boards, their faces flushed with alcohol and excitement. Eventually, they came to a final set of steps, and here another member of staff took their tokens.

'Through the last door,' she said, in a bored tone. 'You'll have to wait your turn.'

'How do you know this is where he'll be?'

'Poison,' said Vintage, trying to sound more confident than she felt. 'He has a particular interest in poisons. Come on, let's have a look.'

The room wasn't very large, and in comparison to some of the other rooms they had seen, it was somewhat bare. The walls were covered in dark purple cloth, and the floor was bare floorboards. There were two screens at the back of the room, and a long table in the middle. This table was, to Vintage's eye, the sort of thing you might find in a kitchen. The surface had seen a lot of wear, with stains and knife marks and dark burned patches. There were two staff members standing by the door, both burly men, and a small crowd of punters; rather like the room, they were more serious than the revellers they had seen in other parts of The Shining Coin. These men and women looked worried, with teeth gnawing at lips and sweat on foreheads. The last figure wore a cloak with a deep hood and thick black gloves. They emerged from behind the screens with a wooden tray full of anonymous beakers, which they placed on the table. Vintage smiled.

'What do we do now?' asked Chenlo.

'Let's watch for a bit. See what happens.'

A man stepped up to the table. At a gesture from the hooded man, he picked up one of the beakers and pressed it to his lips. Without hesitating, he drank whatever was in the cup and then turned to the small audience, his eyes wild. A tense silence stretched out for several long moments, until finally the hooded person nodded, and the man slammed his chosen beaker back on the table. The small crowd clapped politely, and the hooded figure passed the man a bag of coins from within his robe.

'Ah,' said Vintage softly. 'You choose your poison, and if you survive, you win.'

'That,' said Chenlo, 'is a very stupid game.'

A woman standing just in front of them turned and gave them an outraged look.

'I agree, dear, although surely not much more foolish than other games of chance,' said Vintage. 'I wonder what happens when someone chooses the wrong brew.'

Another woman, young with heavy black make-up around her eyes, leaned in towards them, her voice low. 'They can be sick, bring up all their dinner, or fall down suddenly blind. Supposedly it passes eventually.' She shrugged. 'I have seen men shit themselves, really explosively, you know?' Vintage raised her eyebrows to indicate that yes, she did indeed know. 'Once in every game, though, it's something *really* bad. People can die, and you never know when it might happen. That's why the prizes are so high.'

Chenlo frowned, turning to the woman with real concern on her face. 'And you play this too?'

The young woman shrugged. 'Like I said, you can win a lot of money. And I don't know if you've noticed, but the worm people are back, and Ebora are dead on their feet. We're all fucked already, so why not have fun now?'

Vintage exchanged a look with Chenlo. 'I have a friend back in Ebora who would quite agree with you.'

'How much coin?' asked Chenlo. In front of them, another man had stepped up to the table. He was taking longer to choose his beaker. 'How much coin to make you leave this room without drinking the poison?'

'What?' The woman shrugged, looking bemused. 'I already paid my way in here, lady.'

'My friend here will give you that back, and more,' said Chenlo. 'If you leave, and don't come back to this place.'

'Will I?' Vintage saw the look on Chenlo's face, and nodded solemnly. 'I will.'

By the time the young woman had left with her new bag of coins, the man had finally chosen his beaker. He held it up to the light and then sniffed it. For the first time, the man in the hood spoke, his voice bearing a heavy Jarlsbad accent.

'Once you have picked the beaker up, you cannot change it.'

'What was that all about?' asked Vintage. 'She'll only come back tomorrow night, or the night after, you know.'

'She was young, and foolish.' Chenlo looked uncomfortable. She plucked at the collar of her red silk shirt. 'She should be shown another path, at least. Maybe she will leave now and meet a future lover, and not think of this place again, or she will decide to travel, far from here. Or she will come back tomorrow. We all deserve at least a glimpse of these other paths.'

Vintage nodded, feeling slightly ashamed. 'You are right, of course, my friend,' she said softly.

In front of them, the man drank the contents of his beaker. He was hesitant, taking sips and stealing glances at the hooded man, as if trying to guess its contents. Eventually, he put the beaker down on the table and turned to the small crowd, his face flushing with triumph, but the hooded man did not reach into his robes, and abruptly the man doubled over, his face growing dark red. He let out a single shout of pain and dropped to the floor. After a moment, he began to shake violently all over. Vintage began to push her way to the front of the small crowd, determined to help the man, when the two burly guards got in front of her. Quite efficiently they scooped him up between them, paying no attention to his trembling or his guttural howls. He was taken from the room, and the little crowd muttered amongst each other.

'Sarn's bloody bones,' said Vintage. 'What will happen to the fool?'

No one answered. The hooded figure had retreated behind the screen, and returned with a fresh batch of beakers. A few of them were steaming softly. Vintage felt a great wave of dismay, a feeling of sadness for all of them; the men and women willing to risk an agonising death for a few more coins. *This is what it does to us, this endless war*, she thought bitterly. *I talk all the time about how our land is poisoned, but what about our minds? When you know that the land itself may kill you, and that an unkillable enemy may return at any moment, what does that do to you? There's no peace in Sarn, even during peacetime.*

'Right!' She held her hands up. 'I've had enough of this little spectacle. The lot of you, piss off. Go downstairs and have another drink. I've got business up here.'

The small crowd reacted with anger, several people protesting that they had paid a great deal of money to play the game. Vintage turned away from them and walked over to the table. The hooded figure was watching her.

'Enough of this, my dear,' she said. 'I need a word.'

When the hooded figure didn't respond, Vintage sighed heavily. 'I know it's you, and let's be clear, I owe you one. I also respect your safety too much to start shouting your name from the rooftops, so do please stop messing about. Or –' she turned to glance at Chenlo, who had moved away from the little crowd towards the screens – 'maybe I will get Agent Chenlo here to start throwing some fire about. I don't imagine The Shining Coin will continue to employ you if you get the place burned down.'

'Hey, I don't know what you're on about.' The hooded figure whipped down his hood to reveal a young man with blond hair the colour of wet straw. The Jarlsbad accent had entirely vanished. 'But you can't just come in here messing up my game and threatening to set people on fire!'

'Oh Sarn's bloody arse . . .'

'Vintage?' Chenlo was peering behind the screen. 'Would this perhaps be who you're looking for?'

Vintage joined her at the screen. Behind it was another table, this one crowded with flasks and powders and pots, and sitting in a chair was Okaar, his face partially hidden by a number of silk bandages. They left his eyes, mouth and nose free, and at the sight of Vintage, he flashed her a quick grin.

'What trouble you make, Lady Vintage. But I am glad to see you survived our mutual friend.'

Despite herself, she laughed a little. 'What is all this, my dear?'

He shrugged. 'I used to do both, once upon a time – be the mysterious man in the hood, mix the poisons. But since I met your war-beast friend, I find being on my feet for too long painful, and, well –' he gestured to the laden table – 'I was always best at this part.'

Vintage nodded seriously. It did well to remember that Helcate might look like the most harmless war-beast, but his gift could deal a devastating amount of damage.

'You know why I'm here, I expect,' she said.

Okaar shifted in his chair, and picked up the cane that rested on the screen. 'I suppose that I do, Lady Vintage. Come. I will find a better place for us to talk business.'

Chapter Twenty-seven

The place sang with wrongness.

Tor could almost hear it, a high-pitched whine that shifted uncomfortably on the edge of awareness. They had been flying when they'd spotted it, a vast swathe of jungle that was more than Wild-touched: it was the Wild given true form. Bern had insisted they land, and Tor had agreed with a nod, his eyes rooted to the poisoned trees. It wasn't the sort of place you flew into without having a good think about it first.

'This is where they are,' said Bern. His voice was flat, full of a weight of knowledge Tor didn't want to ask about, but had to.

'You can feel them?'

'Stones help me, I can practically feel them crawling against my skin.' Next to them, Sharrik opened and closed his beak to produce a snapping sound; an odd, nervous gesture. 'They are close.'

'Then perhaps we should continue on foot.' Beneath Tor, Kirune gave a low growl. 'I know, I don't want to any more than you do, but I can't help feeling like flying overhead is giving them the best possible warning that we're coming.'

'They can feel Bern,' Kirune added in a low voice. 'Is his presence not also a warning?'

Bern shook his head. 'Since we broke their memory crystal, they pay almost no attention to me. I don't know how to describe it . . . It's like they're too busy trying to put out the fire we set. And in the end, I am a tiny part of their web. Unless they decide to look for me, I don't think they will notice.' He glanced at Tor. 'And we're just here to get a look at them, right? That's what we told Aldasair.'

'Yes,' said Tor, not looking at him. 'I know. Come on, let's get it over with. Keep your eyes open. We might not have to deal with parasite spirits anymore, but I dread to think what might have spawned in that mess.'

He and Bern dismounted, giving Kirune and Sharrik more freedom to move, and they stepped into the Wild forest. Tor loosened his sword, ignoring the mild tremor of annoyance at the fact that it wasn't the Ninth Rain he carried. Beyond the treeline was a world of shadows and shafts of yellow, buttery light. Motes of dust, pollen and spores spiralled through the patches of light, while long, fleshy vines hung from the trees, crawling with flies. The place smelled rotten and strange, and Tor was reminded of summer days with his sister, chasing leaping bugs in the gardens. Mostly the bugs were much too fast for them, but every now and then one of them would get lucky, and once caught in a hand the bugs would release a watery yellow liquid that smelled terrible. That scent seemed to be everywhere here.

As they moved forward, the vines grew more numerous, until Tor found that he was having to part them with his sword. Moving them, he noted that they were sticky and covered all over with tiny insects, trapped in a glistening orange slime.

'I don't like the look of that.'

Tor looked up to see what Bern was pointing at, only to

witness several of the vines moving slowly upwards, retreating back into the branches of the trees.

'What *are* these things?'

'A carnivorous plant, maybe.' At Tor's curious look, Bern shrugged. 'I've seen pictures of them in books. They trap insects, then eat them. Unfortunately, I don't think this is going to be the worst thing we see today.'

They moved on. The deeper they went, the thicker the atmosphere became. Soon Tor could feel a steady trickle of sweat moving down between his shoulder blades. Bern, with his fair complexion, had gone bright pink across his cheeks, and his face grew shiny with sweat. The sound of insects was incredibly loud.

'This is not an honourable place,' said Sharrik. 'It is foul.' He snorted and tossed his head like an agitated horse. 'We should leave and find battle elsewhere.'

To Tor's surprise, it was Kirune who replied to him. 'Steady, brother,' he said. 'We'll need your strength soon.'

Sharrik fluffed out the feathers on his chest, looking pleased with himself, and Tor leaned over to place his hand briefly on Kirune's shoulder.

Thank you.

He feels his human's fears, and it is making him skittish.

'Are we heading in the right direction, Bern?'

The tall human grimaced. 'I can't help feeling that the right direction is always going to be heading very far from this place but, aye . . . the worm people lie ahead.'

In amongst the general cacophony of insect calls there came a new one, loud and guttural. Tor felt the tiny hairs on the back of his neck stand up, and he touched the hilt of his sword again.

'Do you hear that?'

As if he had summoned it, a large shape buzzed through the air over their heads. It was around two feet long and

299

looked like a beetle, with a thick carapace held out of the way of its wings. However, when it landed on the trunk of a nearby tree, Tor saw that it had an oddly fleshy head – where the mandibles of a beetle might be, there was instead a head covered in what looked like greyish skin, and it opened a pair of jaws to reveal two rows of suspiciously human-looking teeth.

'By the stones,' Bern slipped his axe from its belt, 'what is that?'

The thing shifted where it clung to the bark, hiding its delicate wings away. Spiny grey legs with a claw at each end dug themselves in deeper, and it clicked its teeth together, so rapidly it became a clattering buzz.

'Honestly.' Tor motioned them all away from the thing, heading on a wide path around the tree. 'If I never see another Wild-touched fucking monstrosity in my life I will consider myself blessed by the roots themselves.'

They walked rapidly on, eager to put a reasonable distance between themselves and the mutant insect, but instead they came across more of the things; flying from tree branch to tree branch above their heads, or clattering to themselves on tree trunks. Most of them were smaller, perhaps only a foot long, but several were much larger. One monstrous example had to drag itself through the undergrowth, too heavy to fly. Tor drew his sword and carried it loosely in one hand.

Eventually, they came to a place where the trees were more spread out, although it was difficult to call them trees by this time – many of them had smooth, shining surfaces, strangely oil-like, and they leaned and curled around each other, their networks of branches joining overhead. Rather than leaves in the canopy there were thick swathes of a white, fibrous material, and Tor frowned at it as they walked under, thinking of piles of nets in fishing boats. The further on they travelled, the thicker the white material became, until Tor began to see darker

300

shapes nestling within it. A crawling sensation marched up his spine.

'Can you see what those are?' he said to Bern, although it was a stupid question; Eboran eyesight had always been vastly superior to that of humans. Yet he didn't want to say it out loud himself.

'Spiders,' said Bern, squinting up at the fibrous canopy. 'Really, really big spiders. Why did we come here again?'

'Because we are idiots,' mumbled Kirune.

They were big and fat, grey-blue in colour, with smooth, slightly flabby skins. Most of them were curled up on themselves, as if sleeping, while a few sprawled with their legs out, as if ready to scamper somewhere. They did not have the comforting symmetrical shapes of normal spiders. These Wild-touched things had legs that were longer on one side than the other, and clutches of odd-numbered eyes on various places on their bloated bodies.

'Quickly,' said Tor, his neck prickling. 'Let's just move out of their way as soon as we can.'

They did, all thought of moving quietly thrown to the wind as they tramped rapidly through the undergrowth. They were almost to the far side of that particular clearing when Bern gave a low cry, pointing upwards. Several of the giant spiders were silently spooling down towards them, long clasping legs outstretched.

Tor slashed upwards with his sword and slit one spider in two as it reached him. It fell apart like a piece of rotten fruit, while the one that had been next to it landed heavily on his left arm. Its legs locked around him like he was an absent mother and it was a needy child. Swearing repeatedly, Tor brought his sword around, but the angle was all wrong and he couldn't strike it with any strength. In the meantime, the thing had increased its grip to the point where he could feel the painful thud of his own pulse in his biceps.

'The bastard thing is going to squeeze my arm off!'

Bern was having his own problems. Three of the fleshy spiders had landed on Sharrik, and the big griffin was frantically beating his wings while Bern tried to drag the things off. Tor dropped his replacement sword and pulled a short dagger from his belt. With this he stabbed the fleshy pouch that was the spider's gut, and the thing let go, bleeding a dark purple blood. It fell to the ground with a heavy, wet sound. Snatching up his sword, Tor went to Sharrik and began peeling the spiders off. Kirune had one of the things in his mouth, shaking it back and forth like a dog with a rabbit.

'That's the last of them,' said Bern. 'Move!'

They left the twisted trees at a pace. Glancing once more behind him, Tor saw more of the Wild-touched spiders floating down from their webs, and he put his back to them with relief. Once they were a decent distance away, he took off his coat and rolled up his sleeve. There was a dark band of bruising around the top of his arm, just above where the bandages for the crimson flux ended.

'That looks nasty,' said Bern. 'It'll hurt for a few days yet, I expect. What have you done to your forearm?'

Tor rolled his sleeve back down, looking away. 'Oh, nothing. Just a scratch from training. Don't want to catch an infection from being out in this armpit of a forest.'

Bern frowned, but said nothing further. They walked on.

The trees continued, closing in around them again. Tor saw more strange insects, although these ones at least were smaller. There were fat, pinkish things the size of his hand, with thousands of hard, translucent legs, and centipedes, their segmented bodies covered in short, brownish hair. Eventually, they began to come across pieces of heavy stone littered across the dark earth. These seemed out of place, but Tor thought nothing further of it until Bern stopped to kneel by two that happened to be together. He looked unsettled.

'Here, look at this.'

Tor joined him. Up close, the two stones looked too regular, and there were vague shapes on the pitted surface.

'These stones,' said Bern, 'have been cut and shaped to fit together. Do you see? There are even some tool marks on here, and a decorative pattern. There's something like mortar, just at the bottom here.' He picked at a pale crusted substance on the edge of one stone.

'What are you saying?'

'It's part of a building. All around here, are ruins. See?' He stood up and pointed at some more rocks nearby, sunk mostly into the earth.

'You mean there was a settlement? Out *here*?'

Bern shrugged. 'A very, very old one, aye. I couldn't say for sure, but my people know a lot about shaping stone, and once you start looking . . .' His voice trailed off. 'There was a building here, and a path. Once.'

Tor touched his hand to the hilt of his sword. Many humans made their homes within Wild territory – they hardly had much choice – but this place was something else.

'Imagine,' he said. 'Imagine walking through that grove of spiders and thinking, "what a lovely place to settle down and raise some kids".'

'Even the air smells wrong,' said Bern, his face creased with displeasure. 'I don't think you could breathe it every day and remain well.'

'Perhaps the humans were here before,' said Kirune.

'Before what?' asked Tor, but the big cat refused to be drawn further. They followed the submerged stones as if they were a path, and soon it was clear that Bern was right. The scattering of stones became more regular, until they were seeing the remains of broken-down walls, half lost under creeping vines and vast, muscular fungi. Several of the walls came together at the corners, suggesting a few closely built dwellings.

'Vintage would love this,' he said, trying to inject some jollity into his tone, but the truth was the ruins made him deeply uneasy. He could not picture anyone living in these poisoned woods, yet someone had spent enough time here to bring stone and shape it to make a place to live.

'Look at this.'

Bern had stepped over one broken-down wall into a clearer section, and there on the ground was, unmistakably, a small stone bowl, and next to it, a pile of flint arrowheads. There were things carved into the wall here, slightly hidden from the elements, symbols of some sort, although if it was writing, Tor didn't recognise it.

'How old is this place?'

'There is something here,' Kirune's tone was sharp, and Tor went to him immediately. He was also exploring the ruins and had found a place where the walls were almost standing to shoulder height. Crouched next to the wall was a skinny figure about the size of a child. It had greyish skin and a distended belly, and its head . . . Again Tor thought of the giant beetles with their oddly human teeth. His stomach lurched sourly.

'Stones curse me dead, what is *that*?'

The thing's head was riddled with slippery mandibles and black, shining eyes. On the back of its smooth pate, several thick black hairs poked through the grey skin, and these quivered as it sheltered by the wall. Tor wasn't even sure it knew they were there. It raised stick-thin arms and patted at its face with fingers that were smooth and free of fingernails. After a moment, another one rounded the corner of the wall, and made a series of clicking noises with its mandibles. The original creature shuffled towards it, repeatedly bowing its head. Tor and Kirune moved back instinctively, watching as the two creatures came together. Their mandibles met, quivering, as if they were smelling each other, and then they moved slowly away.

'I have a horrible, horrible feeling I know what they are,' said Tor. It was Vintage's fault, he thought absently. She had taught him to think like this. 'This place,' he gestured around at the low stone walls, 'it has been here for a very long time. I think it must have been here before the Jure'lia even arrived. This was a normal forest once, like the rest of Sarn, and then they came. Their ships landed here, all that time ago, and now this is where they hide when the battles are over. Somewhere very close. So the land has just been poisoned more than anywhere else. The people, the plants, the insects and the animals – poisoned over and over, for generations. They've changed and they've . . . become each other. Do you see?'

Bern looked a shade paler than he had before they'd entered the forest. 'I am trying very hard not to.'

'They don't know what they are,' said Kirune, with feeling. 'They have been left, halfway between beings. It is terrible, to not truly know what you are.'

Tor leaned down and briefly placed his cheek to the top of Kirune's head.

I know what you are, he thought to Kirune. *You are my brother.*

They walked on through the ruins of the town, moving slowly so as not to startle the strange insect-people. There were many more of them, hiding in amongst the stones and the fungus. To Tor they seemed confused and lost, clinging to the ruins as though some half-forgotten memory was still telling them it was home. In one place they found a group of around ten of them, all pressed closely together, their grey heads in the dull light looking like the eggs of some vast spider, and a soft clicking sound arose from them as their mandibles quivered.

When finally they left the ruins behind, Bern stopped to wipe some of the sweat from his face. Sharrik was carrying his head low. The big griffin had not spoken in some time.

'Do you think we'll be able to forget any of this?' said Bern. He looked as miserable as Tor had ever seen him. 'The things we've seen. They haunt me. And not just because of this.' He held up the hand with the Jure'lia crystal embedded in it.

Tor shook his head, uncertain what to say. He was thinking of everything he had seen: a little boy butchered by his own sister, bleeding out on the roots of Ygseril; men and women turned inside out by the merest touch of a parasite spirit; people eaten alive by scuttling carnivorous beetles; the terrible prisoners of Origin, kept alive and senseless by alien roots; the boy Eri lying with his guts in the snow; and Noon, vanishing in a blossom of her own fire. Four hundred years old, and not even the oldest of these memories had dimmed, or grown less painful. If he lived for another four hundred years, he doubted they would fade. Unconsciously, he touched his bandaged arm. Not that he would live that long, of course. Not now.

They walked on further through the jungle, avoiding anywhere with the fibrous spider webs in the canopy and skirting around anything that looked like a ruin. The day was dying, and Tor began to wonder what it would be like to walk through such a place in the dark.

'How far away are they? If you had to guess.'

Bern did not lift his head. The big man was still sweating. 'Very close now,' was all he would say.

An hour or so after they'd left the insect people behind, Tor felt his left arm begin to prickle. He set his jaw, determined to ignore it, but soon waves of pain were throbbing in his arm and his chest, hot and constrictive. It became difficult to breathe. Cursing himself even as he did it, he stumbled over a thick wad of vines and fell to his knees.

'Tor!' Bern was at his side in an instant. 'What is it? Are you wounded?'

Tor clutched at his chest and shook his head, unable to force any words out. Bern looked stricken.

306

'Is it the blood? Do you need some? By the stones, you should have just asked.'

Tor smiled weakly and shook his head again. The flesh of his left arm felt like it was splitting open.

'No,' he managed eventually. 'Blood is the last thing I need.'

'You're sick.'

Tor said nothing. He stayed on his knees, waiting for the pain to pass. Kirune came and pushed his head against Tor's shoulder. When eventually the splitting sensation in his arm stopped and his chest ceased throbbing, he held out his hand and Bern pulled him to his feet. The human's face was very sombre.

'I know what that is,' he said quietly. 'Aldasair told me all about it.'

'Well, it could hardly be anything else, could it?' Tor said brightly. He wiped a hand across his forehead, his fingers trembling. 'Eborans aren't known for catching sniffles.'

'Tor –'

'Bern, can I ask a favour of you? Do not mention this to the others.' When Bern opened his mouth to protest, Tor shook his head. 'I mean it. We're in a precarious enough position as it is, and there's nothing to be done about it anyway.'

'But your tree-god . . .'

'Ygseril still sleeps, as well we both know. He sends all his available energy into the war-beasts, and let's be honest, they are a lot more useful than me at the moment. Come on. I don't want to talk about this right now.'

The powdery light of dusk was filtering through the trees when finally they found it. They came out of a thick band of Wild-touched foliage to see the ground dropping away below them. There was a vast chasm in the earth, so huge Tor felt an odd sense of vertigo just looking at it. They were still some distance away, and they could see several clumps of Wild-forest between them and the chasm.

'That's it,' said Bern. 'That's where they are hiding.'

'All these centuries, and the bastards have been hiding underground. Do you think we—'

Tor stopped as an enormous shape rose out of the chasm. It was a Behemoth, looking oddly small against the crack of darkness below it.

'Fuck.'

It moved up through the air slowly, as fat and as lazy as a bee in autumn, and another emerged just below it, following its kin. Together, the two Behemoths rose into the darkening sky and moved to the west. From what Tor could see, both ships looked in good working order, with no ragged holes or torn places.

'By the stones . . . if we needed evidence, there it is,' said Bern. He rubbed at his beard. 'This is useful to know. I'm sure the Lady Vintage will be thrilled. Now, I'd prefer to get some distance from here before we fly back to Ebora. I don't fancy being spotted by anything on the ground.'

'Or –' Tor stood up, loosening his sword in its scabbard – 'or we could go and have a closer look?'

Bern crossed his arms over his chest. 'You want to get closer to that?'

Tor nodded, smiling again. There was an echo of pain in his arm, a faint but constant reminder of his oncoming death. 'Let's go and see what the worm people are like when they're at home.'

Chapter Twenty-eight

Our journey back to the Winnowry today was an especially unpleasant one. We had been to a small settlement on the outskirts of the Sown territories, expecting to pick up a girl of thirteen to take back with us. However, on arrival we were told that she had been killed – caught by a gang of extremists and murdered. The Sown territories butt onto the foothills of the western range of the Bloodless Mountains, and they're dangerous, full of people who have lived hard lives. Once we had seen the body for ourselves, Agent Lin was ready to leave immediately, clearly disgusted with them, but I demanded to speak to the leader of the settlement. It is not right, I told them. The girl could have been safe with us. And they would have been safe from her. My words were seeds falling on rocks, as they so often are.

On our way back we paused at Greenslick to give our bats a rest. It is a terrible place, a ravaged landscape with vast stretches of varnish in all directions. It is hard to look on that and feel hope. Feeling especially melancholic, I asked Agent Lin if there could ever be a brighter future for the children of Sarn. I regretted saying it immediately, as it is always wiser to keep your feelings to yourself in the Winnowry, even amongst other agents, and Agent Lin is hardly known for her caring nature. But to my surprise, her shoulders dropped, and something changed in her face. It was then that I remembered, much too late, that she had had a child once, and they had taken it from her.

'There's no hope for any of us,' she said eventually. 'Not in this cursed land.'

Extract from the private records of Agent Chenlo

'This is a little more civilised.'

Okaar had taken them, via a winding route through streets and alleyways, to a tall tower, and up a winding set of stairs to a small roof garden. The place was stuffed with multitudes of flowering plants as well as several small blossoming trees; it was like stepping into a cloud of floral perfume. Chenlo sneezed twice in quick succession.

'It's a quiet place, and private.' He nodded towards the balcony wall, which was around chest height. 'It's also the tallest tower in this region of the city, so it's difficult to spy on it from other towers. It's used for perfumes, as you've probably guessed.'

'It is *very* fragrant,' said Chenlo, a touch sourly.

Okaar nodded, and led them over to a small wooden table and chairs neatly nestled under one of the blossoming trees. The space had been lit with a number of elegant lamps. Venturing out into the streets he had put on a deeply hooded cloak, and only now did he twitch it back from his face. Once again, Vintage winced at the discoloured purple patches that showed in the gaps between his bandages.

'That section there,' he gestured to a less colourful part of the garden, 'contains my own special selection of plants. They do not tend to be used in perfumes.'

'Your own little poison garden!' Vintage smiled, pleased with the thought of such a thing hidden above the roofs of Jarlsbad.

'What if the people gathering blossoms for the perfumes gather the wrong ones?' asked Chenlo.

Okaar smiled. 'This place is my own. Only I gather the flowers here – sometimes poisons can be sweet-smelling, of course.'

There was a bottle waiting on the table with a set of short glasses sitting in a wooden tray. Vintage recognised the drink as kyern, the same restorative Okaar had given her on the day she'd fallen on her broken ankle in the Eboran palace gardens. As they sat down, Okaar picked up the bottle and looked at them enquiringly.

'Darling, I would love some, thank you.'

'Not for me,' said Chenlo. She looked uncomfortable, plucking at the sleeves of her jacket.

'You know, if Okaar wanted to kill us, he could have done it several times on the way over here. Or he could have just let Tyranny murder us instead.'

'It's all right,' said Okaar. 'I know well that kyern is an acquired taste. Since you spent so much money on finding me, may I ask what it is you want?'

Vintage took a deep breath, marvelling at the various scents. It was just possible, underneath it all, to smell the busy city spread out around them.

'First, I must say thank you for your most timely intervention. It was very welcome indeed. May I ask why you did it?'

Okaar looked down at the drink in his glass, swirling it around. Eventually, he shrugged one shoulder. 'Do I need a reason?'

'You're an assassin. Generally you don't *save* lives.'

'Granted. Lady Vintage, some of the things I have been instructed to do over the years, in the service of Tyranny and in the service of the Winnowry, have been things that have left, shall we say, a stain on my soul? The war-beasts of Ebora are a wonder, a thing that when I was a child I very much hoped to see with my own eyes. They were creatures out of stories, and yet when finally I met one, I poisoned it and took a sample of its blood. I helped to steal one of its siblings, and separate it from its family. I might argue that I had little choice, Lady Vintage, but recently life has given me some new choices. I am not beholden to the Winnowry anymore, for one,' he lifted his glass in a mock salute, 'for which, I believe, I have your colleague to thank.'

Vintage nodded, wondering if she believed any of it. She could tell from Chenlo's face that the agent did not.

'If I save a few lives here and there, perhaps it is . . . I don't know. A way to soak out the stains? Or to paint over them.'

'And I suppose that if by saving those lives, you really, really annoy Tyranny Munk, that's all to the good? What about Jhef? If she's still with Tyranny . . .'

Okaar smiled, although it was a cold thing. 'Jhef chose to stay with the new queen, and she is old enough to make those choices now.'

Silence fell for a moment. The sounds of the busy street below floated up to them. Vintage had a sip of her drink, savouring the kick of sweetness that filled her mouth. Chenlo slipped the final vial from her pocket and placed it carefully on the table. She leaned forward, her eyes on the assassin.

'What is this? Where did you get it?'

'Yes, I can see why you would be interested in that.' Okaar folded his hands neatly on the table. 'It's a drug Tyranny started to make during her time as the leader of the Salts in Mushenska. When I came to know her, we spent some time working together to perfect it. It's still not quite there, but it does the job, as I'm sure you noticed. The name we once sold it under was heartbright. It magnifies the natural qualities of winnowfire.'

'And did the Winnowry know about this?' demanded Chenlo.

'Not at all. We did many things the Winnowry were not aware of.'

312

'Who was Tyranny selling it to, out of interest?' asked Vintage.

'She kept a great deal of it for herself, although she was often wary of using it. The drug makes you feel quite ill, and Tyranny has always mistrusted anything that makes her weak. There were also a number of fell-witches Tyranny was in contact with, a tight-knit and secret circle, who had managed to avoid detection over the years.'

Vintage sat up. 'Really? Who were these women?'

'I did not see them often myself, as they only trusted Tyranny, and they were extremely anxious not to be exposed, but from what Tyranny told me, they were almost a religious order of a sort, a counterpoint to the Winnowry. She did not have much time for them. They treated the winnowflame as a kind of deity, and Tyranny thought them foolish.'

'I have heard of such,' said Chenlo quietly. 'There are always whispers of them, but never anything solid. When Tyranny was brought in, she told us all about them, offered to lead us to them if we let her go. Mother Cressin dismissed it as nonsense.' She raised her eyes to Okaar. 'But that is not why we are here.'

Okaar nodded. 'Of course. When Tyranny herself was captured by the Winnowry and eventually allowed to move freely as an agent –'

Chenlo made a disgusted noise.

'– she began to blackmail all of her old customers. These women vanished immediately.' Okaar shook his head a little. 'Tyranny has never had a friend or an acquaintance that she wouldn't stab in the back at a moment's notice. I should have known better, but so often we are willing to look the other way when the truth is an ugly thing.'

Vintage thought of Nanthema, her face stony as she stood at the side of the throne. 'It seems that Tyranny turns on everyone eventually. Her newly loyal subjects may be about to learn a painful lesson.'

Okaar bowed his head in acquiescence.

Vintage poured herself another shot of the kyern and drank it down in one gulp. 'Okaar, darling, we need this heartbright of yours and we need it in large quantities, as soon as possible. I assume you don't mind talking a little business?'

Okaar shrugged one shoulder. 'I do not need money. I was careful to hide away a great deal of coin when I worked with Tyranny, mostly without her knowledge. And I would have to manufacture the drug from scratch. In large quantities, this will get me noticed. I do not wish to be noticed, currently.' He gestured around at the garden. 'Being noticed will get me killed.'

'What else can we offer you, then?' asked Vintage. 'Name your price.'

'I like you, Lady Vintage. You are sharp.' Okaar looked away across the garden, his dark eyes narrowed. 'Can I ask what you would need so much heartbright for?'

'We have a fell-witch army in Ebora,' said Vintage quickly. 'One that could help us win the fight against the worm people – if they were given the ability to produce such destructive fire.'

'*Not* an army,' protested Chenlo. 'They are refugees. They need our help. The help that Lady Noon promised them.'

'When the Jure'lia come, having the winnowfire that can destroy them will help, I promise you that.' Vintage turned back to Okaar. 'We'll need enough for around fifty women, enough to last over a sustained campaign. You will know best the actual quantities of that.'

From below them, a loud argument erupted, curse words floating up into the air. The language was native Jarlsbadian, and Vintage caught a few phrases here and there: *beer like horse piss* and *sodden pig-brained idiot*.

'I saw the worm people, not long ago,' said Okaar. A scattering of blossoms from the tree above had fallen onto the table, and he touched his fingers to the delicate petals. In the bright sunshine, the scarring on his face was uncomfortable to look at. Vintage thought of Tor, and how much of his scarring had healed, thanks to the application of Noon's blood. *The history of the Eborans might have been a lie, but they still have so many advantages over us dowdy humans.* 'I had taken my leave of Tyranny, and Tygrish was crawling with guards eager to part my head from my body, so I rode out onto the plains to wait for the situation to, how would you say? Cool off. It was night-time, and I was attempting to stay awake in case of bandits. I saw three Behemoths in the sky, moving across the stars so slowly. Have you ever seen them at night? I expect you have. Light crawls across the moon-metal, like it turns to oil when it touches them, and they are utterly sound-less. It was like finding yourself in the woods with a predator so huge it does not notice you, yet you know that if it does, you will be dead.'

'That is the future for all of Sarn,' said Vintage quietly. 'If we do not fight them.'

Okaar nodded. 'I do not know that I can make enough heartbright for you. Who knows, after all, how long this war will last? However, I will make as much as I can, with the time I have and the materials available. In exchange for this, I will require an amnesty from any crimes I have been thought to commit by the peoples of Ebora. I will require sanctuary in Ebora, and protection from the worm people. If there is a safe place, that is where I want to be. I wish there to be a place open for my sister also, if she should ever leave the side of Queen Tyranny.'

Vintage pursed her lips. She was thinking of the other war-beasts, and specifically Vostok. How would they feel if she brought into their midst one of the thieves responsible for taking their sibling from them? Not to mention the destruction of a good part of the forest, and the attempted theft of other valuable items. It was going to be a difficult conversation, at the very least.

'Done. When can you have it ready?'

'A few days at the most. You will, however, need a way to get it to Ebora. Heartbright in the quantities you require will be bulky, and even your war-beast will struggle to transport both you and it.'

Vintage sat back in her chair, taking a deep breath of the scented garden air. 'Darling, such quibbles will hardly stop me. Besides, I think I have an idea.'

Chapter Twenty-nine

'This is a really bad idea.'

'Now then, Bern, surely you're not adverse to some danger and excitement.' Tor pulled his hair back and quickly restrung it into a braid. They were crouched at the edge of the great hole in the earth, in a rocky space where a few twisted trees were still clinging to life. 'We're just going to have a little look around.'

'You suggest that we are cowards?' boomed Sharrik. The three of them immediately shushed the big griffin, and he clucked his beak in protest.

Bern grinned, looking more like himself than he had in weeks. 'I've seen a fair bit of danger and excitement, aye, and I'm not worried about seeing a little more. I'm simply stating for the sake of any nearby gods who might be listening, I thought it was a bad idea. It will be of great comfort to me when my body has been hollowed out by burrowers.'

'That's the spirit. And if my sister isn't down there, I think we've got a better chance of getting in and out unnoticed.'

After the first two Behemoths had left, they had watched a third one rise out of the crevasse, followed by the enormous purple dragon called Celaphon. They had all shrank back at the sight of the beast who had killed Eri so cruelly, but the

317

dragon had not noticed them or felt their presence. Bern was certain that this last Behemoth carried Hestillion herself – he had felt her, very faintly, down the link they shared.

'I do not see why I must wait here,' said Sharrik, taking care to speak in a very rough whisper that was not much quieter than his usual speaking voice. 'I do not wait on the edges of the battle.'

'This isn't a battle, my brother,' said Bern, patting the griffin's shoulder. 'A battle is the last thing we want here, in the heart of enemy territory.'

'And besides, Sharrik, you are enormous and bright blue, and not especially made for stealth. Instead, you will wait here in case we need sudden backup. Bern, Kirune and I will be gathering information,' said Tor. 'Vintage taught me all about it. Come on.'

In the end, Tor and Bern climbed up onto Kirune's back – with a few growled protests from Kirune – and the big cat glided slowly down into the darkness. At first, Tor could see nothing at all, just vast walls of earth and rock to either side, scarred here and there with gnarled, Wild-touched roots from ancient trees, and then below them he began to see faint lights, yellow and white.

'Can you feel them?' he murmured to Bern.

The human, who was sitting behind him, shifted slightly, and Tor felt his discomfort through the link they shared as war-beast kin.

'Yeah. It's – it's like sinking into a bath filled with snakes. I'm doing my best to hide us from them.'

Tor nodded, glad that the human had agreed to come. Slowly, more shapes began to emerge below them. The rounded forms of the Behemoths, lit in eerie yellowish light, looked like no more than strange deformed fruits at this height.

'This cavern is so deep,' murmured Bern, awestruck. 'By the stones, it must reach into the very heart of the world.'

In time, it became possible to see movement too. Tor recognised the skittering movements of various Jure'lia creatures, crawling over the vast Behemoths skins. Some of them appeared to be making repairs, stitching up tears and holes in the moon-metal, while others just moved around listlessly, their many-jointed legs ungainly and unsettling.

There was silence, too, eerie and thick. Every now and then a piece of rock would crumble from the sides, bouncing down into the dark, and it would send echoes across the cavern that seemed deafening to Tor. He winced at every one.

'What is that?' rumbled Kirune when they were more than halfway down.

'What is what?'

Kirune had been descending in spirals, but now he pushed them out across the cavern to the far side. The Behemoths were lost behind them, and suddenly they were flying out over a cave within a cave, and below them were thousands of greenish mounds, all too regular to be rocks. Tor felt his skin go cold, and wondered if this was what Vintage felt when she found something especially significant.

'Land on the edge,' he said. 'I want to take a closer look.'

'I'm not sure that's a great idea either,' murmured Bern from behind him.

'Come on,' said Tor, leaning forward over Kirune's shoulders. 'I want to know what this is.'

They landed on the ground, Kirune's huge paws making no sound at all, and carefully they climbed down from his back. Up close and lit by the faintly glowing fronds that sprouted all over, it was possible to see that the mounds were ovoid, and they were the same greenish black as much of the Jure'lia. They sat in a vast lake of shining black fluid, stuff that looked very similar to the dark ooze that formed the body of the Jure'lia queen. A cold hand walked up Tor's spine: he had been enclosed in that stuff, almost suffocated in it, when the queen

319

had plucked him from the air. He still had nightmares about it surging up his nostrils and closing his throat.

'I have a terrible feeling I know what these are. Bern?'

He nodded and closed his eyes. 'I can feel them in the web of Jure'lia minds, but they are . . . sleeping? What's the word?'

'Dormant.'

'Aye. They are waiting to be something. Waiting to be born.'

'Eggs,' said Tor, half wonderingly. 'They're fucking *eggs*. How long have they been here?'

'I don't know, it's – I can feel the life of the web flowing to them, around them, as though every part of the worm-people web feels some sort of responsibility towards them.' He opened his eyes. 'I don't think I have the right words for it, Tor, but they've been here a very long time. As long as the worm people have, I reckon.'

Tor pressed his fingers to his mouth. He felt the need to laugh suddenly. 'And they won't hatch, or whatever it is they do, until the Jure'lia have taken Sarn. Just waiting down here for thousands of years. Vintage is going to go spare.'

Bern, meanwhile, had gone very pale. 'Thousands of years, the endless quiet, the agony of never quite becoming . . .'

'Bern, are you all right?'

Suddenly, the darkness on all sides of them became a solid thing, rushing towards them. Kirune roared and leapt up into the air, but strings of black fluid fell over them like a net, catching the war-beast and dragging him back down to the ground. Tor drew his sword and slashed at it, while Bern did the same with his axe, but the stuff reformed instantly, only drawing more tightly around them.

'It is you.'

A figure approached, caught in the eerie lights. The Jure'lia queen looked different, although Tor could not have said how. She moved more hesitantly, her head cocked to one side, as though she wasn't quite sure what she was looking at. The

320

white mask that was her face looked yellowed, dirty almost, and lined with cracks at the mouth and eyes.

'That's right, it's me, Tormalin the Oathless, and I'd like to have a word with you about my sister –'

'Not you,' snapped the queen. She turned her face to Bern. 'You are the one who broke us. Who broke the memory chain with your own memory. That should not be possible, human. How did you do it?'

Bern was standing very still, the muscles in his big shoulders bunched. His face had gone an alarming shade of grey. Kirune had pressed himself flat to the ground to avoid the tendrils of black ooze.

'We can feel you,' continued the queen, in a conversational tone of voice. 'Pushing against us. You are telling us, *let us go, let us go*. As though you could command us. It is very interesting, Bern of the Shining Axe.' She placed one long-fingered hand against the black netting, and a tendril of the substance slid around Bern's neck, a rustling snake. 'Tell us how you broke the memory, human.'

'Leave him alone,' said Tor.

'I'm not telling you anything,' said Bern.

The tendril moved up his cheek and slid across his face, but Bern did not move. Tor went to go to him, but the stuff whipped around his arms and dragged him back.

'Bern!'

'We could just tear it from your mind. We don't know if that's possible, but we are willing to try. It would not be pleasant for you, we suspect.'

'Go piss on a rock, you hag-witch,' spat Bern.

Tor opened his mouth, again filled with the terrible urge to laugh, but the black fluid around them spasmed away, throwing him to the floor. He scrambled to his feet in time to see the queen retreating rapidly, Bern pulled along behind her in a pulsing net of strands.

321

'Wait!'

She gestured roughly over her shoulder. 'I do not want you here, bloodkin of Hestillion Eskt, and you will die now.'

Scuttling shapes that had been tending the Behemoths loomed out of the darkness. These were things that Tor had not seen before, larger versions of spider-mothers, strange segmented things that were somewhere between worms and beetles. A swarm of burrowers, each as big as fists, converged on Kirune.

'Shit!' Tor kicked away a creature that was curling its legs around his boot and made to run after Bern, but almost instantly he was pushed back. There was a bellowing from above, and Sharrik crashed into them all, throwing Tor to the ground for the second time. Kirune was shaking his head back and forth, backing away towards the eggs as several creatures crawled over the war-beast's back and wings.

Sharrik dispatched a host of spider-mothers with a few lethal darts from his beak, and then he was in the air again, heading for the queen. Tor got up to follow, trying to ignore a soft bloom of pain in his chest as the crimson flux uncurled itself a little deeper inside him, but the queen had reached the nearest Behemoth. Bern was clutched to her, barely visible inside a writhing net of the Jure'lia fluid, and the moon-metal behind them flexed open.

Tor had time to glimpse the fleshy grey interior of the place, and then Bern and the queen were gone, hidden behind the hardened metal-skin of the Behemoth. A bare second later, Sharrik crashed into the place where they had vanished, his claws raking over the surface frantically. The big griffin's panic and horror washed through them, as cold and as threatening as an unseen current in a fast-flowing river.

'My brother!'

Tor turned and ran back to Kirune, who was in danger of being overwhelmed and tipped over the edge into the egg pit. Sword slashing, he chopped away at the segmented hide of a vast centipede-like thing; it had curled itself around Kirune's middle, preventing the big cat from flying away. Meanwhile, there were other things approaching from the dark corners of the cavern, huge, shambling things with many glistening eyes and sharp, knife-like legs. One of these things seemed to split in half, revealing a pulsating interior lined with serrated bands, until Tor realised it was simply opening its mouth.

'Sharrik, we have to go! Now!'

'I will not leave my brother!'

The segmented creature fell away from Kirune's midsection in bloody lumps, and Tor gladly scrambled back onto the harness.

'We'll come back for him, Sharrik, I promise, but if we stay, we're all going to be torn to pieces.'

Kirune jumped up into the air, his wings opening with a sharp crack, and somewhat awkwardly they began to rise. Sharrik was still attacking the side of the Behemoth, crashing his beak and claws into the moon-metal. He had barely made a dent in the surface, while all kinds of Jure'lia minions converged on him.

Go. Get away.

It was faint, but Tor felt Bern's presence nonetheless – a brief touching of minds. Sharrik bellowed in protest, but Kirune called out to him, his voice uncharacteristically loud.

'You heard him, brother. The human is wise! We must not die here.'

'No!' Yet Sharrik did leap away from the Behemoth, and when they rose up through the cavern walls, the great griffin came with them. Tor could feel his anguish bleeding through into his own heart, heavy and hot. He looked up and focussed on the thin strip of sky high above them; darker now, and stippled with the first stars of the evening, it was still a beacon against the black cave walls.

'We're nearly there,' he said aloud, unsure if he was comforting himself, or comforting Sharrik. 'We're nearly there.' The Jure'lia minions fell away the higher they got, as though the queen had lost interest in them, and once they had cleared the chasm and landed some distance from it, nothing followed them. Tor jumped down from Kirune's back and fell to his knees on the ground. For a long moment no one spoke. Sharrik paced back and forth, his head moving from side to side in distress.

'Ah, curse Sarn, curse the tree-father, curse all of it.' Tor leaned forward, planting one hand in the black earth. His arm was on fire, and his chest felt as though it had been flayed open. 'Ah, fuck. Bern. *Bern*.'

'It is your fault,' thundered Sharrik. His eyes were wild, showing a white circle at the very edge, like a horse driven mad by the smell of wolves. 'This was your idea! And we have lost him. Because of you, we have lost my brother! My companion!'

'He's not dead,' said Kirune quietly. He was splashed all over with Jure'lia gore. 'I can feel him. We can all feel him, still.'

Tor shook his head. His hair had come loose in the fight, and now it hung in his face. 'What have we left him to, though? Why didn't she take us, too?'

'Useless questions,' snapped Kirune, a clear note of disgust in his voice. 'Better ask, how quickly can we get home? How quickly can we get help?'

The pain in Tor's chest was a liquid thing, running down through his arms and legs, filling up his throat. The cough that he knew must come eventually was close, lurking somewhere deep inside. With a great deal of difficulty, he got to his feet and staggered to Kirune's side. There was an alarming sensation of falling, and then he pressed his hands to the big cat's fur and some of the disorientation fled. Kirune, always so solid, so dependable.

'You're right,' he said, forcing some certainty into his tone.

'We need to get help, so that we can rescue our friend. We'll fly through the night, and rest only when it's absolutely needed.'

'Tor –' Kirune turned his big yellow eyes to meet him. 'You are –'

'I am fine,' he said quickly. 'Let's get going.'

They rose up into the air again swiftly, not looking back at the chasm that lay behind them. The night sky felt welcoming after the sticky humidity of the Jure'lia base, and the wind against Tor's face felt very fine indeed. Yet none of it could ease the dread in his stomach, or the knowledge that he was about to break his cousin's heart.

Chapter Thirty

Such a strange case today.

We arrived in the humid region of Liguilia, just south-east of Catalen, after many days of weary travel. I was sore from flying and Agent Lin was in an even worse mood than usual, but it is a beautiful part of Sarn, and my spirits lifted as we flew over those densely forested hills. Most of the larger settlements in Liguilia have a single, tall white tower at their heart, so that travellers on the roads can navigate safely towards them, and I understand that at night the towers send messages via a series of lamps in their upper windows. We saw some of this as we reached its borders: white lights flickering on and off like hesitant stars, across a great blanket of darkness.

The girl we had travelled so far for was gone, however. Her family seemed as confused about it as we did, at first. The girl, named Russini, had been confined to her rooms for the last week, and had seen no one. By her family's reports, she was a good, obedient girl, not one to go against the wishes of her elders. And then I caught the eye of an old woman, apparently the great-grandmother of the girl, and her eyes were bright with some other emotion. I asked her what had happened to Fell-Russini, and she bared her teeth at me and said: 'The Good Women have taken her, and thankful I am too.'

After some lengthy questioning, I discovered that the 'Good Women' are something of a folktale in rural Liguilia, a secret order of women and girls who live out in the forest somewhere, appearing only in times of great need. Sometimes, it is said, they leave treats for good children, and if the Liguinese offer up prayers for them, they keep the worst of the Wild-touched creatures at bay. It reminds me very much of the stories I heard growing up in Yuron-Kai about sand spirits and water sprites, but the old woman claims they are very real, and what's more, that they have a connection to the winnowfire.

During this time Agent Lin had been investigating the estate and found a trail leading into the woods. We went together, on foot, but very quickly it was clear that if the girl had gone into the trees, she would never be found again – the paths are treacherous and bewildering. I asked Agent Lin what she thought about the 'Good Women', and to my surprise she told me that she had heard stories like it before, in many parts of Sarn.

'They worship the winnowfire as a kind of god,' she said. 'Can you believe that? Idiots.'

But I find that part of me does believe it.

When night fell, we made our way back to the settlement, picking our way through a forest that had grown dark and unfriendly. At one point I looked up into the trees and saw a green light that wasn't our own, and a face suspended above it, watching. Our eyes met for a handful of moments, and then whoever she was, she was gone. I did not mention it to Agent Lin.

Extract from the private records of Agent Chenlo

The fever had burned through Noon so fiercely that she had lost all sense of time. When she came back to herself, they were down on the coast, looking out across a vast stretch of sea. For an entire day and night she watched the sky and clouds changing, the colours – blue, grey, green, yellow, pink, velvet black – moving across the restless water. Vostok made fires – somewhat awkwardly pushing driftwood into a pile with her nose and igniting it – and brought water, and when Noon felt ready, fish to eat. The sulphur stink of the island no longer seemed so strange.

'Where are we?' Noon asked eventually, when she could sit up by herself.

'You asked that before,' said Vostok. 'An island. Nowhere interesting, bright weapon. You slept a lot, and you raved a great deal in your sleep. It was very strange.'

'I'm ill.'

'Yes,' said Vostok, with clear distaste. 'It's unseemly.'

Noon smiled. 'War-beasts are not nursemaids.'

'I should think not.' But Vostok bent her head and pressed her warm scales to Noon's cheek. 'The world moves on without us, bright weapon.'

'Yeah, I know.' Using Vostok to balance herself, Noon got to her feet. The wind was blowing in across the sea, bringing cold air and salt with it. She opened her mouth to taste it, and she was reminded of eating her first tomato when she'd escaped from the Winnowry. Life was full of extraordinary things, even when they looked like normal things. Especially so, perhaps. 'Do you have any idea what's happening?'

'They are all too distant, and too chaotic,' said Vostok, a touch sourly. 'But something is happening. We should go back to them, bright weapon. We must go back soon.'

'We should.' But as she said it, a new wave of fear moved through Noon. She knew what she was now. She knew the full horror of what she had done. How could they look at her

328

and not see it, too? She imagined the smell of burned flesh hanging over her like a shroud, the last screams of her people echoing in her every footfall. How could they know her, and love her?

'They will,' said Vostok, very quietly, her voice softer than the surf. 'They do.'

Noon swayed on her feet. Standing up no longer seemed like a good idea, and her vision was dimming at the edges again. Warmth, too close and prickly against her skin, swarmed up from her feet and she felt a fresh coating of sweat break out across her forehead.

'Noon?'

Vostok's voice was distant, as though she were shouting down a long, echoing tunnel.

'I don't think . . .'

The sea slipped away and darkness claimed her again.

Vintage crashed into the wall behind her, propelled there by the force of her stolen crossbow. Her bolt clattered against the wall opposite, but it had the desired effect of forcing back the guards who were trying to make their way into the tower chamber.

'Sarn's arse, this thing has a kick to it! Do you have the bats yet?'

'Almost there.' There were four giant bats in the makeshift chirot tower, and Agent Chenlo had loosened their ties. She had four silver whistles around her neck, and she was stepping over the unconscious body of a fellow fell-witch. 'Will these be enough to carry everything as far as Ebora?'

'I think it'll have to be, darling.' Vintage reloaded the crossbow. From the noise on the stairs, the guards had summoned reinforcements. 'We've got exactly as long as it takes for someone to alert Queen Windfall, and if we're not out of here by then –'

'Right.' Chenlo blew some sharp notes on the whistles, taking turns on each. One of the bats, a great grey creature with delicate pink folds in his ears, shuffled over to the wall that was open to the sky and was gone, into the night. Two more followed. Vintage lifted the bow and fired another bolt, remembering to brace herself this time, and then Chenlo was in the harness of the final bat. 'Ready to go!'

Vintage abandoned her post and headed to the open wall.

'This is a very dangerous plan,' said Chenlo as she passed. 'I'm not sure you can even call it a plan. It is more like barefaced cheek.'

'My darling,' Vintage shuffled to the edge; the drop beyond the ledge was dizzying, 'I think that's the nicest thing anyone's ever said to me.'

To her surprise, Chenlo grinned. 'I did not say it wasn't fun.'

Below her, Helcate appeared, his leathery wings keeping him just below the ledge. It wasn't a big drop at all, but the thought of making that small jump was turning Vintage's knees to water. She turned and steadied herself, sparing a quick wave to the guards who had belatedly stormed into the chamber.

'Cheerio!' She leapt, landing solidly on Helcate's back, and he immediately peeled away from the tower, followed by Chenlo and the bats. As quickly as she could, Vintage swung herself round in the harness and began to strap herself in. A shower of arrows flew from the tower, but they were already out of range and they fell harmlessly into space.

As they flew out across the packed rooftops of Tygrish, Vintage spared a quick glance back towards the palace. There were lights on in the central tower, the one that she knew to be the roosting place of Windfall, yet no giant bat emerged to chase after them. Chenlo had torn away the life energy of both the fell-witches who had been in the chirot tower at the time, and she imagined the others would be off duty, asleep even. Finding them and rousing them would take time, and perhaps

330

Windfall herself was out hunting for the night. It seemed that, finally, they had found themselves a piece of luck.

Eventually, Tygrish dropped behind them, and it was still the middle of the night when they arrived on the outskirts of Jarlsbad. Okaar met them outside a vast warehouse, where Helcate and the bats quickly hid themselves. He was wearing the deep hood again, and half bowed to them in greeting.

'I would not have thought it possible to steal from the queen of Tygrish so openly, but here you are. She won't be happy about this.'

'What a tragedy,' remarked Vintage. Despite the long flight her nerves were still thrumming with adrenalin. 'Have you got what we agreed, Okaar?'

He took them to a series of crates, which were filled with rows and rows of glass vials, all filled with the black and orange liquid. Next to them were several hessian sacks with sturdy leather straps.

'You will have to be careful,' he said, indicating the crates. 'The substance isn't explosive, but the glass isn't as strong as I would like it to be, and it is unpleasant if you get it on your skin. It can cause scarring.' He grimaced a little, as if remembering the scarring on his own face. 'Don't knock the packages around.'

'We will have to be careful, you mean,' said Vintage. At his look of surprise, Vintage raised her eyebrows. 'If you want sanctuary in Ebora, you'll have to come with us now. There's no guarantee we'll ever come back this way, after all.'

'Are things really so bad? I had hoped that perhaps I could win my sister over eventually.'

'The Jure'lia are being organised, methodical. It's only so long before they work their way up to tackling a city the size of Jarlsbad.' Vintage shrugged. 'I cannot even promise you that Ebora will be safe, but it is at least a long way from Tyranny. Your sister, my friend, will have to make her own decisions.

Leave a message for her, if you feel it's safe, but you must come with us now if you wish to leave Jarlsbad.'

Okaar pushed his hood back and ran his hands quickly through his hair, causing it to stand up in wild black corkscrews. Chenlo was already loading up the sacks, carefully packing the vials in straw as she did so. Vintage suspected this wasn't the first time the Winnowry agent had needed to transport drugs on the backs of the giant bats.

'I will do as you suggest,' Okaar said eventually. 'Give me a moment to arrange for a message to be sent to Jhef, and I will be with you.'

He left the warehouse for a time, and Vintage and Chenlo got the bats and Helcate loaded up with the heartbright and their own supplies. Once it was all packed away, Vintage couldn't help feeling like it was all just a desperate shot in the dark. Would this be enough to make up for her own mistakes? Would the fell-witches at Ebora even consent to use such a thing? Some of her doubts must have shown on her face, as Chenlo briefly touched her arm, then turned away, her cheeks flushed.

'It is worth a try,' she said, not quite looking at Vintage. 'You were right about that.'

When Okaar returned, he was carrying a small pack of his own and had changed into dark travelling clothes. He no longer concealed his face behind a hood and bandages, and Vintage thought that some of his old grace had returned to his frame.

'I've done what I can for my sister,' he said, his face set and solemn. 'Now, we should leave before Tyranny finds out where we are.'

The woman was so tall she almost looked Eboran to Aldasair's eyes, and she certainly had the regal bearing he associated with dim memories of the palace when it rang with music and his people had yet to succumb to the crimson flux. Yet she shot him a very human expression of impatience as he poured another cup of tea.

'Lord Aldasair, I feel we have been chasing this same point in circles for days. Why should my people give you anything, when you have done little but take from us?'

Aldasair nodded, although he did not completely agree. He was learning that diplomacy was often the art of recognising the small places where you did not agree, and then very politely ignoring them.

'And when I say take,' she continued, 'I mean, murder our people.'

'The Carrion Wars,' said Aldasair. 'Commander Morota, please do not feel that you cannot name them here. I am very, *painfully* aware of our history, and where we have failed.'

'Well –' the commander sniffed. She glanced at the cup of tea, and scowled faintly before continuing. 'I am sure that Reidn is more painfully aware than you are. People forget that it wasn't just the plains folk who suffered when you experienced your blood lust and swept down from the mountains. Our small colonies to the north were largely wiped out. We do not forget that.'

'And you shouldn't. And, I might suggest, you would do well to cast your mind back further too – to previous Rains, when it wasn't us but the Jure'lia who crept up to your doors.'

The point hovered between them, unspoken. Ebora had saved Reidn, just as it had saved the rest of Sarn, over and over. Commander Morota took a sharp breath, preparing to speak, and Aldasair spoke over her smoothly.

'We could, as you say, spend days carefully adding up old scores, commander, but with all due respect, I don't think either of us has the time. You have at your disposal one of the largest armies to grace Sarn. What I am proposing—'

'What you are proposing is ludicrous,' she cut in, 'and I think you know that, Lord Aldasair. The worm people are in the skies again, and the city state of Reidn is preparing itself for war, yet you suggest I merrily march half our forces from the northernmost territories across the mountains to sit on your front lawn.'

'Not half.' Aldasair took a sip of his tea. In truth, he was heartily sick of tea, but he found the ritual of it useful; it seemed to calm humans, or distract them. Or, at least, it gave them the impression that he had the time to drink cups of tea. 'A small portion to help defend Ygseril, should the Jure'lia arrive here.'

'Because your own people are all dead.'

Aldasair paused, surprised by the anger he felt flare up within his own chest. This woman was a leader of armies, he reminded himself, who likely had no time for tact. What did it matter to her that Aldasair had watched everyone he ever knew die slowly, raving and coughing to the last, years before she had even been born? What did Commander Morota care if he had lost his mind in this palace, listening to the dust settle and his future wind down along with the clocks? Even so, he found his own patience was in shorter supply than he expected.

'As you so kindly point out, yes, because my people are almost all dead. You might think this is hearty justice for a race of murderers, commander, but the death of Ebora will have dire consequences for Sarn. If the Jure'lia destroy our tree-father, the war-beasts will all die, and then our best hope of defeating them will be gone. Your army will fight on alone, and history suggests they will not win.'

Commander Morota sat back in her chair, conceding the point. She was alone; the one manservant she had brought with her from Reidn was back in her room. Despite everything, Aldasair found he liked the woman, with her smooth, shaved head and her stern face. There were scars on her muscled arms and her sword belt had the look of an item that had been well-used and well cared for. This was a leader who led from the front lines. And ultimately he understood her stance all too well.

'You must admit though, Lord Aldasair, the situation is not as clear-cut as it has been in previous Rains. You have a mere handful of war-beasts, and no standing army of your own. It may not be enough to defeat the worm people this time. It may be that this time Sarn must stand alone. And if that is the case, can I afford to give you part of my own forces? Forgive me, but defending your tree-god may be a waste of our lives. Lives that are precious to us.'

Aldasair nodded. This was what it came down to. Indeed, it had been the sticking point from every leader he had spoken to. Were the war-beasts even worth saving? Was Ebora's time over before the war had even started? The truth was, they desperately needed Reidn's help. They needed everyone's help.

'You are right, commander. I will not sit here and lie to you. The situation is dire. But this is exactly why we must take full advantage of everything we have. You know what Ebora is capable of. Would you really throw . . . really throw away –'

He got to his feet abruptly, the chair dropping to the floor behind him. Startled, Commander Morota sat back.

'What is it?'

Aldasair shook his head. A wave of panic and despair had flooded through him, knocking all other concerns away. He could sense nothing specific, only that something terrible had happened. He reached out for Jessen, even as he turned to bow briskly to the Reidn commander.

'I . . . forgive me, I must leave you for a moment.'

He left the woman spluttering at the table and stumbled into the corridor. Over everything else he could feel the panic of Sharrik, the griffin's anger and fright battering at him from all angles. Somehow he found himself outside, standing in the grounds of the palace gardens, and then Jessen was there, her black fur comforting under his hands.

'What has happened?'

'Bern.' Jessen hooked her head over Aldasair's shoulder, pulling him to her. 'It's Bern, he—'

'No.' The world seemed to spin sickly underneath him, as though time had suddenly begun to turn faster. He felt himself being pulled away from his own carefully rooted anchors. 'Please don't tell me that. Anyone but him.'

'He's been captured, the worm people have him. I don't know any more than that. Sharrik is frantic, broken . . .'

Aldasair leaned against the great wolf. He did not trust his legs to hold him.

'They are coming back here now, coming back to get help, but I can barely feel Kirune through Sharrik's distress.'

In desperation, Aldasair opened himself fully to the connection they all shared, hoping to get a hint of what had happened to Bern, but he was met with the cacophony of Sharrik's mind. The griffin was angry and frightened, a terrible combination, and any shred of Bern was drowned out.

'He's not dead, then?'

'Not dead,' said Jessen quickly.

'Then we must go to him, now, meet them before they get here and go back.'

Jessen was shaking her head. 'I don't know where they are, and I don't know where they lost Bern. We have to wait, brother, and then we must all go together. At our strongest.'

Aldasair stepped away, pressing his hands to his face. Waiting was something he had wasted enough of his life on. To sit by while his people died once was bad enough – to wait while Bern suffered an unknowable fate was intolerable.

'I told them not to go,' he said. 'I *told* them, but Tor would not listen.'

Chapter Thirty-one

Something had changed within the Jure'lia web. Hestillion felt it as she came back on board the corpse moon, peeling her leather gloves from her hands with a distracted expression. When she flew with her circle, it was becoming easier and easier to put the rest of the Jure'lia aside, so that they were an insistent buzz in the back of her mind, while her carefully crafted team were close and vital. Whatever this new thing was, it was not unknown to them, and it was being held close by the queen herself. Not a fly caught in their web, but some other part of it, perhaps.

'Celaphon? Do you feel that?'

The dragon lowered his head, his jaws hanging open slightly. His foul breath seemed to fill the chamber, vast as it was.

'Yes,' he said, although he sounded uncertain. 'Does she hide something from us?'

'Never mind,' said Hestillion. 'You stay here while I go and see what is happening. You did fine work today, my sweet.'

Celaphon rumbled his appreciation, while Hestillion left the chamber, flicking aside walls with barely a thought. The queen was tucked away somewhere deep inside the ship, and Hestillion made her way there automatically, moving towards her as though seeking out a single voice singing in the forest. Her head was

337

still full of their last battle, images like bright flags flittering across her mind's eye; the town as it was before they took it, a prosperous place built with handsome blue stone, the windows all bright with glass; her circle moving to her each command, the Behemoths rising and falling through the sky with her every thought; fields full of well-tended crops, turned upside down and fed into the elastic mouths of the maggots. When they had left, the place was an unrecognisable mess of rubble and varnish. One more part of the map that belonged to her.

She paused, images of war breaking apart as she realised she was deep in the heart of Behemoth, in a place she had never ventured before. It was quieter here, the ever-present hum of the worm people oddly restrained. She flexed apart the final wall to find herself in a small chamber lit with several large frond-lights growing from the ceiling. The gently sloping walls were covered in long shards of cloudy white glass, or crystal, all different sizes and shapes. Slumped on the floor with his back against the wall was the human man Bern, and the queen was crouched over him, her long hands cupped carefully around his head. He didn't appear to be conscious.

'What is this?' snapped Hestillion. 'What are you doing? Where did he come from?'

The queen turned her white mask-face to her. Eyes of pond-scum blinked owlishly, as though she were waking from a long sleep.

'We had visitors,' she said. 'Your blood, here. Tormalin Eskt the Oathless, and their loud beasts.'

'My *brother* was here?' Hestillion took a step forward. 'In this cavern? You swore this place was a secret.'

The queen tipped her head to one side, a movement Hestillion was starting to recognise as a sort of shrug.

'We have been here a long time, in human terms. And this is a small world.'

'And where is he now?'

The queen turned back to Bern, her hands tightening around his head. 'Gone. But we caught this one, this one who broke us. Now we have his mind here, we can find out how. There will be something here, in his mind.'

The milky crystal shards around Bern's head flickered with reflections, and Hestillion found herself peering at them more closely. There were images there, pictures moving and changing all the time, like smaller versions of the giant memory crystal at the heart of every Behemoth.

'What are you doing to him?'

'Peeling it all back,' said the queen, absently. She reached up with one hand and laid a single finger against one of the crystal shards. It filled with hectic colour, and Hestillion saw a green land, filled with gently rolling hills and thick swatches of dark forest. Here and there it was punctuated with standing stones carved into the shapes of smiling women. 'Each piece of his mind. We will lay it all open, and then we will understand why the memory he gave to the web broke it so efficiently.'

'This, again?' Hestillion glanced uneasily at the other shards. They were all filling up with images – she saw a large man rather like Bern himself, his beard darker and braided in places, and a short human woman riding a bear, of all things. A ship cut through rough waves, and huge fish rose up to taste the air, Wild-touched things with horns growing out of their backs. 'You must let it go. It's done, there's nothing you can do –' She stopped as an image of Ebora filled another of the crystal shards. 'You said my brother was here, and you let him escape? We are not safe. We'll have to go elsewhere, take the Behemoths and all your creatures, and the eggs.' She disliked saying that word. 'Take it all and go elsewhere. Are you listening? It isn't safe here anymore, not if Tormalin knows where we are.'

On the ground, the man called Bern groaned, trying to turn his head away from the queen's touch, but she moved it back as easily as a child tormenting a baby bird.

'What can he do?' the queen said dismissively. 'They are weak, no real threat. And I have you, my warrior queen. You are so strong now, with your own creatures and your power. You command the smaller minds as easily as we do.'

Hestillion looked away, uncertain what to do with this unasked-for praise. 'I have only taken this role because you have stepped away from it.'

'Have you? Is that the only reason why?'

'You are changing the subject,' said Hestillion. 'We have to move. And I can't do that by myself . . .' *Not yet*, she added silently. 'To move all the Behemoths, you must command it.'

'We are busy,' the queen said dismissively. 'We are already beginning to see differences here, in this human's mind. Look – there are so many, so many memories at his core.' All the shards of crystal on the walls lit up, flickering with images. 'And they are all different. Whereas we had one each, a single memory of each world, carried in the heart of us.'

'You have nothing else?' Despite her own concerns, Hestillion found herself struck by this thought. 'Just those paintings of barren worlds?'

'Eating. Changing. Moving. Those are our memories, and they are all much the same.' Under the queen's hands, Bern groaned again, and Hestillion looked back to the crystals. She could see Tor there now, little glimpses of him with his newly scarred face, laughing from the back of his war-beast or repairing a leather harness. The witch human was there too, small and unremarkable. To her shock she saw herself, a fearsome warrior riding a monstrous dragon, her face oddly blank, her red eyes bright with some unreadable emotion. She saw her cousin too, many images of her cousin, some of them . . .

She blinked. 'They are in love. That is your answer. That is why the memory is so strong – this human man desires my cousin.' Her mouth twisted. 'Not just affection or the bond between war-beast companions. The two of them were sleeping together.'

'Sleeping?'

Hestillion started to roll her eyes, and stopped herself. 'Rutting. Whatever you want to call it. Some Eborans do take human lovers, a dirty little habit, of which my brother was especially fond, unfortunately.' The thought of Tormalin brought all her previous worries back. 'Think on what I've said, *if* you can spare the time.'

She left the queen where she was, endlessly spooling the human's memories onto shards of crystal, and made her way back outside. She summoned Celaphon, and together they flew up through the cavern into the daylight. It was an overcast day, and the Wild-touched forest seemed especially quiet. Although she knew Tormalin and his beast must be long gone, she looked around the clearing half expecting to see him there; his black hair loose over his shoulders, his familiar expression of mockery.

'The human is back,' said Celaphon into the silence. Hestillion frowned a little, annoyed at having her thoughts disrupted. 'The man who is a weapon in my mind.'

'Yes.'

'Why?'

'The queen has caught him.'

The forest simmered in the heat. Hestillion cast her mind out to her circle, almost for comfort. They responded immediately, eager to hear her orders.

'Will you free him again?' asked Celaphon.

'What? No.' Hestillion scowled. 'That idiot had his chance to live. If he and my brother are stupid enough to come here, after everything I have done, then that is their choice. The queen will pull his mind to pieces chasing after an answer she cannot possibly understand, and then his body will die, I expect. Humans are very weak.'

341

Celaphon said nothing, but Hestillion could sense a certain reticence from him. She was about to ask him what he was thinking when something bright and out of character with the landscape caught her eye on the far side of the chasm. She urged the dragon to fly there, and then climbed down from the harness. It was a bright blue feather, as long as her forearm and undoubtedly from a war-beast. She remembered the griffin Sharrik as he had been when they held him within the corpse moon: angry, defiant, beautiful. He was a page out of history come to life. She looked back to Celaphon, with his mottled face and ungainly limbs, the odd starbursts of pale yellow, like mould, across his belly. He was as much Jure'lia as war-beast now, and no Eboran would ever paint a mural celebrating his victories. Still, history was changing all the time. That was the point of it.

She threw the feather back down into the mud and went to her dragon.

For Vintage, returning to Ebora was like descending into a pool of dread. She knew from her link to Helcate that something terrible had happened, but thanks to his limited abilities in that direction, she did not know what. However, the closer they got to the palace, the sharper the sense of grief became. She thought of their faces as the streets of Ebora passed below; Noon, Tor, Aldasair, Bern. A new family to her, a connection she had never known. Had she lost them already?

Their flight from the west had been uneventful, without even a distant sighting of the Jure'lia to send them off their path in an effort to hide. Yet she had also spotted many signs that the worm people were active, streaks of varnish here and there like eldritch scars, abandoned settlements and groups of refugees on the roads. Chenlo and Okaar had both been quiet, picking up on her own subdued mood, and as the huge form of Ygseril came into sight, the assassin broke his silence for the first time in hours.

'It is never not surprising, is it?' he shouted from the back of his bat.

As comforting as it was to see the tree-god's branches still spread to the sky, and still covered with shimmering leaves, Vintage's sense of dread only increased when they reached the palace. She dismounted and looked around at the people, and she saw many grim faces, men and women who looked like they weren't getting enough sleep. *It's a time of war*, she reminded herself, but when she spotted Aldasair and Jessen coming across the grass towards them, it was as if her bones turned to water. The young Eboran man looked stricken, his handsome face pale and drawn, as though he had aged overnight, and Jessen walked with her nose to the ground.

'Sarn's bones, what is it?' She went to him and took his hand. 'What's happened?'

'Vintage.' He squeezed her fingers. 'There's a lot to tell you, I'm afraid.'

It did not take so long to tell in the end. Afterwards, Vintage went to her rooms, her arms full of scrolls – she wanted to examine for herself this evidence that Tor had thought he had found – which she dumped onto the bed, unread. She unpinned her hair and dragged out a case of wine bottles that Tor hadn't managed to find, and poured a glass, which she drank in one slow movement, her chin tipped back and tears leaking from the corners of her eyes.

It was Noon she kept returning to. What had happened to her? Nothing that Aldasair told her made any sense. She had never heard of a fell-witch blowing themselves up, and even if she had, Vostok surely would have been injured too, or even covered in pieces of . . .

She sat heavily on the bed, empty glass cradled in her hands. 'Oh Noon, my darling.'

Noon dead, Bern missing, Tor broken. Vostok out looking

for her bonded companion, and Hestillion directing the Jure'lia. She thought of when she and Tor had first seen Noon, when she had been a bedraggled figure in the Shroom Flats, with no proper shoes and no idea what she was doing. Suddenly, with a fierceness that surprised her, she wished that she could go back there – take that lost girl and her ridiculous Eboran friend and hide them away somewhere, instead of getting them embroiled in all this nonsense. The world would have to learn to look after itself.

There was a hesitant knock at her door. Vintage rubbed a hand quickly across her face.

'Come in, please.'

It was Chenlo. She had worn her old Winnowry travelling clothes back, but had since changed into the red silk shirt again, her sleeves rolled up to her elbows. She hung by the doorway, the thick braid of her hair falling over one shoulder.

'Are you well?'

Vintage stood up and went back to the small table, where she found another glass. 'I'm not sure I know what well means anymore. Will you have a glass of wine with me?'

'Many things have changed since we left,' said Chenlo. She came over to the table, her gaze moving quickly around the room. Vintage felt a brief moment of embarrassment – she had never been a tidy person – and then filed it away as unimportant. Let Agent Chenlo think whatever she liked. 'I have spoken to the fell-witches who are still here. Some of them, after the Lady Noon vanished, decided to go away. I don't know where. They saw her as a leader, and now –'

Vintage poured two fresh glasses of wine, and passed one to Chenlo.

'We still need them,' she said simply. 'We need them even more now, if that's possible.'

Chenlo frowned. 'I'm not sure you have them. Your friend Aldasair is adamant that we should be heading towards the place they've found, and only the war-beast keeps him from leaving, I think.' She took a sip of her wine, barely touching her lips to the liquid. 'At least Okaar doesn't seem to have caused the stir you thought he would.'

'That is true.' The assassin had been given his own room quickly and quietly, far from the Hatchery and the courtyard frequented by the war-beasts. 'Aldasair has nothing in his head but saving Bern, and Jessen follows him.'

Chenlo was quiet for a moment. 'The Lady Noon was important to the fell-witches because she freed them. Because she told them their lives were their own. She is important to you for different reasons.'

'She was my friend. Is my friend. You don't have those in the Winnowry, I suppose?' Vintage felt a stab of guilt at the wince that pursed the corner of Chenlo's mouth. 'When I found her, I thought she would be useful. Her winnowfire was an extraordinary weapon against the parasite spirits, even though she didn't really know how to control it, not then. I offered her safety, someone to watch her back.' She took a big swallow of wine. 'And how safe did she turn out to be? Sarn's bastard bones, I should have kept a closer eye on her, I should have been there . . .' She clamped her mouth down on the words, suddenly sure she was going to cry, and she very much did not want to do that.

'You cannot always watch the backs of friends,' said Chenlo carefully. 'You cannot protect them from all things. Even in the Winnowry, there were women who were under my care, who I could not always save. It's a hard truth. Possibly the hardest. And the more we care, the more painful it is.'

Vintage looked up at the woman, uncertain what to say, but Agent Chenlo was already excusing herself. She left her glass of wine on the side, still mostly full.

Chapter Thirty-two

Tor and the two war-beasts arrived back late the next day. All three of them looked ragged and exhausted, Tor especially so. Vintage elbowed her way through the small crowd that had gathered and grabbed a hold of him as he clambered down from Kirune's harness.

'What did you do?' she said fiercely, before wrapping her arms around him and squeezing him as tightly as she could. 'You idiot.'

'Do you mind? You're creasing my shirt.' But he wrapped one arm around her and squeezed her back anyway. 'Did you hear about Noon?'

'Yes.' She looked up at him, searching his careworn face. There were dark circles under his eyes, and his normally luminous skin was dull. 'My darling, come inside.'

Before she could get him into the palace, Aldasair appeared with Jessen at his heels. The young Eboran had a face like thunder, and Vintage found herself jumping between the two.

'What happened?' demanded Aldasair. 'Why did you leave him?'

'Now, we all need a rest before anyone starts saying things they might regret, so let's –'

Tor stepped neatly around her. He took hold of his cousin by his arms. 'Forgive me, Al. She took him, the queen, and I couldn't get to him in time. We were swarmed and –'

'He is right,' said Sharrik, his voice uncharacteristically soft. 'We would have all died if we'd stayed. The creature that is the queen wants him for something. Bern is not dead, brother Aldasair.'

'We have to go back for him,' said Aldasair. 'Now that we're all back, we have to go. Now.'

'We do, and we will,' said Vintage. 'Now let's get indoors and figure out exactly how we're going to do that.'

Aldasair nodded, although his need to be gone already was plain in the lines of his face. He stepped stiffly aside and they made their way back to the gates, but Tor stumbled awkwardly, going to his knees. Vintage went to him but he seemed unable to get up.

'Whatever is the matter, darling?'

'I'm just tired, that's all. Kirune?' The big cat came alongside him, growling faintly in the back of his throat, and Tor managed to pull himself to his feet by clinging to Kirune's shoulder. 'It was a long journey, and we didn't stop to rest.'

'Aldasair darling, I think we'd be better off if we let Tor sleep for a spell, he's clearly on his last legs.'

'No.' There were two points of pinkish colour, high on Aldasair's cheeks. 'Bern is suffering, and we can't wait. We'll talk about this now.'

In the end they talked about it all night, ensconced together in the war-beasts' courtyard. Tor spent it sitting, his long legs stretched out in front of him, and despite the warm night he did not remove his cloak. Chenlo joined them, her face solemn. When all the news was recounted and all the fresh information shaken out, Vintage found herself sitting cross-legged on the flagstones, Helcate curled up next to her. Tor and Aldasair were talking about the journey to the cavern, about how to

347

get there quickly, and Kirune was comforting Sharrik in a low voice she couldn't quite make out.

'Eggs,' she said eventually, breaking into their talk. They all stopped and looked at her. Chenlo raised her eyebrows.

'We sent for food already, Vintage, and ate it.' Tor had eaten enthusiastically, but she still didn't like the pallor of his skin. 'If you're still hungry . . .'

'Eggs in the cavern. The Jure'lia eggs. This is why they're here. This is what I've been looking for all these years, do you see?' She laughed to herself, and shook her head. 'I could never figure it out. Why come here over and over, to be driven back, again and again? Why not give up, or go somewhere else? Because they can't. They've already laid their eggs, and now they must make this place work, regardless of the local hostility. They must make Sarn their nest, because once the eggs have been laid, they cannot move them.'

'I'm glad for you, Vintage,' Tor ran a hand over his face quickly, 'I really am. But we have more urgent problems than the motives of the worm people.'

'I'm not sure that we do.' Seeing Aldasair open his mouth in protest, she held her hand up. 'I know, dear, of course I know, but listen to me. What is most precious to any living being that can procreate, that wants to procreate? Its offspring. My darlings, we know where they are, and we know what is most precious to them. We can deal them the most devastating blow. We can remove their very reason for being here.'

Silence fell briefly on the courtyard.

'The egg field was vast,' said Tor eventually. 'How would we even begin to do something like that? If we had Vostok, perhaps, we might have a chance, but no one knows where she is. Without her, without Noon . . .' An expression of pain passed over his face that Vintage was quite sure he was unaware of. 'Without the two of them, our firepower is greatly reduced.'

'Actually, it has recently been given something of a revival.'

She glanced at Chenlo, who was watching her warily. 'Heartbright. We found a drug in Jarlsbad that increases the destructive abilities of winnowfire tenfold. Tor, I have seen it destroy moon-metal. The stuff is bloody explosive.'

'You assume that you will have fell-witches to use it,' said Chenlo quietly.

'We have fell-witches here,' said Vintage. 'And, forgive me for saying it, they owe us.'

'If they owe any debt, it is to the Lady Noon,' Chenlo uncrossed her arms. 'And even then, I'm not sure exactly what she gave them, aside from homelessness and an uncertain future.'

Tor sat up. 'She gave them freedom, witch.'

'Us, Noon, it doesn't matter.' Vintage stood up, suddenly impatient with them all. 'Those women are not stupid. However uncertain their futures might be, I am quite sure they understand that a future with the Jure'lia in it is the worst of all outcomes. They will fly with us. They will fight with us. I know it.'

'And what of Bern?' Aldasair stepped forward, his face set into a stubborn expression that looked unfamiliar on him. 'In the midst of your great plan, what of Bern?'

Vintage went to him and took his arm, looking up into his crimson eyes. 'We will not leave without him. What better distraction than the destruction of their great horde of offspring? Between us we will find him, and get him out. Remember, Bern himself is probably the safest any of us would be in that situation. His link to them will protect him to some extent, my darling, and our connection to him will keep us together.'

Some of the stubbornness in his face softened. 'I cannot lose him, Vintage. I won't.' He turned to Chenlo. 'You will talk to the fell-witches, and see which of them will help us. I will go to the kitchens and the tents, see what supplies I can get together for this journey. We'll be travelling light, and, if at all possible, before sunset.'

He left immediately, striding purposefully from the courtyard, and Vintage watched him go, wondering what had happened to the quiet, meek young man she had first met in the Hatchery.

'Sunset?' Tor rubbed a hand over his face. 'What time is it? Surely he means sunset tomorrow? The day after tomorrow?'

Vintage held out a hand and he took it before levering himself to his feet. The sky above them was still dark, but it had taken on the tell-tale ghostly hue that hinted that dawn was not far off.

'You, get to bed. I'll come and wake you myself when it looks like you might have to get dressed.'

When she'd chased him from the courtyard and the war-beasts had left to find their own roosting places in the grounds of the palace, Vintage turned to find Chenlo watching her. In the pre-dawn shadows, the tattoo around the woman's neck looked dark and strangely alive.

'It's not right to ask this of them,' she said. Vintage didn't have to ask who she was talking about. 'They've suffered, they've been tortured, they have only just found what it means to be alive, and you ask them to risk dying. When the woman who freed them isn't even here to lead them.'

'Noon –' Vintage took a breath, stamping down on the immediate anger that flared inside her. 'Noon did absolutely the right thing, and it's hardly her choice that she – that she isn't here now. Be cautious how you talk about her. She was very dear to us. That includes me, it includes all the war-beasts, and it certainly includes Tormalin, the great useless fool.' Distantly, Vintage was aware that her own grief was lying in wait for her; a dark pool of despair and guilt waiting for her to put a foot wrong. *There is no time for that*, she told herself firmly.

'You loved her?'

Dizziness moved through Vintage, and she gritted her teeth, cursing Chenlo for giving her such a hard shove towards that insidious pool.

'She was my dear friend,' she said. 'Of course I loved her.'

Chenlo looked away, her face cast into darkness by the lingering shadows. Vintage sensed there was more she wished to say, and when finally she did speak, the words were brittle, as if they barely covered up something else.

'I'll talk to them for you,' she said. 'I'll ask them, but I can't tell you whether they'll follow you or not.'

'And you?' asked Vintage. 'Will you come with us?'

'I will follow you,' she said simply. 'For my sins.' And then she too left the courtyard, leaving Vintage in the slowly warming half-light.

'Explain this to us. Make it clear.'

Bern shifted against his bonds, but they were rigidly tight, adjusting to fit him more closely every time he moved. His hand, the one with the crystal embedded in it, was a white hot agony, but it was nothing compared to the shifting pain in his head. With every crystal on the wall that lit up with images, he felt as though the queen had slid a pane of lethal glass into his skull, neatly dissecting it.

'I've been telling you, hag, you just aren't listening. Or –' he winced as more pain throbbed through his body – 'stones curse you, you just don't bloody understand. You can't bloody understand, because your head is full of oozing pus –'

'Explain,' the queen said again. This time she pressed her finger to the crystal panel in the wall, and with a lurch of vertigo he was somewhere else. He stood with his parents, inside a vast wooden building that smelled of sawdust and straw. Despite the pain, a residue of old emotion leaked through; he had been demanding to come here all summer, had begged and pleaded, promised to do unending tasks, and his father

351

had finally relented. There was a wide arena in front of them, circled with stone, and in the middle of it a great bear plodded slowly around the ring, ridden by a stocky woman with neatly cropped black hair. The animal was huge, clearly Wild-touched, and wore a thick stone collar around its neck. The woman sat straight-backed and proud, and Bern – *he could still feel it, through all the pain* – was in awe of her.

'They get easier to train every year,' his father said. In this memory he was a huge, looming presence, yet to lose either his leg or his eye. 'The cubs are raised for it now, as calm and as happy as ponies. Not mine though.' He looked down at Bern with a twinkle in his blue eyes. 'My bear-mount I caught in the forest myself, a fierce she-bear I had to wrestle into submission. We fought for days, me and that bear, but she recognised the better warrior in the end.'

'Ah so, you do talk a lot of nonsense,' his mother put in. She was watching the bear rider too, her eyes bright.

'Aye, well, maybe you remember our courtship differently.'

She punched him on the arm, hard enough to make him wince through his laughter. Bern looked at them both: impossible, beloved, irreplaceable. They were his whole world. Then, his father reached down and snatched him up, placing him easily on the top of the stone wall.

'Look, lad, the little ones are here.'

Smaller bears had come into the ring, little lolloping cubs with ungainly legs. They scampered to be near the bigger bear, and Bern felt the weight of his father's hand on his shoulder. Impossible, beloved, irreplaceable.

'*Explain.*'

Bern gasped, the pain rolling over him again and briefly driving out all thought. He was back in the small room of crystals, and his mother and father were very, very far away.

'My parents,' he said. 'It's a memory of my mother and father. As a treat they took me to see the training grounds of the stone-bears. I wanted my own bear so badly then, and I'd been on about it for weeks.' He pressed his lips together, tasting his own sour sweat. 'That's it, that's all it is.'

'Your blood kin,' said the queen. She turned her lean body towards him. 'You are blood to them, part of the same great web. Yes. This is what connects you, although it is a very limited, very weak version of what we experience. We understand this.' She held up her arm, and a thin spur of black fluid sped out from it to touch the wall. There it joined the endless teaming lines of fluid that were present all over the Behemoth. 'That which runs liquid inside you, joins you.'

Despite himself, Bern frowned slightly and shook his head. 'In a way, aye, but it isn't just about blood. If my mother and father had found me in the woods, and raised me, we would still share our bonds.'

The mask-like face of the queen barely changed, yet Bern registered her displeasure anyway. 'Lady Hestillion Eskt, born in the year of the green bird, shares blood with Tormalin Eskt the Oathless. It is why she cannot separate herself from him, not truly. It is why she creates life with his face. This fluid inside them is at fault.'

'She's done what?'

But the queen had already moved to a different crystal panel. 'This one. Explain it.'

In this new memory, Bern found himself on board a ship, the sea around him grey and choppy. It was the old whaling ship, the *Foundation*; he knew it from its dark wood and the greasy smell of whale oil and salt, blood and sweat. He had served on board it for a few years in his adolescence, the sort of service kings' sons and daughters were often loaned out for, on the understanding it gave them some useful skills, and got them out from under their mother's feet. All around him men and women were busy at tasks, while the sky above them got ready to bless them with rain. A young man scampered across

353

the deck towards him, grinning readily. He had hair so blond it was almost white, but all Bern could see of it were a few stray curls from under his thick woollen hat.

'Alya,' he said, remembering.

'Come on.' Alya grabbed his arm and yanked him towards the hold, having absolutely no effect. Even at the tender age of fifteen, Bern was already taller and stronger than most. 'Our shift's over, you great stone head. Stew will get cold.'

They went below, into a cramped room thick with the scent of fish. A sour-faced woman with fish hooks pinched through her ears served them up bowls of thick brownish muck and they sat at a bench together, spooning the mixture into their mouths as fast as they could. Before his bowl was finished, Alya pulled a thick wad of paper from his inside coat pocket, and brandished it at Bern, grinning around a mouthful of stew.

'Your letters?'

Alya nodded. He was the son of another king, in another warlord kingdom of Finneral, and he had an enormous and complicated family, all very dedicated to writing to him. At their last port stop, he had picked up his latest packet, and finally had got around to reading through them all. He rifled through some, and extracted one piece of particularly creased parchment.

'She wrote to me again. See? She hasn't forgotten me.'

He passed the letter to Bern, who raised his eyebrows, impressed. 'This is Katyyin? The redhead?'

Alya made a disgusted noise. 'She has brown hair, like otters' fur, and freckles, and brown eyes, like . . . like a bear's eyes.'

Bern laughed. 'I don't think girls like it when you compare them to furry animals, Alya.'

His friend grinned, the tops of his cheeks turning faintly pink. 'Like you would know, Bern the Younger. Speaking of which, my brother asks me to remember him to you. As if you would forget.'

354

'He does?' Bern put his spoon down, suddenly interested. 'Which one? Show me the letter.'

'*Explain.*'

The eerie frond-lights were too bright after the gloominess of the ship's mess. Bern squeezed his eyes shut and opened them again, his head thumping.

'My friend, Alya. We knew each other when we were lads. That's it. That's all there is to know.'

'But this memory is so *strong*.' The queen sounded agitated. 'No blood link between you and this human, so why does it matter?'

'He was my closest friend. We spent months together on that miserable boat, stinking of oil and whale muck. We were cold and overworked and we made each other laugh.' He paused. He hadn't thought of Alya in years. 'He ended up loving it. The sea. I was glad to go back home, at least for a break, but Alya stayed, convinced his family to start their own fishing business. We wrote to each other sometimes, but I was never much good at it, and then a few years ago my mother told me he had died.' For a moment the relentless pain of the queen's torture lessened, dulled a little by another type of pain. 'Something Wild-touched in the sea dragged him from his deck. His crew barely even saw it.'

'We will make you look at another,' said the queen. 'And another. Until we understand it.'

'What is there to understand? You don't understand because you've the brain of a weevil, because you –'

'Explain.'

This memory was a recent one, so close it made him ache. He had woken in the night, in the bed he shared with Aldasair in the Eboran palace. It was too warm, and he'd kicked the covers off in the night – he never slept peacefully, these days – and his lover was not beside him. Despite the heavy weight of recent sleep that hung over him, Bern had been curious, so he had rolled out of bed and left the chamber. Aldasair had been standing by the tall windows that looked out on a small, forgotten courtyard, wearing only a loose pair of silk bed-trousers that hung low on his narrow hips.

Bern had stood where he was, caught by this vision of the man he loved. Aldasair's face was turned to the window, and the cold moonlight seemed to find and illuminate everything that Bern found most extraordinary about him: the strange, radiant hue of his skin, the delicate line of his brow, his spare frame and the way he held himself. His auburn hair, midnight-blue in the shadows, was a tousled mess, and a wild section of curls lay across his forehead. They made Bern think of the elaborate inky brushstrokes he'd seen on the few paintings that could still be found in remote corners of the palace.

The endless muttering chatter of the Jure'lia had quietened for him, and he'd even forgotten about the awkward lump of crystal embedded in his hand. In that moment there had just been their room, and Aldasair, standing in the window.

'This.' The queen tore him from the memory and he tried to roll onto his side, gasping with the shock of it. 'This is the root. You will explain it.'

Bern shook his head. Seeing Aldasair so clearly, and then having him taken from him, was too much. 'No. I'll not be talking to you anymore. Not about my memories, and not about Aldasair. Do whatever you like. By the stones, I'm done.'

The queen looked at him for long, quiet moment, her fingers flexing and unflexing like the legs of dying spiders.

'Attachments outside of blood,' she said eventually. 'Connections. This is what humans build.'

Despite himself, Bern replied. 'It's what makes us stronger. Stronger than you, anyway.'

'That is where you are wrong, human. We do not die when one part of us is destroyed – our body and mind are, always, truly, one. But if we kill you now, squeeze the life out of you or pierce your flesh with our body, the connections you have made die also. It is so easily broken, everything that you are.'

Bern thought of Eri and the pain they had all felt when he died. He thought of the deepening of bonds that came after.

'You still don't get it,' he said.

The queen reached down for him, and Bern braced himself to be throttled or torn to bloody shreds, but instead she yanked him from his bonds and, trapping him inside a net of shifting black ooze, dragged him to another chamber. She dropped him to the floor and then left, the tendrils of the Jure'lia fluid slithering after her like an army of obedient snakes.

'Bern?'

There was a series of thumps as something huge hauled its weight towards him. Bern lifted his head wearily and saw Celaphon, the enormous black and purple dragon that Tor's sister had ridden into battle. Again, the memory of Eri was very close; this creature had murdered the boy, left nothing but a ruined corpse staining the mud and snow of the Bloodless Mountains. Curiously, the dragon did not look so fearsome now. He was crouched low to the floor, his blocky head held at a slight angle. Bern thought of a curious dog in an alley, uncertain if the hand before it held meat or a stick.

'She's left me here with you?' He looked away, disgusted. 'The queen says she doesn't understand us, but I reckon she understands well enough what an insult is.'

'I am to guard you,' said Celaphon. Bern sat up. Every part of his body felt abused, but equally he did not want to lie prone in front of such a creature.

'Aye, that makes sense. I mean, as a human man with no weapons or allies I am obviously a very serious threat that needs to be guarded by an enormous, murderous dragon that can vomit lightning bolts.'

Celaphon raised his head at this, clearly uncertain what to make of it. Bern noticed that he still bore the discoloured marks across his horned face where Helcate had spat acid over him.

'I am very mighty,' the dragon rumbled eventually.

'You are certainly very large,' said Bern. He picked himself up and walked slowly to the far wall, where he sat down again, his back to it. 'But where I'm from, mighty is a word kept for champions and heroes. Don't talk to me, worm-lizard.'

Chapter Thirty-three

The hill was teeming with activity. The war-beasts were there, their harnesses being attended to by a handful of men and women who had become a kind of team over the last few months. They were humans who had stayed to help, only to become attached to Ebora and its strange, unlikely heroes. More humans were there with supplies, handing out breakfast to anyone who hadn't eaten, or loading up beasts and bats alike with enough food and water to keep them going for days. Tor was there, looking tense and unusually serious in the first light of the day; he was examining his sword, hefting its weight. The fell-witches who had come were a ragtag bunch – Aldasair saw that a few of them wore similar clothes of green and grey, the colours of the Winnowry agents, he assumed, while an even smaller number wore shirts and trousers and travelling jackets that looked like they had been begged and borrowed from any number of sources. Each of them had the bat-wing tattoo emblazoned across their foreheads. They all looked nervous, uncertain, but they also looked ready, attending to the bats that sat in a neat, almost military row.

And none of it was happening fast enough for Aldasair.

'Are we ready?' He addressed the question to Vintage, who,

as ever, seemed to be at the heart of all the activity. 'We have already wasted one day.'

'Darling, we're almost there.' She squeezed his arm briefly. 'We're just getting the heartbright where it needs to be, and then we'll be off.'

Aldasair nodded and met the eyes of the human woman Chenlo. She seemed to take this gesture as a demand for an explanation, as she planted her feet on the ground, arms behind her back, and addressed Aldasair directly.

'Even the fell-witches I could convince to come are not happy about it,' she said, a touch tersely. 'I hesitate to say it, but I suspect that they're mostly doing it out of a sense of loyalty to me.' She paused. 'I will not lie to you, Lord Aldasair, I am concerned that I am leading them to their deaths. Can you give me any assurances –?'

'I can give you nothing.' Aldasair took a breath. He did not want to snap at the woman, but now they were so close to leaving, his impatience had become an almost physical weight. 'This is the Ninth Rain, Agent Chenlo, and all our lives are in danger. I can only tell you we desperately need your help.'

The woman nodded once, her lips set into a grim line. Aldasair felt a shiver of some unexpected emotion from Jessen – anger? – and turned to see the man Okaar making his way up the hill, carrying several leather bags over his shoulder. He looked wary, approaching the mounts cautiously, despite Vintage waving him forward.

'The thief!' boomed Sharrik. The big griffin pawed at the ground, his claws tearing the grass up in clumps. 'A lying, lowly scoundrel. You are not fit for my sight!'

Kirune too had crouched low to the ground, the enormous muscles in his shoulders and flanks bunching as though he were contemplating leaping at the slim human man.

Okaar stopped, clearly believing he was about to be disembowelled. Aldasair went to them, his temper prickling with

360

both the anger of the war-beasts and his own desperate need for everyone to hurry up.

'They won't kill you,' he said to Okaar. 'Not yet, anyway. If you could please get the drug packed away swiftly, I would be most grateful.'

A murmur of dissatisfaction arose from the war-beasts, so Aldasair sent them a plea via their connection. *Bern*, he reminded them. *That is all we must think of for now.*

Eventually, they were ready to go. Tormalin took them up, leading on Kirune, and after the war-beasts came the fell-witches, led by Agent Chenlo. Once they were up in the sky, Aldasair allowed himself a glance back over his shoulder to see them all. The bats were a mixture of black, white and grey animals, and the women on their backs looked like they had come from every part of Sarn imaginable. Something about the sight caused a twist of excitement to uncurl in his stomach; the peoples of Sarn flying with the Eboran champions. It was like something out of one of his oldest history books, except of course, their numbers were greatly reduced and they had little idea what they were doing. Grimacing, he turned back in the harness and settled his gaze back on the far horizon. Find Bern, bring him back to safety. Then they could worry about everything else.

They flew during the long, hot days, and rested for a few hours each night, camping anywhere with shelter, or at least a good view of the sky; they didn't want to be caught unawares by Hestillion and her tame Behemoths. Tor, who felt as though he'd only just done this journey – and twice, at that – found himself struggling to keep track of the days and nights, or even what hour of the day it was. His arms ached continually, and there was a growing tightness in his chest that was particularly ominous.

'Do you have enough energy for a quick walk with me, darling?'

Tor stumbled down from Kirune's back to find Vintage waiting, Helcate already drinking from a big bucket of water someone had fetched for him. It was a clear, cool evening, and they had stopped at the very edge of a wide river, one of many that seemed to spread through the area like the veins in a leaf. The land itself was a strange region of clay and soft, sticky sand; belatedly Tor realised that he remembered flying over it – from far above it had looked unfinished, a scribble on a forgotten map. With some effort, Tor forced all thought of his own discomforts from his mind and straightened his back.

'You don't want to rest?'

'My arse is every bit as tired as yours, I promise you, but you see that sandbank over there? I think it's a settlement.'

Tor looked where she pointed. Some distance from the river the land rose into a lip of dark orange clay. There were odd marks and formations there – holes in the side of it, places where the wind had formed strange shapes in the sand – but certainly no people that he could see, or even any cooking fires.

'Settlements usually require people to populate them,' he said. 'Also, places for them to live. Shelter. Those are the sorts of things that add up to a settlement, Vintage.'

'Come on.' She grabbed his arm, none too gently, and they began to walk together, leaving the makeshift campsite behind them. 'We've time to be a little curious.'

It was a quiet place, where even the wind seemed hushed. The sound of the multiple rivers, a tracery of water and life, was oddly reassuring, and in the far distance it was possible to see a thick band of black that marked the beginning of the deep jungle territory that eventually led to the poisoned forest. Tor found himself wondering what Noon would make of such a place, so different to the plains and to Ebora, and his ever-present sorrow grew a little sharper. As if sensing his thoughts, Vintage sighed abruptly.

'You miss her,' she said. 'I miss her. A huge amount, which is strange really, given that I didn't know her for very long at all, in the scheme of things. For you, your time together must have seemed like the tiniest drop in the ocean. I don't understand it. For her to just . . . vanish like that. It's the cruellest possible blow.'

There were lights ahead after all, a soft glow that seemed to come from the ground itself. Tor made himself focus on those, not quite ready to speak. It wasn't like Vintage to be so insensitive, which meant that she was trying to trick him into saying something he wouldn't normally admit.

After a long pause, he said, 'Who are you talking about again?'

Vintage snorted, although it was a sound without any real mirth. 'My dear –'

'Because whoever it is, I'm sure I've already forgotten them. I can barely keep track of your brief human lives, you know – here one moment, gone the next. I should keep a list, so I can tick the names off as they depart.' He turned to her, his voice becoming softer. 'I beg you, Vintage, please don't make me talk about this. You share your sorrow to make it smaller, I know, but I can't even begin to look it in the face. Not yet. I'm not strong enough.'

'Darling –' Vintage opened her mouth to say more, but in the end simply shook her head. The lights ahead had grown a little stronger, and it was possible to see holes in the ground. They looked regular and solid, entrances that had been built to some specific design and not simply natural occurrences.

'You were right,' said Tor, nodding to places in the clay where channels had been cut. There were footprints in the sand too, lots of them. 'Are you ever not right about these things?'

'I have yet to find myself in the sorry situation of being incorrect, that's true.' Vintage walked closer to the holes. 'Hello? Anyone home?'

Tor looked down into the darkness. There was a ladder attached to the sheer side of the shaft, and it was just about possible to see something moving, deep in the depths of it. He leaned closer, trying to make out what it was.

'I can see something. Is someone coming up the ladder?'

Abruptly, a shiny body erupted up from the hole, not using the ladder at all, and skittered straight over Tor's boots. He gave a somewhat high-pitched yelp and jumped backwards. The thing was a huge ant, the size of a dog at least, and it was followed by two more. All of them were shiny, and a dark red-orange in colour. Mandibles and antennae waggled at them as the creatures circled their legs.

'Jure'lia?'

'No,' said Vintage quickly. She had taken several steps backwards herself, although she looked more curious than alarmed. 'Look at them, they're just big ants. Wild-touched, probably. The Jure'lia queen could never make something so colourful.'

'What do you want? What are you doing here?'

The voice came from the shaft. A short woman with copper-brown skin was pulling herself up on the ladder one-handed; in the other she held a long, wicked-looking knife. Her black hair was cut short and it stuck up at all angles; it was thick with clay dust. She spoke the plains speech with an odd scattering of Catalen – perhaps, Tor reasoned, the southern language had moved west with the natural migrations of people.

'Are these yours?' Vintage gestured to the ants, who were circling her boots. 'We mean you no harm, dear, we're just passing through and wondered who could be living out here, in this extraordinary place.' She was letting her own Catalen accent come through a little stronger than usual, Tor noticed.

The woman narrowed her eyes, looking past them to the place where the rest of their party had made camp. There was a pair of large campfires going already, and Tor saw very clearly the look of amazement that passed over her face as she saw what the firelight illuminated.

'No . . .' She looked sharply at Tor, who she seemed to see properly for the first time. She made a sharp clicking noise with her tongue, and immediately the three ants trooped back to her side. 'This is Deeptown. If you've come to steal from us, there's nothing left, and certainly nothing that could feed that.' Closer to the river, Sharrik could be seen shaking his wings and coat out.

'A town? I don't see a town. A hole in the ground, maybe.' Tor turned to Vintage. 'Really, you humans need to have a think about how you use these words, it's all very misleading.'

'It's beneath,' snapped the woman. 'Below your feet. Deeptown extends for miles, all around here. But the entrances are guarded.'

Vintage's face lit up. 'And your ants, did they help you build it? Are they obedient to you? How extraordinary. I would love to see such a thing.' She cleared her throat. 'I am Lady Vincenza de Grazon, and this is my friend Tormalin, but do call me Vintage. Please forgive us for being so nosy, but what you're describing sounds absolutely fascinating.'

The woman tipped her head to one side. 'You're fighting the worm people? Is that what you're doing?'

'We are,' said Tor. 'As much as we can, anyway.'

'These are bad times,' said the woman, nodding seriously. 'What you're doing is a sacred duty. Maybe your visit here is a blessing?'

Tor struggled to keep his face solemn. It was hard to remember a time when anyone had thought a visit from an Eboran was a blessing.

'We can hope so,' said Vintage in a carefully level tone.

'Then I will take you to see our pathfinder. Come on.' She turned back to the shaft, then paused. 'My name is Treen.'

Tor glanced at Vintage, who looked brighter than she had done since she'd heard the news about Noon. He reached out to Kirune briefly, reassuring him.

We're just exploring. We won't go far.

Treen took them past the shaft she had emerged from, and instead they moved towards a larger, more permanent-looking entrance nearer the sandbank. This one had been reinforced with wooden struts, and as they climbed down the first ladder into the gloom, Tor saw that the walls were scratched all over with writing. At first he thought it must be some sort of decorative motif, but when his eyes grew more accustomed to the light he saw that it was more akin to the sort of writing you often saw daubed on the walls of Mushenskan taverns – declarations of love or enmity, rude poems, swear words, opinions on the sexual prowess of acquaintances.

At first they saw only a connecting series of tunnels, lit with neat spherical oil lamps – here and there the red ants moved past them, intent on their own business – but then Deeptown revealed itself in glimpses; a great hall full of people eating and drinking; rounded chambers packed with those bedding down for the night; a room where several neat little stoves cooked flat loaves of bread, the steam and smoke disappearing up into a series of long, narrow chimneys.

Eventually, they came to another chamber. This one was wide and low, and lit with so many oil lamps that the warmth from them was stifling. It looked like a place of teaching, with low stools, a long shelf filled with old books, and many flat trays covered with slate, yet the only people in the room were an old woman seated in an over-stuffed chair, and a man and a woman standing with her. There was also an enormous ant in the room, four times as big as any they'd seen before, and this one was a deep dark red, like human blood. It was curled at the feet of the old woman like a faithful dog. All of them looked up as they came into the room.

Treen scampered forward to have a quick whispered conversation with the group, and then she waved at them to come over. Tor couldn't help glancing at the ant as they came. It had an elongated, swollen body, and its eyes were like fat blobs of oil.

'It's the queen of this colony,' murmured Vintage, so he alone could hear. 'She's the mother of all these ants.'

'You are Eboran?' The standing woman spoke first. She looked worried, her mouth pinched into an uncertain frown.

'Tormalin here is,' said Vintage smoothly. 'You can tell well enough that I'm not, but the lost lands are my new home, and I fly with a war-beast. Thank you for seeing us, Pathfinder.'

The woman smiled, a slightly pained expression, while the man next to her openly scowled.

'I am not the pathfinder.' She gestured to the elderly woman in the chair. 'Mother, some strangers have come to see you.'

The old woman shifted, her jaw working. She was small and somehow soft, her skinny legs hanging off the end of the chair, leather slippers dangling into space. Her skin was brown, like her daughter and Treen, but her hair was pearly white and wispy, curling up towards the ceiling as though it were caught in some errant breeze. With one hand she reached down to the ant, and smoothed her fingers across its broad head.

'They tell me the Ninth Rain has fallen,' she said. 'The old enemy, creeping back. They say even the corpse moon fell from the sky. I haven't been above ground in twenty years, so I don't know, but all my children tell me.'

'You run Deeptown?' asked Tor. The pathfinder lifted one bony shoulder.

'Deeptown runs itself, mostly. I just listen to my children, and tell them where to build.' Again she stroked the head of the giant queen ant. 'The earth has its dangers, so you have to listen – unless you want to find yourself burrowing into a dead drop, or a cave full of flood water.' She seemed to brighten a little. 'There are worm-touched rodents around here, you know. Great ugly bastards. Have to keep away from them and their dens, too.'

'These are dark times we live in,' said Vintage.

'But we still have some heroes, it seems.' The old woman smiled, her cheeks creasing with wrinkles. 'You fight the worm people?'

'We're trying to,' said Tor. 'We're taking the fight to the jungle south of here. If we're lucky, the worm people will regret this latest Rain.'

The pathfinder sat back in her chair, glancing at the woman and Treen, who both looked somewhat stricken.

'The Dead Wood is haunted,' said Treen. 'Not safe for anyone, the Dead Wood.'

'It's true, there will be terrible things beyond the woods, but we have to go there anyway.' Vintage smiled at the small figure in the chair. 'Pathfinder, would you bless us for our journey? It would be a great honour.'

The old woman gestured, and Vintage went to kneel before the chair. The pathfinder scooted forward and reached down to take her hand. As she did so, the great queen ant brought its head round, mandibles moving busily. It almost looked like it was smelling Vintage, its big bristly head nudging her elbow.

'Go with the blessings of Deeptown, for what it's worth.' The pathfinder and Vintage exchanged a smile. 'Now then, young man. Come closer. I've never seen an Eboran – I would like to see what all the fuss is about.'

Tor plastered a smile on his face, and knelt before the woman. The ant ran its mandibles up and down his leather coat, while the pathfinder took his hand and squeezed it. Up close her eyes were as black as the ant's, and glittered with a wily intelligence.

'A hero out of stories,' she said softly. 'I never thought I would see such.' She closed her eyes, and Tor was alarmed to see the glitter of tears on her cheeks. All at once he longed to be elsewhere, out of this hot little room and back above ground with the sky a comforting darkness overhead. The woman's grip on his hand tightened, and her eyes popped open. 'You're suffering, old one,' she said. 'She can taste it, you see. Smell and taste, they're all the same for our ants, and what she tastes from you is bitter, bitter. So much pain. It seeps through you.'

Tor pulled his hand out of her grip, and stood up, ignoring the way the ant's antennae followed his movements.

'Thank you,' he said tersely. 'Thank you for your blessing.'

Later, when they had climbed the final ladder and said their farewells to Treen, Vintage turned to look at him.

'What did the pathfinder mean, do you think? About you being in pain?'

With some difficulty, Tor resisted clutching his arm, still bandaged under his coat sleeve.

'She's an old woman who talks to ants, Vin, I don't think she means anything.' Somewhere ahead of them, the two camp-fires they had left behind were still burning. Tor could make out the familiar shape of Kirune, standing silhouetted against the flames. He was watching them come, his keen eyes no doubt seeing their every movement in the dark. 'Shouldn't we have told them more about the Jure'lia in the jungle? Or the poisoned creatures that live there? Hardly seems fair to let them carry on thinking the place is haunted.'

'So, we tell them that they are neighbours with the ancient and feared enemy, that the worm people have been under their noses all along,' Vintage shrugged, 'and then what? Where do they go, Tor? Deeptown is their home, they've all lived there for generations, and it's just as safe as anywhere else. Safer, even, given it's so hidden.'

Tor thought of the Jure'lia's maggots, pumping varnish down the entrances to Deeptown. He thought of being in those corridors when the green resin slowly closed off any chance of escape – hundreds of people and ants, crushed and suffocating together.

He could think of better places to be if the worm people came. Yet he did not want to argue the point. After the pathfinder's grim words to him, he was happy to leave the discussion of Deeptown for the time being. Forever, hopefully.

'Come on,' he said. 'We should get some rest while we can.'

Chapter Thirty-four

The pain was too much.

Bern had always considered himself a strong man; physically capable, level-headed in most aspects. But he was no fool. Every few hours or so the queen would drag him back into the chamber of crystal shards, and methodically, relentlessly, she peeled his mind back to the core, siphoning off his every memory and thought. He watched through eyes streaming with tears of agony as his life made a strange, fragmented parade across the walls, the only distraction from the pain the occasional glimpse of a face he'd thought he'd forgotten, or places he hadn't visited since he was a child.

And then the queen would question him, poring over each memory like a weaver examining substandard thread. What did this mean? Why had he done this? Why was he so connected to people and places that he had not seen for years? Above all, what was his bond to the Eboran Aldasair, what did it mean?

After every session he would be slung back in the chamber with the dragon, left to try and reconstruct what was left of his mind. His understanding of who he was, of where and *when* he was, felt broken, as though he were a delicate vase, his pieces shattered on the floor, no way to put it back together. Once or twice he had tried to leave the chamber, gathering what small amounts of energy he had left to try and use his connection to the Jure'lia to peel the walls back and escape, but each time Celaphon would lumber after him, shove him back with his big blunt head, or, if the dragon happened to be absent, various minions of the queen watched him instead, spidery things with multiple, pale eyes.

The pain was too much, and he wouldn't survive much longer.

'You know,' he said, staring up at the ceiling. 'I haven't eaten in days. I will die of that if nothing else.'

Celaphon lifted his head. Bern had been lying in silence for some time, and the dragon had seemed content to ignore him.

'Humans are fragile,' said Celaphon. 'My Lady Hestillion is not. I have learned this now.'

'I reckon you'll find she still has to eat.' Bern took a slow breath. His body felt incredibly heavy, impossible to move, almost as though he were sewn to the floor. There were a series of heavy thumps as Celaphon moved across the chamber to look down on him.

'You look bad,' the dragon said. 'Not how you were before. There was colour to you, before. I thought you were a weapon.'

'Your queen won't stop until I'm dead. I'm nothing to her but a puzzle to be solved, but she doesn't have the wit to understand the pieces, let alone the picture.' He swallowed hard. Speaking too much made his head spin. Increasingly, his sense of where he was felt wrong. Was he back in the dragon chamber, truly? Or was he still languishing in the room of crystals, his mind splayed across the walls? He couldn't be sure.

'It is a sad end for a warrior,' said Celaphon. 'I should like to have killed you in battle. Instead you will die here, quietly. Alone.' The dragon sounded genuinely regretful, although still far from sad – rather as though he'd been denied a favourite game.

'Not alone,' said Bern. 'They're still with me. It's very dim, the link, in the middle of this pit of arses, but I can feel them. Sharrik and Aldasair, and the others.' He flexed his sore hand. Each time the queen used the Jure'lia crystal to tear apart his mind, his hand burned with pain. 'I got to do that, at least. A boy from Finneral rode a griffin, loved an Eboran prince . . .' His voice trailed off as his mind tried to retreat to happier times, but Celaphon was abruptly much closer, his hot stinking breath blasting over Bern's face. He grimaced and turned away.

'They are with you, here? How do you feel them? What is it like?' He nudged Bern's arm, almost flipping him onto his front. 'Tell me.'

Bern groaned. The lack of food and the stench of the dragon's breath had combined to fill the back of his throat with bile.

'If you're not going to feed me or kill me, leave me alone, monster.'

The walls flexed open and the queen stalked back inside, her mask-face set. Celaphon shuffled back, and Bern made half an attempt to get to his feet, but the queen had no patience for such dignities. With a flick of her long arms, loops of the black fluid slid around him like a net, and he was hauled from the chamber.

Hours later he found himself back. He had no memory of the journey from the room of crystals, but at some point he had crawled to the wall and was curled up there, his hands over his head. Gradually, as he came back to himself, he pushed his back against the wall and sat up. Even that small movement caused waves of black spots to burst in front of his eyes.

'Ah, shit,' he croaked.

This time the queen had gone back to his earliest memories, ripping from him images and sounds that he could barely process as belonging to him. Some of these had been almost comforting – his mother carrying him back and forth under a wooden-beamed ceiling, singing some nonsense song – while others were just unsettling, such as the memory of a childhood fever where the walls of his room had seemed to liquefy and reach out to him.

The dragon was a dark presence at the far end of the room, but seeing that Bern was awake, Celaphon came forward again, his white eyes wide and eager.

'You still live,' he said, sounding pleased.

'Only just,' muttered Bern. He lifted up his hand and looked at it. The flesh around the blue crystal was inflamed and pain seemed to radiate out from the thing, coursing down his arm and his fingers with each heartbeat. 'I knew this would bloody kill me eventually, but I wasn't brave enough to do what had to be done.' He thought briefly of his axe, but he had no idea where it was. Had the queen taken it from him when she'd caught him? Regardless, he doubted he had the strength now to chop his own hand off.

'My siblings,' said Celaphon, 'do you feel them still?' There was, Bern thought, a different energy about the dragon. In so far as it was possible to guess a mood from a face that was covered in scales and horns, the dragon seemed unsettled, excited even.

'I feel them all the time,' said Bern. 'Although I'm not sure *you* can call them siblings. Not now, anyway.'

'We were born on the tree together,' said Celaphon, a trifle indignantly. 'I've been told that. The tree-god birthed us.'

'And you killed one of us. Remember that? The boy, Eri, who was bonded with Helcate.' Anger made him sit up straighter, although immediately his head swam. 'Tore him apart. Not to mention all the others you've killed since. You're a murderer, a traitor.'

Celaphon snorted, shaking his head. A glimmer of blue light

danced around his teeth, and Bern wondered if he was about to be blasted with lightning, or simply torn apart.

'He burned me,' the dragon said. He sounded absurdly sulky, a child accused of some injustice. 'My face, my eyes. And,' he added, more confidently, 'we are at war.'

'You've got that right.'

For a time, they both fell quiet. The ever-present hum of the corpse moon, still slightly discordant, filled the giant chamber. Bern thought of Aldasair and Sharrik, wondered what they were doing, where they were. Underneath the continual interference of the Jure'lia web he could sense them, a distant warmth.

'I can feel you reaching out to them,' said Celaphon suddenly. 'A tiny thread of . . . of gold, runs from you.'

'What are you talking about?'

'It's so small, and fragile, but it is in me still. Despite what I am, and how I am, the poison song cannot deafen everything. You say I am not their brother, but that gold thread says differently.'

Bern ran a hand over his face. Even in such a brief gesture he could tell that the bones under his skin were becoming more prominent.

'By the stones, I don't care, dragon. Think what you like. Any chance you had to be a war-beast with them was lost when you took one of our own from us. You're a creature of the worm people now.'

Celaphon snorted again, taking more steps until he loomed over Bern.

'But that thread is still there. Show me. Reach out to them and I will follow it. Let me touch that connection again.'

'No.' Bern paused, and laughed, although it hurt his chest to do so. 'Never.'

'I will kill you.'

'So? Do it. I am dying anyway.' Bern shook his head. 'You'd

be doing me a favour, really, although I reckon it would piss your queen off some.'

Celaphon lowered his head until the end of his huge snout rested on Bern's chest. After a moment, he pressed down, pushing Bern against the wall with so much strength that the big man could not free himself.

'Do it,' the dragon rumbled, 'or I will go from here, and find them. I will kill the griffin – you know I can do it – by snapping my jaws once. And then I will find the other, the man who was here before, and him I will bite slowly into small pieces. I will *eat* him. I promise you this.'

Bern pushed at the snout; it was as immovable as a standing stone. Looking up into the dragon's baleful, silvery eyes, he saw that he meant every word.

'It makes no difference,' he said again. 'You might have come from the same tree, but they won't have you back.'

Celaphon did not move. Reluctantly, Bern closed his eyes, and sought out the warmth that ran beneath the taint of the worm people. He reached out for them as he hadn't since he'd been captured, and as he did so his own need to be close to them again took over – *Aldasair, Sharrik, Tor, Kirune, Vintage, Helcate, Jessen. Family.*

He found them, briefly, and the passenger that travelled with him found them too.

Aldasair scrambled to his feet, half tangling himself in his ragged blanket. The campsite was quiet, the twin fires burning low, yet he had been certain for a moment that they were under attack; the sense of violation was overwhelming. Around him, he could see the others waking up too. Tor sprang up with more grace than Aldasair had, although he looked terribly old in the moonlight, his brow furrowed with worry. He snatched up his sword from where it lay beside him.

'What was that?' said Vintage. She was sitting up with her

arms wrapped around herself, although it was hardly cold. 'Did you all feel it?'

Sharrik strutted forward, tossing his head from side to side in agitation. 'It was Bern! He was with us then, I felt it! And then –'

'And then it was the dragon,' finished Jessen. 'The poisoned one.'

The fell-witches were waking up, roused by the confusion and fuss.

'What's happened?' Agent Chenlo's hair was loose over her shoulders. 'Are we in danger?'

Aldasair ignored her, turning instead to Tor. 'What does it mean?'

Tor wiped a hand across his mouth, frowning as he did so. 'I don't know, Al, but I can still feel him there. Like a bad taste. He was sharing space with us then, and he was closer than he's ever been.'

'He seeks to join with us,' said Kirune. 'Even after –'

'Helcate,' said Helcate. Belatedly, Aldasair realised that the smallest war-beast was trembling all over, and sorrow and fright emanated from him like a slow, thick fog. Vintage got up from her bedroll and went to him, throwing her arms around his neck.

'Oh my darling, I'm sorry,' she said, her voice muffled slightly as she pressed her face to his snout. After a moment, Aldasair joined her, patting the curly fur on the war-beast's flank.

'Little brother,' rumbled Sharrik, 'you do not need to fear him. He is nothing to us.'

Aldasair nodded, although he could hardly blame Helcate for being afraid. The sense of being violated, of their bonds being soiled somehow, was palpable even as the presence of Celaphon retreated. Kirune shook himself all over, as if trying to throw off the sensation. Aldasair reached out for Bern again, but the sense of him had gone.

'What does this mean?'

'It means, cousin, that Bern is still alive, and that he still has the strength to reach us.' Tor grasped his shoulder and squeezed it, briefly. 'I suspect it also means that he's getting desperate.'

Aldasair nodded. 'As soon as there's light in the sky, we go. And we don't stop until we have him safe again.'

Chapter Thirty-five

Hestillion stood over the map, her paintbrush in one hand. They had taken it from the ruins of a sizeable town in Triskenteth, a surprising place of tall stone towers and glass windows. She had been half regretful as the maggots and the spider-mothers had pulled it down into pieces, this town full of libraries and commerce, but there was no real way of stopping the process once it was started. Or at least, that was what she had told herself before putting the matter from her mind again.

She and the First had made their way through the central tower of the town, taking whatever seemed interesting and useful, and that was when she had come across the map. It was the most complete map of Sarn she had ever seen, more detailed and more beautifully inscribed than even the maps her father had owned in Ebora. Now, armed with a pot of green ink, she carefully filled in and covered over all the places she had taken with her circle; great splotches of green for all the varnish. Varnish vomited forth by *her* maggots.

It made for a pleasing scene. With her methodical plan, she had erased Sarn settlements by the dozen, wiping them from the map and leaving roads that led to nothing but eerie, eldritch graveyards. The next step, of course, was to take the largest cities. The multiple kingdoms of Jarlsbad, the glittering jewel of Reidn, the vital and bustling stink of Mushenska. When they were gone, Sarn – and therefore Ebora – would be brought to its knees.

'The map turns green,' murmured the First. Hestillion turned to him, pleased. All of them had started talking now, comments and observations, the occasional question. None of them would ever be giants of wit, that was true, but she was fascinated that they were beginning to learn. Their link to her, to the Jure'lia, her thoughts coursing through them . . . their minds were starting to form around these things, like a river running over rocks.

'It does. Look, come here, all of you.' They were all with her in the chamber, her entire circle. The Behemoths they controlled had been drifting for a few days while Hestillion considered their next target. One by one, the circle came over to the table. 'We are making tremendous progress, much faster than the queen ever managed. It's because we're being careful about our targets. Now, this place,' she tapped the region of Jarlsbad, which was a thick collection of place names and roads, 'what do we know about it? Green Bird?'

The woman-shaped creature with a bird daubed on her bony chest tipped her head slightly to one side, considering.

'Many small kingdoms,' she said. Her voice was thick, as though her throat closed over when she wasn't speaking. 'Fruit. Land bridges. Tall towers. Scents. Wild-touched cats. Grass . . .'

'Yes, that's all true. Anything else? Grey Root?'

Another of the circle stepped forward. Jure'lia armour flowed across her shoulders and up over her throat. The grey roots of her name were a sprawling pattern across her bald head.

'The separate kingdoms war,' she said. 'They fight. But –'

she looked lost for a moment – 'it is talking-fighting, mostly.'

'Politics,' agreed Hestillion. 'They're all prosperous, producing fruits, perfumes, steel – all trade that bolsters Sarn. But it's this place that interests me in particular at the moment.' She tapped her finger against the parchment.

'Tygrish,' said Red Moth.

'Tygrish,' said Hestillion, falling silent for a moment. With the maps and the other loot they had taken from the tower, she had come across a pile of recently opened letters. Whoever lived in the tower had had family in Jarlsbad, and they reported that the royal family in Tygrish had fallen – displaced by a fell-witch. And her war-beast.

'Is this my brother's pet, and her dragon? Or someone else? Is my brother there with her? Why would they take a kingdom of Jarlsbad, and by force?' She sighed. 'That letter has raised a lot of questions, a lot of questions I wish to have the answers to. It could all be confused gossip, of course – this sort of thing is rife during war, I should think – yet I wanted to take my first piece of Jarlsbad soon. Perhaps this is a sign. Our next step of the journey lies to the west.'

'We return first?' asked Grey Root. 'To the Under. For *our* dragon.'

Hestillion thinned her lips. Of course Celaphon was a mighty force in their arsenal, but he had also proven to be somewhat unpredictable when it came to the war-beasts. There was a great conflict within him; he was unable to truly decide if they were his blood kin or his enemy. She felt it in him sometimes, as a deep fluttering uncertainty at his very heart. Faced with this other dragon, or even another, unknown war-beast, how would he react? She couldn't say for sure.

'No,' she said eventually. 'We will let Celaphon rest for a little while longer. My circle, together we can easily take Tygrish, and I'll have the answers to my questions.' She smiled at them.

'It will be our largest victory yet, and our biggest test. Prepare yourselves.'

'Are you dead yet?'

Bern opened his eyes a crack. The soft light of the vast room was too much for him to take. He closed them again.

'Not quite.'

The dragon snorted, and stomped around his prone body. It was an unnerving sensation, to know that such an enormous creature was in the same room as you and so close to stamping you into paste, but Bern no longer had the energy or the will to stand.

'Soon, though, I think.' Celaphon made a rumbling noise in the back of his throat. 'When I joined with them, I felt them. They were horrified. They did not want me there.'

Bern said nothing. He did not have to ask who the dragon meant.

'But even underneath the anger, I felt . . . connected. Like there was a bond that they could not stop. Or deny. Because we *are* kin.'

'Family,' murmured Bern. 'It's just like family. Even when you hate them, you still have to – they're still just *there*. So hard to stop having the same blood.'

'I will always be a creature of two worlds,' said Celaphon. For the first time, the dragon sounded quiet, sad almost. Against his will, Bern found himself opening his eyes again to look at the creature. He was not looking at Bern; instead he had turned towards the wall, his blind-looking eyes examining something Bern could not see. 'I grew too different, too strange. My body hurts,' he said simply. 'It hurts all the time.'

Bern lifted his head. 'This wasn't supposed to happen to you,' he said. His mouth was so dry. The rolling weight of hunger in his gut had become one long cramp. He lifted his injured hand off the floor briefly. 'Or me. You should have been birthed in Ebora, next to your brothers and sisters.'

'I am mighty,' said Celaphon, although to Bern the words sounded especially hollow.

Silence fell between them for a while. Bern drifted, the acrid scent of the Jure'lia and the dragon in his nostrils, the discordant murmur of the corpse moon yammering in his ears. He was remembering burying the little clay statues of war-beasts in the black Eboran earth, how Aldasair had told him this was to help their souls return to the roots of the tree-god.

'What if,' the words were out before he even knew he was going to speak aloud, 'what if I die here, with the worm people still in my head and my blood. Will my soul be trapped here?'

Celaphon lowered his head and sent a blast of hot breath across Bern's face.

'Your soul?'

'In Finneral, we believe that when we die, our souls return to the stones of the hearth –' He coughed. His throat was raw and talking was rapidly becoming very painful. 'The hearth stone. All families have one. We go back to it when we die, and then when new children are born, we start again. All our – all the –' He swallowed. 'All our thoughts and memories gone, the soul all clean, like a pebble in the river . . .'

'Stones?' Celaphon did not sound convinced.

'I never paid much mind to it, but the Stone Talker told us that the hearth stone was the heart of Finneral. If we missed the ones who died, we had to remember they were always there. I didn't believe in it, but . . .' An unexpected sob rose up in his throat. 'What if I can't go back to the stone? The worm people will keep me here, I know it, because of this.' He flexed his fingers around the crystal shard in his hand. 'Even dying won't get me away from them.'

The dragon lowered his head until his snout was hanging over Bern's outstretched hand. Bern could feel the creature's hot breath moving across his skin. Then, the walls drew back in one muscular movement and the queen appeared again.

Taking no notice of Celaphon, she snatched up Bern in her net and dragged him back to the crystal chamber.

'There will be more,' she said as the ropes of fluid bound him back in place. 'I feel that we are close now to understanding.'

Bern shook his head, conjuring a rueful look for her even as his heart began hammering in his chest. 'You'll understand nothing. It's not in your nature, worm-queen.'

She didn't bother replying. Instead, a rippling wave of pain moved down through Bern's body – *that's new*, he thought dimly, *can't be a good sign* – and then he was with his father under a fat yellow moon. In this memory they were together on a hillside, Bern the Elder riding his bear mount, and Bern – in his early teens – riding a small horse. They were both watching the movements around a hearth-house, a low building nestled at the bottom of the hill. Lamps burned softly in the windows, and dark figures were by the stables, mounting their own horses. In the deep quiet of the night, Bern could almost hear their voices, and the clatter of horseshoes on cobbles.

'I still don't know why we have to do this at night-time,' said Bern. He shifted in his saddle, too aware that his father would see straight through this complaint. He tried to put more sulky indifference into his voice. 'It just makes us look more suspicious.'

His father, Bern the Elder, minor king of Finneral, chuckled warmly. 'Alliances between war-bands are made at night, under the sky-stone.' He nodded to the moon. 'As well you bloody know, lad.'

Bern rolled his eyes. 'It's just the moon. If it's so important, what does it mean that we make an alliance under *that*?' He pointed to the corpse moon, hanging silvery and ominous to the east. 'That doesn't seem like a particularly good omen to me.'

'Blast the stones, aren't children a joy?' His father seemed to be addressing the world in general, or perhaps imagined hordes hiding in the shadows. 'Been around for less time than a bear's fart and they're full of their own cleverness. Why listen to your father, bear's-fart? I've only led my people for decades, only fought with my back against the stones, only raised you from a tiny mewling cub –'

'I'm fairly sure Ma did that.'

'But let us all pause and listen to the staggering wisdom of Bern the Younger, who thinks himself a Stone Talker, I reckon. Don't think I don't know this is because you're nervous.'

'What?' Bern blinked, taken aback by this sudden change of attack. 'Nervous? I don't know what you're talking about.'

Bern's father snorted laughter. 'Here, look, they're coming. Sit up straight, Bern Stone-Talker.'

There were people at the base of the hill now, coming towards them. Bern saw another large figure, like his father, riding on a bear-mount, and two on foot. At the sight of one of them, his heart did a little stumble in his chest, and he forced himself not to glance at his father. He had the terrible suspicion that Bern the Elder knew very well what his heart was up to.

'Ho!' The call came from the central figure on the bear. 'Well met, Bern the Elder.' As they drew closer, Bern could see that she was a broad-shouldered woman with wild brown hair that seemed a part of her own horse-hair cloak. She had a war hammer at her waist, but she was grinning widely as they came on. Walking next to her was a girl of around twenty summers, her thickly boned face and freckles marking her out as the daughter of the bear-rider, and next to her came a slim young man around Bern's age. He had dark hair shaved at the sides, curls of ink tattooed under the fine fuzz of stubble there, and although Bern could not have seen them so clearly in the moonlight, he knew he had eyes like pale, fine granite.

'Rig, my friend, it's good to see you,' said his father. 'All these years, and finally a peace between us.'

The big woman shrugged one shoulder. 'Those last pockets

of the Sown resistance have been nothing but a pain in my arse, Bern, and my people want to get back to their farming and hunting. Anything we can do to make that happen faster –' She paused to gesture to the two who stood with her. 'You've met my daughter, Jorg, and my brother's lad, Rold. They come as my witnesses.'

'Fine young people,' said Bern's father. 'My boy Bern is here as witness also – he was so excited to come, like a young pup out sniffing for hares. Can't imagine why.'

Bern felt the slow crawl of his blush moving up over his neck and across his cheeks. At least, he thought, in this light they can't see it, yet he couldn't help noticing a very knowing look pass between his father and the war-queen Rig. He kept his back very straight, trying not to look too obviously at Rold, but then the boy spoke.

'Perhaps we can hunt while the elders talk,' he said, looking directly at Bern. 'Night hunting in these woods serves up more prey than you would think.'

He grinned, and Bern felt his heart turn over in his chest, and that was when Rold's throat burst open, spilling a gout of black blood down his front and onto the grass. For a terrible long second, Bern could not understand what he had just seen; one moment Rold had been smiling at him, impossibly hand-some, and the next he was a boy on his knees, already close to death. The arrow that had torn his throat out was embedded in the leg of Rig's bear-mount, and more arrows were flying, stuttering over the small hill like lethal hail.

'It's the fucking Sown!' shouted Bern the Elder, and, too late, Bern spotted other shadowy figures on the brow of the hill. Rig was already riding towards them, bellowing, her war hammer held above her head, and his father was turning his own mount. The girl Jorg had left her cousin in the grass and was following her mother.

'Rold?'

'He's gone, son.' His father took a moment to lean across from his bear, grasping Bern by the forearm. Arrows zipped over their heads, too close, too close. 'Now we make them pay. Do you understand? We kill them all, quickly. None of them will see sunrise.'

He let go and was off, a huge, terrifying shape barrelling towards the scattering figures at the top of the hill. There were more people on the edges of Bern's vision, not just archers but warriors, their faces grim and streaked with Sown ink. From above him, a horn was being blown; Jorg was summoning the house guard.

Abruptly, his horror and sorrow were blown away like the last remnants of tattered pennants, and Bern felt himself fill up with something else instead, something hot and hard-edged, red-eyed and frantic. He would kill them all, he would taste their blood, and the future they had denied Rold would be denied them too. That was all that mattered . . .

'What is this, then?' asked the queen. Bern took a huge, watery breath. The surging rage had felt so real, so present. 'What is this new feeling?'

'We did kill them,' he said, not really listening. He was remembering Rold, who had been so good at hunting. 'Took apart every one of them, and before the sun came up. I was covered in blood after, and it felt – right.'

'And you condemn us.'

'This was different.' Bern shook his head. 'This was revenge. What they had done was an enormous insult to our clans – an attempt on the life of a king and queen? They were lucky we just killed them.'

'It was more than that to you,' said the queen. Bern looked at her for the first time, surprised by this accurate observation.

'Aye. I liked Rold, I liked him a lot. An early crush, I suppose. And they killed him without even thinking about it.' He licked his lower lip with a dry tongue. 'Stones curse them, the arrow was meant for Rig's bear, not him, but that mattered nothing to them. All that promise, snuffed out. I wanted to kill them all. It was important, and right, that I did.'

'Such attachments, again,' said the queen. 'To that which is not blood kin.'

Bern laid his head back against the soft, slightly yielding surface he was tied to. 'You'll never understand us. Just let me die, worm-queen.'

'Perhaps you are right,' said the queen. The relentless buzz of her voice, always, to Bern's ear, humming with the discordant harmonies of a thousand other voices, had taken on an odd, dreamy quality. 'But recently we have learned the value of change, and of trying new things. And when we need to understand something, we have learned that you just take it apart first.'

She brushed a long, curved finger across Bern's forehead, and a bolt of pain moved from the space between his eyes down to the crystal embedded in his hand. He screamed.

Chapter Thirty-six

'I can hardly believe it.'

Vintage stared intently at the enormous crevasse that broke the jungle floor into two jagged pieces, half sure it would vanish if she looked away. Tor, on the back of Kirune, was descending slowly into the darkness, while Aldasair was already gone, Sharrik leading him and Jessen down into the Jure'lia lair. The forest surrounding them was lush and strange almost beyond imagining, and the tiny glimpse she had got of it had made Vintage eager to come back with her notebooks and glass jars, but there was no time. Even her muffled and broken connection to Helcate was telling her that Bern was in a lot of pain, and as strong as he was, she couldn't see how he could survive it much longer.

'All these years,' she said softly, 'and they were just hiding underground. In the arse-end of nowhere, of course, but that hardly matters.'

'Lady Vintage.' Chenlo looked tense. Behind her, their handful of willing fell-witches were tending to their bats. Those who had been agents in their previous lives wore expressions of grim patience, while the few who had, until recently, been imprisoned in the Winnowry, looked largely terrified. Vintage forced herself to turn away from the crevasse and meet Chenlo's gaze. 'You will tell us as soon as the signal comes?'

'As soon as I hear it, you will know.' She addressed the women now, still keeping her voice low. They were some distance from the opening of the crevasse, and all of Tor's reports suggested that the worm people were nestled deep in the dark earth, yet something about the place asked for quiet. There was danger in the line of every warped tree and swollen leaf. 'Remember, my darlings, we are sneaking in, so you must be absolutely quiet. Listen for me. When I tell you to drink the heartbright, do it, but not until then – we have a limited supply, and I will not waste it if the opportunity to destroy their eggs is not there. Likewise, do not summon your winnow-fire until I tell you so. Tormalin tells us it's dark down there, and we don't want you all lit up like a whore's bedroom.'

Sweaty faces looked back at her, saying nothing.

'We can make such a difference here. We can hurt the worm people in a way they've never been hurt, but I won't lie to you. This is dangerous, very dangerous. Most of you won't have seen the worm people up close before, and they are not something you generally wish to see on an empty stomach. The consequences of being caught down there will be very dire indeed.'

'Yet we're going down there and chucking fire about,' said one of the ex-agents, a woman with a face like a brick and a Mushenskan accent. 'Lucky us.'

'Some of us have barely even flown with a bat before.' This was one of the younger girls, her eyes wide with uncertainty. 'What should we do if something goes wrong?'

Vintage caught a glance from Chenlo, and cleared her throat.

'Listen. If things should go tits up, keep your eyes on that strip of sky and get out as fast as you can. Don't wait around the crevasse either – get away, head north, and we'll do our best to meet up again elsewhere. I –'

Helcate lifted his head, his snout quivering, and at the same time Vintage felt it: not quite words, just a sense of urgency. *Come on*, it was saying. *Follow us. It's time.*

'Helcate,' said Helcate.

'That's it,' said Vintage, scrambling back into the harness. 'That's the signal. Follow me, and remember everything I said. We'll be quiet now, as much as we can. Chenlo?'

The agent nodded and went to her bat. In moments they were all in the air. To Vintage, the leathery wing beats of the bats sounded much too loud – surely the Jure'lia would hear them coming and tear them to bits – but they sank down past the craggy stone walls of the crevasse without incident. For a time they were caught in a suffocating dark, then, as her eyes adjusted, Vintage saw the strange glowing plant-like fronds that were growing directly out of the walls. They afforded only a ghostly, yellowish glow, but it was enough to hint at the huge scale of the space they were in. The walls fell away abruptly, revealing an area that seemed to stretch in all directions, and nestled in its rocky bosom was an army of horrors. Behemoths clustered together like fat, milk-fed puppies, while cavernous passageways, each easily as big as the Eboran palace, led on to other enormous chambers. The place was silent, filled only with the faint dripping of water somewhere nearby, and a discordant low-level hum that Vintage assumed must be the sound of the Jure'lia at rest. Remembering Tor's instructions, she led them down towards the north-western chamber, already noting the faint green glow that came from that direction.

'Tomas save us,' murmured someone. 'We're flying into our own tombs.'

Vintage felt rather than heard Agent Chenlo admonish the speaker, although Vintage could hardly blame the woman. Now that they were here, sinking into the abyss, it felt rather like they'd found a snake's nest and were preparing to lay down naked in it. Vintage glanced up at the retreating slither of sky far above them; already it looked like nothing more than a discarded blue ribbon.

'Movement on the ground,' said Chenlo, her voice barely more than a whisper. Vintage looked down and saw what she meant; an alarming sea of Jure'lia creatures shuffled and clicked below, like a carpet made of shining beetles. She saw spider-mothers in there, giant burrowers, and other less identifiable things. When she spoke, her throat was tight.

'I think it's all right,' she murmured. 'They're just going about their business. They're not going to take any notice of us just yet.'

The north-west chamber loomed into sight, and Vintage swallowed hard, her heart thudding in her chest. Here, stretching as far back as they could see, were the rounded forms of the Jure'lia eggs, just as Tor had promised. Each one looked easily as big as Vostok, and they were surrounded by a teeming mass of the black Jure'lia fluid. A strange chemical stink rose up off them, and quite distinctly she heard one of the young women gag on the stench of it. In her mind, Vintage tried to picture the life cycle of the Jure'lia, and how these eggs fitted into it: an endlessly hungry army that travels through the skies to a new world, lays its eggs within its warm flesh, then sets about eating away anything on the surface that might do it harm. Then what? *Then, the great circle of life*, thought Vintage, smiling grimly. The eggs hatch, and a new army sets out on its quest to find a world to consume.

One new army? Several thousand, more like. The shadows in the vast cavern were deep and thick, but already it was evident that they had an enormous job ahead of them.

There was a shout from across the cavern, loud and mocking – it was Tormalin, making a racket as usual, but one that was for once a part of the plan. From behind them Vintage heard the Jure'lia surge into life. The background hum became a shriek, and there was the unholy sound of thousands of insectile legs coming to life – clicking, skittering, buzzing life.

'Sarn's bloody roots, it's time. Ladies, drink your heartbright and follow me.'

Kirune alighted on top of the Behemoth just behind Sharrik and Jessen. The place was as gloomy and as unpleasant as Tor remembered, yet there was a tight knot of excitement in his chest. For the time being at least, the weakness of the crimson flux had retreated, and he felt feverish with the need to fight.

'How will I find him?' Aldasair was frowning around at the enormous cavern, as if Bern might be standing in plain sight somewhere. 'She could have him anywhere.'

'He is close.' Sharrik shook his head, fluffing up the feathers on his neck. 'I feel him, nearby. Within this fat thing, I think.' He stamped his heavy paws on the surface of the Behemoth.

'It's a place to start,' agreed Aldasair. 'But how do we even get inside?'

'We crawl up its arsehole,' said Sharrik, in a very serious tone. 'Before, over the mountains, the scholar Vintage took Bern up the arsehole of this monster. That is how she described it.'

'Oh.'

For a very dangerous moment, Tor was seized with the urge to laugh. He swallowed it down with some difficulty, and clapped his cousin on the back.

'It seems your path is clear,' he said. 'I'll get down there and cause some trouble, and bring all the little beasties running. You, Sharrik and Jessen find Bern.'

'Sharrik should stay here with you.' Aldasair's face was pale, two hectic splashes of colour across the tops of his cheeks. 'You cannot possibly deal with that horde alone.'

'I must find Bern!' Sharrik raised his voice, then just as rapidly lowered it. 'I can feel him, clearer than any other. You must take me.'

'I will be fine.' Tor smiled at them. 'Don't worry about me, just get him out and as far away from here as you can.'

With that, he touched his hand to Kirune's fur and they trotted over to the sloping edge of the Behemoth. Below them, the teeming minions of the Jure'lia squirmed and skittered. Tor saw bulbous white and yellow eyes, mandibles like iron traps, many-jointed legs tipped with blade-like claws.

'No one asks if I will be fine,' said Kirune.

Tor smiled again, and buried his hands in the thick fur across the big cat's shoulders.

'Brother,' he said. 'This will be fun, won't it? All we need to do is fight. We were made to fight, you and I.'

'You mean to die here,' rumbled Kirune. 'I can feel it.'

Tor unsheathed his sword. 'I can hide very little from you these days. Would that be so terrible? I am dying anyway.'

'You are a fool.'

'Come on, old friend,' Tor leaned back in the harness, bracing for the jump, 'Vintage will be waiting.'

The powerful muscles bunched and they sprang outward into the gloom, landing in the midst of the crawling horrors, scattering enough to briefly create a free space around them. Tor grinned and waved his sword.

'Come and face your doom, you ugly worm bastards!' His shout echoed around the cavern, fluttering against the walls and bouncing back like a frightened bird, but something about it made him grin all the wider. *Here we are, in your secret den*, he thought. *Crawling right up your arsehole*.

Slumped on the floor of the chamber, Bern rolled to a stop, his cheek pressed to the slightly porous floor. For a time he knew nothing but a swarming darkness behind his eyes – the Jure'lia were so loud and close, he could almost believe he was one of them – and then he snapped back to consciousness with the realisation that he couldn't breathe. He gasped, trying to get some air back into his lungs, but the muscles across his chest wouldn't obey him. Instead he thrashed on the floor, fingernails tearing at the soft material beneath.

'You gasp like a fish.' Celaphon was watching him again, his huge malformed head hanging above him like a dark cloud.

In desperation, Bern tried to roll away. Bright bands of white pain were circling his chest and arms, and more than anything he didn't want to be looking at Celaphon when he died. A thin trickle of air wheezed into his throat, but it wasn't enough.

'You are dying,' said Celaphon.

Bern squeezed his eyes shut, trying to summon an image of Aldasair, or even his parents, but his body betrayed him, bringing forth only the roar of the worm people, deafening and inhuman. *I'm going to die, and that's where I'll be stuck forever*, he thought in between gasps. *I'll be a tiny strand in their giant, diseased web.*

Dimly, he was aware that Celaphon was still talking, although he could make no sense of it, and then he felt his arm being lifted by something wet. There was a sense of pressure, and abruptly the pain in his chest was dwarfed by a crushing sensation at his wrist. He could breathe again, taking great gulps of air into his lungs only to scream it back out again as a pain unlike anything he had ever felt travelled up his arm. Through eyes streaming with water he saw the dragon Celaphon with the end of his arm in his mouth; saw his own blood streaming between the dragon's teeth as he patiently chewed his hand off. There was a terrible wet crunching that seemed to travel through his body in a wave, and then his arm dropped away. Where his hand had been with its jagged blue crystal was a ragged stump, pumping bright arcs of arterial blood onto the floor.

In the next moment, the pain was replaced with something else: sweet, blessed silence. For the first time since the queen had forcibly joined him to the Jure'lia, his mind was quiet, safe – clean. And more so, he could fully feel his connection to the war-beasts again, and through them, to Aldasair.

'You are free now,' said Celaphon. The dragon threw his head back, and in a motion like that of a greedy seabird, swallowed down the remains of Bern's hand.

'Free,' croaked Bern. Already, the floor around him was covered in a crimson slick of blood, and his vision was dimming at the edges. He felt unutterably tired, and the heaviness that crowded his brow, closing his eyes, promised the longest possible sleep. Aldasair came into his mind, and Sharrik, as they had been when he had first seen them: Aldasair a lost figure in a crowd, looking for all the world like a painting come to life; and Sharrik as he tore himself free of the silvery pod, covered in sap and already fierce, his blue feathers the brightest thing Bern had ever seen. 'That will do . . .'

'What have you done?'

The queen swept into the room on strings of fluid, and the brief glimpse Bern got of her mask-face was unsettling – he wasn't sure he had ever seen her so obviously angry before. It didn't matter. He turned away from her, feeling cold, and waited for the darkness to become complete. Celaphon stepped around him, snorting and stamping.

'You do not command me,' the dragon said, an odd hint of triumph in his voice. 'Hestillion might, but she is not here.'

'I need this creature alive!'

'You are killing him anyway,' Celaphon pointed out, quite reasonably, to Bern's mind, and then slim feelers of black fluid were curling around his body. He no longer had the energy to move against them, but when they flowed over the ragged stump where his hand had been, he gave a low, disgusted cry. There was heat, and a strangely lively sensation, as though a thousand tiny fish were biting at his skin.

'If he dies, Celaphon of the corpse moon, we will tear your skin from you and use it . . .' The queen stopped, her attention

396

elsewhere. Bern shifted in the puddle of his own blood, trying to see what she was doing, but she had moved away from both him and Celaphon, and then without a word she vanished back through the wall.

The burning pain in his chest and arms was back, but Tor barely felt it as the Jure'lia swarms fell back before him. Kirune leapt from patch to patch, tearing anything that got too close to pieces, while Tor dragged his sword through the bodies of anything tall enough for him to reach from the big cat's back. There were things here he had never seen before, shambling beetle creatures that walked on two spindly legs, pulsating worm-things, segmented and grub-yellow, that tried to curl around Kirune's paws. Tor laughed at them and slaughtered them all, his sword growing thick and heavy with ichor.

'How much longer must we do this for?' growled Kirune.

'Listen out for it,' said Tor between gritted teeth. 'We'll soon know when Vintage has started causing trouble.'

The horde was growing every moment, even as they stood on the bodies of those minions they had already killed, and it was evident to Tor that eventually they must be overwhelmed. The thought of that was thrilling somehow, it was right. It was as it should be. All except for one thing.

'Listen Kirune, when I tell you to, you must go and help Vintage.' He kept his voice level, casual almost, even as he paused to drag his sword across the throat of a lumbering maggot-man. 'Once they've exposed themselves, I've no doubt that the Jure'lia will be after them too, and if they don't make it out, all of this will have been a waste.'

'You speak to me as if I am an idiot,' snapped Kirune. They leapt over a crowd of spider-mothers and then span around to cut their legs out from under them. 'Like I cannot tell what you mean to do.'

'It's just what has to happen, Kirune.' Tor thought of Egron, wasting away in his suite in the Eboran palace, diseased blood oozing from his wounds as he coughed away his life. That, or a warrior's death, his sword in his hand and defiance on his lips. There was little contest. 'They will need your help, and I will need to stay here. We've only got a short—'

The cavern filled with white light, and there was sound a little like an enormous cough. Half a second later and the light grew so bright that Tor had to hold his arm up to shield his eyes.

'I'll give you two guesses what that was.'

Chapter Thirty-seven

Together Vintage and the fell-witches had flown to the very back of the egg chamber; it had taken a worryingly long time to do so. Finally, it was possible to see the craggy surface of the interior wall, pocked with strange fungus and a few outcrops of the straggling fronds with their soft, eerie lights. Below them, the eggs seemed to steam slightly, their slimy casings glistening unpleasantly.

'We should space out, in a line,' called Vintage. She was no longer concerned about alerting the worm people; it was clear from the racket Tor was causing that their attentions were currently elsewhere, and the eggs themselves did not seem to be sentient. 'Those of you unfamiliar with this, be careful not to take too much life energy from your mounts. An unconscious bat is going to land you right in the shitter. Then, ladies, you should direct your winnowfire downwards, whilst moving back towards the entrance. Helcate and I will do what we can with his acid spit. Does that make sense?'

Chenlo nodded tersely. 'We shall have to be cautious, at least to begin with.'

'Very wise. Chenlo, I shall leave you to direct, in that case.'

The woman nodded. Too late, Vintage noticed she had

changed into the red silk shirt Vintage had bought her in Jarlsbad. When had she taken the time to change into that, and why? Forcing such irrelevant questions to the back of her mind, Vintage turned Helcate away from the back wall, and waited. The fell-witches flew out, spacing themselves along the length of the wall, becoming tiny moth-like shapes in the greenish gloom.

'My darling, there's every chance we will have to get out of here very fucking quickly,' she murmured into the war-beast's ear. 'I shall trust you to get us to safety.'

'Helcate,' agreed Helcate.

'Are we ready?' called Chenlo. There was a chorus of affirmatives, some more enthusiastic than others, and she raised her hand, which was doused in a guttering flame. 'Fire!'

The stream of her winnowfire shot down into the dark, followed by the streams of the other fell-witches. Just as it had been in Jarlsbad, the heartbright-enhanced fire was strange and unstable, more black than green and fizzing with embers that poured in all directions, yet Vintage could see immediately that it was working; the greenish moon-metal casings of the eggs blistered and broke apart, spurting a greyish substance that burst into yellow, oily flames.

'That's it!'

The fell-witches moved back, bats' wings beating so quickly they were blurs, and the next row of eggs went up. Beneath her, eager to join in, Helcate hiccupped a long stream of clear acid, which spattered all over the nearest eggs. The effect wasn't as impressive as the winnowfire, but she saw the casings turn black and buckle, almost appearing to wilt. Quickly, huge gouts of a foul-smelling smoke began to unfurl towards the ceiling, and Vintage could see that the super-heated contents of the burning eggs was even causing the black fluid to boil. She leaned down, trying to get a closer look, and her mouth turned down at the corners. The things were bursting into

400

flame faster and faster, catching each other alight before the fell-witches had even got to them. The conflagration below them roared higher and higher, yellowish flames licking at the walls.

'The bastard stuff is too flammable. It's going to overwhelm us before we get back to the entrance.' She cupped her hands around her mouth. 'Chenlo!'

But the Winnowry agent had already figured it out, and was shouting at the fell-witches to get away. Abruptly, several of the eggs below them exploded from the heat, sending gouts of boiling liquid up towards the ceiling. Several women screamed as they came very close to being knocked out of the air, and below them the fire raced.

'Shit! Shit shit shit.'

As one they flew for the far side of the cavern, lungs now itchy with the foul smoke, but the eggs were exploding one after another, so quickly they made Vintage think of the little red strips of popping crackers her family had bought on festival days. *Pop, pop, pop.*

'As fast as you can!' she called, urging Helcate forward. Boiling fluid filled the air around them, haloed with flame, and one of the women was caught by it. Vintage saw the splash of light to her left, and then the fell-witch was gone and the bat was on fire, shrieking and flying blindly up into the roof. Vintage cried out wordlessly, and saw Chenlo swoop to catch the woman, but it was too late. The fell-witch was lost in the steaming fire and fluid below.

'Sarn's bloody bones curse us all. Chenlo, get away from there!'

The Winnowry agent swooped back up just slightly too late. Another explosion caught her, searing her bat with fire and nearly knocking her from its back. Helcate surged forward, his narrow snout pointed like an arrow, and as they reached the bat – collided with it, more truthfully – Vintage yanked the woman from her harness and bundled her onto Helcate. The little war-beast dipped once, but with a few powerful beats from his leathery wings was back on course.

'I couldn't save her.' Chenlo looked deathly pale under the soot smudging her face. 'Vintage, I saw her burn, I saw her . . .'

'There was nothing you could do. Hold on!'

The entrance to the egg chamber was in sight, although the roaring wall of fire that came on behind them threatened to beat them to it.

'What the fuck is that?'

The cry came from one of the Winnowry agents, and it took a moment for Vintage to realise what she was talking about. Something pale and sinuous was unfurling itself from the top of the entrance – long white fingers of something that looked like wax but wasn't, oozing down from somewhere above.

'It's covering the way out,' said Chenlo. 'It's going to trap us all in here with the fire!'

'Can you feel him, Sharrik?'

The griffin tossed his head with agitation. They were in a corridor, although Aldasair hardly thought that was the right name for it; the walls were curved and yellow-white, porous and moist to the touch. It was more like being inside the bones of a living animal, and the continual scratching hum that filled the place only added to the sensation. They had been searching blindly for what felt like hours, although he knew that in truth that was very far from the case, and Aldasair was filled with the creeping suspicion that they were lost; children in a garden maze who had boasted they knew the way to the centre.

'I can,' said Sharrik. He sounded more certain than he had before, and Aldasair cast him a quizzical look.

'Brother?' Jessen nudged his shoulder with her snout. 'What is it?'

'He is close, and growing closer,' he replied. 'But more than that. His mind – it's free of the Jure'lia taint!'

'How can that be?' Together, they moved a little faster down the corridor. Perhaps, reasoned Aldasair, the queen had broken the connection between Bern and the worm people. Perhaps she had not wanted a human in their web after all – which still led to the question: what was she doing with him?

He was just dreaming up all manner of tortures when the wall to their right abruptly flexed apart to reveal Celaphon, the huge worm-touched dragon. Immediately, Sharrik roared, leaping to the front of their small group with his head lowered and shoulder muscles bunched.

'Murderer!' cried Sharrik. 'Villain, it is time for you to pay for your outrageous strike against us!'

Curiously, the dragon did not react with the howling fury Aldasair was expecting. Instead, he looked at them closely, as though seeing them properly for the first time. The discoloured scales across his face where Helcate had burned him looked like scorched copper pennies.

'The boy, Eri,' said the dragon. 'I saw all that when I joined with you, so briefly. This is why you hate me.'

'He was one of ours,' said Jessen, coldly. Aldasair joined his hatred to hers, flowing so clearly in the bond between them, and he felt clean. 'He was our family. You are not.'

'You will not use his name,' added Aldasair, surprised at the venom in his own voice. 'You have no right to it.'

'Will you not fight, coward?' bellowed Sharrik. Somewhere up the corridor there was the sound of something with many legs approaching. The dragon did not look like he was about to fight, however. Instead, he curled his long neck back over his shoulder and tugged at something lying on his back. At first, Aldasair thought it was a strange pile of bloody rags, and when it hit the floor with a solid thump, he felt a wave of shock pass through him that seemed to drain all the strength from his legs.

'Bern!'

He scrambled down from Jessen's back and fell to his knees next to Bern. The big human man looked dead already, even though Aldasair could feel the faint flutter of his presence through the connection they shared. His skin was white as parchment, and there were dark shadows on his cheeks, eyes and throat. His right hand, the one that had been merged with the crystal, was gone; instead his arm ended in a ragged stump that appeared to have been sealed with tar. Except that Aldasair knew very well what it was.

'What have you done?' thundered Sharrik.

'I have done exactly what he wanted,' said the dragon, in a mild tone of voice. He paused, before fetching something else from his back. Bern's axe dropped onto the floor next to him. 'I have freed him from us so that he did not lose himself here when he died. He wants to die elsewhere, free. Under the sky, I expect.' The dragon's big-horned head dipped up, gesturing to the outside world they could not see. 'Take him up there, so he can die in peace. That's what I want for him, brother-who-will-not-be. But I should hurry – humans leak a lot when they lose a part.'

'Bern? Bern, my love?' Aldasair touched the big man's face, feeling his heart sink further at how cold and clammy his skin was. There was no response from the human, and Aldasair forced himself to look at the ragged stump again. An Eboran might survive such an injury, but a human? Even one as strong as Bern would die quickly from the loss of blood. He got his arms under Bern's shoulders and lifted him, carrying him back to Sharrik's harness.

'Sharrik, leave now and get out of the caves. Head north, back to Deeptown. It's the closest place and someone might be able to help him there.'

'But . . .' The griffin looked stricken. He tossed his head back towards the dragon, who was still sitting placidly in the opening to the corridor. 'We must destroy the abomination! For what he did to Eri, and for what he has done to my Bern!'

'There's no time, brave one.' Aldasair picked up the axe and pushed it through the loop at Bern's belt, before glancing down at his own hands. They were smudged and ruddy with Bern's blood. The terrible, cold idea that Bern might die on the way to Deeptown – that he might die without Aldasair at his side – had wedged in his heart like a cold blade. 'You must fly as fast as you possibly can, stop for nothing. Go now!'

With one more half-reluctant glance at Celaphon, Sharrik went back down the corridor, picking up speed as he went.

'And us?' demanded Jessen. Aldasair could feel the scrutiny of her gaze – she knew what it would mean to all of them if Bern didn't survive.

'We would slow them down. Bern has one chance now, and there's little I can do about it.' Aldasair turned back to the dragon. 'You. What were you planning to do?'

'To take him outside,' said Celaphon. 'That is all. The queen will be angry, but . . .' He shifted his enormous bulk. 'For the sake of the small voice that links us, I would have done that much.'

For a moment, Aldasair could think of nothing to say. This was a creature he had only ever met in battle. He could not understand where this new kindness had come from, if that was even what it was. Jessen growled low in her throat, although Aldasair recognised it as a noise of discomfort rather than anger.

'And what will you do now?' she asked Celaphon.

'When I meet you next on the battlefield, I will fight you,' the dragon said without hesitation. 'There is no changing what they have made me, it seems. But . . .' He lowered his head and shook it slightly. 'I long for battle, to fight. What the queen did to Bern the warrior was not battle. It is something else. He was a weapon, and she made him into a tool.'

There was a rumble from beyond the Behemoth, moving through the walls and the floor. Celaphon lifted his head up again like a dog finding a scent.

'You are causing trouble, it seems,' he said. 'The queen will not be pleased about that, either.'

Aldasair climbed back into Jessen's harness, trying to ignore the smears of Bern's blood on the floor.

'Come on, we need to get back out there. I imagine Tor will need our help by now.'

'I'm having the time of my life!'

Somewhere behind him, Kirune roared in irritation at that, but Tor kept moving, slicing his way merrily through the insectoid hordes. He had jumped down from Kirune's harness when the big cat had refused to leave him, and was now attempting to get as deep into the mess as he could. He had taken several cuts and scratches, including a reasonably deep wound on his arm that had soaked his sleeve in clear blood, but nothing yet had come close to taking him down. He had to find something bigger.

Kicking the remains of a spider-mother aside, he finally spotted something with potential. It looked a little like a scorpion, the strange, fast little beasts they had in the high grasses of Yuron-Kai, but it was the size of a horse, and several whip-thin tentacles waved like seaweed from its shining carapace. Eagerly, Tor ran towards it, his heart beating rapidly in his chest. This could be it, his final moments, impaled on the end of its spear-like stinger, or trampled under by its needle-legs.

But before he reached it, there was another bright cough of flame from across the cavern, and the place was briefly lit up as bright as a summer's afternoon. In the same moment, a tall black spidery shape slid down from the side of one of the Behemoths – it was the Jure'lia queen, stretched and long, her mask-face a thumbnail of white balanced on the confusion of her almost-humanoid body. She was looking towards the egg cavern, where a huge conflagration was now burning out of control.

'What have you done?' Tor heard her words clearly despite all the chaos. 'WHAT HAVE YOU DONE?'

The strange waxy substance had dropped like a curtain across the entrance, and they were seconds away from colliding with it, seconds away from the fire consuming them. Vintage reached for Helcate with every part of her being, but the small war-beast was already taking action. His body convulsed and he spat a long stream of acid straight ahead, spattering against the waxy curtain and burning a hole straight through it. Almost immediately the stuff began to heal itself in sticky white strands, but it was enough of a gap for them, and they shot through, closely followed by the fell-witches on their bats. A second later and the full force of the explosive fire hit the curtain and it dissolved into nothing, while flaming chunks of egg and fluid flew out into the wider cavern space. As one, the witches began to fly up towards the strip of sky, while Vintage found herself hanging back, desperately scanning the teeming mess below. What she saw clutched at her heart.

'What is it?' demanded Chenlo. 'What are you waiting for?'
'Look!'

Vintage pointed. Below them the floor of the cavern was carpeted with Jure'lia creatures, and in the very midst of them was Tor. His face was shining with battle joy and his sword was thick with greenish blood, yet it was obvious that at any moment he would be overwhelmed – even as they watched, some sort of abomination armed with a huge piercing stinger turned its attention towards him.

'I can't leave him there . . .'

'You have to – look!'

The queen was surging towards them, a nightmare of grasping limbs and fury. Flaming debris from the eggs was now alighting on the Behemoths and, to Vintage's shock, they were beginning to burn too. Very quickly the cavern was turning into an inferno.

'Helcate!' cried Helcate.

'Sarn's cursed heart. Fly, darling, fly!'

They shot upwards, barely avoiding the grasping fingers of the Jure'lia queen. Ahead of them they could see the fell-witches, silhouetted against the tiny piece of sky. Helcate stretched out his neck and picked up speed, intending to catch up with their allies.

The place was burning down. Tor could barely believe it. Vintage's heartbright had proved every bit as lethal as she'd promised. All around, the Behemoths were burning with a bright, eerie flame, oily and yellow-green, and the heat and smoke were such that he could barely breathe. He grinned and wiped a hand over his face, turning back to the scorpion thing and raising his sword over his head. It was a ridiculous manoeuvre that bared his chest to the creature's waiting stinger, but, he reflected, it hardly mattered.

'Take this, you ugly, worm-infested piece of—'

His words were cut off as he was knocked back by a bulky shape landing in front of him. He looked up to see Aldasair lopping off the creature's stumpy head with his axe, before turning Jessen towards him.

'What are you doing?' demanded his cousin. 'We have to get out of here!'

'Where's Bern?'

'He's outside already,' said Aldasair shortly. 'Come on, Jessen can carry us both, if Kirune is –'

'No!' Tor took a few steps backwards, half falling over the bodies of the creatures he'd already killed. 'I'm to stay here, this is where it *ends*, this is where it stops.'

There was a roar from behind them as part of a Behemoth collapsed in on itself, and Tor staggered, hit by a wave of heat. Aldasair and Jessen shrank back from it too, and Tor took the opportunity to turn and run away from them, only to collide with the solid form of Kirune. The big cat knocked him down as easily as a kitten batting a ball.

'Wait, you don't understand –'

'I understand you are a fool,' growled Kirune. The big cat lunged for him, grasping the back of his leather coat between his teeth, before forcibly yanking him into the air. The ground dropped away and they made their way up, joined shortly by Aldasair and Jessen.

Tor struggled briefly, thinking that perhaps he could wiggle out of his coat and drop to the ground, but he knew in his heart that Kirune would come after him – that the cat would keep coming after him, again and again, until they both died; torn apart by the Jure'lia or cooked by the fire that was burning out of control in every part of the cavern.

As they rose up, Tor saw something that chilled him: strands of the Jure'lia fluid were stretching from one side of the cavern to the other, clinging to rocks and outcroppings of stone like pieces of a spider's web, and it was spreading, racing them up to the crevasse. It was the queen, he realised, the queen stripped down to her most basic form, and it was chasing the tiny figures of the fell-witches ahead of them.

'It looks like we're all going to die down here anyway.'

Chapter Thirty-eight

Vintage gasped as they cleared the crevasse, the air impossibly sweet and clean after the smoky nightmare of the cavern. Above them, the sky was blue and blameless and they were out, they were out. Below her, Helcate gave a strangled cry, and for a moment his own panic seemed to flood through her.

'What is it, darling?'

Chenlo was already shaking her arm and pointing. Next to them the surviving fell-witches were shooting out of the huge crack in the ground, only for long tentacles of black Jure'lia fluid to follow them. As she watched, they were caught, the fluid flowing up and around the bats' smaller back legs, catching them and pulling them back down. With her heart in her throat she leaned over and looked down. Helcate was similarly caught, the black fluid tangling in his legs and flowing across his fur with eager, possessive fingers. Already, the sky was receding as they were dragged back towards the fiery abyss.

'It's the fucking queen,' Vintage spat through clenched teeth. There was a cry from below, and she saw that Jessen and Kirune had been caught in the same trap. Aldasair and Tor were both there too, their pale faces turned up towards her,

410

but her relief at seeing them was short-lived. The queen herself, a strange distended spider shape with a white mask-face tossed in the centre, was howling with rage, a discordant strangled note that seemed to go on and on.

'What do we do?'

'Darling, I don't know . . .'

A few of the fell-witches had turned in their harnesses and were attempting to throw fireballs down at the queen, but for every one that landed, more of her flowing elastic body appeared, stretching and oozing to fill the space. Helcate gave a yelp of frustration as they were yanked backwards, closer and closer to the crevasse.

'Chenlo, you can jump.' Vintage was staring at the ground, trying to calculate how much of a drop there would be. 'Just before she takes us inside, jump for the side – you might make it.'

'Are you out of your mind?' Chenlo looked, for some reason, deeply insulted. 'And what of you?'

'I'm not leaving Helcate, we'll—'

There was a chorus of cries from below, and something, some instinct that they were now sharing the sky with something else, made Vintage look up.

It was Vostok. The white dragon, half dream-like to Vintage's smoke-sore eyes, turned in the sunlight, her scales glittering like a shower of gold coins. She banked around, meaning to come around closer to them, and Vintage saw that there was a figure on her back – a young woman with untidy black hair, her face set and determined.

'Noon! Oh Noon!'

The dragon and her girl came on fast, the dragon's jaws opening to release a terrifying blast of violet fire. The beam hit the queen dead in the centre of her spidery body, and a second later it was followed by a blast of pure war-beast-fuelled winnowfire, green as emeralds and bright as hope. There was

411

another howl from the queen, and abruptly Helcate surged forward – he was free, the clinging ropes of Jure'lia fluid abruptly severed. The fell-witches flew up into the sky and away, and then Jessen and Kirune were with them too.

'What is happening?' called Aldasair.

Vintage shook her head. She didn't trust herself to speak. Belatedly she saw that rather than riding in Kirune's harness, Tor was dangling from the big cat's mouth – the expression on the Eboran's face was one of complete and total shock.

'She's alive,' he said. 'Noon's alive.'

As if to prove him right, Vostok and Noon flew past for another attack, both viciously intent on their target. This time they followed the remnants of the queen down, blasting the stringy portions of her body with an endless stream of twinned fires. The elastic fluid bubbled and boiled and stretched, clearly looking to escape, but behind her was the inferno of the cavern, and above, the relentless fury of the dragon.

'Helcate,' Vintage leaned over the war-beast's neck, 'take us closer, darling, as close as you dare.'

The queen wilted, falling back against the ragged edge of the cliff face like a splash of spilled ink, and still the dragon came on. Noon's face was still and composed as she poured her winnowfire down and down, beating the Jure'lia queen into a smear, a stain. Eventually, there was a shudder that seemed to move through the ground, as if Sarn itself were sighing, and the queen stopped moving. Her mask-face clattered onto the rocks, blistered and cracked, and only then did the dragon stop. Noon sat back in the harness, looking vaguely confused about where she was; she looked older to Vintage, with a few more careworn lines at the corners of her eyes.

Vintage urged Helcate forward, unable to keep from grinning.

'Noon, darling! What time do you call this?'

Noon looked up and as her eyes met theirs, something

seemed to come back to her. She smiled, and a ragged cheer from the fell-witches floated down towards them.

Kirune dropped Tor to the ground, although he barely felt it. He stumbled a little, caught by the strange suspicion that he was in a dream. There seemed no earthly way that they could have escaped the cavern, that they could have been pulled from the jaws of a fiery death by a dragon . . . or that Noon could still be alive. Yet there she was. Her hair was a little longer, and she looked a little like she had been living under open skies for months – the tops of her cheeks and the bridge of her nose were sunburned – yet it was undeniably her. Vostok was standing proudly, her long tail lashing back and forth behind her as they perched on the edge of the crevasse. *Vostok was right all along*, he thought, still trying to get the idea to fit into his head. *She wasn't dead at all.*

'Noon?'

She glanced over to him, and then untied the straps on her harness before climbing down. He watched her do it, still half in wonder – the busy efficiency of her neat, tanned hands. Nearby, Vintage was standing with her hands pushed into her wild cloud of hair, laughing softly to herself.

'Noon,' he said again. 'We thought you were dead. I thought you'd died. I . . .'

Free of the dragon, Noon marched over to him and reached up – half standing on tiptoes to do it – and kissed him hungrily on the mouth. It took Tor a moment to respond – he thought of when he'd been recovering from the battle over the mountains, when he'd been so close to telling her, and she had walked away – and then he bent his head and kissed her back. She tasted of salt and fire, somehow. Dimly, he heard Vintage laughing, more loudly now, joyfully, and even heard a couple of whistles from the fell-witches. The kiss broke into a disbelieving smile, nose to nose.

'It's good to see you, bloodsucker.' Noon touched the scarred portion of his face, as if framing it.

'What happened to you?' He meant her disappearance, but all at once the question seemed to have other meanings: the Noon he had known would never have kissed him so passionately in front of others; the Noon he had known did not look so haunted. Noon opened her mouth to answer, when Vintage appeared at their elbows.

'My darlings, as utterly romantic as this is, I think we need to get moving. The ground under our feet is feeling less than stable, and I suspect there are lots of places in Sarn safer than this one.'

For the first time, Tor noticed that the earth was trembling slightly, and an ominous rumbling from the crevasse was growing louder all the time. Gouts of oily fire were sticking bright fingers up through the broken rock. With some reluctance, he let Noon go, although she squeezed his hand before they parted.

'I told Sharrik to take Bern to Deeptown.' Aldasair was still with Jessen. He looked shaken and pale, but he spared a smile for Noon. 'I suggest we go there and gather ourselves.'

'Excellent, lead the way.' Vintage jumped back onto Helcate, and waved to the fell-witches who still hovered above. 'All of us back together under the same roof – that's a bloody good end to this mess if you ask me.'

Aldasair nodded, although to Tor he looked ill with worry. One by one they left the clearing, rising into the air and turning north. Tor glanced down before the crevasse dropped out of sight, and the blackened mess that had been the queen of the Jure'lia was still there, steaming on the broken rocks. He fixed the image in his mind: the worm people, beaten. It was possible after all.

There was a group from Deeptown waiting for them when they arrived, along with Sharrik, who looked tense and alert.

Tor recognised the woman Treen, with her three dog-sized ants at her ankles, and as they landed she went straight to Vintage.

'Your friend is with our pathfinder now,' she said. 'They're doing their best to help him.'

Aldasair, who had jumped down from the back of Jessen, marched over to her. 'Can you take me to him?'

'Aldasair?' Vintage looked worried. 'How badly was Bern hurt?'

Treen took them below, with the war-beasts and bats staying above ground. Quickly they were enveloped into the world of Deeptown, with its softly lit corridors and earthy scent. Tor saw people standing around watchfully, their faces tense and worried, and eventually they were led into a small, rounded chamber brightly lit with small, round lamps. Bern was there, lying unconscious on a low bed, and the pathfinder knelt with him, her old bony knees in the dirt. Tor's stomach turned over; Bern's arm ended in a ragged mess, a horror of flesh and bone and blood splotched here and there with a rubbery black substance.

'Roots save us, what happened to him?'

Aldasair and Vintage had gone straight to Bern's bedside, while Noon hung back in the doorway, her eyes wide.

'Celaphon the dragon bit his hand off, the one the crystal was grafted to,' said Aldasair bitterly. 'He was already weak, and he has lost so much blood.'

'That bastard dragon,' said Vintage, with feeling. She took Bern's remaining hand and pressed it to her cheek. 'I can hope it burned to death in that cavern, but I doubt I will be that fortunate.'

'The dragon thought it was helping Bern, I think.' Aldasair pursed his lips and shook his head slightly. 'I'm still trying to understand it, but Bern was desperate to be free of the Jure'lia, and . . . and he was dying anyway, as Celaphon put it.'

'A bite from such a beast explains a lot,' said the pathfinder. 'It's made a terrible mess of this young man's wrist – turned the bones into pulp, shredded the muscles – and this stuff –' she picked with tiny shrivelled fingers at the shreds of black material – 'this stuff is evil. It has saved his life by stopping the bleeding, but it is evil. Already it is poisoning his blood.'

'It's from the worm people,' said Aldasair. 'The queen herself.'

The pathfinder raised her head, her eyes wide. 'Evil times we are living in.'

'And the Dead Woods are burning,' said Treen quietly. 'A huge tower of smoke hangs over the forest, which can only be an evil omen.'

'That's our fault, sorry,' said Noon, from the back of the room. 'We set the worm people on fire.'

Treen and the pathfinder exchanged a look. 'They are so close?'

'Listen.' Aldasair paused in pushing strands of sweaty hair off Bern's pale forehead. 'Can you help him? Will he live?'

The old woman sat back, her hands lying palm up on the tops of her thighs. 'We can't leave the wound as it is, this is the problem. All that shattered bone, the torn muscle, it won't heal like that, no.'

'And the worm substance is essentially dirt in the wound,' said Vintage grimly. The old woman nodded.

'What we shall have to do, is remove this portion of the arm . . .'

'You mean to cut him again?' Aldasair sounded close to panic. Silently, Tor went and stood with him, one hand on his shoulder.

'They must, my dear, can you not see?' Vintage looked less than happy about it herself. 'It's the only way to save him.'

'It's risky,' said the pathfinder. She tapped one thin finger at a point halfway up Bern's forearm. 'We cut here, cleanly and quickly. The skin we pull over, and we seal. Then we wait, and hope.'

'It sounds like you've done this before,' said Tor.

Treen nodded. 'When you live in a city of tunnels, crushing injuries are quite common.'

'But he has already lost so much blood,' said Aldasair. 'How can he live through being cut open again?' To Tor, he suddenly sounded very much like the young man who had spent so many decades wandering the corridors of the palace, lost and frightened. 'He's a human, he's not . . . He only has so much blood.'

'That is the danger.' The pathfinder nodded. 'Normally, we would let him recover a little first, but this stuff – if it is in his veins too long, it will make him sick, will kill him. We have to get it away from him, quickly.' With some difficulty, she got to her feet; the sound of her knees popping was very loud in the crowded room. 'Our healer is on his way here now.'

'Then we shall give you some space,' said Vintage, suddenly all business. 'Aldasair will want to stay here, of course. Is there somewhere we can wait? And please, we'd very much appreciate it if you keep us aware of what is happening to our dear friend.'

They were shuffled away down more corridors, with Treen quickly showing them to tiny little dorms in some quiet, secluded part of the town, with the fell-witches following Agent Chenlo. Vintage, despite her words to the pathfinder, insisted on staying with Bern and Aldasair, and so Tor found himself alone with Noon in a small mud-walled room. It was warm and cosy, the floor covered in a tightly woven mat, the circular door made of pale, varnished wood. There was a low bed and a couple of stools, a stone basin wedged directly into the wall, along with little alcoves for storage. Someone had thoughtfully put some thick seed cakes in them, and a jug of water.

He turned to her, ready to face all manner of awkward conversations, but she closed his mouth with more kisses, just as hungry as she had been in the forest. She took his hand

417

and slid it inside her shirt to find the soft mound of her breast, and he felt himself grow hard almost immediately.

'Noon . . .' He murmured into her neck, trailing kisses down across her shoulder, baring more of her skin. 'Are you sure?'

'Please,' she said, tugging urgently at his clothes, 'I've been alone, I've been to some awful places, Tor, and I need you. Please.'

He nodded, removing her shirt and dropping it to the floor. He kissed her breasts, and then moved down, trailing his lips over the soft angle of her ribs, the hollow of her belly. As he tugged her trousers down, she pushed her fingers into his hair, trembling slightly in his hands, and when he bent his head to the place between her legs, she said his name in a whisper, urging him, begging him. All the complex lessons of the House of the Long Night seemed vaguely silly in the face of their closeness – what could be simpler than this?

She shuddered, opening herself to him, and abruptly he was dizzy with need. He picked her up in one quick movement – she laughed, her feet briefly pointed at the ceiling – and placed her down on the bed.

'You still have too many clothes on,' she said, pulling at his shirt. He yanked it off, and he saw her glance at the bandages on his arm, but it clearly wasn't the time for questions. Instead, he brought his hips to meet hers, gasping as she wrapped her legs tightly around him. In small movements they came together; her face was flushed, her dark eyes shining.

'Noon. Noon.' He became aware he was saying her name in time to the movements of his hips, but there seemed to be nothing he could do about that. He was already lost. 'Noon, I love you, Noon.'

She moaned, her back arching, and he felt her reaching her climax underneath him. He held on as best he could, until she opened her eyes again and pulled him back in deep.

'I love you, Tor.'

He cried out as waves of pleasure so sharp it was akin to

pain moved through him, and she whispered her words again and again into his ear. It was an exultant spell against all things, against all sadness and horror.

Later, they lay together in a sweaty heap. Tor had reached up into one of the alcoves for the flat cakes, and they were eating them in small pieces. They were made from seeds and something very like honey, but much darker in colour, and Tor found that he was ravenous. Despite everything – the crimson flux, Bern being close to death, the actions of his sister – he felt at peace. He had told her. Whatever else happened, he had done that.

'What happened to you?' he said eventually. 'Where did you go? It almost destroyed us, you know. You just vanished, or, well, it looked like you exploded. It was only Vostok who really believed you could have survived it.'

Noon chewed for a while, considering her answer.

'You remember the Aborans, and how they got here? To Sarn?'

Tor frowned, tearing off another piece of the cake. 'I could hardly forget.'

'The being of energy that powered their ship, or whatever they called it: I met her. It was her that took me, and she's – well, *she's* winnowfire. She's the reason we have it, that it exists on Sarn at all.'

'It's possible I am just delirious from a mixture of blood loss and, uh, overexcitement, but none of what you just said makes any sense to me. I doubt, somehow, it would even make sense to Vintage, and she loves this sort of thing.'

He had expected her to laugh, but she just nodded slowly, still thinking. 'I don't think it makes any sense to me either,' she said eventually. 'But that was the truth. She exists in a glass castle, in the middle of the Singing Eye Desert, and I think . . . I think time there is strange. She takes on different bodies, and wears them out, and she – she gave the winnowfire to us. She

419

thinks it's a gift. I think she did it partly because she hates the Aborans – hated their superior attitude – and because she wants to be a god too. A better god than them, maybe.'

'And what did she want with you?'

Noon shifted on the bed, looping one leg over his comfortably. 'I'm not sure I know. I was amusing to her, I suppose. She felt it when I accidentally brought their ship to life on Origin, felt it through the fire, I think. She wanted to know who had done that. It's like proof of what she did, in a way. That I reactivated their ship, and then left them again – I bet that feels like a victory, to her.'

'Well.' Tor sensed strongly that Noon wasn't telling the whole story, but he didn't want to push her. 'We are living in strange times.'

She pressed her head to his chest and he kissed the top of her head. 'I wanted to leave. I knew I'd left you all in the middle of a fight, that you'd have no idea what had happened to me, so I demanded to be taken back. She wouldn't do it. She kept me there. Until . . .' She shifted again. Tor looked at her back, the line of stippled shadows where her spine sat. He felt like he could look at it all day. 'Until she'd had enough. And then she sent me back to Vostok.'

'She kept looking for you, you know,' said Tor. 'Wouldn't give up. So stubborn.'

'That sounds like her,' agreed Noon, and he could hear the smile in her voice. 'When I found her again I was very ill for a while, some sort of fever, and as much as I wanted to, we couldn't go anywhere. Eventually, when it had burned through me, we started to fly back to Ebora, but Vostok felt very strongly that you weren't there. She insisted instead on flying to the south, across that jungle.'

'We're bloody lucky she did,' said Tor. The image of the cavern, busy with shadows and fire, would not leave him. 'We'd all be dead otherwise.'

'And now . . .' Noon shook her head, then moved to face him. Her eyes were wide, and she looked younger than she had a moment ago; the face of a child who has braved the darkness of the night and found it free of monsters after all. 'Do you think we killed them, Tor? Do you think we killed *her*? Do you think it's over?'

'Honestly? I don't know.' A thin thread of fiery pain worked its way down his right arm, and he resisted the urge to rub it with his free hand. 'There was no sign of my sister or even the dragon at the end, and I'm not sure if that's good or bad. After all, the recent attacks have all been orchestrated by her. When Bern wakes up –' *If Bern wakes up*, his mind added traitorously – 'I'm hoping he'll be able to tell us more about what was happening.'

Chapter Thirty-nine

Hours later, her eyes thick with grit and hands still covered in dried blood, Vintage walked slowly back to the small room Treen had allocated her. Inside she was surprised to find Chenlo sitting waiting for her – not on the small bed, but sitting on the floor with her knees up to her chin. She looked oddly childlike for a moment, and not at all like the fierce and stern Winnowry agent Vintage had come to know.

'How is he?' she asked.

'Oh, well.' Vintage looked down at her hands, and grimaced. 'He is still with us, at least.'

'Here –' Chenlo got up from the floor in one fluid movement – Vintage had to admire her grace after such a long and tiring day – and went to the basin in the corner, into which she poured some water. 'I have some soap you can use.'

It was a small waxy white cube, which Chenlo produced from her belt, and it quickly made a thin sort of lather that smelled rather wonderfully of tea-roses and spice.

'Thank you,' she said, meaning it. Chenlo just nodded, slightly awkwardly, and gestured to the small table by the bed. On it was a small clay pot, which was steaming slightly.

'I thought it likely you would want some tea.'

Vintage smiled, and then found that she felt perilously close to crying. Instead of speaking, she nodded and went and sat on the bed. After a moment Chenlo brought her over a small cup of fragrant tea, her own cup held carefully in her other hand.

'This is your own tea,' said Vintage, when she had tasted it. 'The one from Yuron-Kai.' It seemed a silly thing to say, but the thoughtfulness of the gesture had touched her, and she wasn't sure how to let the woman know it. 'It's expensive.'

Chenlo shrugged one shoulder. 'My once-sister used to say that tea was best for shocks.'

'Your . . . once-sister?'

Chenlo had sat on the very edge of the bed, the cup cradled in her hands, and now she shifted uncomfortably. 'In Yuron-Kai, when a child is taken for the Winnowry, in all the ways that matter she no longer exists to her family. I had a family once, but not for a long time. Do you see?'

Vintage pursed her lips, trying to think of the right thing to say. As if sensing her objections, Chenlo looked away.

'None of which matters now. Tell me what happened with Bern, please.'

'Ah, that poor boy.' Vintage looked down into her tea. 'They did as the pathfinder said they had to. I have seen some unpleasant things in my time, but that . . . To watch as someone dear to you is hurt, and then hurt worse in an attempt to heal them . . . I knew perfectly well what they did was to help him, but even so I almost had to sit on my hands to stop myself wrenching their tools away.' She sighed, trying to gather her thoughts. 'They strapped him down, and brought in a couple of burly young men to help, just in case he should wake up while they were doing what needed to be done, and they tied a belt around his arm, just under his shoulder, very tight. Aldasair was there of course, standing behind his head, talking to him all the time. They had a very fine saw, thin and tough with an incredibly sharp edge, and with it they cut off the lower portion of his arm.' She glanced up at Chenlo, her voice hushed. 'It was so quick! I'd never even have guessed it was possible, but, well, I suppose they are used to dealing with such injuries after all. They had it off and – and I think I could quite happily go the rest of my life without seeing such a thing again.'

'He did not bleed to death?'

'No, although I am sure that he is not quite safe from that fate just yet. They sealed the end of his arm with a brand – again so fast I barely saw it – and then they covered it with this thick brownish stuff, like treacle. It's made by the queen ant here, apparently, and it will dry quite hard. He was as white as chalk by the time they'd finished, and the dark shadows on his face looked like bruises. Aldasair was with him still when I left, he won't leave his side, but hopefully the two of them will sleep now.' She swallowed the last of her tea. 'And Sharrik! I should go and speak to him, let him know how it's gone too.'

'Enough.' Chenlo plucked the empty cup from her hands. 'You need to sleep also. I will go and speak to the griffin for you.'

'You will?'

Chenlo nodded, and once Vintage had lain down on the bed she left, slipping out into the tunnels as silently as a ghost. Vintage was certain that despite the exhaustion that hung over her she would not sleep, but very quickly she was lost in a blankness thankfully free of dreams. At some point she became aware of someone in the room again, and she opened her eyes a crack to see Chenlo, her black and white hair hanging loose over her shoulders. The woman turned the lamps to their lowest glow and resumed her place at the foot of Vintage's bed, her knees drawn up to her chin, her head bent in thought.

Vintage half thought to speak to her, to offer some of her own warmth in return, but sleep surged up like a floodwater and took her away again.

The enormous tower of black smoke hung over the distant line of forest like an ominous sentry. Noon stood and watched it, waiting to see the familiar shapes of the Behemoths moving through it, or perhaps some small movement that could be the dragon Celaphon, but she saw nothing. The sky otherwise was a deep blue, unmarked by clouds save for one lost lamb far to the east.

'We should go and look at it properly,' she said to Vintage. The older woman grimaced.

'Not while it's smoking like that, we won't,' she said. 'We won't be able to get close enough to see anything, and I don't like to think what that sort of muck would do to your lungs.'

'You're right,' said Noon. She turned to look at where Vostok and Sharrik stood together, drinking from one of the shallow rivers. The big griffin was miserable; you could see it in every line of his body. 'How's Bern?'

'He's sleeping still, but the pathfinder is hopeful. He's bloody strong, she says, and, well, *we* certainly know that. He woke up earlier this morning and said a few words.' Vintage smiled a little ruefully. 'Aldasair said he was quite grumpy, like he'd had too much ale the night before, but Tor got some information out of him. Hestillion wasn't there, he claims, even though Celaphon was. He said that the queen was trying to understand how he had broken their memory crystals – she couldn't believe that his memories of Aldasair were so strong they overwhelmed the memory the crystal already contained. He said she was slowly pulling his mind apart.' Vintage took a big breath and sighed it out. 'It'll be a few days before we can think about moving him.'

'Well, then,' Noon looked back at the smoke; on this windless

425

day, it didn't appear to be moving at all, 'I suppose we'll just have to wait.'

In the end, it was three whole days before the tower of smoke became nothing more than a half-remembered smudge on the horizon. Noon and Vintage flew out there together on Vostok and Helcate, staying high and close to the clouds until they got to the crevasse, or at least, what used to be the crevasse. The jungle immediately surrounding the broken ground was covered in a greasy black soot, and the earth itself appeared to have caved in – it was no longer possible to see the huge rent in the ground that had led to the Jure'lia caverns. Now there was a thick black soup on the ground, dried hard and covered in odd bulbous shapes, and the rest of it was a confusion of stone and mud. Nothing moved in that broken landscape; not even flies.

They stayed there for a little while, poking around and making notes, but eventually Noon met Vintage's gaze and a mutual shiver passed through them both. This was not a place to stay for long.

When they returned to Deeptown it was early evening, with the sky just shading into mauve, and Tor was waiting for them next to a line of oil lamps.

'The Jure'lia have met their end, it seems,' said Vostok as Noon climbed down from her harness. The dragon was tossing her head as though proud, but Noon sensed an undercurrent to her emotions that made her uneasy. 'The Ninth Rain was their last war.'

Tor didn't look convinced by this either. 'I was there, I saw the queen shrivel up like a leaf caught in a flame, but even so –' He shrugged. 'My sister wasn't there. Where is Hestillion? What is she up to?'

'Perhaps she has cut ties with the worm people,' said Vintage. 'It's not impossible, is it?'

'I don't know. Once my sister gets an idea in her head . . .'

'We should go back to Ebora.' Noon pushed her hands back through her hair. The blackened trees and plants had reminded her uncomfortably of her own recently recovered memories, and if she closed her eyes too long she could see it all again; the blinding light, her mother's hair a halo of fire, the twisted burned things that were left after. She wondered what She Who Laughs was doing, if she wondered what Noon was doing with her newly rediscovered knowledge, or if she even cared that the people of Sarn might have finally won their war.

'I agree, my darling. I have had more than enough of this strange corner of Sarn, and more than enough of Deeptown and its ants. As wonderful as they have been,' Vintage added hurriedly. 'As soon as Bern can travel, we'll go. And let's hope your sister has decided to dedicate her life to embroidery or collecting seashells, Tor.'

Chapter Forty

'Kill them all!'

Much to Hestillion's annoyance, Tygrish was resisting, and they were doing a reasonable job of it too. When she looked out the translucent panel in the Behemoth's wall, she saw lines and lines of soldiers on the tall, white walls, and beyond them, trebuchets armed with debris and enormous boulders. Every few moments she and her other two ships were being pelted with a rain of fire and rocks – not enough to damage a Behemoth, not even close, but it was enough to knock some of her creatures out of the sky. And then there was the bat.

'The war-beast is approaching again,' murmured the First. Hestillion narrowed her eyes. The enormous snow-white bat was so fast it was difficult to spot, often getting close to them and blasting them with its icy breath before Hestillion even knew it was there. A flutter in the corner of her vision and it loomed suddenly close, an ugly thing with eerie blue eyes and a mouth full of sharp teeth. An arc of blue light shot across the screen, striking one of Hestillion's grey men, and the thing fell out of the sky like a rock. She caught a brief glimpse of the woman who rode the war-beast – *the human woman*, she

428

fumed to herself – and then the viewing screen was obscured with a blast of bright green witch-fire.

'My circle, are you watching? Can you see it?'

'I see it.' It was the voice of Red Moth, as clear as if she were standing in the room with Hestillion. The Behemoth to Hestillion's right began to bleed flying creatures, all of them heading towards the war-beast, who was already swooping back over the white walls, to the cheers of the people below. 'We will take it down.'

The grey men and the great beetles with serrated mouths were flying into a firestorm though, and to Hestillion's annoyance she watched as they were knocked out of the sky, or flew up out of range, confused by the fire eating up their delicate insectoid wings. Her third Behemoth had moved into position beyond the city walls, and it was taking the brunt of the humans' attacks. Periodically, alcoves would open in its shiny walls and spider-mothers would crawl their way out to float down towards the city streets, but the bat would come back, freezing them with a blast of her icy breath.

'Ridiculous,' spat Hestillion. She had a terrible sneaking suspicion she should have brought Celaphon; she quickly pushed that thought aside. 'All these humans are doing is prolonging the inevitable. They should be fleeing, like the others. If they had any sense. Green Bird, draw back again. We need to take down this war-beast, or we shall waste all of our creatures.'

It mattered little to Hestillion if they lost every spider-mother on board the ship, but the truth was that it would take her time to create more monsters from the crafting pools, time that they didn't have if they wished to take Tygrish in one attack. As she watched, the Behemoth controlled by Green Bird moved up and away from the city walls, briefly attracting a flurry of flaming arrows. The bat came past again, and she saw, quite clearly, the human woman who rode on the

429

war-beast's back: she had hair a shade paler than Hestillion's but cut very short, and the tops of her cheeks were flushed a bright, hectic pink. She opened her mouth and hollered, clearly an expression of victory, and she dared to punch the air with one closed fist gloved in green fire. Not her brother's pet witch after all, and no war-beast that she knew, either. Not that it mattered.

Hestillion hissed through her teeth. 'My circle, I will go out there myself. Grey Root, you will join me.'

She felt their reactions like the brush of a moth's wing against her cheek. There was blind acceptance from four of them, and then . . . something else, from the last.

'What is it?' she snapped.

'Your armour,' said the First. 'Is it ready? For combat.'

'It will have to be.' She left the translucent viewing screen and the chamber, stalking down corridors until she came to another room, one very close to the skin of the Behemoth. In here, she kept her armour. She had made it for herself, quietly and without fuss, and out of sight of the queen. Something about it made her feel vulnerable, as though the very fact of it revealed a desire or a dream she would rather keep to herself. Grey Root was there waiting for her, already stepping into the smaller version of the armour Hestillion had crafted for whichever member of the circle needed it.

Hestillion raised her hand, intending to reach for the suit, when a shiver of some strange emotion moved through the Jure'lia web. It did not originate from her circle, or any of her Behemoths; it was very far away, impossibly distant. It felt like chaos, panic even, and it threatened to engulf her.

'No,' she muttered. Grey Root tipped her head to one side, curious. 'No. I don't have time for the queen's chaos now. I have worked so hard to make us efficient. If she will not fix their brokenness, that is her problem.'

She squeezed her hands into fists at her sides, and forcibly put the larger Jure'lia link from her mind. The battle was so close to hand, and the presence of her circle made it easier than it had been to turn it aside. Satisfied, Hestillion turned her attention to Grey Root.

'You will go out first,' she said. 'Through your eyes I will see how the battle progresses. Then I will join you.'

Grey Root nodded once. The Jure'lia armour closed around her, a close-fitting thing of chitinous plates and grey, fibrous padding. An aperture opened in the wall, letting in a blast of warm air that smelled of grass, and she was gone.

Hestillion turned to her own armour, and began to strap herself in. It did not fit as closely as that which the circle wore – their bodies were already half made of the same stuff, after all – but she had spent a long time crafting it and tweaking it until it cupped her body like a gauntlet. Within the armour, she was stronger, hardier. Black and green moon-metal turned her arms into lethal knives, transformed her head into a sleek shell. Her torso was covered in interlocking plates of the springy Jure'lia hide, meaning she could still move as easily as when she was wearing her old silk robes, and the whole thing was light; nothing like the bulky plate armour her father had worn during the Eighth Rain.

She stepped up to the aperture, reaching out via the Jure'lia network to her circle. In a flickering of images, she saw where they all were; the First remained in the central command chamber, standing utterly still; Green Bird was moving her Behemoth out, her head bent in concentration; Red Moth was still commanding the flight of the spider-mothers, while Yellow Leaf waited with her. And Grey Root – Hestillion got a sense of chaos beneath her, swarms of arrows arching up through humid air, and, circling around to attack, was the war-beast.

Hestillion smiled. The tiny, flickering consciousness of the armour came to life, a sensation like being bombarded by fireflies in the dark. She reached out to it, and the back portion of the armour flexed, revealing two sets of thin, diaphanous wings. Hestillion spread her arms wide, and jumped out into the sky.

Noise and light, the sensation of wind pressing against her. She flew with real speed, darting out of the path of several projectiles before she had even gained her bearings, and then she soared up and away, taking a moment to collate all the information she had: everything that her circle saw, everything that the Jure'lia felt, and all that she could see with her own Eboran eyes. Tygrish lay below her, a teeming city of white walls and fruit trees – even flooded with armed humans it was a beautiful place – and immediately it was possible for her to see where the weak places were, the places where the humans were too thin in numbers to be effective.

Red Moth, go to the southernmost gate – it's where they're hiding the civilians. An attack there will send them into a panic. Green Bird, and the First – wait on me. I will end this war-beast.

The thought of it caused a curl of horror to move through her stomach, but then the air was full of arrows again, followed by a blast of freezing air that briefly caused one side of her body to go numb. Hestillion cursed herself even as she flitted away; the usefulness of the circle was enormous, but it was easy to be distracted by it. The great white bat was in the air with her, circling to get closer, and Hestillion saw the human woman again. To her surprise, she was laughing.

'Who are you,' shouted Hestillion, 'to ride a war-beast?'

The woman looked shocked for a moment – she had clearly taken Hestillion to be another voiceless worm-creature. Then she grinned.

'I am Tyranny, queen of Tygrish,' she called, 'and this is Windfall. We're here to ruin your day, worm bitch!'

'A queen?' Hestillion shook her head lightly just before a barrage of green flame headed her way. She flew up, glass-like wings buzzing. 'You do not look like a queen. Not even a human one.'

The woman who called herself Tyranny didn't reply. Instead, the bat flew screaming up, enormous jaws so wide they almost looked unhinged. Hestillion stretched, her body and mind conveying to the armour how she wanted to move, and where. For some time, she and the bat danced around each other, creating a spiral of leathery wings and glinting moon-metal, punctuated with blasts of fire and ice. Hestillion caught glimpses of how they looked from below, relayed to her by her circle, and for a dangerous moment she became dizzy – did she fly through the air over Tygrish, or did she stand within a Behemoth? She reminded herself of the First's subtle warning: the armour was mostly untested. She could not allow this to continue.

Finding herself momentarily above the bat, Hestillion flexed her left arm, releasing the weapon hidden there. A long segmented ribbon shot out of the Jure'lia gauntlet, expanding as it went. The thing was lined with wicked thorns and it slapped across the war-beast's broad chest like a whip, piercing skin and digging in instantly. Hestillion threw herself upwards with all her strength, dragging the flail after her, and the bat screamed; a terrible, piercing noise that shredded the air like a hawk's cry. Daring to glance down, Hestillion saw the bat's white fur now running with black blood. The woman Tyranny looked dumbstruck.

'Tygrish falls to us, *Your Majesty*!' Hestillion yanked the flail free, and watched with satisfaction as the war-beast tumbled through the air. She was only falling for moments, but the effect on the people below was immediate. Hestillion saw soldiers breaking for cover, archers lowering their bows, uncertain expressions on their faces.

Green fire filled her vision. Hestillion ducked away, but the bat had recovered and the queen of Tygrish kept coming, a look of fury on her face that was very far from sane. Hestillion folded her wings close to her body and let herself fall, dropping down out of the range of fire before surging back up behind the bat. She leapt forward, slashing her armoured arm, and caught the back portion of Windfall's left wing. More black blood leapt into the air, but the war-beast spun round to grapple with her. The woman who had called herself Tyranny reached out and grabbed Hestillion around the throat, and she had time to think that she was surprisingly strong, for a human.

'What even *are* you?' hissed the woman. Up close, Hestillion could see discoloured scars across the woman's neck. *Just like Celaphon*, she thought. 'You look Eboran, so why are you covered in that muck?'

'Why do you fight alone?' The Jure'lia armour covered Hestillion's neck and the top portion of her head, but she could feel the moon-metal getting hot where the fell-witch touched her. This could not be sustained for long. 'Where's my brother? The other war-beasts? The little one threw its acid on you, didn't it?' She grinned wolfishly. 'You war with them, too. What idiots you are.'

Tyranny made an inarticulate noise of rage, and her hand began to glow a bright, emerald green. Sparks spat into life against the armour.

'The First! On me, the burrowers. Bring them here directly.'

The war-beast screeched, a high-pitched noise that seemed to stab directly into Hestillion's ears; the creature was clearly annoyed that she was out of range of her ice beam. It would be easy, Hestillion noted, to push away and break the hold the human woman had – she was only a human woman, after all, as strong as she was – but her presence made it easier for the First to know where they were. And besides which, she wanted to see this. Bright green veins crept across the Jure'lia armour, like delicate threads of lightning. Hestillion grinned.

'What are you smiling about, you mad bitch?' spat Tyranny.

'I'm going to rip your head right off! I've done it before, and to people tougher than you . . .'

'This,' said Hestillion. 'I'm smiling at this.'

From above, a dark rain began to fall on them. Hundreds of burrowers, black and shining, their sharp legs wriggling, pelted down onto the woman and her war-beast. Hestillion felt them crawling over her too, tiny feelers tasting her skin and rejecting it before seeking out the flesh they were trained to eat. Tyranny dropped her hand and began frantically brushing at herself, but the beetles were fast and hungry. The war-beast was beating her wings frantically, taking them away from Hestillion, but she moved with them, eager to see what would happen. Tyranny was yanking the things out of her hair and popping them in short, sharp blasts of winnowfire, but the bat had no such defence. Her beams of freezing ice shot harmlessly into the sky, causing brief flurries of ice particles but no damage to the burrowers.

In the last clear glimpse Hestillion had of them, she saw that a beetle had started to eat one of the bat's huge, blue eyes, munching down through a white, viscous jelly – and then both queen and war-beast were falling down, spiralling towards their doomed city like an old dead leaf.

'Green Bird, you do the rest.' Hestillion touched the neck of her armour, which was still hot enough for it to glow. 'The city is ours for the taking now.'

Chapter Forty-one

It was a slow and painful journey back to Ebora.

For Aldasair, it was one of the most excruciating experiences of his life. Bern was well enough by that time to walk around unaided, his injured arm kept close to his chest in a sling, yet he was still not quite back to himself. They travelled in short bursts, hopping across the landscape of Sarn for a few hours each day, before resting and finding food. The fell-witches, led by Agent Chenlo, went on ahead, and they soon lost sight of them beyond the rolling hills and the dark grey blur of the distant Reidn mountains. For reasons he couldn't quite identify, Aldasair had become sure that if they could just get Bern home, get him beyond the Tarah-hut Mountains and back under the shadow of Ygseril, then the big man would come back to himself. But he was weak, easily tired, and they had to travel slowly.

On the third day of travel, when they had stopped at the edge of a vast patch of varnish, Aldasair found himself shivering for no reason he could name. Looking up, he saw Bern – who had climbed carefully down from Sharrik's side to stand on the scrubby grass – shudder violently.

'What was that?' called Noon. She came over to them. 'Did you feel it?'

'I think we all did,' said Vintage uneasily. 'A shared feeling between us. It was . . . panic? Horror?'

'But we're all here,' said Tor. Aldasair's cousin had brightened somewhat since the return of the fell-witch, although there was still a thinness to his face that Aldasair did not like. He gestured around to the war-beasts. 'The five of us, and all the war-beasts. What could we be feeling? From who?'

No one had an answer, until Kirune came slinking up. The great cat raised his head, bearing huge curved fangs.

'We might not want to think of them as family,' he said quietly. 'But we five were not the only ones birthed by the tree-father.'

An uneasy silence settled over the group.

The next morning they all flew on, with Bern leaning too far forward in his harness, his face grey. When they made camp again, Aldasair went to him while the others set up the fire and made food.

'I'm worried about you. Sometimes I look at you on Sharrik's back and you look like you might be about to pass out.'

Bern smiled wanly. 'Me? What could there be to worry about?' He sighed heavily. 'Here, let's sit by the water. I like the sound of it.'

It was a rare patch of untouched forest, calm and green and refreshingly normal. The Wild had not spread its corrupting fingers here yet, and the shallow stream ran over pebbles so clean they looked almost jewel-like to Aldasair. The banks were sandy, and as they sat, Bern pushed the fingers of his left hand into the damp sand. *His only hand*, thought Aldasair, his stomach turning over.

'How is it?' he asked hesitantly, nodding at the place where Bern's right arm ended abruptly. The pathfinder's resin had begun to crack and flake; she had assured them that by the time it came off completely, the rounded stump should have healed over. 'Does it pain you still?'

Bern looked down at the stump as if he'd forgotten it was there. 'Pain? Not pain as such. It's bloody sore at times, I'll give you that. But I'm not rightly sure how to tell you what it is like. There's –' he sighed again – 'there's a lot to tell.'

'Try, my love.' Aldasair put his hand on his thigh. 'Please.'

Bern nodded and sat back a little, looking out across the stream. His beard, Aldasair noticed, was becoming a wild tangle. It had been some time since any of them had had time for personal grooming.

'Part of me thinks it's bloody typical.' To Aldasair's surprise, Bern grinned, suddenly looking more like his old self than he had in days. 'My ma always said I was like my dad born again, and now she'll say I'm as careless as him too.'

Aldasair frowned slightly. Human humour was sometimes very strange.

'I do not think she will say that,' he said carefully. 'I think she will be very sad for you, and your father will be too. They are fine people.'

'Oh, aye.' Some of the merriment faded from Bern's face. 'She'll break her heart over it, I've no doubt about that. Both of them have always known we live in a dangerous world, but I'm not going to enjoy letting them know how right they were about that. As for how it actually feels?' He lifted up his foreshortened arm and looked at it; underneath the brownish resin, it was possible to see the flap of skin where it had been pinned in place, along with the neat stitches done by the healer of Deeptown. 'Sometimes, I swear I can feel the hand still there. I catch myself going to scratch my head, or pat Sharrik, or even grab for my axe, and I'm just gesturing with nothing. Sometimes it even hurts – I don't mean my arm, I mean the *hand*. Like I've fallen asleep on it and it's tingling, except it's not there at all. By the stones, it's annoying.' He scowled, then shook his head, as if changing his mind about being angry. 'But aside from all that – listen.'

'What?'

'Just listen.'

Perplexed, Aldasair sat back on the sand and listened. It was a quiet forest, filled with only the gentle noises of small birds and the murmur of water across pebbles. A little way behind them, he could hear Vintage talking. He couldn't make out her words, but the sound of her voice – steady, merry, confident that those listening would be interested – brought a little warmth to his heart.

'I can't hear anything.'

'And neither can I,' said Bern triumphantly. 'My link to the Jure'lia is completely gone. When Celaphon chomped off my hand and swallowed it, he cut me off from them. Their terrible chaos, the endless whispering voices, the sense that I was . . . that I was tainted by them – it's gone. I'm free of them, my love. And as awful as the price was, I'm glad.'

'You nearly died,' said Aldasair, feeling like this particular fact should not be brushed over so easily. 'And if we had not arrived moments after he'd done it, you *would* be dead. Celaphon doesn't care for you, or any of us.'

Bern picked up a pebble and threw it into the stream. 'I wonder about that. What your cousin did to him, what the worm people did to him. He had no choice. I think if he had had a real choice, then he would have been here, with us. A brother to us all, instead of a monster.'

For a time, they sat together, immersed in the gentle quiet of the forest. Small brightly coloured birds hopped around in the shallow waters on the far side of the stream – one of them was as green as the leaves above them. Aldasair watched it closely, thinking long thoughts.

'There's something else,' Bern said eventually. He sounded hesitant, as though the words pained him. 'She – the worm-queen. She was inside my head, Al, so deep, pulling my memories apart, dragging up things I haven't thought about in years and turning them over as though she expected to find some hidden treasure under them. That's the worst of it really – the memory of her grasping, hungry fingers in my head. I keep worrying that she might have broken my mind somehow, that there could be memories I've lost, and how would I know? What if I've lost memories, Al?'

Aldasair reached up and brushed Bern's hair away from his face. 'Then we'll make new ones, my love.'

Ebora brooded under a shimmering heat haze as they made their way over the foothills of the Bloodless Mountains, yet as they drew closer, Vintage saw that the human campsites had grown since they had left. The roads leading to the palace were thronged with people, and new tents had sprouted up all over, like wildflowers in a stretch of featureless meadow.

As they came in towards the palace, they flew closer to each other, naturally flying in formation over the great, wide street that cut the city in half and led to Ygseril.

'Do you see what I'm seeing?' Tor called across. 'I can hardly believe it.'

'I see it,' said Vintage, and although the sight should have warmed her heart, she felt uneasy.

The crowds below them were cheering and waving, and when they landed on the palace lawn, they were immediately met by a surge of people. There were colourful pennants all over, made from – at Vintage's guess – the silks of various tents, and as she climbed down from Helcate's back, Vintage was greeted by an excited throng, all desperate to wish her well and shake her hand.

'We heard what you did,' said one man with a grizzled grey face. 'Who'd have thought it? Who'd have thought I'd live to see the end of them.'

A woman with a baby in her arms was crying, and she pressed a somewhat damp kiss to Vintage's cheek. Two little boys with identical mops of blond hair tried to give her some flowers they had picked. She glanced up to see the others being given the same treatment – some brave soul was attempting to put a garland of bright red leaves around Vostok's neck, and Noon was already surrounded by fell-witches; she caught a brief glimpse of the young woman's face, and saw that she looked somewhat alarmed.

'My darlings, please, I . . .' Vintage found that for once she didn't know what to say. Could she tell them that they were uncertain of their victory? That it seemed, in her heart, to be too easily won? Did she want to be the person to take this joyous day from them, when the truth could be on their side? She smiled fixedly at them instead, and accepted their embraces, patted their hands and kept her mouth carefully shut. Eventually, a slim, dark figure eased itself out of the crowd, and she took Okaar's hand gladly.

'Your witch friends, they told us the good news when they arrived,' he said. He was smiling slightly, as if amused by her perplexed expression.

'And what did they tell you, exactly?'

'That the lost witch had been returned. That the worm-queen was dead, blasted into a smear by the great Lady Noon and Lady Vostok, that the hiding place of the worm people was destroyed also.' He looked at her closely. 'Is that not the truth?'

'It's not *not* true.' She glanced upwards, catching sight of Ygseril's spreading branches. The leaves were still there, silvery and green, rustling slightly in the summer winds. Looking at them, it was almost possible to believe that they had survived. That Sarn might be free. 'My dear, let's get inside. We all need a bloody rest, I know that much.'

Instead, there was a feast. They held it in one of the central ballrooms, although it spilled out into the corridors and neighbouring rooms, and the humans brought so much food and drink that Tor began to wonder what they were going to eat for the rest of the year. The ballroom opened on one side to a spacious courtyard, and Jessen and Vostok joined them there, allowing themselves to be fed and congratulated by a series of increasingly inebriated humans. Tor watched them for a while, and stood and talked with a few well-wishers. Noon had been fully abducted by the fell-witches, who were drinking ever more elaborate toasts in her honour – he caught her eye at one point and acknowledged the faintly irritated expression on her face by raising his glass to her. Eventually, although the moon was still up and the party still very lively, Tor eased his way out of the room and away from the still-teeming corridors. He felt, in short, unutterably tired, and it was no longer possible to ignore the fierce ache in his arms and chest.

Outside under the stars, he walked out towards the more untamed sections of the palace garden. Despite his pain and weariness, he felt reluctant to retire to his rooms.

'I'll be spending more than enough time in bed, sooner rather than later,' he said to the quiet trees. To his own ears his voice sounded cheery, very much his old self, but the words summoned a surge of panic that was like drowning. He gripped his bandaged arm tightly and squeezed it, as if he could squeeze out the poison that was growing there.

'When will you tell them?'

Tor sighed, and looked at the ground. Kirune slunk out of the shadows, his yellow eyes like ghostly moons in the dark.

'I can hardly tell them now,' he said. The tightness in his chest was growing. 'Did you not see? We're celebrating our victory. I might be vain, but I won't spoil this moment for them.'

'You cannot hide it,' said Kirune. 'Not for much longer.'

To Tor's surprise, the big cat came alongside him and pressed his head to his side. Tor rested his arm on his back, and sank his fingers into the cat's thick, grey fur.

'If it *is* all over, perhaps I'll go away,' he said. 'It's not like I'm not known for my tendency to run away, and they will think I've had enough of the responsibility. Tormalin the Oathless was my given name for a reason. I'll just go away, find the furthest corner of Sarn, and die there, hopefully with a bellyful of wine and no real idea what's going on.'

Kirune said nothing.

'It's better than dying here, coughing up my lungs in those rooms, just like everyone else I knew. Better than Noon and Vintage having to watch me die. Instead . . .'

'Instead,' rumbled Kirune, 'they will think you did not love them.'

It was Tor's turn for silence. Eventually, they walked together through the trees, saying nothing, simply listening to the sounds of a forest at night. At one point, the pain in Tor's chest grew so bad that he fell to his knees, and for a while he knelt with his arms around Kirune's neck, waiting for the agony to subside.

Wherever you go, brother, Kirune said inside his head, *I will go also.*

In time they worked their way back inside the palace, and ended up in the Hall of Roots. The huge space seemed oddly threatening in the dark, so Tor went to and fro lighting lanterns, until the hall glowed with a warm, yellow light. Ygseril's huge, gnarled roots looked the same as they ever had, and the vast shape of the trunk was so familiar it made his heart ache. How many years was it since he had come here to find his sister kneeling on these roots, her silk dress sodden with human blood? He reached out a hand to brush away some of the dust from one twisted outcropping of root when a noise at the doors made him turn. Vintage and Noon were there, peering around the door like uncertain children.

'Darling, there you are. Not like you to leave a party early.'

'Looks like you've brought the party to me.'

They came over to the roots, Noon carrying a bottle of

443

pilfered wine under one arm, and they sat cross-legged together before the vast snake's nest of the tree-father's roots. Kirune slunk off into the shadows, sniffing at the corners and generally ignoring them. Not long afterwards, Aldasair also appeared at the door.

'I looked in on Bern,' he said as he joined them. 'He's sleeping very deeply, but it is a good sleep, I think. There is colour returning to his cheeks.'

'It must be his first truly restful night in months,' said Tor. 'I doubt he's had a moment's peace since the worm-queen put that crystal in his hand.'

'Of course, if he still had the crystal, and the connection to the Jure'lia, we might be more certain of their demise.' Vintage flapped a hand at Aldasair's outraged look. 'I know, darling, I wouldn't wish that on our dear Bern, but all the same, I would like a bit of certainty.'

'Our party-throwers certainly seem to think the worm people are dead,' said Tor.

'That's thanks to the fell-witches,' said Noon, the corners of her mouth turning down. 'They came straight back here and told everyone what they'd seen. Chenlo did try to get them to tone it down a little, but once it was out . . .'

'We can hardly blame them for that,' said Vintage. 'We all almost died in that place, and they saw the queen shrivel up into nothing. It seems like a hard-won victory.'

'So why doesn't it feel like it?' Noon took a quick gulp of the wine straight from the neck of the bottle, and passed it to Tor. 'I mean, shouldn't we feel it? If they were really gone?'

Aldasair shrugged. 'We drove them off at the end of every Rain, but they were never really gone – just hiding. We don't know what victory is supposed to feel like.'

'When your world has been at war forever, how do you know peace?' Vintage took the bottle from Tor, and shook her head.

'So what do we do now?' asked Noon.

'We watch, and we wait,' said Vintage. The words were firm, although the expression on her face was anything but. 'I'll have messages sent beyond Ebora in the morning, see if we can figure out what your sister is up to, Tor. If the worm people are still around in some capacity, I'm sure we'll know about it soon enough.'

'I will continue our diplomatic efforts,' added Aldasair. 'Even if the Jure'lia are gone, Ebora has been isolated too long. It's time we were on better terms with the rest of Sarn.' He paused. 'It's likely that we will never be forgiven for the Carrion Wars – and nor should we – but as long as there are humans who want to come here, to see what Ebora is and was, and learn from it, then we should be here with open arms.'

Tor smiled. 'Cousin, who would have thought you would grow up to be such a leader?' Seeing that Aldasair looked embarrassed, Tor leaned across and took his shoulder, squeezing it briefly. 'I don't jest, Al. I am proud of you. You always were the best of us.'

Aldasair looked away, a flush of colour in his cheeks.

'It won't hurt to encourage our neighbours to leave some heavily armoured people here, if they can,' added Vintage. 'A standing army around Ygseril seems like a reasonably sensible idea, and we're nowhere near close to being self-sufficient. The fell-witches at least seem keen to stay here, thanks to the presence of the illustrious Lady Noon, their liberator.' Vintage shot a wicked grin at Noon, who pressed her lips together in a grimace. 'With the heartbright, they make a formidable weapon against the worm people all by themselves.'

'From what you've told me, they did an incredible thing,' Noon said reluctantly. 'They didn't need me to do any of it.'

Vintage looked like she might say something to that, but in the end she took the wine bottle and drank from it instead. For a time they sat together in silence, the only sounds the soft padding of Kirune's paws as he moved through the shadows, and the distant, muffled sounds of merrymaking from the other side of the palace. Tor looked at them all in turn: Vintage, examining the label on the wine bottle with a sceptical expression; Aldasair with his hands folded neatly in front of him, deep in thought; and Noon, her eyes turned up to the newly repaired glass ceiling. He wished that he could capture this moment and keep it with him forever, just as the Jure'lia queen kept her own precious memories in a shard of crystal – this moment of peace, before any of them knew that he was dying, before he had to look at them and see that knowledge in their eyes.

'What's that?' Noon was still looking up, frowning slightly. Tor glanced up too, but a second later something landed on the floor between them – a single silvery leaf, turned brown and delicate at its edges. There was a heartbeat's pause, and another landed, just next to Tor's foot. He stared at it.

'What does that mean?' Vintage asked sharply. She had leapt to her feet and was peering up into the darkness of Ygseril's branches, but there were no more leaves falling that Tor could see.

'I'm not certain,' said Aldasair, a crease appearing between his brows. 'The leaves fell when Ygseril died at the end of the Eighth Rain, but they fell all at once, a great shower of them, still green and silver. This . . .' He picked up the leaf nearest to him and held it up between two fingers. 'Look at it, it's turning brown.'

'Like a normal leaf,' said Noon.

'It could be a true autumn,' Aldasair said. 'I don't know what that means for the tree-father, but it certainly suggests that something is coming to an end, doesn't it?'

'Here –' Tor gestured to Vintage. 'Pass me that wine. I need a drink.'

Chapter Forty-two

It was not smoke that alerted Hestillion to the disaster – that had long since dissipated. It was a taste in the air, something detected by the Behemoths themselves and communicated through them to the circle. A soft shiver of confusion and horror seemed to vibrate through the walls, a keening noise through the Jure'lia network that turned Hestillion's stomach over.

'What is it?' Yellow Leaf was with her, so she turned on the woman-shaped creature, a prickle of sweat breaking out across her shoulders. 'What's causing this?'

'There is death in the air,' said Yellow Leaf. 'We taste its foulness.'

When they came to the crevasse, Hestillion went to the Behemoth wall and turned it translucent. The huge rent in the ground was barely recognisable. Instead she saw fresh raw earth where parts of it had collapsed, and a thick, solid-looking black mass, strange and bulbous, as if it had boiled before turning solid.

'How did I not feel this?'

Except she thought that perhaps she had, after all. Had there not been a swell of confusion, a disturbance to the Jure'lia just before she had destroyed Tygrish? She had dismissed the feelings as unimportant, something happening very far away. All that had mattered was her circle. *Her* victory.

'I'm going outside.'

Standing on the rubble under a bright blue sky, the air smelled fresh to Hestillion, but her Jure'lia senses, the connections that tugged and scratched at her skin, were telling her something was terribly wrong. Hesitantly, she walked over to where the black tar-like taint began and pressed the toe of her foot to it, noting that it was still tacky enough to leave an imprint. A little distance away, a few pieces of rubble seemed to call out to her; they were white and chalky-looking, much paler than the pieces of grey and brown rock that populated the wider jungle. For a long time, Hestillion did not move. Instead she stood and looked at the shards of white rock, her chest rising and falling with ragged breaths.

'It's not rock though, is it?' she said to no one in particular.

Eventually, she went over and picked up a piece, holding it up to the light. The queen's mask-face was pitted and yellowed in places, with fine greyish cracks radiating across it, but it was still perfectly recognisable for what it was. Hestillion touched her fingers to the curved lip that hinted at the edge of an eye socket.

'You should have been here.'

Celaphon emerged from the far side of the jungle, his huge head lowered. He was not quiet as he moved – the great dragon had never been one for stealth – and she could not figure out how she hadn't heard him coming.

You're not paying attention, she told herself fiercely. *You need to focus.*

'What happened?'

The dragon crossed the broken crevasse towards her, leaving huge, clawed imprints in the solid black covering. Behind her, Hestillion could hear various Jure'lia creatures exiting the

Behemoth that had landed, scuttling out onto the grass and rocks. There was some impulse at work here, something seeded deep within them, to gather and witness.

'My brothers, my sisters. Their warriors,' rumbled Celaphon. 'They came here and destroyed the eggs, setting a fire like the sun. It burned so quick and bright, I think it surprised them.'

'And you didn't stop them?'

Celaphon was silent for a moment, rearranging the huge leathery wings on his back. Now that she looked, he was darker in colour than she remembered, as though he were covered in a light covering of soot.

'The white dragon came suddenly from the sky, and she and the witch burned our queen. So relentless, so angry. I felt a little of their fury and their triumph, I think. Just a little.'

'Celaphon,' Hestillion held up the piece of mask, admonishing him with it, 'why didn't you *stop* them? You are the mightiest of all the war-beasts! How could they possibly stand against you?' Yet even as she said it, Hestillion felt a cold unfurling of guilt in her gut, tangled with the strands of another emotion she wasn't ready to name. Celaphon watched her, his silvery-white eyes difficult to read. Eventually, he snorted and sank his claws into the mud.

'When I was small,' he said, 'and weak, and dying, you promised me we would go to a great lake, and eat only fresh fish. When I had grown, you thought of flying far with me, to a remote part of Sarn, where we would live for the rest of our days, alone. We never did that, little bird. Why didn't we?'

Hestillion looked down at the broken piece of mask in her hands.

'I . . . that was . . .'

There were too many thoughts and images in her head. Celaphon before he was grown, small and wrong, her desperation

449

to save him, and the strange work the Jure'lia growth fluid did on his body; the Eboran boy, lying in the dirt, his face spattered with black blood; flying on the back of Celaphon with the joy of battle surging through her veins, their enemies scattered and dying; the queen's hand closing around her neck; her circle, standing and listening and obeying – even now.

'You would not have gone with me,' she said tersely. 'One thing or another would have stopped you. Loyalty to the queen, your need to see your brothers and sisters. I would not have been enough.'

Celaphon took a few steps across the remains of the crevasse until he was standing above her, casting her into shadow.

'And what do we do now? How do we go on, little bird?'

Hestillion shook her head. *It's over*, part of her insisted. *All of it.* And yet, some dark part of her, the same part that had created her own private army in the steaming crafting pools, that had flown Celaphon into combat and thrilled at the power of it, that had taken a blade to the throat of a human child – that part of her did not want it to be over. Not after all her *work*.

'I don't know,' she said, truthfully enough, and one of the Jure'lia creatures tottered forward into her line of sight. It was one of the larger burrowers, a beetle the size of her fist with jagged serrated plates across its back. As she watched, the thing fell over onto its back, sharp legs scrambling at the air. Hestillion frowned at it. 'I have to think. I've just destroyed a clutch of cities. We've had a string of victories.' *My victories*, she added silently. That seemed important. 'We've conquered so much of Sarn, we're on the brink of . . . the brink of taking it.'

The burrower was convulsing violently, its frantic movements leaving marks in the dirt. Hestillion felt an overwhelming desire to crush the thing under her boot, but even as she raised her foot the thing began to pull itself apart.

'What –?'

A thin thread of black fluid spooled itself out from the body of the bug, touching the dirt tentatively, as if feeling its way, or tasting it. Another thread followed that, and then another. The body of the burrower became a busy, teeming mass, as more and more threads of black fluid leapt from it. Already, the shape of the thing was lost, and instead there was something agonised and frantic, a form that was changing all the time. It grew larger and larger, until Hestillion had to step away from it, concerned she would be caught up in its twisting, snake-like body. Another burrower appeared and ran to it, only to be immediately snatched up and pulled apart, contributing what it was to the pulsating mass.

'It's you, isn't it?' Hestillion swallowed hard. 'You're still here. Of course you're still here.'

The thing on the ground rose up, briefly becoming taller than her before collapsing again. Something like a head thrust out of the general mess; something like a mouth opened, gaping and infirm. One flailing appendage scraped across the ground, apparently at random, scooping up the broken pieces of her old mask, some random shards of rock, even the tiny scattered bones of some dead animal. These it pressed into the stringy fluid around the mouth, and those broken pieces formed a face of sorts; nothing as recognisable as her old mask, but the suggestion was enough for Hestillion to need to suppress a shudder. A sharp splinter of grey rock served as a cheekbone, an old piece of the mask had been repurposed as her chin, and the skull of a bird hung crooked over the place where her eye might have been – a sinister eyebrow.

'While any part of us still exists, we are here,' said the queen, her voice a thing of buzzes and clicks. There was a light, trickling sound from behind Hestillion, and a swarm of burrowers swept forward to be absorbed by the thing that was the queen. She became larger, almost taking on a humanoid

451

form, but not quite. The thing that she was now was looser, less contained. More pieces were added to her patchwork face.

'What happened?' asked Hestillion. The crystal sunk into her chest felt like a blade wedged there.

'Your people, your brother . . .'

'They are not my people,' Hestillion added quickly.

'They came here and destroyed us, the heart of what we are. Poured fire on – poured fire on –' The queen shook all over, a violent convulsion that made Hestillion take a step back. 'They destroyed *my* eggs. Our future, gone. There will be no travelling form, no leaving this world, not for our future selves. The great unending chain is severed. We thought that change would break us from this prison. You taught us that, Lady Hestillion Eskt, born in the year of the green bird, but it was wrong. You lied.'

Hestillion held her hands up, glancing at Celaphon, who had not moved.

'This is not my responsibility,' she said sharply. 'You have always made your own mind up.'

Long arms of black fluid whipped out from the queen, wrapping around Hestillion before she had a chance to move, holding her tight and pinning her arms at her sides. Moments ago, it had seemed like her life had many paths, and now it seemed there was only one – the same dark path that had always led to this.

'If you're going to kill me, hurry up,' she said.

The queen ignored her. 'We changed our form, let you take part of us away, brought, for the first time, new shapes forth and shared our memories with flesh that was not ours. This way, we thought, this world would be scoured and warmed, finally. But we opened ourselves to infection.' The queen lowered her broken face towards Hestillion. 'The infection that is you, little war-queen. We thought that if we could understand the connection between the false memory in the crystal and the human, we could understand what you have done to us. But knowledge comes too late.'

The coils around her tightened and very quickly it was painful to breathe. Hestillion wondered what would happen if she summoned her circle now. Could she turn them against the Jure'lia queen herself? 'What are you going to do?'

Next to them, Celaphon snorted, pawing at the ground. The pieces of the queen's makeshift face trembled; a tarnished ribcage, probably from a large rodent, had given her the suggestion of long, thin teeth.

'We learned some things from the man when we opened his mind. One of those was the satisfaction of revenge.'

Abruptly the coils of Jure'lia fluid dropped away, and Hestillion stumbled backwards, only narrowly avoiding falling back into the dirt. The thing that was the queen beckoned, and more creatures oozed from the Behemoth, falling into her coils and disintegrating. There was a strange, strangled noise, like metal being slowly crumpled, and Hestillion turned to see the thick stretch of black tar opening up. A shard of crystal, once the heart of a Behemoth now lost within the broken chasm, was being pushed out like a child spitting out an unwanted cherry stone. The queen reached down for it, and Hestillion got a brief glimpse of the memory it contained, a strange barren world of boiling pink skies.

'What are you doing?'

The queen turned the memory crystal over and over in her arms, examining it from all angles. She had grown much larger in a matter of moments, Hestillion realised with some alarm.

'A new memory.' The queen caressed the crystal, and the imagery within it flickered, becoming something else. The arid grey deserts were gone, and in their place were boiling flames, white and yellow and fiercer than anything Hestillion had ever seen. They spoke of infinite destruction, of an end to everything. The death of all hope. 'The memory of how we died. It will carry us on to revenge, little war-queen, holding us together until we can taste the death of Ebora in our mouths.' The queen pushed the shard into her twisted, changing body, making it a part of her.

'Ebora will fall, finally,' she said. 'That is our revenge.'

Chapter Forty-three

Vintage stopped as she reached the summit of the small hill and looked back behind her. It was a fine day, and the central city of Ebora seemed to shine like something polished, while the regal form of Ygseril continued to spread his branches over the sprawling palace. It had been around a week since they had seen the first leaves fall from the tree-god, and in that time Vintage found herself looking at it often, trying to spot a more robust sign of autumn amongst the branches. Out here, on the lonely stretches of untamed countryside, the changing of the season was more apparent. Green was slowly being replaced with yellow, gold, orange and red, and there was a freshening in the air that promised sharper mornings and, eventually, darker nights.

'It's quite beautiful, isn't it?'

Chenlo came up beside her, carrying their basket of food under one arm. She was wearing the scarlet shirt Vintage had bought her in Jarlsbad, and her striking hair was tied back into a very loose braid.

'It is,' she agreed. 'Shall we eat here?'

They laid down a blanket and unpacked a series of things Vintage had bought and traded for that morning – a loaf of bread studded with seeds, two small meat pies that were slightly greasy to the touch, two boiled eggs dusted with salt, a punnet of purple berries, a thick slice of a kind of jam tart from the Finneral contingent of the palace guard. To that she added a bottle of wine from her own vine forest, one of the very last she had left. She looked at it for a long moment, turning it over in her hands and staring at the label.

'Tell me,' said Chenlo, 'about your home.' She nodded to the bottle of wine.

'Well, I haven't seen it in so long . . .' To avoid looking at Chenlo's face, Vintage began searching in the basket for the carefully wrapped glass goblets.

'I do not think you've forgotten it.'

'No, I suppose not.' Vintage pulled out the glasses and poured the wine. 'Catalen is hot, and complicated. We've had three revolutions in the last two decades, moving from emperors to kings to republics to, honestly, a general population who no longer really cares who is in charge. My family are, to be blunt, rich, and we've made our money from the rich, black soil, and the cheerfully constant sun.' She sighed. 'I feel such guilt when I think about it. About home. What's happened to them all? Are they all right? They have answered none of my letters. My nephew Marin – we were very close when he was little, and once we wrote to each other all the time.'

'We have heard of no major attacks in Catalen.'

'None we have heard of, no. Can I tell you something, Chenlo?'

'Anything you like.'

Vintage glanced up from her glass, surprised by this casual tone from the agent, but Chenlo was carefully cutting the jam tart up into neat pieces.

'I left my home in the vine forest somewhat . . . abruptly. I had been thinking about it, dreaming about it really, for years, but there were always too many responsibilities, too many reasons not to go. Then, one day, I saw a parasite spirit in our forest – it was, is, a place poisoned by the Wild – and that was it. Something closed inside me, or opened up or . . .' Vintage placed her glass on the blanket. 'I felt no regret when I walked away from them, none at all. And I never have. What does that say about me, if I am able to so completely and painlessly sever ties with the place I have lived all my life?'

Chenlo sipped her own wine, considering her answer. When she spoke she looked directly at Vintage, her dark eyes serious.

'Perhaps it says that you should have been out here all along.'

'Perhaps.' Vintage dared herself to hold the other woman's gaze, but something about her face, caught in the pure sunshine of summer's slow dwindling, made her look away. She realised that her heart was beating too fast, so she took a breath to slow it. 'I did always miss my nephew though, Marin. Curious, inquisitive, a trouble-maker. A child after my own heart. The last I heard, he was studying in Reidn, and I must hope he has remained safe behind those thick city walls.'

'You could visit,' said Chenlo. 'Go to Reidn, or back home to Catalen. See for yourself that your home still stands.'

'I couldn't leave Ebora, not yet. We don't know that we are safe, not really, and, well . . .'

She ran out of words, but Chenlo nodded slightly, as if she knew exactly what she was going to say.

'Sometimes,' she said quietly, 'it is not so easy to go home.'

'Quite.'

They sat for a time together, nibbling at the pies and passing each other pieces of tart. The wine was sweet and golden and silky, and Vintage found she was glad she had brought it after all; it seemed to be made for this golden afternoon, and this company.

'I've brought something for you,' said Chenlo eventually. Some of the old formality had entered her voice, and Vintage found herself sitting up curiously. 'After seeing how familiar you were with the gaming houses of Jarlsbad, I thought that you would like it.'

From within her own pack Chenlo pulled out a grey silk bag with a drawstring at its throat, which she passed to Vintage with a slight nod; a ghost of her more formal bows. Inside it, Vintage found a folded wooden board with brass hinges, and a stack of cards made from thin pieces of bone. Each card had been painted with an elaborate figure or scene, surrounded by a number of different symbols, symbols which were reflected on the wooden board.

'Oh, my darling, it's a tarak set! And a beautiful one at that. Where did you get it?'

Chenlo smiled, a faint blush colouring the tops of her cheeks. 'There is a Jarlsbad trader here, with his family. He told me it is one of the most popular games in the kingdoms.'

'It certainly is. On a very basic level, it's essentially a game of matching symbols and images before your opponent does, but you can play different versions depending on how familiar you are with the game, and in places like The Shining Coin the stakes can be very high indeed. The imagery on the cards is fascinating in itself really, all these different figures and symbols. They're thought to come from bastardisations of myths and stories from all over Sarn, but most significantly, the game itself is thought to be related to the Eboran tarla cards, which I'm sure you must have seen.'

Vintage glanced up to see Chenlo grinning at her, delighted.

'Have you played before?' Chenlo shook her head. 'I will teach you, then. Come on, let's make some space on the blanket.'

At this Chenlo looked vaguely panicked.

'I've rarely had the chance to play games, Vintage, I'm not sure I will be any fun to play with.'

'Of course you will.' Impulsively, Vintage reached over and kissed the woman on the cheek. When she sat back, they were both blushing fiercely, and Vintage found her lips were tingling with the memory of Chenlo's skin. 'Here,' she said, trying not to think about the sudden tension between them. 'I will show you.'

'I would like you to show me,' agreed Chenlo.

Lonefell stood within its tangle of a garden, hot and silent, the windows black and dusty. The home of Eri's parents looked strange to Noon, with its multiple stories and peaked roofs; another sign, she supposed, that she was starting to feel at home in Ebora. The palace was a sprawling thing of just one level, as were the vast majority of the grand houses that lined the streets of the city, but Eri's parents had had a fascination with human art and architecture, and had built their own house to reflect this. Hidden within a dense thicket of forest and sheltered from any of the cooling breezes that suggested autumn was on its way, the place felt dreamy and hot, the only sound the dim buzzing of insects.

She came to the part of the garden that was still reasonably tidy, and there he was: a tall, still figure, black hair loose across his shoulders. Her heart lightened at the sight of him even as she felt a sharp stab of annoyance.

'I'm beginning to feel like you're avoiding me.'

She saw his shoulders jerk as she surprised him, and a moment later he turned, smiling faintly.

'It's so noisy at the palace. I almost miss the days when everyone there was dead.' He gestured around at the garden. 'I wanted some peace and quiet.'

'Peace and quiet? You?' But she went over to him, and for a while stood next to him in silence, looking down at the place they had cleared for Eri's grave. As soon as they could, she and Vintage, along with Helcate and Vostok, had gone back to the foothills of the Bloodless Mountains to find the boy's remains. It had taken a while – it turned out that one slope covered in stones and scrubby grass looked very much like any other – but Helcate at least had had a very powerful memory of where Celaphon had attacked them both, so he had led them. Weather and the interest of small animals had reduced Eri's body to a sad pile of bones and ragged clothes, scattered and painfully hard to look at.

'When we found him, I thought –' Noon cleared her throat, suddenly embarrassed.

'You thought what?'

'That there was something magical about him, or about the place where he was. The snow had all gone by then, and it was a bare, miserable place, but Helcate was so sure he was around there somewhere. Then, I saw glinting lights by the ground, a haze of shimmering red stars. And I thought, oh, of course – when Eborans die, they turn into lights or something like that. It made sense to me, for a second, because you were always so magical and mysterious to us all, when I was a child.' She pushed her hair out of her face. 'But it was the armour he had. Do you remember? A kind of jacket made of copper and rubies. It was twisted and broken in the mud, but the rain had washed it, and then the sun lit it up. That's what I could see. Just reflections.'

Tor said nothing.

'His bones were there, so we gathered them up and brought them home.' She wanted to say more, about how she had wrapped them in cloth, so carefully, trying not to think about the bucket the boy had had once, the bucket that had contained his father's bones, yellowed and polished. They had buried him here, near his parents, in the garden that he had tended for so many decades, and Aldasair had chosen a small marble sculpture from the Eboran archive, which they had placed out here by his grave. It came up to Noon's hip, and it depicted a whirl of falling leaves, artfully carved so that they looked weightless and free, caught in a gust of wind. In the middle of the leaves was a laughing Eboran boy, one hand lifted to catch the leaves that were moving too fast for him. 'I know that Helcate still comes out here all the time. Tor, what are you doing here? Really? We've barely seen you all week.'

'He was my friend too, however briefly.'

'The plains folk are going to have a festival,' she said. 'It's a new one. With the full moon tomorrow, they want to celebrate the fact that the true moon is finally alone in the sky. They're going to do it every year from now on, apparently, as the summer ends. And they want us all to be there, so they can, I don't know, honour us, I suppose. There will be food and a lot of drink,' she added hopefully. 'Although I recommend steering clear of the stonefeet. It's made from mare's milk.'

For the first time since he had seen her arrive, Tor turned and looked at her. She was struck again by the hollow places on his cheeks, and the faint lines at the corners of his eyes. More than once since the Jure'lia cavern she had offered him her own blood, but he had refused.

'You should go,' he said. 'Throw yourself in with them, get to know your people again.'

'What?' Noon grimaced. 'Blood and fire, why would I do that? I'm still half a monster to them, you know that.'

'No, you're a hero to them, just as you are to the fell-witches. You need to get over these ideas, Noon, let go of that past. It's not you anymore. If the Ninth Rain has really ended, don't you need to reconnect with your people?' He paused, then shrugged, as if it were the most natural thing in the world. 'What about when you want to settle down? There will be young men falling over themselves to wed the hero of Sarn now.'

Noon turned on him, a hot prickle of horror moving down her back. '*Wed?* What the fuck are you talking about? What the fuck do you mean, *settle down?*'

He shrugged, completely unmoved by her sudden rage. 'I'm just being realistic, Noon.'

461

'Why are you doing this?' Her throat felt thick suddenly, as though her anger and confusion were bile rising up from her stomach. 'What is it you're not telling me?'

'Noon —' To her surprise, he touched her hair, smoothing his hand along her cheek. He looked so sad, so lost, that in one cold moment all her anger turned to fear. 'How I feel about you is real, I promise you that. I didn't lie when I said . . . what I said.'

'Then what are you keeping from me?'

Somewhere nearby, a bird was making a racket in the trees, chasing off a predator perhaps. The heat of the day was a weight, making it harder to move or speak. Noon felt like she was an insect, trapped in a jar; too warm, with a doom surrounding her that was so large she couldn't see it. Tor dropped his hand.

'What are you keeping from *me*?' The flippancy was back in his voice, although it didn't ring true. 'I know there is more behind your time with She Who Laughs than you are telling. Vintage is just thrilled to hear the details, hungry for any knowledge on a god from another world, but she's too excited to see the gaps in your story.'

Noon stepped away from him. The last thing she wanted to think about was She Who Laughs, or the memories she had forced her to recover. They still felt dangerous to her, a nest of snakes that mustn't be touched. That and the new power that lay dormant inside her.

'You don't want to talk to me about whatever it is that has you brooding about like a figure in a painting, that's fine.' She stomped away across the garden, leaving him standing by Eri's grave. 'But don't accuse me of your tricks.'

Later, as the sun sank from the sky and the heat drained away, Noon sought out Vostok. The dragon had sprawled herself on part of the palace roof, looking out across the city like a terrifyingly lifelike statue. When Noon called up to her, she lowered her tail down the side of the building into the courtyard, allowing Noon to climb up onto the roof next to her. The tiles still retained a little of the warmth of the day, and thanks to the slight hill the palace sat on, it was possible to see a portion of the newly busy city. Every day, as word spread of the defeat of the Jure'lia, more people came, and lights from multiple campfires burned fierce in the gathering dark. Noon could hear a faint murmur, the sound of lots of people nearby talking and living their lives.

'Bright weapon.' Vostok shifted on the roof, giving Noon room to come and sit curled by her forearm. 'It is not easy for me to tell when something is wrong. Human emotions are strange, fast things, like fish in a river. And since the fiery one took you, that has been even harder.' The dragon bent her head round to better look at Noon. 'But this I do feel. Something new. A barb in your flesh.'

Noon pressed her hand against Vostok's scales, taking comfort in the presence of the war-beast. 'You told me once that Tor was unreliable. That it was the nature of relationships between humans and Eborans to be, I don't know, short-lived.'

'I see.' So close to each other, it was difficult for Noon not to feel the press of Vostok's emotions. Pity, sorrow, a certain amount of satisfaction. 'It is because you, yourself, are short-lived. That's not his fault, bright weapon. It's simply his nature.'

'Well he's chosen a weird time to feel that way. Sarn is peaceful, and it looks like we might no longer be in danger of dying in a variety of horrible ways, and now he's started disappearing, avoiding talking to us, finding reasons to be alone.' The impulse to keep talking was strong – to tell Vostok that it was the thought of her, Vintage and Tor that had stopped her from stepping into her own abyss when She Who Laughs had forced her to look again at her own terrible past. That she longed for Tor in ways she didn't entirely understand, in ways that almost shamed her. For so long her people had feared and hated Eborans, and here she was, in love with one. But instead she leaned against Vostok's shoulder.

'What happens to you?' she asked softly. 'If the Ninth Rain really is over, what happens to the war-beasts? I've never heard anyone talk about it.'

Vostok chuckled. 'We remain, in peace, for a while. In the past we have helped to rebuild cities and towns, moved supplies to those places that needed it. And then eventually, when we have no more tasks, we lay down to sleep, our souls returning to the roots of the tree-father, until a time when we might be needed again.'

'Lay down to sleep?' Noon sat up and looked at Vostok. 'What does that mean? You mean you just decide to *die*?'

'Bright weapon, there is no need to take that tone. You forget, that for us to die means something quite different. There is no mystery or ending for us, just a period of waiting. Eventually there will be another time, another form to take.'

'But . . .' Noon reached up to curl her arm around Vostok's neck. 'I don't want you to go anywhere. And what if the worm people really are gone, forever? Does that mean the tree-god won't grow any new pods, ever again?'

Vostok shifted against the tiles, and Noon knew with a sudden sinking certainty that the proud war-beast hadn't considered such a possibility. Nevertheless, when she spoke again her voice was measured and unconcerned.

'Then we will have lived in glory, and died in victory.'

'Bollocks to that,' said Noon. 'Bollocks to all this death and glory stuff. I will think of tasks for you. So many tasks you'll have to stay until I'm old and grey, at least.' Her arm still awkwardly slung over the dragon's neck, she did her best to pull Vostok to her. 'If Sarn doesn't need you anymore, I still will.'

Chapter Forty-four

The sweet fluting sound of a horn cut through the air.

Vintage put down the journal she had been studying – more of Micanal's personal writings, all the more fascinating since they had learned his fate – and turned curiously to the window. The single note was followed by a series of more frantic calls, and she felt a flicker of alarm move through the connection she shared with Helcate. Something was happening. She left the chamber and quickly made her way to the palace grounds, where Kirune, Tor, Noon and Aldasair were already waiting, their eyes on the sky. Next to them one of the Finneral guards was standing, one hand held over his eyes even as the last light faded from the day. In his other he clutched an elegant horn, carved all over with the complex geometric shapes of the Finneral written language.

'What is it?' She glanced at the others. Noon was frowning, her forehead wrinkled so that the bat-wing tattoo became a confused smudge. 'Anyone care to enlighten me? Are the worm people about to vomit on us from above?'

The Finneral guard raised the hand with the horn and pointed with it. 'We've something flying over the city, Lady Vintage, but it's all over the place. We're not sure what it is.'

There was, Vintage saw, a bright pale dot flying over the outskirts of the city. It wove back and forth, like a drunkard trying to find the bits of the street that weren't moving, yet it was growing closer all the time. Whatever it was, it was trying to head towards the palace.

Vintage pulled the spying glass from her belt and held it up to her eye, twisting and untwisting the lenses until the thing came into focus. It was still difficult to see, because it was moving too much, but even so, there was no mistaking it.

'It's Queen Tyranny,' she said flatly. 'Or at least, that's Windfall, and she has someone on her back, but she looks injured.'

'Tyranny?' Tor looked at her. 'The woman who stole our war-beast?'

'Our sister comes home,' added Kirune.

'Should we . . . go up and help her?' asked Noon.

Vintage pressed her lips together and shrugged. 'Darling, she stole from us, tried to have me and Eri killed, stole an entire kingdom, tried to feed me and Chenlo to some Wild-touched cats, and kept a war-beast from her destiny. If she's going to fall, let her.' Vintage turned to the guard. 'Go and find Okaar, if you can. Let him know what's about to take a big shit on our doorstep.' Catching Noon's look, she shook her head slightly. 'Noon darling, it would be dangerous anyway. Windfall possesses an extraordinarily powerful ice beam, and we are certainly not her friends. We should wait and see what happens.'

They watched the pale dot grow closer, watched as it resolved into a giant white bat. Vintage still couldn't quite make out the figure riding in the harness, partly because the angle was wrong and partly because whoever it was had slumped forward, their face obscured by the bulk of the war-beast's head. The creature was over the edges of the palace gardens when it started to drop, falling out of control before a few flaps of its enormous wings bore it briefly up again.

'Fire and blood,' muttered Noon. 'What's the matter with it?'

The bat made it to the outer garden and then dropped a final time, crashing down behind the treeline. Without discussing it, Vintage and the others ran forward.

'Where did she go?'

'Here,' Tor was in the lead, his sword held loosely in one hand, 'I can see it through the trees.'

'Be careful.' Vintage touched her belt, missing her crossbow once again. 'Remember, this one is dangerous.'

However, as they emerged into a small clearing, littered with freshly broken branches, Vintage had to admit that Windfall did not look especially dangerous. The great white bat was pressed to the ground, her wings spread out as though she could not cope with her own weight, and her huge blocky head was bowed. On her back, a woman was trying to untie herself from the harness. She managed it just before they reached her, and Tyranny fell awkwardly into the long grass.

Despite all her words of anger and caution, Vintage found herself going over to the woman.

'Tyranny? What's happened? What are you doing here?'

The young woman raised her head. The fine jewellery and robes were gone, and instead she was dressed in a sweat-stained vest and patched trousers. All the hectic colour had left her cheeks, leaving her skin oddly grey-looking, and the acid scars across her neck looked livid and sore. Worst of all, when she met Vintage's eyes, Vintage had a crawling sensation that, for a moment, Tyranny didn't know who she was.

'Are we here?' she said. The confident Mushenskan drawl was absent. 'Is this Ebora?'

'You are in Ebora.' Tor lowered his sword so that the point of it hung in front of the blonde woman's face. 'I don't know why a thief would return to the scene of her crime, but if you

467

think we've forgotten what you did, you are very much mistaken.'

Tyranny glared at the sword, then looked away again. Instead, she dug her hand into the thick white fur of the war-beast.

'You see? We're here. Are you bloody happy now?'

Windfall raised her head, and Vintage felt her stomach turn over. Where the bat's right eye should've been was a deep black hole, ragged and bloody. Her other eye, still blue and intact, looked wild and lost.

'Tyranny,' Vintage leaned down and, taking a risk, shook the woman's shoulder, 'Tyranny, what happened? Was it Tygrish? Has Tygrish fallen?'

Tyranny shuddered violently, and her mouth turned down at the corners. To Vintage's astonishment, the woman started to cry.

'Not just Tygrish,' she choked out between sobs. 'All of Jarlsbad. All of Jarlsbad is gone.'

Having established that Tyranny wasn't going to be an immediate threat, they took the woman and her war-beast into the palace via the rear gate and through to the biggest courtyard – the easiest space for the war-beasts to gather within the palace. Aldasair sank into the background, fetching food and drink and quietly talking to the guards who had gathered at the doors. Vintage, meanwhile, was watching the woman and her war-beast very closely, her face set and stern. Tor could see that she was conflicted – her anger at Tyranny's behaviour was fighting against her usual curiosity.

'Tell us what happened.' Tor put his sword away, and shared a glance with Noon, who was standing with her arms crossed over her chest. The war-beast called Windfall had crept into the corner, her head weaving back and forth in a manner that sent cold fingers walking down Tor's back; she made him think of his mother, when the horror of their situation had eroded her mind to a single point of bright confusion. 'It was the worm people, yes? When did they attack?'

Tyranny sat forward with her elbows on her knees, her head down. There were dark scuff marks on her skin, dried blood behind her ears. She clearly hadn't washed for some time.

'I am cold,' she said in a very small voice. 'Do you have a blanket or something?'

'A blanket? We sent you diplomats and your response was to lock them up and try to have them eaten alive. You're lucky we didn't burn you from the skies on sight.' Even so, Tor nodded to Aldasair, who vanished back through the doors. 'Why are you here, Queen Tyranny of Tygrish?'

She shuddered at the name of her kingdom and raised her head. Tor, who had been far from Ebora when Tyranny had tried her tricks and stolen their war-beast pod, had built a picture of the woman in his head, and it was very far from this scrawny, dirty, shivering creature. Yet there was a steeliness in her eyes, and he could see her attempting to control her own fear.

'Windfall wanted to come here. It's all she's spoken of since – since we were attacked. She thinks that we'll be safe here.' Her mouth twitched up at the corner in a bitter smile. 'But all of Sarn is fucked, as far as I can see.'

Aldasair returned with Bern, both carrying supplies. Bern, who had regained some weight in the days since their return, stood over Tyranny for a moment, frowning, before throwing a thick blanket over her shoulders. Aldasair gave her a cup of water, which she immediately drained.

'It's the worm people, of course it's the fucking worm people.' Tyranny looked into the bottom of the cup. 'They came, three of their ships, but we were ready. I wasn't about to let just anyone walk in and take my kingdom from me, so I'd been preparing our army, and my guard, to meet any threat.' She looked up at them, her pale-blue eyes defiant again. 'And I had a *war-beast*. Of all of Jarlsbad, Tygrish was best defended. I knew, I *knew* we could hold them off by ourselves, we would be the first to do it, to show that humans are strong – I've never needed anyone else.'

'And how did that work out for you, Tyranny?' Vintage sighed. 'Sarn's bones, I never took you for an idiot, but here you are, by the skin of your arse.'

Tyranny scowled. 'Three ships,' she continued. 'We got into positions. We readied ourselves. Our walls are high, my people are brave –'

Tor exchanged a look with Vintage, who had raised her eyebrows. *My people.*

'There was no dragon?' he asked. 'A huge, dark dragon?'

Tyranny looked annoyed that she had been interrupted. 'A dragon? There was no dragon. We fought well, and I think we gave them a bit of a shock, you know? To start with. They thought they could just walk in, sweep us aside, and they were wrong. But –' she swallowed hard – 'the ships moved. They went to where we were weakest, and they rained their fucking shit all over us. And then, when Windfall and I were in the sky, someone came out to fight us, one to one.'

'The queen?'

'No, it was a bloody Eboran of all things. Some woman wearing this weird flying armour, all made from the same stuff their crawling bugs are made from.'

Tor held himself very still. He could sense both Vintage and Noon looking at him, but he kept his eyes on Tyranny.

'An Eboran was wearing Jure'lia armour?'

'Yeah. She had knives inside it, and a kind of flail, and she attacked me and Windfall directly, trying to beat us out of the sky.'

'Then what happened?' asked Noon.

'One of the ships moved above us, and she ordered it to

puke its nasty crawling things all over us. They were everywhere, crawling and biting and –' Tyranny shuddered, even more of the colour seeping from her face. 'They tried to eat Windfall's eyes, and they were so fast, *so fast*. I had to – I reached inside the hole they'd made and pulled them out again, the bugs. Pulled them out of her head and blasted them, but I couldn't save her eye.'

In the corner, Windfall gave a high, piercing cry. 'Inside my head,' she said, her voice harsh. 'I felt them inside my head.'

Kirune went over and sat next to the war-beast, his huge bulk resting just next to her wings, and Windfall's alarming sobs quietened again.

'By the roots, you are lucky to be alive,' said Aldasair softly.

'The rest of Tygrish wasn't so lucky,' said Tyranny. 'We fell towards the ground, and that's when they swarmed us. All our armies, my guard, all chewed up and eaten by the worm-people filth. We got outside the city walls and hid in the long grass, and I . . . I thought Windfall was dying. The noises she made, the pain she was in. I felt it.' Tyranny touched her breastbone with her fingers. 'I felt it here, too. I thought I was going mad. I kept touching my own eyes, because I thought I had been blinded too. But she lived. We both lived.'

'War-beasts are hardy,' said Vintage. 'What happened then?'

Tyranny shook her head. 'I'm not sure how long we were in the grass for. I don't know how we didn't get eaten by the Wild-cats there, unless they were all frightened off by the worm people. We were feverish I think, I lost time, and then eventually I realised we weren't dead, and that was when Windfall started talking about coming back here. I wouldn't. I told her that Tygrish was our home, that there was nothing for us in Ebora.' Tyranny ran a hand through her closely cropped hair. 'She'd never even seen it, for fuck's sake. It's a dead city full of relics.'

'Relics you stole,' added Vintage.

471

'I said no. I said, we'll find shelter nearby, someone to help us. And then we got up in the air again.'

A small silence filled the courtyard. Tor pressed the back of his hand to his mouth to conceal a wince; a new flash of pain was slowly burning its way through his chest, uncurling down his arms. All at once the very act of standing up seemed too much, but he kept his back straight. There wasn't time.

'Tygrish was gone. The towers had been pulled down into rubble, the houses and the town squares, the markets and the streets – all gone, all lost under varnish. The walls had been broken down too, the land bridges shattered. And no one there. No movement from anywhere. It was just – gone.' Tyranny lifted her hands and looked at them, as though the glittering city of Tygrish had been cradled in her palms just moments before. 'Windfall began shrieking then, "Ebora! Ebora!" over and over, but I told her to shut up, that there were closer places, better places, places with humans in them, so we flew west, seeking out the rest of Jarlsbad but . . .'

Her voice trailed off.

'Sarn's bloody bones,' muttered Vintage. 'The kingdoms of Jarlsbad have stood for hundreds of years. Are you telling me they are gone? All of them?'

'From Tygrish to the Kerakus Sea is a wasteland,' said Tyranny. 'Even the land has changed. The grasses have become marshland, where the rivers have been stopped. We saw no one, no animals, not even anything Wild-touched.'

'Thousands of people, it must be,' said Vintage weakly. 'Hundreds of thousands of people, wiped out by three Jure'lia ships.'

Wiped out by my sister, thought Tor. A ripping pain shot down his forearms, and he pictured his skin splitting open, oozing the dark red pus of the crimson flux. He clenched his fists, and put the vision from his mind.

'So you came here.'

'What else was I supposed to do? It's the only place Windfall would go, and at least we knew people here. I –'

Okaar appeared at the door, his thin face a shade paler than it had been. He went and stood in front of Tyranny, although the woman shrank away from him.

'If you are here, where is my sister? Where is Jhef?'

Tyranny turned her head, not looking at him. She looked, to Tor, as though she might cry again, but when she spoke her voice was tight with anger.

'I don't know! I don't know where she is. If she had stayed with me, she would have been safe, I know that, but her bloody loyalty to you meant she was forever keeping just out of reach.'

'But she was in Tygrish?' Vintage came forward and put her hand on Okaar's shoulder. Tor suspected that she too thought the assassin was on the verge of striking Tyranny. 'And Nanthema too, I assume?'

'I don't know where they are. Yeah, they were in the palace, as far as I knew but –' She shrugged, and shook her head. 'There was no palace left. Nothing could have lived through that.'

'And to think Nan wanted to leave Ebora because she felt it wasn't safe. Because there were too many bad memories here.' Vintage looked ill. 'What a stupid loss.'

'You as good as killed my sister!' Okaar shook Vintage's hand off and slipped a long thin blade from within his jerkin. Instantly, Windfall struggled to her feet, screeching a warning even as her jaws fell open to reveal the boiling blue light at the back of her throat. Tor pushed Okaar back none too gently and stood between him and the queen of Tygrish.

'That's enough,' he snapped. 'We haven't got the time for this.' He turned to Vintage and the others, seeing his own worried expression reflected in their faces. 'What does this mean for us?'

As ever, Vintage knew exactly what he meant. 'We know

473

Hestillion was not at the Jure'lia cave when we were there. I suspect that the attack on Jarlsbad was happening at roughly the same time we destroyed the queen's eggs. And, my dear, it does sound as though your sister was in charge of it.'

'Then there are three Behemoths still out there,' added Noon. 'That's what we're saying, isn't it? Three worm-people ships that weren't in the cavern when we burned it down.'

'What are you talking about?' snapped Tyranny.

'Three ships, it seems, can still cause a lot of damage,' said Aldasair, ignoring Tyranny. 'But the odds have levelled out a little, I would say.'

'Have they? Hestillion has proven herself to be a far more lethal commander than the Jure'lia queen.' Vintage looked at Tor, her face grim. 'Will she come for Ebora, Tor? Will she seek to wipe us out? Once Ygseril has gone, the war-beasts will be no more.'

'You ask me as though I should know what my sister wants.' He swallowed. The pain in his chest was becoming hard to ignore, and a fine sweat had broken out across his back and forehead. 'When we were children she would have given her life to bring the tree-father back, but now? I stopped under-standing Hestillion a long time ago.' He pressed one trembling hand to his throat – the pain was searing its way up his neck now. It was like drowning. 'Excuse me, I just have to –' He turned and headed for the doorway, intending to get out of their sight. 'I just need to –' Desperately he staggered forward, his eyes on the darkness of the corridor, but the strength that had been in his legs just moments before drained away and he fell down into the dirt, pain reverberating through his body like a struck bell.

'Tor?'

He heard Noon's voice, frightened and close, and felt strong hands on his shoulders, and then everything was lost in a rising tide of pain and heat.

Chapter Forty-five

'You must be the biggest fool I have ever known, and it has been my dubious lot in life to know a great number of fools, Tormalin the Oathless.'

Vintage was fussing over the bandages on Tor's left arm, her face set in an expression of forbearance. Noon found herself unable to look away from his right arm, which was currently bare of the coverings Tor had been using to hide his illness from them. There was a series of red lines there, like livid veins, and the skin around them was turning chalky and white. They had taken his shirt off, and to their mutual horror had discovered another small patch of the affliction, just over his breastbone. Tor himself was asleep, or he had been; at Vintage's strident tone his eyelids were flickering, and he groaned.

'Oh there you are, darling. With us now, are you?'

He opened his eyes. 'Where am I?'

'*Where am I?* Really? You can't think of anything better than that to say?' Vintage shook her head. 'How about, "Hello, Vintage, I am a prize idiot"? Or, "I am sorry I chose to hide from you information that would obviously be vitally important to you, because my pride is apparently more important than your feelings or the well-being of our home"?'

'You're in my room,' said Noon. She touched his shoulder, worried that perhaps he wouldn't realise she was there. 'In my bed. We've changed your dressings. Why didn't you tell us, Tor?'

He lifted his bandaged arm and peered at it. 'You did a better job than I did, anyway. Not easy to bandage your own arm, you know.' He sighed. 'What would be the point in telling you? Or do you crave more disasters?'

'Stubborn,' snapped Vintage. 'I used to think it was a charming quality of yours, but it turns out it is spectacularly unhelpful.'

'If I'm stubborn, Vintage, it's because I learned it from you.' Tor groaned and pulled himself up a little. 'Blessed roots, I ache.'

'We've called for all the healers,' said Noon. 'They're gathering supplies now, and then they'll want to examine you.'

Tor chuckled weakly. 'You know as well as I do that there is no cure for the crimson flux – it's killed enough of my people for us to be sure of that – and this is no time to be lounging in bed.'

He made to get up, and Vintage pushed him roughly back down.

'Shut up. You don't get to tell us anything for now, you idiot.' Noon realised that Vintage was close to crying, and she felt a cold hand close around her own heart. If Vintage was so desperate – optimistic, cheerful Vintage – then surely there was no hope at all. 'You're going to bloody lie there and let them poke you about and apply their salves, and you're going to do it with good grace and humour.'

She made a show of straightening his sheets, then marched over to the door. 'I'll go and see who's ready to poke you about. I have asked them to bring their biggest, pointiest needles.'

When she had closed the door, Noon turned back to Tor.

'She's about as angry as I've ever seen her. What do you think you were playing at?' She bit her lip briefly and savoured the pain; a distraction from the sorrow. 'Why didn't you tell us? Why didn't you tell *me*?'

'Noon, you knew this could happen. It's practically inevitable.' He sighed and looked down at the marks on his arm. 'Kirune knew. I made him promise not to tell the rest of you. It's a distraction, and roots be cursed, we don't have time to be distracted right now. What happened to Tyranny and Windfall? Do we have any more news?'

Noon shook her head. Tyranny was being kept in a room under guard, while Windfall had been accepted by the other war-beasts – she was with them now, being shown her rightful home and legacy.

'We've not heard anything else. Aldasair sent more fell-witch sentries out to the borders and beyond, to watch for any worm-people activity, and Bern is asking anyone who arrives in Ebora for news. I'm not sure what else we can do for the moment.'

'We can get ready for war. That's what we can do.'

'You're right about that, at least.' Noon slipped a small sharp knife from her belt and held it up so that Tor could see it. 'I don't know anything about healing, and it's possible the healers will be useless, but I do know what helps you.'

He smiled ruefully, but there was a hunger in his eyes. 'The thing that doomed me in the first place.'

'And as you once told me, what difference can it make now?'

She held her arm up and cut it in the way that he had once showed her. Bright beads of blood grew across her skin, and without needing further prompting, Tor bent his head and drank from her. With her free hand, she smoothed his hair back from his forehead.

'Take what you need.'

His arm circled around her waist, pulling her closer, and

Noon was forcibly reminded of the time they had spent in Esiah Godwort's house; when she had laid down next to him day after day to give him her blood, to bring him back to consciousness. It had been a nightmarish time – she had been so convinced that he would die, that she had killed both him and Vintage with her tainted ability – but it had also been the first time she had felt close to him. They had walked in dreams together, shared memories and shared blood. Feeling the press of his mouth against her skin again was, despite everything, a joy.

There was a series of knocks at the door, and Tor broke away. There was a smear of blood on his lips, and his eyes were brighter than they had been in days.

'Tell them to go away,' he said, his voice husky. 'I have everything I need here already. Noon, if you are with me . . .'

'All you ever had to do was ask.' Noon picked up some of the spare bandages. 'But you know that if you don't let them in, Vintage will kick the door down.'

Chapter Forty-six

Treen ran to the top of a dune and looked down across the river-scape. The ants were on the move, and she'd never seen so many above ground at once before. They swept over the clay, turning it into a living carpet of red, black, brown and orange bodies, all shiny and hot under the sun. Moving slowly amongst them were the loaded sleds of Deeptown, each one piled high with food, belongings, furniture and people.

'How far do we have to go, do you think?'

She turned to see Tchai, one of the young ant herders, his broad shoulders glistening with sweat. Like she had, he had grown up with the ants, learning how they moved, how they spoke to each other, and how to talk back to them, and, like her, she could see that he was worried. To move all the ants at once like this was to invite all sorts of trouble – stampedes, a break-off colony, sudden fights, or attacks from the various predators that skulked their way around the flats.

'The pathfinder thinks we need to get out of the sight of the Dead Woods if we can.' She caught the sceptical expression that passed over Tchai's face, and she shrugged. The Dead Wood was a thick, dark smudge on the horizon, spreading in both directions as far as they could see. 'I know. But you saw

479

the smoke. You heard what the Eboran warriors said. And you have heard the same noises, felt the same tremors. Deeptown isn't safe.'

In recent days, Deeptown had been shaken by strange movements in the earth. Four tunnels had collapsed, killing a father and his two sons, as well as two ant herders, and the ants themselves had grown increasingly skittish. They were sensing something the humans couldn't, Treen was sure of it, but although the pathfinder had spent many hours trying to get some sense out of them, all she could tell was that they were scared. Very scared. And then there had been the noises, heard above ground, when everything was still.

'Being under the sky for this long isn't safe,' said Tchai. 'And where are we running to? There's nowhere else like Deeptown. You see anywhere else?' He gestured to the flat orange landscape in the distance. Aside from the wide, shallow rivers that cut through it here and there, it looked suspiciously featureless. 'When we stop to rest, the ants will panic. You know this as well as I do.'

Treen bit her lip. 'What do you suggest we do, then, Tchai?'

'We should have stayed,' he said immediately. 'We have supplies and bolt holes, enough to last for months. We should have sealed up our entrances and let whatever horrors are coming roll over us.'

'The pathfinder talks, we obey,' she said, although in her heart she remained uneasy. Like all of those born and raised in Deeptown, she felt safest when there was several feet of thick, clay-packed earth above her head. Being above ground when there was the threat of predators made her feel vulnerable and exposed. 'But also,' she added in a quieter voice, 'we watch and wait. Perhaps we need to make ourselves scarce for a few days just to be safe, and then, when things have quietened, we'll go back. Deeptown will still be waiting for us.'

Tchai tipped his head to one side, not quite agreeing with her.

'We'll have to keep an eye on the sky too, we don't –'

Her words were cut off by a strange, wailing cacophony, followed by a rumble so loud and deep that she felt it through her boots.

'What –?'

Tchai grabbed her arm and pointed. The distant smudge of trees that marked the edge of the Dead Woods was moving, growing bigger somehow. It was bleeding shadows. From all across the migration swarm, ant herders began to blow warning notes on their pipes.

'Sarn's bloody bones, what is it?' Tchai held his spear at the ready, as if he could fight such a thing. 'How do we even –?'

'Tchai, your eyes are better than mine. Are we in its path? Can you tell?'

The young herder shook his head, his eyes very wide. 'I don't know.'

Now that it was moving, it came on very fast. A huge black shadow, taller than the treetops, crashed out of the treeline, unfurling tendrils of darkness as it came. The ground below it was torn up and cast aside. Treen saw trees she knew had stood for hundreds of years picked up and tossed away like toothpicks. Quickly it was clear of the Dead Wood, and it was coming on across the sand flats, oozing and changing shape all the time – it was hard to look at, hard to comprehend. Treen turned back to the herd, to her people with their sturdy but largely slow-moving sleds. If it was coming this way – if it spotted them – she doubted they would be able to get everyone out of the way in time. Nevertheless, they would have to throw caution to the wind.

'Go!' she cried, waving her arms over her head. 'All of you, move!'

Tchai blew more notes on his pipes, and as one the denizens

of Deeptown surged forward. Treen turned back to look again at the approaching monstrosity; now that it was closer, she could make out more details. Floating in the air behind it, like fat pigs' bladders hanging in the sky, were three of the worm people's hideous ships, their skins oily and greenish in the harsh summer light, and another shape came on behind, one that made her think of the extraordinary dragon that had visited them briefly.

'I think it's going to miss us,' said Tchai. He pointed with his spear again. 'Look, it's bending to the west, but that means . . .'

'That means it's going to go straight over Deeptown.'

In the end, they stayed together on top of the small hill, and watched. The huge monstrous shape that, unbeknownst to them, was the Jure'lia queen, seethed forth over the flats, long tendrils of black ooze seeking and crawling like inquisitive fingers. Eventually, they were able to see that the back portion of the monster had a number of strange, pale protuberances, and from these thick varnish poured, ensuring that every part of the landscape the thing covered was sealed behind it in a solid green prison. When it came to the place they both knew to be Deeptown, Treen reached out her hand, and Tchai took it.

Treen found that she could imagine it all too well – being down in the under-streets as a huge, monstrous weight passed over, the dust in the air as the foundations shuddered and burst. Thick rivers of varnish pouring down every entrance, catching and holding people and ants alike, and then slowly, slowly blocking out all light and air.

'Thank all the gods for the pathfinder,' muttered Tchai. 'We would still be down there now.'

'It's heading north,' said Treen, not really listening. 'It has a destination in mind, I think.' Around them, she could hear the cries of the men and women and children who had just watched their home destroyed. 'Deeptown is gone,' she said.

'Come on. We're going to have to think and move fast if we're going to live through this.'

'Can you hear that?'

Pamoz unwound the rags from her head, and pulled the lever on the contraption. After giving a few last strangled gurgles, the thing stopped, wisps of steam curling up towards the ceiling.

'Hear what? I can't hear anything.'

Fell-Erin rolled her eyes at her. 'I'm surprised you can hear *me*, that noise clanging around in your ears all day. Come outside.'

Frowning, Pamoz wiped her hands on a cloth and followed the fell-witch to the door of the dilapidated barn. Outside, the little town was quiet, with no people in sight – but that wasn't anything unusual. Pamoz had chosen the place specifically because it was deserted, and because it had once been the location of a thriving metal-ore mine. This far south, Sarn was too hot and too arid, but it was also wilder, with greater stretches between settlements. This meant that when things went bad – as they often did – people were quicker to leave and find somewhere else to make their homes. No one wanted to be stranded.

'Perhaps there is something . . .' Pamoz scratched the back of her head, resolving that in the evening she would find some water and have a proper bath. There were lots of things about working with the Winnowry that she didn't miss, like their outrageous demands, the close watch they kept on their women, and the general sense that anyone outside of their strange church was inferior in some way . . . but they had always been good about providing her with what she needed, whether that was supplies, workers, or clean bath water. Out here in the arse-end of nowhere, all of those things were harder to find.

'Of course there is something,' snapped Fell-Erin. 'You're half deaf, I keep telling you. I think sometimes that ridiculous contraption will blow up in your face and you'll only notice when your legs fell off.'

'It's close to working,' Pamoz said mildly. 'The wheels are turning, I just need to get them turning steadily. And in the same direction. And then it won't be so ridiculous, will it? A cart that moves without horses.'

'It'll be your triumph, I'm sure,' said Fell-Erin. They were all very careful not to mention the Winnowline, the huge project Pamoz had been constructing for the Winnowry that was now, thanks to an incident the previous year and the absence of the Winnowry itself, permanently on hold.

'What is that?' A younger woman ran across the square towards them, her hair held back from her face in a bright red handkerchief. The bat-wing tattoo on her forehead had been added to since the Winnowry had fallen – now the stark shape was surrounded by delicate blue flowers that trailed down the sides of her face. Fell-Aethe was the other fell-witch who had agreed to come and work directly with Pamoz, and she had been on lookout duty for the afternoon.

Fell-Erin took the woman's hand and squeezed it. 'You saw nothing from the wall?'

'No, but it's coming from the south, I think? I was on the north wall.'

Together they went to the lookout tower, a tall old building built from cool yellow brick, and, climbing the rickety stairs inside, emerged onto the southern wall. Like most settlements in Sarn, the builders of this small town had devoted a lot of time and energy to the defensive walls, and they were in better condition than the tired collection of buildings they protected. The little town was called Goldlodge, according to Pamoz's map, and it was nestled in the midst of a series of steep, rolling green hills. It sat halfway up one, clinging to the side of it like a particularly determined barnacle, and from the walls they looked out across a soft, pleasing landscape, only broken here and there by the thin, winding track of an optimistic road.

'It's coming from over there.' Fell-Aethe pointed to the place where one hill rose out of the shadow of another. 'Can't you hear it? A rolling, hissing sort of noise.'

'Don't ask Pamoz,' said Fell-Erin. 'Her head's full of steam.'

'Now that you say it . . .' Despite the humid warmth of the day, Pamoz felt goosebumps rise on the backs of her arms. She had felt this before, every now and then, when they had been building the Winnowline tracks – the sense that they were being watched by something large, something Wild-touched. 'Can you—'

A shadow fell over them. The three of them looked up to see an enormous bulbous shape passing overhead. Fell-Erin gave a little cry, falling back against the wall and crouching. Pamoz grabbed her arm and shook it.

'Get up,' she hissed. 'We have to get under cover.'

'Look!' Fell-Aethe was still looking out across the far hills. A great dark shape had appeared, creeping out from behind the slope of the land. 'Tomas save us, what the fuck is that?'

Pamoz shook her head. Nothing she was looking at made sense to her. The thing came more than halfway up the hill, and it appeared to be made of a black and greenish oozing material that shifted and changed as it moved. She saw things that could be arms and legs, ten or twenty of them, each fringed with multiple, moving tendrils, and she saw things that were almost bone-like in structure – the jutting shape of ribs here, the suggestion of a curved spine. There were fat protrusions along the back of it that were paler in colour, and oddly segmented; these were pulsing and flexing, squeezing out dribbles of green fluid. The head of the thing was long and narrow, almost like a pickaxe, and although it was too far to see it

485

clearly, Pamoz thought she could see speckles of lighter material, as though certain objects had been caught there, stuck to its face.

'Worm people,' she said through numb lips. 'Hide. We have to hide.'

The three of them ran, descending the tower steps in stumbling jumps before sprinting across the dusty market square back into Pamoz's work barn. Once inside they crouched against the steam-driven contraption she had been building for months, their hands pressed to its slightly warm sides as though it were a bigger animal, something that might protect them when their enemies kicked down the door. They waited there for hours, listening to the rumbled, keening hiss of the Jure'lia procession moving past them, then waited a few hours more to be sure. When they finally emerged, cautiously stepping out under the dangerous sky again, they discovered that whatever the terrible thing was that had passed so close by, it had paid no attention to the tiny settlement of Goldlodge. However, the beautiful green hills, with their lush grasses and small patches of fruit trees, were scarred and broken, trailed and daubed with varnish that was already shining solid under the newly risen moon.

Chapter Forty-seven

In the dream, Tor stood in the foyer of a rambling Eboran mansion. The shadows were deep, and the tapestries on the walls were rotting, the blackened threads revealing here and there little snatches of a lost history. There was dust on the floor and old, dead leaves, and on a long table by the door, the skeleton of some small animal, its bones yellowed and chewed.

'Do I know this place?'

Here, all the pain of the crimson flux had vanished, and he no longer wore the bandages that in waking hours covered him from wrist to shoulder. Instead, he felt young, full of energy, and as he walked down the corridor he plucked at the fine silk jacket he was wearing. It was yellow, not his colour at all, but it was very finely made, and there were black silk birds embroidered at the cuffs. The walls were hung with long, narrow paintings, each depicting a tall, solemn Eboran hero – there was Floriaan the Unlucky, with his lute, and Brochfael the Unending with her shining sword and gauntlets. For a time there had been a fashion in Ebora for these portraits of ancient heroes, each one depicted unsmiling, watching the viewer from eyes of ink and paint, and the owner of this particular home had been an avid collector. Tor touched the canvas of one, placing his fingers against the hilt of Brochfael, and that was when he remembered the place – once, he had made certain to always touch the sword of Brochfael, because he believed it was lucky.

'We used to come here to play.' He looked away up the corridor. Now that he had recognised it, the familiarity settled over him like a shroud. 'Is there a word for the feeling of visiting a place from your childhood that you had completely forgotten? You would think it would be a good feeling, but it's not. It's not at all.'

He turned away from the portraits and kept walking. Slowly, the dust vanished from the floor, as did the old leaves, and the tattered tapestries regrew themselves. The windows became clean, crystal panels that sparkled, and each room he passed became grander and grander. The silk covering the walls was painted with silver and gold; elaborate mirrors with heavy jewelled frames met him at every turn; huge marble fireplaces polished to a gaudy shine promised roaring fires. Eventually, he emerged into a larger chamber, and he laughed, both confused and delighted.

'But this was never here,' he said aloud.

He stood in a vast throne room of creamy yellow marble, with tall windows that stretched from the floor to the balcony that edged its way around the entire room, and from the ceiling hung huge banners of black and yellow silk, each with the symbol of a green bird in the centre. When they had imagined it as children, the throne room had been thronged with lords and ladies, their clothes and hair glittering with fabulous jewels, their faces bright with droll amusement, but in this dream, the court was empty and silent. At the far end of the chamber was a throne, a tall, elegant thing carved of white wood, and in front of it, a long velvet cushion, where supplicants could kneel in relative comfort.

Tor walked over to one of the windows. Instead of an Eboran garden, with its lush manicured grass and carefully placed rocks, he saw an exotic tableau of fountains and fruit trees, complete with strange, sleek animals – a well-fed bird strutted back and forth across gravel of all colours, presenting a huge fan of a tail that was speckled with iridescent greens and reds, and a small spotted cat sat on top of a glazed clay urn, a jewelled collar around its neck. Tor found that he was laughing.

'You remember it?'

The voice behind him was cool and soft, and he found he wasn't at all surprised to hear it. Who else could have made such a dream?

'I do, but obviously not as well as you do.' He turned around. The throne room was still empty. 'Where are you?'

'I was your queen, and you were my bravest champion,' the voice continued. Tor found he couldn't tell where it was coming from. 'I would think of quests for you to do, and you would journey across all of Sarn to perform them. Bring me the head of the Wailing Wyrm of Triskenteth. Fetch the lost silver crown from the ice caves of Targ. I wished to bathe in the enchanted waters of Orlé, so you would bring me a cart, filled with caskets of the purest spring water.'

'You certainly did enjoy telling me what to do, that's true.' Tor looked back to the throne. In their abandoned mansion she had used a chair, one carved with flowers all over. She had been small enough then for it to have looked like a throne when she sat in it. 'And I would run off around this place with my wooden sword, looking for things to present to you. Each room became a new kingdom, a new country to battle my way through. The corridors were packed with ghosts and monsters, all of which I bravely fought, in your name. The silver crown of Targ I made from the kingswort growing all over the garden, and I got the water of Orlé from the bird bath.'

'Yes. It had leaves in it.'

Tor grinned despite himself. 'What was the head of the Wailing Wyrm of Triskenteth? I forget.'

'You brought me a frog. Alive. You hid it up your sleeve until you could throw it at my dress.'

'That's right.' His smile faded, and the darkness of their present stole away the brightness of such memories. 'Why have you brought me here? And why are you hiding from me?'

Slowly, the shadows in the far corner of the throne room resolved themselves into the shape of a tall, slender woman. Her hair in the dull light looked silver.

'I don't have much time,' said Hestillion. 'You have to listen to me.'

Cautiously, Tor walked across the throne room, his footfalls echoing up to the rafters. As he got closer, Hestillion seemed to grow dimmer. She was wearing a simple grey robe, unadorned with any jewellery or embroidery, and something about that caused his stomach to grow tight.

'I will listen, if you show yourself, sister.'

With obvious reluctance, Hestillion stepped into the light. She was thinner than when he had last seen her, her cheeks hollowed, yet her frame spoke of wiry muscle and strength. Her eyes were bright drops of crimson, and the shard of blue crystal at her throat winked and shimmered, yet it was her skin that he could not look away from. Tendrils of greenish black were scratched across it, a fine web of corruption that covered her face, her hands, her neck.

'I can't change it,' she said, peering down in wonder at her own hands. 'Usually I can make myself look however I wish in a dream, but this – it's inside me, through and through.'

'Hestillion . . .'

'Listen, the queen is coming for you. She is coming for Ebora, and she will not be stopped now. She intends to tear Ygseril up by the roots, and kill everything that lives.' She took his hand; her fingers were dry and hot. 'If you ever loved me, brother, leave now. Don't wait. Leave Ebora and don't look back.'

'The queen is alive?'

She shook her head, annoyed. She had always been frustrated by how slow he could be; how he focussed on details instead of the meat. 'Of course she is. Do you think burning down our hiding place would kill her? All you have done is remove her every reason for being cautious! All you have done is make her feel anger for the first time.'

He pulled his hand away. 'Do you expect me to be sorry for that, Hest? The Jure'lia have been destroying Sarn for generations. They've murdered us in the tens of thousands, and I'm supposed to regret that we finally caused them real damage?'

'As usual, you are missing the point. How can you damage them, truly? You have ended their future, yes, but what difference does that make if she kills you all anyway? While any part of the Jure'lia survives – even the smallest, crawling beetle – the queen lives still. I have seen it myself, with my own eyes. She is all of them, *and they are all her.*'

Tor blinked. It had always been an impossible hope, that they might defeat the worm people, as depleted and broken as they were, but with Hestillion's words the true magnitude of the task sent ice water through his veins.

'Are you listening? Go, you must go now. She is coming.'

The light had changed. Above them, the ceiling with its black and yellow banners had gone, and instead they were looking up into a troubled, cloudy sky. A fine snow was falling, yet when it landed on Tor's robe, he saw that it was not snow after all, but ash.

'Why are you warning me, Hest? You've spent the last year trying to kill us. You *did* kill one of us. Not to mention leading their worm-eaten ships into battle, destroying Jarlsbad. Or did you think I had forgotten that? You have no love for Ebora. You only want to see us all dead.'

491

She stared at him. Her face, with its shadowed eyes and dark veins, was mask-like.

'Idiot,' she hissed. 'I don't care about them. None of them, I never cared about anything but . . .'

There was a roaring noise from outside, loud enough to shake the glass in the windows. A moment later, the sky was alive with fleeing birds – thousands of them, in all shapes and sizes, all of them various shades of green. Tor looked up, briefly lost in the wonder of it.

'You really were the greatest dream-walker Ebora ever saw,' he said softly. 'In another, better world, that would have been your calling, sister.'

She grabbed his arm and hissed in his ear. 'And you, brother, were ever its greatest fool!'

Tor woke up with a start, his chest too tight to gasp down a breath. Vintage, who had been slumped in a chair near his bed, gave a sharp cry.

'What is it, darling?'

For a handful of seconds that felt agonisingly like hours, Tor struggled to breathe. When finally the iron rings around his chest eased, he grabbed her hand and squeezed it.

'We have to get ready, Vin. The queen is coming. She's coming for Ebora.'

Chapter Forty-eight

They flew out at the first hint of sunrise, heading south across the city towards the Bloodless Mountains. It had been a cold night and a chilly morning, and Noon noted that they did not speak to each other; each war-beast and each rider were taken up with their own thoughts, intent on their destination. When they reached the southernmost foothills, Vintage called to them all to land, and they came to rest near one of the roads that led into Ebora, close to one of the old broken-down watchtowers. The pigeons that were roosting in it rose in a sudden cloud as they landed. From this spot it was possible to see across the plains for a good distance, and if the light was good, you could even see the faint glimmer, far to the west, of Greenslick, and to the east, the beginnings of the Yuron-Kai territories. They climbed down from their harnesses, and they stood and looked. For a long time, no one said anything.

'They are not here just yet, then,' said Aldasair quietly. 'That's something.'

'I'll take any time we can get,' said Bern. He scratched at the foreshortened end of his right arm. 'When they come, it will be quick.'

Noon noticed that none of them questioned whether Tor's dream had been real or not. Tor himself, who had insisted that his 'rest period' was over, stood next to Kirune, dressed in a heavy black cloak, his face set and serious. Noon was sure she had seen new lines in it since he had dreamed of his sister.

'This is the queen's final assault,' said Vintage. She was standing with her hands on her hips, glaring out across the plains as though they had insulted her personally. 'She will bring everything she has in the effort to destroy us, I think we can rely on that. So. What's our plan? Vostok?'

The dragon lifted her head. Caught in the gaudy rays of the sun, she looked unreal, ethereal almost, her violet eyes full of soft fire.

'If she brings all she has, then so must we.' She looked around at them all. 'I feel it, brothers and sisters. This may be our final battle.'

'We will destroy them!' boomed Sharrik. He pawed at the ground, tearing up clods of grass and earth. 'This is what we were made for.'

'Yes,' agreed Vostok, with feeling. 'We were made to be weapons in this great war, the Ninth Rain. But also, we must use everything that is available to us. We must learn to fight with new allies. This is something I have come to realise.'

'Helcate,' said Helcate.

'I agree,' said Vintage firmly. 'And we do have some. The fell-witches will be a formidable force against the Jure'lia. And the Yuron-Kai, the Finneral, the Reidn troops. The peoples who live in Ebora now, who have kept its lifeblood flowing, despite everything. It's not going to be easy . . .' Vintage pushed at her hair, forcing it out of her eyes and pinning it back. 'It's not going to be easy because we must fight the worm people *and* defend Ygseril, because if the tree-god is destroyed, the war-beasts will fall. We are weaker if we split ourselves, yet I can't see how we can avoid it.'

'Unless we let the worm people come to Ebora,' said Bern quietly. 'Let them walk right in the front gates, and defeat them at our own hearth.'

'My darling, that is a big risk.' Vintage patted her hair some more, shaking her head.

'It's all or nothing,' he admitted. 'But that's what we're facing here, isn't it?'

'I sent messages to the Yuron-Kai and the Finneral before we left the palace,' said Aldasair, 'and I briefly spoke to the Reidn commander. She is waiting on more details, of course, but she has said she will bring every warm body she can.'

Noon sat down on the grass and brought her knees up to her chin. She could feel the joint tension of all of them, thrumming under her skin – the connection they shared was alight with the need to figure this out, to find a way to survive. It was frightening. Tor had told them the details of his dream, had repeated word for word what his sister had told him, and it was clear from the attack on Jarlsbad alone that they were all in enormous danger. Yes, it was frightening. But the sense that they were all striving after the same thing, the feeling that they were pointed in the same direction . . . that was a comfort. It was a sense of *rightness*. She wondered if that was how it was always supposed to feel, this connection between war-beasts and companions. Idly, she rested her hand on the grass. It was damp with dew, and the bright green life of it pressed eagerly against her fingers.

She looked at the grass, and she remembered.

For a little while she let them talk, listening to the warm sounds of their voices – beloved voices – because she knew that when she did speak, she wouldn't be able to take the words back again. Vintage was suggesting that in order to protect both the tree-god and the people who had taken shelter there, they should keep their ground troops, such as they were, stationed throughout the streets of the Eboran city. *All of those people could die*, Noon thought. *We could all die. But I could stop them.*

What is it, bright weapon?

I've got an idea.

'I've got an idea,' Noon said aloud. When they all turned to look at her, she smiled. 'But I need to show you something first. You, uh, you might want to stand back. Just in case.'

She leaned forward and buried both her hands in the short, wet grass. Carefully, very carefully, she recalled the sensation of connectivity that had fallen over her when she was a child – the realisation that so many things were joined in ways that were invisible. First of all, she took the life energy of the grass under her fingers – easy enough – and then she let herself move to the blades of grass that were next to it, and then through the earth itself. She heard a slight gasp from Vintage as the grass turned brown not in a close circle around her hands, but in a jagged series of lines that branched out from her like forks of lightning.

'Darling, what are you –?'

Noon shook her head tersely. The idea that she might lose control, that she might kill this new family as she had killed her own, was too close. Instead, she concentrated on the connections that were opening up to her as she travelled along the tiny green lives under their feet. A thick bush of wild roses crumpled and turned black, the petals falling from its blooms in a sudden miniature snow flurry, and inside the tower, unseen, a number of spiders and rats fainted away. She followed them up and up, each portion of life energy neatly siphoned away inside her, until she found the pigeons' nests in the roof. One, two fell, the rest leaping up into the air in surprise, and she couldn't help following them, until they too dropped from the sky, landing on the grass with soft thuds.

Stop it, she told herself. *Stop it. That's enough.*

She threw her arms up, and winnowfire leapt up from her

hands, a wild gulf of flame which briefly gave the hill its own little corona of mid-afternoon daylight. And then it was gone.

'Sarn's bloody *arse*,' said Vintage faintly. 'What was that?'

Noon took a deep breath and stood up, trying to ignore how shaky her legs were. Over by the tower, a couple of the unconscious pigeons were starting to flutter their wings.

'It's what She Who Laughs made me remember,' she said. 'A new, deeper way of using what I am. When I was a child, I killed everyone I knew.' She looked around at them briefly, still expecting to see disgust in their eyes. 'You all know that by now. But I didn't tell you how, because I didn't know. It was this.' She gestured to the brown grass and the pigeons. 'I realised that all living things are connected, in lots of different ways, and that through the winnowfire touch I can take their life energy.'

'You can take life energy without actually touching the living thing?' asked Aldasair.

She nodded. 'Essentially, yeah. The grass lives through the earth, so through that I can get to any blade of grass, do you see? Beetles that burrow in the earth make their nests in the tower, share the same air as spiders, who get eaten by pigeons, pigeons who hatched from eggs in the same nest . . . Do you see?'

'I'm not sure that I do,' said Bern.

'I do, a little.' Vintage rubbed her finger across her chin. 'At least I think I do. You can drain the life energy from multiple subjects very quickly. That must lead to an enormous build-up of winnowfire.'

'It does.' Noon shrugged. 'I lost control of it, when I was a child. Those I didn't kill when I took their life energy, I burned to death.'

'Noon,' Tor had been quiet so far, his face troubled, 'you mean to use this, don't you? Against the Jure'lia?'

'It is too much,' said Vostok immediately. 'Too much to ask of her. You,' she swung her head around to address the rest of the group, 'you do not understand.'

'But it's the only way, don't you see?' Two of the pigeons had flown off, somewhat erratically. Three of them still lay on the ground, unmoving. Noon thought it very likely that they were dead. 'Hestillion told us that as long as any part of the worm people still lives, then they *all* still live. What else do we know about them? That they are deeply connected.' She looked to Bern, who nodded reluctantly.

'I've felt it,' he said. 'Stones save me, it nearly drove me mad. It's a great web, with that hag at the centre of it.'

'And the memory crystals,' said Vintage. 'Don't forget those.'

'Yes.' Noon nodded hurriedly. 'And I think they are the key. I need to get to a crystal and rip into their connection from there. The queen told Bern and Aldasair that the crystal held them all together, and when I touched Bern's crystal I could feel that it was a living part of them, in a way. We've got to be sure to get all of them, and I think that's how we do it. Every last scuttling bastard one of them.'

'And what?' demanded Tor. 'Drain the life energy of an entire alien army? Enough that you kill them all? What happens to you then?'

'I'll be fine,' she said. 'When I did this on the plains, I was completely unharmed. What will happen is an enormous explosion, so I need to be far away from Ebora, or anyone else who wants to live through it.'

A silence grew between them as they took it all in. Noon could feel Vostok's objections bubbling under the surface, and could see the scepticism in Tor's face, but she stood and waited for them to think about it. While they had been talking the sun had risen, filling the plains beyond with acres of golden light. *It's funny*, she thought. *It looks so much more beautiful from a distance.*

'I can almost see it,' said Vintage eventually. 'But the logistics . . . Noon, we know that fell-witches are not harmed by their own fire, but an explosion that big . . . And if you're going after a crystal, you'll have to be inside a Behemoth when you do this trick of yours. Even if you live through the explosion, what about the fall?'

'I will catch her,' said Vostok softly. Noon caught the dragon's eye. 'I am faster than anything else in the sky, and I've done it before, when she reappeared after she vanished.'

'I'm not saying it won't be dangerous. It's going to be dangerous for all of us,' said Noon. 'But think about it. I can take their lives from them, I know I can. And if I do, if we can wipe the worm people from Sarn forever, then maybe all the misery and pain my winnowfire has caused will mean something after all.'

Vintage sighed noisily and shook her head. 'Fuck my old boots, it's a terrible plan, but what else do we have?'

'Wait.' Tor held up his hand, still frowning. 'I will only agree to this if we're certain that Noon will be unharmed. We do not send one of our own off to die – that's not how this works. It's not who we are.'

'I promise,' Noon said, looking him in the eyes. 'I *can* do this. I won't die. You have to trust me.'

Tor glanced at Vintage, who shrugged. Nearby, a few of the surviving pigeons called to each other softly.

'Very well. Let's get this shit show on the road.'

Later, Chenlo and Vintage put the word around for the fell-witches who were still in Ebora to attend a meeting in the Hall of Roots. Vintage's reasoning had been that the sight of the tree-god might inspire them, or that at least they might feel they were receiving special treatment – generally the doors to the Hall of Roots had remained locked and off-limits. As Noon stood against the wall and watched them come in, she thought the fell-witches looked more unnerved than impressed; their eyes danced often to the huge twisted roots, or up to the glass ceiling where the branches presented their remaining leaves to the sun. And when Vintage, in her loud, confident way, began explaining the situation and their tenuous plan to deal with it, Noon saw many of the women look at each other with obvious fright.

'We can end this now, my darlings, I promise you that.' Vintage looked around at them all, her usually cheery face pinched with worry. 'For the first time, fell-witches will fight alongside Ebora as a truly integrated part of our forces, and this is how we will end the worm people. By working together.' They had, under Noon's advice, not told the fell-witches about her plan to destroy the Jure'lia via her own strange understanding of the winnowfire. She was worried one of them might try it for themselves, and that could be disastrous. 'We need you.'

'Those of you who know me, know that I will not lie to you,' added Agent Chenlo. She stood next to Vintage with her arms behind her back. 'This is dangerous. But our lives are dangerous. They always have been. I tell you it is possible we could do this, and destroy the worm people.'

The women were murmuring amongst themselves. As Noon watched, a few of them moved towards the doors and left. Vintage frowned. Chenlo did not move.

'We already helped you.' A woman moved forward out of the small crowd. Noon recognised her as one of the fell-witches who had been at the Jure'lia cavern. She had not been an agent of the Winnowry – just one of the many women kept prisoner there for much of her life. 'And we nearly bloody died. I like you, Chenlo, you know I always have, but –' She shook her head. 'I've not had a good night's sleep since we went to that cursed place. Every night, nightmares about fire and smoke and *things*, reaching for me . . . I see poor Fell-O'val falling into that boiling mess every time I close my eyes, and that would have been the end for all of us if the Lady Noon hadn't saved us.'

Noon flinched and looked carefully at her boots. She could feel many in the crowd turning to her, expecting her to speak. She kept quiet. *Why did I come here?*

'My heart broke for Fell O'val,' said Vintage. 'She did an incredibly brave thing, and with her help, we have hurt the worm people in a way I didn't even believe was possible. But that was only part of the job. Sarn's bloody bones, I wish that weren't the case, I really do, but if we don't stand up to the worm people here, this is the end for all of us.'

'It's the Eborans' job.' This was another woman, still wearing the greens and greys of the agent colours. 'Let them do it. Let them risk their lives. Haven't we suffered enough?' She gestured around to the crowd, and Noon saw several women nodding their heads. 'We've been abused, and hurt, and we deserve a rest. We're not immortal, we don't fly mythical beasts or have the protection of a magical tree-god. We're not strong enough for this. Leave us be.'

'As ever, you refuse to see the bigger picture, Fell-Dana,' said Chenlo, tersely. 'It is all very well saying, it is not our responsibility, but if the Jure'lia destroy the tree-god,' she pointed at the huge presence behind her, 'then you will all die anyway.'

There were more angry mutters at this. Another woman, who looked close to tears, spoke up from the back.

'We're free now,' she said. 'Can't you let us be? Free to have our own lives, to find homes, have children . . .'

'And how will your children live?' said Vintage. 'Terrified, forever hiding, forever running, until they're caught by the varnish, or hollowed out by burrowers?' She paused and touched her fingers to her forehead, and when she spoke again, the sadness in her voice made Noon's heart ache. 'I wish that I did not have to ask this of you, I truly do.'

'You ask too much,' said Fell-Dana flatly. 'That's all there is to it.'

Without really thinking about what she was doing, Noon walked to the back of the hall, and climbed up onto the roots. They felt strange and slick under her hands, cold and hard. It was difficult to believe that they belonged to a living thing, but the life energy of Ygseril was there nonetheless, a slow and vast presence. She stood up, and looked out across the women.

'Listen!' The murmuring fell silent, and the fell-witches turned to look at her. She saw Vintage's eyebrows shoot up, and even Chenlo looked surprised. 'Listen to me. No one can tell you what to do now. That's the truth. The time when you were controlled by other people is over. When I smashed the Winnowry to pieces and threw open its doors, that's what I wanted for you. Freedom.' She paused, and a strange feeling of weightlessness passed through her. Moments ago the idea of talking to any of these women, let alone addressing them all at once, would have been horrifying, but suddenly it seemed like the only right thing she had *ever* done. 'So we can't tell you to do this. We can't order you to help us. But I do want to tell you something, and if you care for me at all, if you think I've ever helped you, then I will ask you to please believe what I say. That's all. Because it's true.'

The fell-witches were all watching her. Every head, etched with the sign of the bat wing.

'Some of you know that I was missing for a while. It's not easy to explain where I was, but I can tell you that I met the being that is responsible for us – for the winnowfire.' There were some incredulous mutters at this, and then with a start Noon realised that Tyranny had edged into the room. She looked pale and thin, but her blue eyes were like chips of ice. 'This being came to Sarn a long time ago, at the same time as Ygseril.' Noon held her arms out, taking in the enormous trunk

502

that rose behind her. 'She is energy, she is fire, she is . . . impossible to explain, or describe. She is not a good person. In her own way, she is probably as bad as the worm people, but it's her who gave the flame to us. So that's the first thing I have to tell you, that you have to believe – our winnowfire shares a history with Ebora. You think all this has nothing to do with us?' She smiled. 'That's not true, I'm afraid.'

The fell-witches looked confused, and Noon felt a surge of fear, but she pushed it down.

'The other thing I need you to believe is what this being told me. She said that she had given this gift – gift is what she called it, if you can believe that – *only to the strongest people of Sarn*. Only the strongest, she said, could possibly keep it inside themselves, could live with the green fire in their guts. Only the strongest.' Abruptly, she found that she was grinning. 'And it's fucking true, isn't it? I'm standing here, and I can see it when I look at you. We've survived, we're still here, and *we are the strongest*. All of the terrible things the Winnowry did to us, all of the terrible things that people have said and done, all the people who have hated us because of what we are . . . and we live, still. The power is still ours. The flame never died. We are the strongest, and I think you know it too, deep down inside.'

The women were entirely silent. Noon found that she couldn't read their faces, but she could see that there were tears on Vintage's cheeks. That was all right. She knew then that this had been the right thing to do.

'I'm not going to tell you this thing is a gift, that you should be grateful your lives have been so hard, because that's nonsense. The worst kind of nonsense. But I am telling you that it's something we can bloody *use*. So fight with me,' she said. 'We'll be unstoppable. I know you've grown up believing that Eborans are the only true heroes of Sarn, that they are the only ones who can fight, but that's not true. It's us. It's our time to fight. So fight with me.'

'I'll fight with you!' It was Tyranny, from by the doors. She came forward, and her eyes were shining. 'The worm people will wish they'd never been born.'

'It would be my honour,' added Chenlo, 'to fight alongside my sisters.'

All at once, an excited babble grew from the crowd of fell-witches. Noon saw them turning to each other, taking each other's hands. Not all of them looked convinced, she could see that easily enough, but she could see them daring to think of themselves in new way. Noon climbed down from the roots and headed back towards the doors, no longer avoiding their eyes or their questioning glances. Vintage met her halfway there, and threw her arms around her.

Chapter Forty-nine

'That was certainly something.'

Chenlo looked up from the piece of parchment she had been reading and nodded thoughtfully. She and Vintage had been in the study for the last hour or so, talking to each fell-witch who wanted to join the fight, making a note of their name, and trying to figure out how to divide up the supplies they had amongst them: the bats, the armour, the remaining vials of heartbright. More of the women had signed up than Vintage could have hoped for, and it looked like they had the makings of a small squad of dedicated witches.

'Did you know she was going to do that?' asked Chenlo.

'Not at all.' Vintage poured a small measure of brown liquid into a pair of glasses – it was a Yuron-Kai drink called *barakesh*, and she'd bought some from the Yuron-Kai contingent. It tasted to her tongue like something used to clean flagstones, but when Chenlo sipped at it she seemed to savour it. 'As I'm sure you've noticed, she's done her absolute best to avoid talking to or even thinking about the fell-witches – I think it reminded her too keenly of her old life – so I was surprised to even see her in the hall this evening. But these last few months have been strange ones for Noon, and she has changed. I suppose we all have.' She sat down in the chair next to Chenlo with a sigh. 'This bloody poisoned world, it's always changing us.'

'She's their leader,' said Chenlo quietly. 'I thought that perhaps . . . but when they look at me, they will always see one who stood on the outside of their cells. The Lady Noon gave them their freedom, and now she has stepped up to that responsibility.'

'The fell-witches were lucky to have you. I didn't see that at first, because, well, the Winnowry . . .' Vintage waved her hands around vaguely. 'The Winnowry is deeply evil and dangerous. But there are roses growing in the most Wild-touched places.'

Chenlo nodded and looked away, but not before Vintage noticed a flush of colour on her cheeks. The Winnowry agent picked up the sheet of parchment, full of her neat handwriting and Vintage's more elaborate scrawl.

'At first light I will go to the quartermaster and look at how good our harnesses are,' she said, suddenly business-like again. 'There's good Finneral leather available, so we can make more, if we're quick.'

'Yes.' Vintage took the piece of parchment, looking at the names etched there in black ink. Although she had been overjoyed to see so many women at their door, the sight of their names seemed to place a terrible cold weight in her stomach. She couldn't help thinking of Esiah Godwort, lost inside his own compound as it burned to the ground; of little Eri, who would never have come to Ebora in the first place if she hadn't insisted he accompany her; of misguided, cowardly Nanthema, destroyed by the Jure'lia at Jarlsbad. She even thought of Tor, the disease that had killed most of his people now marching hurriedly through his veins. She felt responsible for all of them. How many people would still be alive without her interfering? And how many names on this list would not live to see another summer?

506

'What is it?' Chenlo was looking at her with obvious concern. She took Vintage's free hand and squeezed it.

'Oh. These brave people.' She forced herself to smile and meet Chenlo's eyes. 'We're asking them to risk death. And many of them may well die. What right do I have?'

'You have the right because you will be there with them,' said Chenlo steadily. 'And because I will be there too. We will face the worm people together.' She took a deep breath. 'I will be glad to stand with you, Vintage.'

She leaned forward and brushed her lips against Vintage's cheek, and then rested her forehead against hers. The kiss that came after that seemed as natural as breathing, and quickly Vintage was lost in the scent and the taste of her – the *barakesh* that had been so brash on her tongue now tasted powerful and intoxicating, and when she pushed her fingers through Chenlo's hair it ran through her fingers like silk, river-quick.

'I've had a solitary life,' Chenlo said. 'I'm so tired of it, Vintage. So tired of very carefully feeling nothing.'

'That's no life at all.' Vintage swallowed hard, abruptly nervous. 'Let me show you.'

She kissed her mouth, her throat, the place where the eagle seared her skin. Eventually, they left the study, and, holding hands and laughing together like teenagers, they meandered down the empty corridors, pausing to kiss here and there until they came to Chenlo's room. Inside it was lit with a single lamp, casting a golden light on a bed tidily made up with white and red sheets. The crimson shirt Vintage had bought her was carefully hung over a screen.

'Darling, are you sure . . . ?'

'Please,' Chenlo murmured. 'Show me.'

Vintage showed her, with her lips and her tongue and her clever fingers. She felt dizzy herself, her own desire beating like a newly born heart – the golden tones of Chenlo's skin, the delicious feeling of bare limb against bare limb, the delicate

507

lines at the corners of Chenlo's eyes, creased with pleasure. When she came, she shuddered in her arms, crying out in wonder, and Vintage held her close, wondering if this was it now; if Chenlo would retreat from her again, deciding that she had made terrible mistake. But Chenlo pulled her closer, pulling at her last pieces of clothing.

'Now show me again,' she said, 'so I can show you.'

Tor, from his lonely spot in the courtyard, saw them pass. They were a brief picture of happiness caught through the glass windows, both looking much younger than their years. When they were gone again, he made to get up, thinking that he should go inside and try and get some rest, but the pain in his arms and chest forced him back into his seat. A shadow on the far side of the courtyard caught his eye, and he grimaced.

'I can see you there,' he said. 'Don't you know that Eborans can see very well in the dark?'

A hooded figure eased its way out of the gloom.

'Old habits, forgive me,' said Okaar. 'I wanted somewhere quiet. To be alone, for a time.'

Tor gave a little snort of laughter. 'Ah well, you're a few years too late. A little while ago, you couldn't move for lonely places in the palace. Now, it's as lively as –' He shrugged. 'Actually, I don't remember it ever being this lively. Even when I was a child, our world was fading.'

Okaar pulled back his hood and nodded. The human man looked gaunt, the shadows under his eyes almost as vivid as the scars on his face and throat, and Tor couldn't help noticing that his fingers trembled slightly against the dark material of the robe. He remained standing, as though he wasn't sure what to do with himself.

'Will you not sit with me?' said Tor. He was forcibly reminded of leaving Ebora, decades ago, and coming across the old human man sleeping in the tower. What had he asked him?

Will you not drink with me? And the man had called him a monster. 'Vintage seems to trust you, despite everything, and I'm not sure I have the energy to be suspicious this evening.'

Okaar did not move or speak for a long time. He seemed to be caught in the threads of an invisible web. Eventually, he shook his head, slowly, back and forth.

'I do not feel that I can sit, or sleep, or rest. I don't know what has happened to my sister. I feel that until I have figured that out, there can be no rest for me.'

'The girl Jhef? Vintage mentioned her.'

Okaar nodded. 'It seems very likely that she has died. Crushed deep inside the palace as it fell, or eaten alive by the Jure'lia. I'm not sure what would be worse. I'm not –' He stopped, his voice briefly too strangled to continue. 'The last time I saw Jhef, we argued. There were terrible words exchanged. It was not her fault. She grew up following Tyranny, living a life where we took what we wanted, when we wanted it. A thief's life. Jhef couldn't understand why I would not stand with Tyranny in that palace. Why I could not pretend that she was a queen.' He sighed shakily. 'Ah. The not knowing. It is impossible to bear. Part of me believes that if I think about it hard enough, I can figure out a way to find her, save her. Yet I go –' he lifted a finger and whirled it through the air next to his head – 'around in circles. There is no saving her. There is no figuring it out. I will be caught forever, wondering what happened, what were her last moments like, was she scared, did she suffer. I –' Tor heard the thick click in his throat as the words were swallowed by grief.

'Maybe you're better off not knowing.' The man looked up at that, a flash of something in his eyes, and Tor shook his head, too tired to argue. 'I know very well what my sister is doing, and it certainly doesn't bring me any peace. She flies with the Jure'lia, wears their skin on her skin, and she kills humans like they were stains to be wiped away.' He looked down at his hands. 'When we were children, we were close. Very different from each other, certainly that – Hestillion was always clever, thoughtful, methodical. She figured out what she wanted and then she constructed elaborate plans to get it, usually using me, since I was easily talked into helping her. I was flighty, difficult to pin down, full of my own self-importance, and our parents despaired of me, yet when our world fell to pieces –' he looked up at Okaar, who was still standing in a shard of moonlight – 'she was like you. When everyone began to die, when Ygseril was a cold and remote chunk of wood, she spent her time trying to figure out how to fix it. She wanted, somehow, to bring everyone back, but there is no turning back time. You know, I think that's what turned her into what she is now. Not the dying, the pain, the slow ending of everything – but the fact that she couldn't *fix* it. In her dreams, she could craft anything. But when she woke up, the world was still a rotten husk.'

'Do you ever think about saving her?'

A slither of pain like a blade moved across Tor's heart, although he couldn't have said if it was the crimson flux or not at that moment. Ignoring the renewed agony in his arms, he pushed himself to his feet again.

'Vintage is the one who loves a lost cause, not me,' he said. He walked to the courtyard gates, trying not to think of the expression he had seen on Okaar's face as he left.

The horde moved, and the circle followed.

If Hestillion wanted to, it was possible to see the trail of destruction they were leaving from multiple angles – through the eyes of the First, or Green Bird or Red Moth, each on board one of the remaining Behemoths. Or she could see what Grey Root and Yellow Leaf saw, travelling as they did with the huge amorphous shape that was the Jure'lia queen herself. Mostly, though, she preferred not to; she could see enough from Celaphon's back, riding high in the cold air far above. They had been heading steadily north for some time, crushing, destroying and suffocating anything in their path. If she looked behind them she could see a great long stretch of solid green. On this bright morning, the sky was pocked with chilly grey clouds.

'The sea,' said Celaphon. 'It's coming. What will happen then, do you think?'

Hestillion squinted against the wind and saw that he was right. A thin line of unsteady light on the horizon suggested a great stretch of water, and they were heading straight towards it. As yet, the queen had not turned aside for anything, and it was difficult to imagine her doing so now.

'Can she swim, do you think?' she said. 'Or fly, even?' The thought was alarming.

'She has no wings,' said Celaphon dismissively. 'And she would need very large wings.'

Hestillion pictured a map of the region. They were leaving the great southern continent of Sarn, so ahead of them should be the Lost Sea, whose hot blue waters were said to conceal all manner of Wild-touched monsters. Far to the east, the strip of land grew thin and then fat again, eventually becoming Catalen, a region of thick forests and warm, sunny days. If the queen kept up this trajectory, they would cross the sea to arrive just west of Catalen, possibly near Orlé or Triskenteth, where they could follow the River Tyg inland to the swamps. Further, along that coast, was Mushenska, one of Sarn's biggest and busiest cities. Hestillion had only ever seen it from a distance, but the thought of it – crawling with humans, all living too close together and giving off their stale, human scent – made her grimace.

'What will happen,' asked Celaphon, 'when we get to Ebora?'

'Bad things.' Aware that this was not the answer the dragon was after, she sighed and pushed a strand of blond hair out of her eyes. Her armoured suit was safely stored onboard one of the three remaining Behemoths and she itched to put it on. 'You know what she wants. She wants to wipe it from the map, she wants to suffocate it in varnish, leave nothing there alive.'

'My home,' said Celaphon. 'I've not even seen it, not properly.'

'It's not your home,' snapped Hestillion. 'You were born on the corpse moon, and nourished there. It's not even my home. Not anymore.'

'Then you do not care?' There was a tone to Celaphon's voice she had not heard before; a certain craftiness, like that of a child who thinks they have the key to getting their own way.

'It's a little late for that, do you not think?' The Eboran child lying with its guts in the dirt; her brother, holding his sword to her throat.

'If our queen destroys the tree-father, then I will die too.'

Hestillion narrowed her eyes. Below them, the land was growing drier, more familiar. She saw stretches of long grass dotted with islands of tall, spindly trees.

'How do you know that?'

'It is just a thing that I know,' said Celaphon. 'Or you told me once. I do not remember.'

'She might not destroy Ygseril. She may keep him prisoner, as he kept her prisoner for so many centuries. A final humiliation.' Even as she said it, she knew it was unlikely. And the truth was, she did not know how she would feel if the tree-father was finally destroyed. The thought was just too big to comprehend. Perhaps, part of her reasoned, it would just be a relief. Celaphon was not convinced.

'The tree-god keeps his own prison,' he said, a shade enigmatically, then, 'she'll kill everything there, you know that. How do you even know that *you* will live when the tree-father is gone?'

Hestillion did not answer. Since the incident in the caverns, when Celaphon had spent time unsupervised with the human man Bern, he had seemed more likely to question her, to challenge her words. It was extremely annoying. Instead, she urged him forward until they flew just above the enormous shifting mass that was the queen. She moved over the land like a plague, eating up the grasslands and leaving nothing but death.

'My queen!' Hestillion urged Celaphon lower still, so that they hovered over a simmering mass of black Jure'lia fluid. Shapes and debris moved there; she saw faces in the muck, limbs that reached desperately, sticks and leaves and stones. 'May I speak with you?'

The fluid boiled with movement, and many of the shapes and pieces of rubbish moved together, becoming a mouth and an eye. Hestillion fought down the urge to look away. She missed the white shape of the queen's mask.

'Lady Hestillion Eskt of the corpse moon, born in the year of the green bird. Born again in the year of the Ninth Rain.' The queen's voice was a buzz; it was a thousand voices. 'Our warrior queen. What do you want?'

'To give some advice.' Hestillion nodded to the line of sea ahead of them, which was growing clearer and brighter all the time. 'When we cross the Lost Sea, you may wish to think about turning west, towards the island of Corineth. A great human city lies there, called Mushenska.'

There was a long silence, filled with the wind and the hissing, babbling sound of the Jure'lia on the move.

'Why would we wish to do that?' said the queen eventually.

Hestillion bit down her impatience. 'Remember what I told you before? That to take control of Sarn, you must destroy its infrastructure. Take its allies apart piece by piece, until Ebora has no help at all.' She leaned forward in Celaphon's harness. It was cold so high up, but she was warmed by the thought of her victories. 'I have destroyed so many cities! I have even

513

reduced the kingdoms of Jarlsbad to rubble, and Mushenska is said to be even greater – a place of trade and industry, Sarn's most modern city. To destroy it would be a devastating blow. You need only turn to the west.'

The features of the face, such as they were, twisted and flexed.

'Ebora must be destroyed,' said the queen in her rasping voice. 'There is no other path, Hestillion of the corpse moon.'

'But –'

Black fluid boiled again, and the debris flowed away. The face was gone.

Hestillion urged Celaphon back up into the sky, and for the rest of the day they watched in silence as the queen surged towards the sea. When finally they got to the coast, the light had seeped from the day, leaving a purple night scattered with stars that seemed too close, too interested. The queen did not stop, but flowed directly into the crashing surf, sending up waves that flooded the beach and the grasslands beyond. She shifted as she went, sending up a series of long pole-like fingers above the water while the rest moved below. Several of them, Hestillion noted, sported pale glistening orbs that turned wetly and watched the sea, while other protrusions slid ahead like snakes, feeling their way across the vast ocean. Even for Hestillion, who had largely grown accustomed to the grotesque forms of the Jure'lia, it was a nightmare image – a lively poison seeping out into the water, a thing of serpents and eyes and teeth.

She and Celaphon flew on, their eyes already looking for land.

Chapter Fifty

Bern was certainly right about one thing; when they arrived, they came on fast.

Their first warning was the panicked shout of one of the fell-witches who had been dispatched to the southern regions of Ebora to keep watch. Vintage was with Aldasair, who was supervising the distribution of the modified Eboran armour to Finneral and Yuron-Kai soldiers. The bat nearly fell out of the sky onto the palace lawn, and the woman jumped out of her harness and ran.

'It's them! It's – the fucking worm people are here! Are you listening?'

Vintage went to her and took her firmly by the shoulders.

'Where? How long ago?'

'I came straight here. They're coming down through the foothills.' The woman had gone the colour of chalk, and for a moment she leaned too heavily on Vintage's arms, her eyelids flickering dangerously.

'Wake up,' Vintage gave her a sharp shake. 'Are you with me, darling? Good. Get to your unit. Tell them to get ready. Tell everyone.'

Helcate was a presence in her mind, and through him she could feel the others.

It's time. They're here.

She turned to Aldasair, who nodded brusquely. 'We're lucky we had even this long to prepare,' he said quietly. 'We'll do what we can. That's all we can do.'

Tor and Noon came sprinting across the grass with Kirune, while a dark shadow thrown over them announced Vostok's presence. From somewhere nearby someone was blowing a horn. The mournful notes floated out across the palace grounds, and Vintage suppressed a shiver.

'We all know what we're doing?' Noon was strapping on a short sword as she came. 'It's all clear?'

At that moment Bern arrived on Sharrik's back. The big griffin was already in his armour. Vintage had the idea he had been wearing it constantly, just in case.

'I'll be hanging back in the city,' said Aldasair. 'Jessen and I will be with the human armies, keeping the worm people from the palace as long as we can.'

'Our last ring of defence,' said Vintage. 'Let's hope you have a very peaceful afternoon, darling.'

'And the rest of us –' said Bern.

'The rest of us fly into battle!' bellowed Sharrik.

'We make sure Noon can get to where she needs to be,' said Tor smoothly. To Vintage's eye, he looked better than he had done in days. His crimson eyes were bright, and he had brushed his long black hair back into a tail, which was firmly bound with black silk. He wore a tight-fighting suit of leather armour in dusty reds and browns, something easy to move in, and there was a long, graceful sword strapped to his back.

'And then you all have to be as far away from me as possible,' said Noon. She looked around at them all, her eyes fierce, and Vintage wondered what had happened to the scared young woman she had found in the Shroom Flats. 'I mean it. I have no control over how big this explosion will be.'

516

'You all be sure to take care of yourselves though, aye?' said Bern. He looked worried, and Vintage couldn't blame him. Sharrik snorted, and Bern ruffled the big griffin's neck feathers. 'Tor, if you need help, you call for me. There's no shame in illness, in needing help. I want to see you all back here when we've finished smearing them into paste.'

Vintage wondered if Tor would be offended by Bern's obvious concern, but instead he nodded seriously. 'Thank you, brother.'

'There's no more time,' said Vostok sharply. 'We have to get moving. Now.'

'Wait!' Vintage held up her hand, despite the hiss of impatience it earned her from the dragon. She had the sudden terrible feeling that they would never again stand together as they did now, and she wanted a few more seconds to feel their closeness, their kinship. She threw her feelings towards the link that they shared, hoping that for once she would come through clearly.

Stay strong, my bravest, dearest friends. We fly as one.

She saw Noon and Tor smile, saw Aldasair nod. Bern bowed to her, still atop Sharrik, and Helcate pushed his snout into her shoulder.

'Yes,' said Vostok. 'We fly as one, Lady Vintage. You speak well.'

'Helcate,' said Helcate.

There were a few last scrambled moments as war-beasts were strapped into armour and weapons were fetched, and then they went, while Aldasair and Jessen ran back to join the human troops.

Vintage and Helcate flew up a few moments later, meeting Chenlo in mid-air. The Winnowry agent was on her own bat, her scarlet shirt a fiery note against the blue sky.

'What happens first?'

'First, my love, we go and have a bloody good look at what

we're facing. Bring half of the fell-witches, we may well need them.'

The nightmare swept down from the mountain's shadow, turning everything the colour of a bruise.

Noon pressed her hand against Vostok's scales for comfort even as she narrowed her eyes against the wind. It wasn't easy to look at this. They had faced a lot together, had nearly died, had seen friends die, and now this unstoppable doom was coming for them. And to make things worse, it had changed.

'Fuck my old boots,' shouted Vintage. 'What is that thing?'

'It is her,' called back Vostok. 'Or them. Or it. The being that is the Jure'lia, in all its parts.'

Noon just shook her head, uncertain what to add to that. The shape moving down through the outskirts of Ebora was huge, taller than Ygseril even, and its form seemed to change all the time; tendrils of blackish green flicked out in front of it as if tasting the air, while things like limbs came and went as it moved. Holes appeared in its oozing body, then filled up, and every now and then she thought she could make out a larger shape to it; a spine perhaps, a long, conical shaped head. Above it hung three intact Behemoths, like terrible obedient moons.

'Look below!' called Bern. Noon leaned out over Vostok's pearly wing and saw movement; hundreds of scurrying burrowers, making their busy way into the outer ruins of the Eboran city.

'Blood and fire.' She swallowed hard, her stomach turning over. From behind her she could hear a few of the fell-witches cry out in horror. 'All the people in the city, the soldiers . . .'

'They know how to fight,' said Vostok. And then in a quieter tone, 'It is what it is, bright weapon. All we can do is what we were made to do.'

'You're right.' Noon sat up in the harness and reached for the connection that held them all together.

Aldasair, there are burrowers in the city, perhaps worse. Be ready.

She felt his grim acknowledgement and imagined him informing the human soldiers. They wouldn't be taken by surprise at least.

'So,' she said aloud. 'Which one?'

'The one furthest to the back,' said Bern. 'It'll be the least distance to push.'

'Agreed.' Noon turned and waved to the fell-witches, who were clustered on their bats behind Chenlo. 'Ladies, take your heartbright and follow me! We're going to need your firepower.'

Vostok flew up and around, meaning to avoid the queen as much as possible, and that was the beginning of it. Noon waved at Vintage and Bern as they passed, taking a small moment to savour the sight of their faces – Vintage looked tense but excited, while Bern looked older somehow, like a grizzled veteran fighter – and then Tor joined her with Kirune, the big cat's powerful wings cutting through the air.

'Here we go!' he called.

'You should stay here,' she shouted back. 'Help Vintage and Bern distract the queen.'

He shook his head, and had the cheek to grin at her. 'I go where you go!' Noon gave up. They had had this conversation before, more than once, and at no point had Tor come even close to changing his mind. They flew up and around, edging closer to the monstrous queen. Noon pressed herself to Vostok's back, peering down over the dragon's shoulder. The ubiquitous ooze of the worm people that made up her shifting form looked oily and strange, catching other colours in its reflected light and polluting them.

They passed beyond the creature and shot up towards the Behemoth lingering at the back of the formation. It looked much the same as the other two, although there were some dents and scorch marks in its shining skin, and Noon took this to be a good sign; they had clearly met it in battle before.

'There!' she shouted to the fell-witches. 'Concentrate your fire on its front! Push it away!'

The fell-witches flew up on their bats, their arms held out in front of them. Tor and Kirune flew up and out of their way just as multiple streams of heartbright-fuelled winnowfire poured forth, crashing against the nose of the Behemoth with a spitting fury. Instantly Noon could see that they had done damage; panels of Behemoth skin were peeling back, blackening at the edges and bleeding a strange, clear fluid.

'That's it!' Noon leaned down over Vostok's neck. 'Let's help them, we don't have any time to waste.'

Violet and green fire joined the barrage, and soon the front of the ship was lost in a corona of light too bright to look at.

'It's moving back!' She glanced up to see Tor and Kirune circling above. 'You've got it on the run.'

'A little further,' said Vostok. 'We need to be closer to the mountain and further from the city, to be safe.'

Noon paused in her own stream to shout to Chenlo. 'Keep going a little longer, it's working!'

The fell-witches doubled their efforts and gradually Noon realised that they were moving. Below them, the scattered ruins of the edge of the city were becoming scrubby grasslands and the rockier outcroppings of the foothills. However, apertures in the sides of the ship were opening up, and things with many legs and eyes were crawling out. Noon heard a shout of alarm from one of the fell-witches, and a few of the streams of fire stopped.

'We're almost there, keep going!'

There were a few shouted words from Chenlo that Noon couldn't hear over the flames, and one or two winnowfire streams started up again, but some of the creatures – things

520

that looked like giant, deformed burrowers – were unfurling glassy wings and drifting down towards the women.

'Tor!'

'I told you you'd need me!' Tor and Kirune swept down together, a greyish streak against the bulbous shape of the Behemoth. Light flashed along Tor's sword, and Noon saw pieces of giant burrower falling away to the ground below. Kirune growled, landing on the surface of the ship and disembowelling several more creatures with a sweep from his claws.

'Bright weapon, look!'

The mountains were much closer, and when Noon looked down all she could see was rock and scree, broken up here and there by patches of thorny bushes. They were at the very foot of the Bloodless Mountains, as far as they could get from the Eboran city without leaving the region entirely or crashing into the mountainside. Briefly she entertained the idea of carrying on, pushing the Behemoth out beyond the mountain range to the plains beyond – a mountain in the way of the explosion wasn't an entirely bad idea – but there was just no time.

'Chenlo, go! Take them and help Vintage. It looks like they need it!'

Sharrik's heart was thundering. Bern could feel it through his legs, through his own chest, and through the connection they shared he could feel the sheer dense power of the griffin's battle fury. He readjusted his grip on the axe, and grinned.

'My brother!' bellowed Sharrik. 'This is the battle we were born for!'

Below them, the Jure'lia queen was a strange shifting shape, changing and moving in all directions, but always edging forward through the broken streets of the outer city. Where her liquid body met the ground, Bern could see that parts of it were breaking away and becoming other, scuttling things;

this was where the wave of burrowers and other creatures were coming from.

'She's making them as she goes,' he said, his voice thick with disgust. 'Until she's dead, there will be no stopping them.'

'Never mind all that now, darling, our job here is to distract the queen,' called Vintage from the back of Helcate. She lifted her hand and pointed, and Bern saw that the Winnowry woman was returning, with the fell-witches in formation behind her. 'And it looks like we've got reinforcements!'

'Good.' The queen herself seemed to be paying them no mind, which Bern didn't find all that surprising; to her, he supposed, they were no more than annoying gnats. It was time for that to change. 'Attack the head area, or whatever that's supposed to be.' Bern lifted his remaining axe and pointed. 'Let's remind her that the stones of Sarn are not to be trampled over!'

'And try not to get in each other's way!' added Vintage. Chenlo nodded solemnly and called out a series of instructions to the fell-witches, who immediately flew off in all directions. In moments, streams of fire were pouring down on the queen from every part of the sky. Bern grinned. He had thought of them as gnats, when in fact they were wasps. Deadly ones.

'Come on. Let's remind the queen who we are, shall we?'

Sharrik rumbled his approval and they shot down and across, heading straight for the seething mass of the queen's spiky back. Sharrik tore across it, razor-sharp beak peeling her oozing flesh into two pieces, and to Bern's satisfaction there was a series of outraged shrieks from any number of mouths. Once on the other side, the griffin turned and dove again, and this time Bern reached down with his Bitter Twin, cleaving a ragged wound in the queen's hide alongside the griffin's.

'Nice work!' shouted Vintage. Helcate was following on behind, spitting his streams of acid directly into the wounds Sharrik and Bern had caused. Already the queen was healing herself, sending tendrils of black ooze soaring up to stitch herself back together, but with this onslaught and the ministrations of the witch-wasps, she also wasn't moving forward very quickly or investigating the shapes now attacking one of her Behemoths. It was a rough and dangerous plan, but it was working.

'Let's try the other side,' shouted Bern, 'keep her on her toes!'

Sharrik swerved and tore through the queen's flesh again, but this time the bubbling ooze erupted, coming after them in a wave of reaching black tendrils. Bern saw them writhe up and around Sharrik's rear legs, even felt the pull as they were yanked backwards, and then Chenlo was in the air above them, a series of guttering fireballs crashing into the queen's oozing flesh. There was a deafening hiss and the tendrils snapped back again. Sharrik was free.

'Look out,' called Vintage, somewhat unnecessarily. 'She's up to something!'

The seething oily surface of the queen's body split open in multiple places, holes of all sizes gaping into existence. Bern had a moment to think that perhaps they had got outrageously lucky, wounding the queen in some devastating way that was even now causing her body to fall to pieces – when a thousand voices shouted from a thousand newly formed throats.

'*You destroyed our future – for this insult you will all die.*'

There were cries of horror from the fell-witches. The queen's body flexed and split apart, becoming something not remotely humanoid. Sharrik leapt up and away instinctively, and Bern caught a series of increasingly fraught curse words from Vintage as Helcate scrambled to get clear. Below them now was a thing more like a Wild-touched plant, or a giant mouth made from three huge jaws, and inside long green tongues were emerging, reaching up to pull them inside. One of these huge tentacles snapped up into the air and closed around a bat that failed to get away in time. There was a shriek from the fell-witch, cut short, and then she was gone, sucked back down inside the queen's shifting body.

'No!' Chenlo looked stricken even as she ordered the other fell-witches to keep back. The thing changed again, the mouth falling in on itself – the woman and bat completely lost to view – and then a head appeared once more, a huge elongated thing that twisted round to face them.

'*This war is over,*' hissed the queen. '*We all end here, today. This was your choice.*'

Bern remembered being held down and his mind being torn apart. He remembered the invasive touch of the queen's fingers on his memories, taking them to pieces and fouling them with her presence. He thought of the searing pain in the palm of his hand as she had forced the shard of blue crystal into it, and a phantom shiver of agony moved through his foreshortened arm. He raised his axe above his head and let Sharrik's battle fury move through him.

'Hag, there will only be one ending here today,' he shouted, 'and I will dance on your bloody grave when it's done!'

Chapter Fifty-one

'Here, quickly, now!'

Noon leaned out and added her winnowfire to Vostok's, enlarging the hole in the Behemoth's side created by the vicious fires of the fell-witches. They had blasted their way partially into one of the open corridors inside the ship, and now there was just a layer of blistered grey material between them and it. Tor and Kirune were still busy dealing with the creatures spawned by the ship, and every now and then Noon would hear a shout or a growl from them as they worked together. The connection that ran between them all was taut and alive, and so sensitive it was almost distracting; she could feel, like a persistent breeze against her skin, Bern's anger, Tor's fierce amusement, Vintage's worry, the tension thrumming through Aldasair. It was an incredible thing.

'There, it's done.' They drew away, and Noon saw that Vostok was right. There was a sizeable hole tunnelled into the side of the Behemoth, and it was possible to see its inner spaces, lit with sickly yellow light. 'You will have to go as swiftly as you can, bright weapon, because it won't be long before she tries to seal this breach.'

'I know.'

Vostok perched on the edge of the hole, and Noon untied herself from the harness, carefully climbing down onto the smoking moon-metal. The heat through her boots was tremendous. She turned and placed her hands on Vostok's long snout, marvelling again at the beauty of every pearly scale.

'Vostok . . .'

'I will not argue with you,' said the dragon brusquely. 'My place is on the battlefield, as it has always been. Just go quickly, and do not take unnecessary risks.'

'Thank you. You'll help the others? Get them through the rest of this?'

'I will. And I will be here to catch you, bright weapon.'

There was a clatter from above them, and Kirune skidded to a halt at the edge of the hole. Noon looked up, a mixture of annoyance and fondness briefly closing her throat. Tor was grinning down at her, his face bright and his armour smeared with worm-gore.

'Don't think you're going anywhere without us.'

'I told you –'

'The place is going to be crawling with these crawling bastards. You need us, Noon, if you want to get anywhere close to the memory crystal.'

'Fine. I . . .'

Noon turned to meet Vostok's eye, and then without another word the dragon was gone in a flurry of white feathers, heading back towards the dark, pulsing smudge that was the queen. For a long breath Noon was too filled with wonder to move – *the most extraordinary thing I've ever seen* – and then she was stomping her way down into the ragged tunnel, her eyes on the distant light.

'Fine. But you do what I tell you to do, when it's time.'

An aimless rustling sound moved through the streets of Ebora, like a great tide of dead leaves, or an army of ghosts. On

Jessen's back, standing with the human troops, Aldasair sat up straighter in the harness and set his mind firmly against the idea of ghosts. *I've wasted too much time with spirits, lost too many years listening for the footfalls of the dead.*

You are not alone anymore, brother.

Jessen's voice in his head was reassuring, and he had to admit, she was certainly factually correct. Looking down the rows and rows of soldiers, Aldasair thought it likely he had never been in the company of so many people at once, and certainly not so many humans. On the advice of Commander Morota they had split the troops into two rings; one running through the streets of Ebora, and another closer circle just outside the palace. He and Commander Morota were with the outer ring now, standing on the broken paving slabs of a long abandoned street. On either side stood some of the more extravagant houses, buildings of marble and green slate that were riddled with creeping plants and coloured with rot and moss. Grass still grew up through the cracks in the road, but it was possible to see signs that Ebora was no longer dead. Someone had come and swept away the old leaves and broken branches from the street; a fallen tree was in the process of being chopped up for firewood; a child's toy, something made of soft rags and wool, was lying abandoned in the road. Aldasair found his eyes returning to it again and again.

We are so fortunate they came here, he said to Jessen. *The humans. I spent much of my life in fear of them. In fear of their hatred for us, and fear that they were the disease that had ended us – but what they brought back was life.*

He thought of Bern. Of him introducing himself, of him offering to help. Of him looking at the Hill of Souls and so easily understanding what it would mean to fix it.

'Lord Aldasair, has there been any further word from your comrades?'

Commander Morota looked uneasy. She had turned down the opportunity to wear Eboran armour, preferring to stay in her own Reidn steel and leather, but she had made sure that her soldiers were as fully kitted out as possible. They stood together, spears and short swords at the ready.

'I'm aware of them, commander, but I sense that they're all rather busy with their own battles.' He narrowed his eyes at the far end of the street. 'And it looks like we will be also. The burrowers are coming, I can see movement.'

Morota began shouting orders to the human men and women, and a tremor of noise moved through them as they readied themselves. Jessen moved to the front of the force, and Aldasair slipped his axe from his belt.

'Stand ready!'

Huge barrels were being rolled some distance in front of the lines, and Aldasair caught a whiff of a strange chemical scent as the tops were pried off.

'Give the word, Lord Aldasair,' said Morota in a low voice.

We could fly, suggested Jessen. *We'd have a better view.*

No. These people need to see us on the ground next to them, fighting elbow to elbow. Otherwise they will think we are leaving them to deal with the worst of it alone.

A swarm was moving down across the road towards them, thousands of skittering Jure'lia creatures. Most of them that Aldasair could see were burrowers, but there were other shapes in there, bulkier, stranger things with oversized mandibles and fat, red eyes like Wild-touched berries hanging on a bush. Some of them were coming over the buildings, crawling across broken roofs and swarming over broken windows. The sound of their approach – thousands of knife-sharp legs tapping across stone – was growing louder.

'Now!' called Aldasair. 'Do it now.'

Morota shouted more orders, and the barrels fell, spilling a thin brackish-smelling liquid across the stones in front of the army. People moved back, anxious not to be too close to it, and a number of shouts went up in adjoining streets; barrels were falling there too as the enemy drew closer. Some of the men and women were muttering, and Aldasair could feel their fear like a cushion at his back.

'Now!'

A young fell-witch stepped up to the fluid just as the first burrowers crossed into it, and quickly she bent and touched her fingers to the ground, sparking with green light. There was a soft wumph noise and Jessen took a few instinctive steps backwards as a sheet of flame rose up in front of them. The Jure'lia creatures caught in it immediately burst into flame themselves, and the air was filled with a high-pitched squealing. A number of them staggered out, took a few steps towards the crowd of soldiers, then collapsed, their insides turned to super-hot liquid.

'It's working!' called Commander Morota. Aldasair nodded tersely, hoping the burrowers would keep marching mindlessly into the flames. Okaar had come up with the plan and had even mixed the chemicals for them, given precise instructions about when and how to use it, but thanks to a lack of supplies they had precious few barrels of the stuff. They had to be careful.

As Aldasair had hoped, line after line of the burrowers were streaming straight into the hissing flames, sacrificing themselves, but as their bodies heaped up and up, the flames themselves were beginning to die down. And of course the Jure'lia creatures that were coming over the ruins and not the roads were still lively enough. As he watched, a dark wave of scuttling nightmares began to drip down from the houses on either side of the wide street. Aldasair lifted his axe, and turned to address the soldiers.

'The time to fight is now! Remember what we told you about the drones, and keep as many as you can away from the palace. Help will come eventually – we just have to hold on!'

'We are home.'

Hestillion scowled at Celaphon's sentimental tone. They were following on behind the main attack force, having both grown oddly weary of the endless roar of the queen's consumption. She had put on her suit of Jure'lia armour and sat in Celaphon's harness ready to attack herself, but she remained oddly reluctant. Here was Ebora after all, here was the place she had been avoiding since the battle where the boy had died, and it looked different, although she couldn't have said how exactly. There in the distance were the familiar streets, the silvery spread of the tree-father's branches, all the same as it had ever been, yet she felt distinctly as though Ebora had forgotten her – as though she could walk through the palace corridors and find no trace of her, no sign that she had ever lived there. It was unsettling.

'This is not our home,' she snapped. Without waiting to see Celaphon's reaction, she reached out to her circle and assessed their impressions of the battle so far. Yellow Leaf and Red Moth were on one Behemoth, Grey Root on the other. The First and Green Bird were on the corpse moon, and they were under attack. Hestillion took a sharp breath, shocked that the queen had apparently turned a blind eye to such damage. 'Come on, we're needed.'

As they rounded the front of the corpse moon, Hestillion leaned forward, ready to strike whatever might be waiting there, but whatever had done the damage was gone. Yellowish smoke, tugged away by the wind, floated out of a blackened hole leading directly into the ship itself, and as Hestillion looked at the damage, she swallowed hard. Dragon-fire, winnowfire, and distinctive claw marks in the moon-metal. Already knowing what the answer would be, she reached out along the Jure'lia network for the First, and through his deeper connection to the corpse moon, scanned its corridors for the invaders she knew must be there.

'My brother,' she said. 'And his pet witch. I told him to leave, the fool.'

'What will you do?' asked Celaphon. He sounded crafty again, as if he knew that her answer would amuse him. 'Will you kill them?'

Hissing with impatience, Hestillion unstrapped herself from his harness and dropped neatly into the hole. The twisted moon-metal panels were still warm under her boots, and the stench of burning worm-flesh was overwhelming. She wrinkled her nose and turned back to Celaphon.

'Go and fight, sweet one,' she told him. 'Whatever they are up to, I will stop them, and then I will join you.'

Celaphon lingered by the hole, his white eyes as difficult to read as ever. Hestillion found herself looking over the vast landscape of his face; the discoloured patch where the smaller war-beast had spat over him; the bristling horns and plates that had sprouted from him after the queen had given him the growth fluid. It was hard to picture the tiny creature he had been, when she had torn him from the pod with her own hands and held him to her chest. Had he ever been that small, truly?

'What is it, Celaphon?'

'It's not your fault, what happened to me,' he said.

Hestillion stood very still. She felt caught between anger and bewilderment.

'I . . .'

'I was born into a cursed time. So were you. Try and remember that.'

He unfurled his enormous horned wings and dropped away out of sight. For a long, vertiginous second she felt like she was falling with him, as though there were a rope strung

531

between the two of them and shortly she would be torn into the air after him. Then, from somewhere out of sight, she heard the queen bellowing something with a thousand voices. It seemed to break whatever spell she was under, and, shaking her head briskly, she made her way down the tunnel into the corpse moon.

The corridor had been empty so far – almost eerily so – but as they crept their way deeper into the Behemoth Tor could hear a series of noises that suggested they wouldn't be alone much longer. The deep crackling hum that was ever-present within any Jure'lia vessel had grown louder and more discordant, and there was a rustling, a tapping, growing closer with every step. He weighed his sword in his hand, feeling pleased with both its grace and the lack of pain in his arms. It seemed foolish that he had ever worried so much about losing the Ninth Rain, or even been so horrified by the prospect of dying from the crimson flux. It seemed he would live just long enough, after all. Kirune was walking by his side, his heavy head slowly tracking back and forth, waiting for the inevitable.

'Are we going the right way, do you think?' Noon was walking slightly in front, her hands held up in front of her.

'We are,' said Tor, with more confidence than he felt. 'My guess is that the more trouble we see, the closer we will be to the memory-crystal chamber.'

'Are you suggesting we actively head towards that horrible noise?'

Tor grinned. 'You're the one who suggested this ridiculous plan in the first place.'

'That's a fair point.'

'They are coming,' rumbled Kirune. 'Up this corridor, now. Be ready.'

Noon took a few steps back and appeared to stroke Kirune's

ear, although Tor knew she was taking a little of his life energy to fuel her winnowfire.

'Wait.' Kirune turned around, looking back the way they had come. 'We are being followed –'

They were very nearly overwhelmed immediately. A tide of worm-creatures surged from either end of the corridor, a clicking, rattling, whirring confusion of legs and mandibles and rolling yellow eyes. Tor saw giant burrowers, things like scorpions with multiple tails, and several of the grey men they had previously fought in the skies. Noon turned gracefully, her arms wheeling, and sent several discs of green flame into the heart of the horde, blasting into pieces much of what was coming for them, while Kirune used his bulk to simply crush the larger Jure'lia creatures against the corridor wall.

'Fuck.' Noon waved her arms again, sending a rolling wall of fire up the corridor. Many of the scuttling things burst into flame, but it was clear there were more coming all the time. 'There're tons of the bastards.'

'We must move forward.' Kirune came up next to her, and pushed his head under her arm. 'Use my life source, witch. Fill the space with fire. I will walk with you.'

Tor moved to cover Kirune's back, his sword a restless blur. A burrower ran up his leg and he hopped briefly backwards, shaking it off. Noon meanwhile had done as Kirune suggested, and the space ahead of them was filled with a vortex of bright winnowflame. There were shapes in there, things curling in on themselves and shedding legs, although they were difficult to make out. Heat billowed back at them in an oppressive wave.

'Noon, are you all right? Can you keep this up?'

'I'm fine,' she said without looking at him. 'Just stay close.'

And, he noticed, she did look fine. Her face was serene despite the sheen of sweat across her forehead, and he thought of the dream he'd had of her once, when she had worn a violet cloak and a crown of green fire around her head. Her eyes had been emerald flames in that dream, but her face had looked the same; it had been the face of someone just realising the full potential of their own power. He shivered and turned away in time to split a giant burrower in two.

All was chaos.

Vintage drew back from the main fight, letting Helcate summon more of his acidic spit – he could not simply produce endless amounts of it, and he was already enormously tired. One team of fell-witches was continuing to help Sharrik and Bern attack the queen, while the other, led by Chenlo, was harrying the two Behemoths that continued to move slowly through the skies over Ebora. It had just occurred to her to wonder where Tyranny was when Windfall shot through the air space in front of her, the huge white bat flying much faster than any of its smaller cousins. The queens of Tygrish no longer wore any of their finery. Instead they bristled with armour and weapons, and they were heading straight for the enormous form of the queen.

'Sarn's bloody bones.' Vintage pushed her fingers into the curly fur at Helcate's neck. 'Let's hope she remembers she's flying as part of a team.'

A beam of light shot from the war-beast's mouth, and Vintage watched with satisfaction as a huge flower of ice crystals blossomed on part of what she was choosing to think of as the queen's back. The bat flew closer, the beam growing fatter, and the flower spread, sending fingers of frost down and across to the bulbous maggot shapes growing from the monster's back. The constant stream of varnish thinned to a dribble, then dried up entirely.

'Oh look! Clever girl.' Vintage couldn't help smiling. 'Such a powerful weapon, just as I knew it would be.'

Sharrik and Windfall appeared to be working in tandem now, with Bern and Tyranny shouting instructions and encouragement to each other. The bat was working on creating a ring of ice around the vast queen-monster, while Sharrik continued to plunge himself into the queen's amorphous flesh, ploughing great furrows and tattering her tendrils into scattered pieces.

'How are you feeling, darling? Are you ready to get back to it?'

Helcate made a series of hiccupping noises. 'Helcate!'

'Good work, my brave one.'

They soared down into the milieu only to be met by Chenlo on the back of her own bat. Her shirt was torn and the grey fur of her bat was scorched in places, and her hair was coming loose from its meticulous braid.

A rose in the heart of the Wild, thought Vintage.

'We've run out of the heartbright,' she called. 'The women's fire is starting to have little effect against the moon-metal.'

Vintage saw that she was right. The arcs and streams of winnowfire that criss-crossed the air around them were back to their more usual blue-green, with none of the spitting violence of the chemically enhanced flames.

'Does Okaar have any more?'

Chenlo shook her head. 'We took all of it with us.'

'Helcate,' said Helcate.

'Of course.' Vintage pursed her lips. 'Winnowfire fuelled by war-beast life force is just as effective. My love, tell the women to take life force from Helcate and Sharrik. Warn them it can be overwhelming, warn them not to take too much, to be careful . . .' Vintage shook her head. Telling them to be careful in the midst of this nightmare was laughable. 'And don't swarm us, I don't want Sharrik kept from what he's doing, or Helcate accidentally spitting acid all over a witch who didn't get away in time.'

Bern, Sharrik. Did you catch that?

We did. We'll look out for the witches.

Chenlo nodded once and flew off, shouting new instructions

to the fell-witches. It was a testament to the Winnowry agent's control that they weren't immediately surrounded, but soon women were flying on their bats towards them, hands held out, and Helcate went to them gladly, his neck stretched out to meet them. It was a difficult manoeuvre – too many wings in the same airspace, thought Vintage grimly – but they managed it. After the first two flew away, their hands full of bright green fire, Vintage felt the wave of tiredness that moved through Helcate, and they dipped a little lower in the sky.

'Darling, we must be careful. You will tell me if it's too much?'

'Helcate!' said Helcate, a shade testily.

'Because we can't have you –'

Her words were lost in a roar that almost shook them from the sky. Helcate plummeted briefly, then struggled back up and away. There was something else in the sky with them, something huge. Vintage twisted in the harness and looked up, her stomach turning a slow somersault. It was Celaphon, the enormous purple dragon that had killed Eri, his wings spread and his huge jaws open and crackling with electricity.

'Oh,' she said, fighting against a wave of horror that threatened to stop her heart. 'That particular monster can fuck *right* off.'

Chapter Fifty-two

Aldasair staggered to the ground, wiping a line of clear blood from his chin and redoubling the grip on his axe, which was streaked with Jure'lia gore. He looked up to see Jessen by the gates, the body of a drone clamped between her jaws and one of the remaining human soldiers cowering behind her. The Jure'lia hordes were still coming, and they had been pushed back through the city streets to the grounds of the palace. All around him were the sounds of men and women screaming and shouting, the smell of spilled human blood. There was so much of it, splashed across the grass and on the stones, it was making him dizzy, summoning memories he'd hoped would stay hidden forever.

'Commander!' He got back to his feet, glancing up at the sky as he did so. The situation up there didn't look much better. 'Commander, your soldiers –'

'The last are inside the palace,' said Commander Morota. She had stayed close to him and Jessen throughout the fight, and Aldasair had been impressed. The woman had the stamina of an Eboran, although she looked pale and exhausted now, sweat leaving dirty lines on her cheeks. 'Inside and outside of the Hall of Roots.'

Aldasair nodded. It was what they had agreed. There were a tiny team of fell-witches on the roof too, staying close to Ygseril's branches. If the tree-father fell, then they were likely all doomed anyway.

'Jessen, there are more coming.' A number of freshly made drones were shuffling their way across the palace lawn, their faces still contorted with the expressions of horror the humans had worn when the burrowers crammed down their throats. The wolf leapt from her place by the gates and thundered across the grass towards them, tearing and snapping until pieces of hollowed-out human lay scattered. 'Commander, we may have to move inside the palace.'

'I agree.' She kicked away an insectoid creature the size of a dog, then drove her short sword down through its spine. 'It's more defensible. Seal the entrances, the windows, get more people out on the roof.'

She called to one of her remaining soldiers, and he raised a horn to his lips. A series of short, sharp notes blurted across the gardens, and those who were still able to began to run back towards the gates.

Do we go too?

Jessen came charging back across the grass. Aldasair had never seen her look so wild; her amber eyes were wide, her tongue lolled out of her mouth wetly. The fur on the front of her chest was dark and wet with the interior juices of so many worm-monsters.

We stay with them.

Together they ran through the gates and across the gravel yard, following the remaining soldiers through the wide central doors. Once inside, the doors were slammed shut, and more men and women ran to seal them with planks of wood and old Eboran furniture.

'We just need to slow them down,' Aldasair called to the humans. 'Keep them from the central chambers long enough

538

for our friends to do their work.' He hoped his words were encouraging, but he doubted they were even listening. Their faces were tight with horror, the faces of people who had watched their friends eaten and their makeshift homes trampled under a wave of horrors. When the doors were sealed, they started on the windows, covering them up as best they could, but the palace had always been a warren, an organic sprawling place with no plan and no logic to its layout.

They'll get in somewhere. Jessen's voice in his head was tired. *And if they don't,* she *will.*

Someone took his elbow and Aldasair almost raised his axe before realising it was the man Okaar. He wore a long thin sword at his waist, although the awkwardness of his movements suggested he was unlikely to be able to use it as skilfully as he once had.

'My friend, you are bleeding from a dozen places.'

Aldasair glanced down. A couple of the wounds were oozing black blood, but there was no pain. No pain from any of the cuts. He shrugged, uncertain what to say. What did it matter who was bleeding at this point?

'I don't suppose we have any more of your clever barrels, Okaar?'

The assassin looked grave. 'We had so few ingredients to begin with.' Behind them, the doors began to shake as something outside crashed against them repeatedly. 'It's all gone – on the heartbright, and the fire barrels. I am sorry.'

Aldasair shook his head. 'Without you, we'd be in an even worse state now. You'd best get away if you can, Okaar, if you can't –' He swallowed the last words. *If you can't fight.*

Okaar raised his eyebrows in a rueful expression. 'And go where, Lord Aldasair?' When Aldasair didn't reply, he continued. 'What of Tyranny? And the Lady Vintage? They are still out there?'

'They fight on.' Aldasair thought back to the brief glimpses of the sky he'd managed to get in between the fighting. 'The air is alive with fire and ice. The queen edges forward though, for all their efforts.'

A piercing scream from outside caused them all to turn back to the doors. Aldasair went over to the nearest window with Commander Morota and Okaar at his back. The human troops had nailed a pair of boards over it, but it was still possible to see a strip of the outside world through the dirty glass.

'Sarn's bloody bones,' spat Morota. 'We've barely made a dent.'

To Aldasair, it was like looking through a portal into a vision of a nightmare, or the distant past. The lawn, the gardens, the ornate gates; all were almost completely lost under a swarm of teeming insect creatures. There were human figures out there staggering around, most of them already drones, although the screaming indicated there were a few whose insides were still in the process of being eaten. The city itself was dwarfed under the shadow of the queen, and her tentacles squirmed through the broken windows of houses, across roofs and along the streets. Peering up into the sky, squinting against the light, he could just make out Bern and Sharrik as a flitting shape somewhere up near the queen's head, and there was the shimmering blast of Windfall's ice beam. There were Behemoths up there too, and a great deal of movement around them. Their forces – their brave and desperate team – looked like tiny scraps of broken leaves in the face of the Jure'lia.

'You cannot hope to win against that,' said Okaar. His words were rusty chunks, dry and broken.

'We don't have to.' Aldasair turned away from the window and grabbed the man's arm briefly. 'We just have to hold them off for long enough.'

'There, that roof. It's clear. Land there.'

'I will not,' thundered Sharrik. 'We are in the middle of battle, and I will not –'

'Stones' arses, this is not the time to argue with me!' Bern leaned low over the griffin's neck, shouting the words directly into his tufted ear. 'Bloody well land!'

For a wonder, the war-beast did as he was told. They peeled away from the chaos that was the space around the queen and flew low over the ruined city, coming to rest on a long, low roof lined with green tiles. Once they were down, Bern untied himself from the harness and stepped down, pushing the handle of his axe into one of the straps.

'This is an insult,' grumbled Sharrik.

'You are exhausted. Rest for a moment, brother, or you'll get us both killed.'

The griffin lowered his head, and then sunk down, folding his thickly muscled legs beneath him. Bern ran his hand down the beast's neck, feeling a tide of weariness lap at him through the connection they shared.

'Just a few moments,' Sharrik conceded. 'Such a battle I have never seen.'

There was a long black barb sticking out of the griffin's shoulder – some piece of Jure'lia carapace wedged deep in the fur so that a thin trickle of black blood was leaking from the wound. Bern pulled it free, wincing at the jagged tooth-like spur.

'It's too much.' Inevitably he raised his head and looked back at the shape of the queen. Windfall continued her icy dance around the monster, while Vostok harried the creature's head, yet he wasn't sure they were causing the thing any real damage. A peal of violet flames lit up the sky. Gouts of green and blue fire shot through the air like comets. Another bulky shape circled at a distance; the dragon Celaphon, although he appeared to be riderless, and had yet to attack. 'The fell-witches taking your energy too . . .'

'I can do it,' said Sharrik gruffly, but Bern could see how the griffin's head was nodding even as he spoke. He put his arms around the war-beast's enormous neck, and rested his head against his beak for a moment.

'I know you can, brother,' he said.

For a little while they sat in silence together, surrounded by the noise of war and buffeted by the terrors of their companions. Instinctively, Bern sought out Aldasair amongst the mayhem, and felt him somewhere close. He was distracted, worried, and trying not to show it. There was very little time left for any of them.

'It is not so glorious,' said Sharrik eventually, in an uncharacteristically quiet voice. 'This war. There is so much sorrow, so much pain.'

'That's all war,' said Bern. He was looking at the stump where his wrist had been, but he was thinking of the various little conflicts his people had had with the Sown. All those years of grudges, skirmishes, broken oaths and revenge. It all seemed very small now; the squabbling of children.

'I'm not so sure that I like it after all.'

Bern thumped Sharrik on his meaty shoulder. 'I don't blame you. But after this war, you won't have to fight again. How about that?' He forced himself to smile. 'We will go to Finneral, you and I, and we'll spend our days eating and drinking and get good and fat. How about that?'

Sharrik gave a low chuckle.

'We'll fish, and hunt, and tell stories, just like my father. And there will be peace for us. After this war.'

'After this war,' agreed Sharrik. 'No more fighting. But now –' the griffin stood up again – 'but now our friends need us.'

When they were back in the air again, Sharrik seemed somewhat renewed, fighting with fresh energy and purpose. They dove and swerved through the grasping tendrils of the Jure'lia queen, and more than once they called encouragement to Vostok, who was slathering the enemy in a waterfall of violet fire. Windfall, with her one blind eye, was continuing her spiral of ice, and Bern caught sight of Tyranny, her face wild and flushed. He lifted a hand to her, and saw her grin back at him, and that was when it happened. A flailing black tendril of Jure'lia fluid flew through the air as fast as a whip crack, and abruptly Tyranny and Windfall were no longer there. A second later Bern caught sight of the ex-queen of Tygrish – she had been ripped bodily from her harness and was falling through the air down to the city below.

'Sharrik, quick!'

It was impossibly close. Sharrik shot after her, coming close to a free fall, and Bern, his axe shoved back through his belt, reached out, grabbing her hand with a smack that seemed oddly loud amongst the chaos of everything else.

'Tyranny! Hold on!'

She looked up at him, her eyes so wild they looked like they would fall out of her head.

'Where's Windfall?'

Sharrik had swept round and up, trying to avoid the hordes of Jure'lia creatures on the ground, and they were above the queen again. Windfall was there, flapping steadily in mid-air, not moving. To Bern the war-beast looked stunned, as though she wasn't quite sure where she was. Her huge mouth hung open, but there was no sign of the ice beam.

'Windfall, look out!'

The long pointed head of the queen swept up, like a dog hearing an unexpected noise, and then it split open, revealing rows and rows of nightmarish teeth, marching all the way down her throat. She snapped her jaws shut, and Windfall was sheared in two.

'No!' Still hanging from Bern's hand, Tyranny began to kick violently, her whole body shaking with grief and anger. 'NO!'

'Tyranny, don't, you'll fall!'

A shimmer of sorrow and pain coursed through Bern as the reality of Windfall's death moved through the connection between the war-beasts. Sharrik roared in anger, echoing Tyranny, echoing the pain of all of them.

'You bitch!' In her free hand, Tyranny summoned a glove of green fire. 'You will die for this!'

And then to Bern's horror, she let go of his hand, and she dropped like a stone onto the queen below, trailing flames as she went. There was a blossom of fire as she landed, and Bern saw her throwing fireballs directly at the queen's enormous split head, but if she did any damage, he didn't see it, and the black ooze that she stood on shifted and flowed up her legs, over her waist, and finally dragged her down into the body of the thing itself.

It was easy enough to see where they had been. Dead Jure'lia creatures lay in smoking heaps along the corridors, many of them crushed or sliced to pieces, and the walls themselves were blackened and tainted with winnow-soot. Hestillion wrinkled her nose at it, and walked a little faster. It also seemed obvious enough where they were heading. Perhaps, she reasoned, they meant to break the crystal in the same way that her cousin had, by planting some alien memory inside it.

'It's too late for that,' she muttered. 'Too late for any of that nonsense.'

Nevertheless, she reached out again to the First, instructing him to intercept them before they reached the crystal chamber, but then to her surprise she heard them herself. They were arguing, their voices raised. Hestillion stepped around a corner to see her brother standing with the human witch, his war-beast some distance away, killing the last of the worm minions.

'It's my choice,' he was saying hotly, his face set into its usual stubborn lines. 'What difference does it make to me at this point?'

'What difference?' The young woman's hands were curled into fists at her sides, and she looked furious. 'What about what difference it will make to everyone else? We don't have time for this, Tor, our friends are *dying* out there . . .'

'Your sister is here,' commented the war-beast dryly.

They both turned to look. Tor drew his sword.

'Hest, this is a private conversation.'

'I told you to leave.' She twisted her hand inside the Jure'lia suit, and a pair of long blades made of pale chitinous shell slid out of the forearm casings; they were wickedly sharp and surprisingly strong. '*Not once*, not once in your long, idiotic life have you ever listened to me. I told you to run, and here you are, doing the exact opposite. I don't know why I'm surprised. Why do you never *listen to me*?'

'You're standing there covered in that Jure'lia muck, and you have the cheek to call me an idiot?' Infuriatingly, he laughed. 'That's you all over though, isn't it, Hest? Standing on a heap of shit and declaring yourself the queen of it.'

She was moving before she even knew she had decided to fight him. The suit was a thing made with hate, constructed from the very need to fight and survive, and she let it suggest her movements, leaping from one side of the corridor to the other, blades flashing. Tormalin moved just as fast, his sword crashing against hers repeatedly, pushing her back.

The First, come to me. Bring help.

'You've learned a lot!' Tor actually sounded pleased. 'I always thought you had no taste for the martial arts, sister.'

She slammed her arm across his, tearing leather and skin alike with the barbs on her armour, then thrust upwards, catching him on the chin. He staggered backwards but the sword he held seemed to have a life of its own, skating up under her guard and slashing at her breastplate.

'We don't have time for this!' It was the witch, her hands full of green fire and the war-beast at her back, but at that moment the wall to their right spasmed open and a fresh wave of scuttling creatures fell on them, instantly pushing them away from Hestillion. The First stepped through after them, his pale handsome face serenely blank. Hestillion saw the expression of surprise that moved over Tor's face, saw the horror on the heels of it.

'What the fuck is that supposed to be?'

It was her turn to laugh. 'Someone who actually does what I say. Someone who is actually useful.' She nodded to the First. 'Kill the witch. Do it slowly if you like.'

The corridor erupted into fighting again. This time, Tormalin did not look so amused, and Hestillion could sense that he was distracted. He looked over his shoulder more than once as the witch threw her green fire at the First and desperately fought off a wave of burrowers. She caught him a serious blow on the shoulder that drove him to his knees, and to her surprise, he struggled to get up. Taking advantage of his momentary weakness, she pushed her blade to his exposed throat, forcing him to stay where he was.

'Tor? Tor, are you all right?' The witch was shouting frantically, but the First was keeping her back.

'I told you to go.' Hestillion pressed the blade closer, watching as a thin line of clear blood ran down her brother's throat. There were hot tears rolling down her cheeks, making it difficult to see. 'I didn't want you to be here.'

To her surprise, Tor lowered his arms and smiled. His sword lay loose in his lap. He wasn't quite looking at her.

'What is it?' she spat. 'Roots be damned, Tor, not everything is fucking funny!'

'Oh, I don't know. This world gifts you with a dark sense of humour, I think.' He reached up and pulled at the section of leather armour covering his chest. Hestillion heard the sharp pops as stitching and rivets came away under his hands. Beneath it he was wearing a simple white shirt, which he pulled aside. 'You can kill me if you like, Hestillion. I'm dying anyway. What difference does it make?'

There were livid red lines on his chest, fanned out in a shape a little like the veins on a leaf. The skin between them was a chalky white, and it already looked hard and broken. Hestillion stared at it, unable to move.

'What . . . ?'

'The crimson flux. I mean, you can't be surprised. It was always going to be the end of me, wasn't it?' He shrugged one shoulder. 'The death you will give me with a blade will be much kinder than the one I face, sister.'

She moved the blade away an inch. It was impossible to look away from the infection, and suddenly all those years of silence in the Eboran palace – all those years of watching people coughing themselves to death, of cleaning sheets and bringing water to the doomed, of listening to the mad ravings of Eborans driven to feverish insanity by the sheer weight of their combined devastation – all those years seemed terrifyingly close. As though in a blink of an eye she could be back there again, trapped in those dusty corridors and entombed in silence. As though she'd never got away from it at all. She had changed nothing. The crimson flux was always waiting.

'No,' she said. 'Tor . . .'

Behind them, the war-beast Kirune leapt at the First and sank his teeth into her creation's neck, tearing it out in one savage movement. The sight of the being with her brother's face sinking to its knees, seeping Jure'lia fluid, was too much. She slid her blades away, and felt the queen's eye fall upon her, suddenly watchful.

You told us you had cut all ties with your blood. The queen's voice in her head. *You swore it to us. You swore it to me.*

Hestillion looked up and met her brother's eyes. He looked sad, even though he was still smiling, and she found herself trying to remember the palace they had built together, when she was the queen, and he was her faithful knight. Such a long time ago.

That's not how blood works, I'm afraid.

She felt the spike of the queen's rage like an arrow to her heart, and then the witch was stepping between her and her brother. The human woman's hand on her forehead was cold and damp.

'We haven't got time for this, Tor.'

Darkness.

Chapter Fifty-three

'How many – how many of us are left?'

The look that passed over Chenlo's face told Vintage all she needed to know. They had been trying to push the two Behemoths still flanking the queen back, as they were producing an unholy tide of horrors and dropping them down onto the city below, but the various flying monsters spawned from the queen's oozing body were taking them out, one by one. Moments ago Vintage had watched with horror as a fell-witch was ripped from the back of her bat by an unsettlingly humanoid figure with wings, too far away to help. Helcate himself was exhausted, both from producing his acid spit and providing life energy for the witches.

'Most of us are on the roof now,' Chenlo shouted back. 'They stand ready to defend the tree-god. We should join them!'

Vintage paused to raise her new crossbow, shooting a fleeing grey-man in the back.

'If we leave off the pressure on the Behemoths, they will swarm in.' In truth, she didn't know what to do. Retreat felt like a dangerous option, yet with every second that ticked by they were closer to failing entirely. Not for the first time, she looked back to the Behemoth that hung over the mountains still. It was impossible to see what was happening there, and her link to the war-beasts and the rest of them had grown unstable again, filled with anger and fright. The Jure'lia queen herself was at the gates of the palace, her vast form close to blocking out the sight of Ygseril.

'Helcate!'

'What is it, my darling?'

It was the dragon again. So far Celaphon had remained strangely distant from the battle, flying back and forth around the outskirts of the city as though he were sight-seeing, a fact which had been playing havoc with Vintage's nerves. Now, the vast purple dragon was flying in a straight line right towards them, his huge jaws hanging open to reveal a shifting blue light at the back of his throat.

'Get away, get out of his line of sight!' She signalled desperately to the other fell-witches. Chenlo and her bat flew up and in front of them, trying to shield them. 'All of you, move!'

Vintage heard a roar from Vostok, and Celaphon opened his jaws wider in response. A jagged bolt of electricity shot from his jaws, yet instead of striking the white dragon – or, as Vintage had initially thought, blasting her and Helcate from the sky – it hit the nearest Behemoth.

'What –'

Blue and white light crawled over the Jure'lia ship in a vast net, growing brighter and brighter as they watched, until the thing looked like a huge, misshapen star. Celaphon flew next to it, continuing to spit line after line of lightning at the thing until –

'Watch out!'

There was a huge crumping noise, and the lightning winked out of existence. The Behemoth, which had gone a dull, rusted colour, began to fall out of the sky, heading down into the midst of the ruined city. It crashed in a vast cloud of dust and fire, instantly turning several large buildings into powder and rolling partially away towards the outskirts. Beneath her own shock, Vintage could feel the confusion and consternation of the other war-beasts. And then, a new voice on the connection, strange and triumphant.

See how mighty I am?

Celaphon turned a loop in the sky and shot another blast of lightning at the other Behemoth, capturing it in a web of shifting power. The vast shape that was the queen, oozing its way across the palace buildings, stopped, quivering slightly. Vintage had the impression of communication happening that was hidden from them, and then the second Behemoth was crashing to the ground, destroying several buildings and rolling into the forest to the north-west of the palace. Celaphon roared his triumph and soared back up into the sky.

'What is happening?' shouted Chenlo.

'I've no fucking idea, my love, but I don't think we need to worry about the Behemoths anymore. Quickly, to the palace roof!'

What they saw as they flew over turned Vintage's heart to ice. With Celaphon's help they had destroyed the Behemoths, but the queen herself was the heart of the Jure'lia, and all they had done so far was slow her down. The front half of the palace was lost under the huge, oozing form of her, and the maggots that were somehow embedded in the monster's back were spewing out long streamers of varnish again. Anything or anyone that had been in the gardens was dead, either eaten alive by burrowers or suffocated under the Jure'lia resin. In her slow movements, the queen had become partially humanoid again, with two arms reaching out towards the spreading branches of Ygseril, her long head splitting open as if to swallow the whole thing in one bite. Parts of her seeped down through windows and into courtyards, inquisitive fingers seeking every possible entry point. They were, Vintage reasoned, minutes away from disaster.

Aldasair? Aldasair, are you still with us?

Vintage's voice was like a cold hand on his forehead. Aldasair, who had fallen into a trance-like rhythm of fighting and shouting orders, blinked rapidly and took a breath.

We're in the Hall of Roots, everywhere else is lost. I –

Some of the human soldiers who had been attempting to hold the larger Jure'lia creatures at the doors were thrown back, tossed to one side by a huge spider-mother. The pale sac at the centre of its abdomen began to pulsate wildly, and a stream of freshly spawned burrowers surged over the human warriors. Aldasair ran forward and buried his axe in the creature's soft stomach, very nearly splitting it in two, but there were more behind it. Jessen leapt into the fray, growling and snarling, and Aldasair fell back. Commander Morota had been with them, but he had lost sight of her.

'Commander? We're losing the doors –'

'Lord Aldasair! Over here!'

The Reidn soldier was standing on Ygseril's roots, looking up to the glass ceiling. Aldasair had a brief moment to consider what an outrage that would have been, once upon a time – a human with their feet on the tree-father – when he spotted the dark shapes moving across the panels of grass. There were fell-witches up there, fighting desperately with gouts of green flame, and tendrils of the queen's body were oozing between them, pushing them aside or crushing them – heading towards the place where Ygseril's trunk met the glass. Commander Morota grabbed his arm and pulled him up onto the roots.

'What do we do?' All her military poise was gone, he noticed.

She sees her end coming, said Jessen in his head. *And worse, she sees that we are losing.*

Fingers of oily black were spreading down the trunk, coming

faster now, as though the queen could sense that she was close. At the doors, Jessen and the remaining human soldiers had fallen back, overwhelmed by the sheer number of Jure'lia monsters.

'We stand together,' said Aldasair. He held his axe in one hand, an old short sword in the other. 'It's all we can do.'

My friends, we're running out of time!

The light from the crystal chamber played over their faces, turning them both a sickly shade of yellow. The crystal itself was full of fire, a vision of destruction and terror that Noon could almost feel the heat from. She turned back to Tor, knowing already the look that would be on his face.

'Here we are,' he said, smiling.

'Yeah, and you need to get out of here. Now.'

He didn't move.

'How sure are you that you'll be able to survive such an explosion?'

'I'm sure.' But some of the truth must have shown in her face, and he shook his head. 'Reasonably sure. Either way, you have to go now, Tor. Both of you need to get far away from here.' She looked at Kirune, who was standing watching them with the unconscious form of Hestillion slung over his back. 'It's the only chance we have to end this. I've lived through it before, right? And I can't do it if you are here.'

Tor stepped forward and took her face in his hands, gently tipping her head to look up at him. He brushed the hair back from her face with his thumbs, and after a moment she covered one of his hands with her own.

'I'm dying anyway,' he said softly. 'What I said to my sister was true. Any death that isn't the crimson flux, that isn't slowly wasting away in a bed somewhere, my mind full of dust, is a blessing. I will not leave you to do this alone.'

'You could still live.' To her own horror, her voice was thick, and her face was wet with tears. 'There could still be sap to heal you. We don't know . . .'

'I'll send Kirune away.' There was a growl as he said this, which Tor ignored. 'But I won't leave you now. Noon, it's taken four hundred years for me to understand what this is.' He leaned his head down so that it rested against her own. 'Let me do the honourable thing, this once.'

She kissed him. They kissed for some time, briefly lost in the idea that they could be somewhere else, in a different life. His tears tasted like wine.

My friends, we're running out of time!

They broke apart, Aldasair's voice ringing in their heads.

'I love you, Noon. I always have.'

'I love you, Tor.' She squeezed his hand. 'Don't forget it.'

She tore the life energy from him as fast as she could, so as not to see the expression of betrayal grow in his eyes, and she held him as he fell to the floor.

'Kirune, you have to – you have to take him.' She stopped to rub her sleeve across her eyes. 'As fast as you can. Please?'

The big cat came over to her and lowered his head. She kissed him on the end of his nose.

'He will be angry when he wakes up.'

'I know. But whatever happens next, he has to be far away from here.' She dragged Tor and slung him over Kirune's back, tying him in place with the harness straps. 'Can you take them both? You can always leave Hestillion behind. I wouldn't mind at all.'

'I can take them.' Kirune paused, seeming to struggle with his words. 'You are brave, witch-warrior. Tell me truthfully. Will you make it?'

'There's only one way to find out, isn't there?' She took a breath and looked at the slow rise and fall of Tor's chest. He looked almost serene in sleep, and she hoped he was having good dreams: the one where they walked together in a field of wild flowers perhaps, or the one where they found each other for the first time, in a cave surrounded by snow and wolves. 'Please. Go now, quickly, as fast as you can.'

When Kirune had left with his precious cargo, Noon turned back to the crystal and its fiery rage. With Tor's life energy quietly banked inside her, she felt stronger than she had.

'Time to end all of this.'

She pressed her hands to the surface of the crystal, which was perfectly cool despite the images of fire dancing inside it. There was a strange energy to it, alien and unlike anything else she had felt, but it *was* still recognisable, all the same – the same as any plant, or animal, any human or Eboran. And through that energy she could already feel the millions of dancing connections it carried, the web that linked it to every part of the Jure'lia, the network that held all of them together. It was even simpler than the chain of connections she had sensed on the day she had killed her people, because it wasn't complicated by human emotions or any sort of food chain. There was just the Jure'lia, both the singular and the many.

She grinned, surprising herself.

'Oh, this is going to be easy.'

The crystal flickered uneasily as she tore the life energy from it, and then sought beyond it, moving from crystal to crystal and every place in between. The winnow-thirst roared inside her, suddenly awake, and this time she gave it free rein, opening it up to consume as much as it liked. This was the secret she had glimpsed, and the thing that She Who Laughs had been trying to get her to understand: that her capacity was infinite. That there were entire universes inside everyone.

Standing with her hands pressed to the crystal, Noon began to laugh.

'Look!'

Flying burrowers were beginning to drop out of the sky.

Several of the spiky insectoid things Helcate had been fighting stopped moving, falling onto the glass as though they were made of stone. The queen herself had her head in Ygseril's branches, her jaws slowly pulverising their way through the tree-father's outer arms, but many of her smaller minions were collapsing.

'What does it mean?' Chenlo was bleeding from her forehead, her face a sheet of blood as bright as her shirt.

'I think it means that Noon is where she needs to be.' Vintage reloaded her crossbow. 'There's still a chance we could all live through this!'

Noon moved from connection to connection, siphoning it all within herself and feeling the power building there. Each little crawling thing she supped from offered up its strange alien mind so easily – each one so simple, so uncomplicated – and as she leapt from creature to creature, she began to glimpse echoes of their history, stretching so far back into the past it made her dizzy.

There were other worlds; a few were lush and green like Sarn, but most were acrid, hot balls of rock with pools of hissing acid, or storms that lasted for centuries, the only life tiny crawling things with shells like lumps of metal. She saw frozen worlds, places where the ice was miles deep, where history slept in its layers, and worlds that hardly seemed like they were there at all, places of pressure and scent and a strange, violent magic. The Jure'lia had been to all of them, had taken each one and pierced it with eggs before covering it in varnish so that the world became hotter, more stable, until the time of birthing came and they could travel again.

Then there were unimaginable stretches of time, time so stretched and changed it almost became something else, and the Jure'lia revelled in this time of cold and darkness. Here they witnessed a breadth of creation Noon could not fathom;

holes of swirling purple light, pulsing stars that grew and died, over and over, and the brittle-bright light of comets. This was where the Jure'lia belonged, in this cold unfeeling nothingness, where beauty came and went with the aeons.

So many different bodies, one continuous mind – born again from the eggs, over and over.

And that mind was noticing her now, she realised. How could it not?

Noon raced towards it.

Aldasair stood over Commander Morota's body. He had lost his sword somewhere, and his arms ached so much he could barely lift the axe. The Hall of Roots was filling with the tendrils of the queen's body, a pulsating mass of evil. He could see no way out.

Bern?

Jessen came to him and licked the palm of his hand.

Al! Stay with us. Bern's voice was like a bell inside his head. *Things are happening out here . . .*

'You.'

The queen in her mind was not the creature Noon had seen in battle – not a huge amorphous shape of slime and tentacles, but a more human thing. She stood with two arms and two legs, and the face she wore was a cleverly crafted mask that looked almost real. It looked, Noon realised, a lot like Hestillion.

'Me,' agreed Noon. 'I don't think I know you, actually.'

'We saw you in the human's memories,' the queen said dismissively. 'Just another small living thing, another part of the pestilence. You helped to destroy our future.'

'And I'm going to kill you now, too.'

'You? You are nothing.'

Noon shrugged at that. The majority of the Jure'lia life force was already within her, a cold and vast energy that longed to burst her apart. Yet here stood the real core of the worm people – the singular mind that powered the rest. She could sense the real shape of it, the iron-hard will and the infinite energy required to build it.

'This is the end. I'm almost sorry, because this wasn't where you were supposed to be. Any other world, and you could have carried on as you were, probably forever. But Sarn isn't here for you to consume and throw away. Do you understand? We won't be used.' Noon opened her arms. 'You've come such a long way. But so have I.'

Too late the queen realised the real threat that she was, and for a brief second Noon struggled to consume her. But the weight of the Jure'lia was already within her, and suddenly so was the queen too – her life energy was a hundred thousand stars, living and dying, over and over.

Oh it's too much, it's too much.

She reached out along her link to the others.

Vostok?

Bright weapon.

You saved me, Vostok. You brought me out of the dark. Thank you.

You will ever be in my heart, bright weapon. Go and do what you were made for. Be our greatest, and our brightest.

She thought of Tor and the others, hoping that they were far enough away, that they would live through the battle. She had thought her capacity was infinite, but she saw that wasn't quite the case; the energy inside would need to be released soon, and that would be the end of it after all. Her very last purging. The last flicker of winnowflame.

I can't keep it. It's too much.

Then don't keep it. It was her mother's voice, or it was Vintage's; she couldn't tell. *You can let go now, little frog.*

Noon let go.

*

Tor woke up on the mountainside, lying in a patch of earth and grass. Kirune was sitting next to him, and his sister lay a few feet away, still unconscious. He had time to see that the corpse moon was some distance away, looming by the furthest of the Tarah-hut Mountains, and then he was thrown back into the dirt by a flash of light and sound that briefly turned everything white.

'Noon . . .'

A flash of heat kissed his face, as though she were saying goodbye, and a roaring noise filled his ears. When he could look up again it was to see a landscape utterly changed. A good portion of the mountain was gone, and the sky was dark with smoke and dust as the vaporised rock seethed up through the air. Of the Behemoth itself there was no sign, although already he could see pieces of molten debris falling back to earth, livid points of orange light trailing black, oily smoke.

She was gone. A presence in the connection between them all had been severed, and the absence was an agony. Tor rolled over onto his side, a sob lodged in his throat. The pain was unbearable, unlike anything he had ever felt.

'Ah no. Please, no.'

A weight on his side let him know that Kirune was there; the big cat was resting his head on him, and Tor could feel his own sorrow reflected back at him – reflected back at him multiple times.

'She did it,' Kirune said softly. When Tor didn't answer, the war-beast nudged him, nearly rolling him down the hill. 'She has destroyed them, where we couldn't. Get up and look. She would want you to see.'

Reluctantly, Tor uncurled himself and stood up shakily. The city was painful to look at. Already a collection of ruins, it now looked like it was covered in a giant, virulent mould, a grasping poisonous plant of black tendrils that had seeped into every building and up every street. Even the palace was covered in it, and Ygseril – he felt his stomach turn over – Ygseril's great silvery branches were entangled in it too.

But something was happening there. The slippery stretches of greenish-black were growing fuzzy at the edges, less defined. As he watched, a dark smoke began to rise off the ruins of Ebora. And there was Vostok. The great white dragon was flying in a wide circle, her rage and sorrow a terrible thing – hot and endless like the sun, it was impossible to look at for long.

'Come on.' A fragment of melted moon-metal struck the ground some feet away from them, setting the grass alight briefly. Kirune nudged him again. 'It's not safe here, brother. The mountains are broken. Let us go.'

Standing on the roof of the palace with her feet firmly planted on the glass, Vintage felt the loss of Noon like a sudden aching dizziness. She dropped her crossbow and fell to her knees, blinking rapidly to keep from passing out. Next to her, Helcate gave a low mournful cry.

'What is it?' Chenlo grabbed her elbow and tried to pull her back to her feet. 'What's happened?'

'Noon . . .' Vintage raised her head. She suddenly felt more tired than she ever had. 'She did it. But . . .'

The black tendrils of the Jure'lia queen, surrounding them like a great pulsating cage, shivered violently, and then began to turn an odd, rusty black. The shimmering oil colours vanished and instead the surface took on an old, cracked look, like an elderly woman's face covered with too much powder. And then they all began to fall apart, turning to a fibrous dust in front of their eyes.

'Sarn's bastard bones, what . . . ?'

Vintage scrambled to the edge of the glass, to the place where Ygseril's enormous trunk erupted up into the daylight. All around them, the remains of the Jure'lia queen fell on them like a strange, dry rain. She could feel it sticking in her hair and covering her skin, and she felt a weird spike of combined joy and revulsion.

'Aldasair?'

She peered down into the Hall of Roots below. The whole place was awash with the dark dust, making it difficult to see, but she caught sight of Aldasair's pale face looking up at her. Already the tear tracks on his face were dirty smudges.

'I'm alive,' he called, his voice breaking. 'So are Bern and Tor, I can feel them. But –'

'I know, darling.' Vintage sat back on the glass. She could feel them all too, their sorrow like thorns in her heart. All around them, the cheering was starting, the celebrations – the fell-witches who had lived, the handful of men and women who had managed to fight to the end, were calling out with joy. *The worm people are dead! We've won!*

Very quietly, Vintage began to cry.

'I know.'

Chapter Fifty-four

Beginnings and endings, flesh and bone, ink and paper. These are what stories are made of. Have we come to the ending yet? I don't know, my darling. Sarn's story continues, at least, even as many of us are left behind in dust and blood.

We found Celaphon's body in the ruins of Ebora. He made quite the impact, I can tell you – that's one street that will forever bear the scars of this war. No one saw him fall, but it seems likely that his connection to the Jure'lia was too deep for him to survive Noon's magic. He was mostly their creature, after all, but at the end he did his best to come back to his family. The crystal embedded in his forehead was cracked and grey, the colour of a winter sea.

Hestillion was a trickier prospect, and perhaps it would have been easier for all concerned if she had died along with her adopted worm people. Her crystal turned dark too, and the skin around it became livid and swollen with infection. For some weeks she was feverish and barely conscious, but she held on – Tor commented that she was just too bloody-minded to die – and eventually, made something of a recovery. To my eye, she is a ghost of a woman, a person formed more of regrets and horrors than skin and blood. I look at her and wonder at the dogged persistence of life. The question of what to do with her was left up to Tor, but she left of her own accord, without goodbyes. I imagine she wanders Sarn now, looking at the things she did. I hope it haunts her. Okaar has gone too. He is making his way back to the ruins of Tygrish, to look for any sign of Jhef. There is little chance of finding out what happened to her, and I think he knows that, too, but sometimes the hopeless course of action is the only one open to us.

Speaking of difficult prospects, there is Tor, of course. Much to our surprise, Ygseril appears to have had a new lease of life, growing bright new leaves, as green as emeralds, and it is producing sap again – just a tiny amount, but an extraordinary thing, nonetheless. The handful of remaining Eborans have been healed of the crimson flux, but for a long time Tor refused to be treated. He grieves so deeply, and he is remarkably stubborn – even as stubborn as me, Helcate has somewhat cheekily suggested – but for many nights I watched Kirune talking to him, quietly and persistently, and some days ago Tormalin the Oathless took his first cup of sap in a few hundred years. The marks of the crimson flux left him – and so did the scars on his face and neck. I found him crying over that, and my darling, I sat and cried with him. It's strange the things you can come to miss.

Bern and Aldasair built a new Hill of Souls together, a place to honour all those we lost in the Ninth Rain: the human soldiers, the fell-witches, and Noon. The Finneral brought their most sacred stones for the foundations of it, and the place has already become a shrine of sorts. Young fell-witches come and lay small stones there, with messages for Noon scratched into them. She would hate it, of course, but a symbol can be a powerful thing. The Winnowry won't rise again within the lifetimes of these young people, I am sure of that.

And it will not be an easy period for Sarn – I am also sure of that. During her most industrious period, the Lady Hestillion did a very good job of ruining much of the landscape, and those scars, mile-wide trails and splotches of varnish, will be with us forever. The places left untouched by the Jure'lia resin are likely to be poisoned, and we will see more Wild-touched creatures, more strange and dangerous things living amongst us, no doubt. The towns and settlements that were destroyed by her and the queen cannot simply be wished back into being, and the loss of the kingdoms of Jarlsbad is unspeakable.

Still, we are here. And free for the first time in human history. It's important to remember that.

Chenlo and I intend to go travelling. Yes, what's so new about that, I hear you asking, but first we must both go home. My love needs to see the Yuron-Kai again to settle her own heart, and I must go back to the vine forests. I need to know what has happened to you all. I am afraid, because I'm not sure that I can bear more grief than what I already carry, but it seems that running from your past can become a rather circular motion. Tor and Noon taught me that.

I hope you will be there to greet me, darling Marin. I hope to see you very soon.

Extract from the private letters of
Master Marin de Grazon,
from Lady Vincenza 'Vintage' de Grazon

She Who Laughs walked out across the plains, enjoying the dry tickle of grass under her bare feet. The desert was very beautiful, but it could also be very boring. And some time ago she had felt her daughter die, that small but fierce light extinguished so entirely, and something about that had made her want to see the place where the girl had been born. The plains were also beautiful, she decided. Like much of this world.

Lately, she had found herself returning to what Noon had said to her, during those days in the glass castle, about responsibility, and power, and change. And there was the sacrifice the girl had made: right at the end her bright mind had been full of those she had loved, and those who had loved her. Perhaps there were things to be learned there that she hadn't considered before. Perhaps there was another way.

With this in mind she had reached out to the last seed of the Aborans, had felt its tired battle to live, and given it something of herself. A little piece of her life to make it grow. It wouldn't be the same as it had been before – it couldn't be – but that was as it should be. Change was neither good nor bad, but it was vital. She thought Noon would have been pleased by that. She hoped so.

Presently she came to a place where the grass had been eaten up by a vast greenish sludge, shining hotly under the sun. It was hard to the touch, and reflected the heat back up at her. She Who Laughs grimaced. The stuff felt wrong; it did not belong here. It was a dead thing, and it suffocated the life under it and around it, life that did not need these extra obstacles.

She knelt down next to it – she wore the body of a child of ten or eleven, with raven-black hair and clever brown fingers – and placing her hands flat against it, summoned the purest form of her fire. Presently, the thick green substance began to bubble and melt, breaking down into a watery fluid that sank harmlessly away into the dirt. She Who Laughs smiled, feeling well satisfied with herself, and looked out across the vast stretch of ugly green.

'It will take a while,' she said aloud. 'But I have plenty of time.'

Acknowledgements

So here we are at the end of a trilogy again. How did this happen? It feels like five minutes ago I was scribbling vague ideas about rogue archaeologists and sexy elves who were not really elves. I set out to challenge myself with these books – a decision I have occasionally cursed myself for – and I feel like I've learned so much. It's been hard work; it's been cheerfully exhausting; it's been a joy.

And as ever, a brilliant gang of brave souls have guided me through it. Huge thanks first of all to my beloved editors, Frankie Edwards and Claire Baldwin, who made sure that the book sang and kicked you in the feels at exactly the right moment (so you can blame them, really). Enormous thanks to Juliet Mushens, my superstar agent – for all the advice, the support, the laughs. My life would be much duller without Juliet.

Thanks also to the fabulous Phoebe Swinburn for being a shining publicity star, and to Patrick Insole and his team for giving *The Poison Song* an absolutely stonking cover (it's my mum's favourite, and not just because she likes cats). Much gratitude and admiration must go to Jot Davies, the brilliant narrator who lends his voice to the audio versions of these books – it was his idea to give the Eborans a slight Welsh accent, and it makes me smile every time I think of it.

I owe a debt, as usual, to all the fantastic writers I also count as friends. Thanks must go to Den Patrick, not just for being a mate, but also for introducing me to Dungeons and Dragons over the last year or so – it's been a blast! Huge thanks as ever to Andrew Reid, my salt mate bestie and daily source of hilarity. Big thanks to Peter Newman, a friend in all weathers. I still owe Adam Christopher that ginger beer, and love and thanks to Alasdair Stuart and Marguerite Kenner – your support means the world. I would also like to throw out a thanks to Dogshit Justice, a support group that has helped me through the outrageous global trash fire of the last few years, and to Jenni, my oldest friend.

I'd never have gotten anywhere without the help of my mum, of course, who taught me how to make the chocolate chip rock cakes for myself this year. And as usual, big love and thanks to my partner Marty, who is there for me every time I climb back out of these fantasy worlds.

Lastly, thank you to all the readers who came on this journey with me. I'm going to miss Vintage, Noon and Tor an awful lot, but I like to think of them still out there with you, having adventures. Darlings, it's been emotional.